A Message to Your Heart

A Message to Your Heart

NIAMH GREENE

PENGUIN
IRELAND

PENGUIN IRELAND

Published by the Penguin Group
Penguin Ireland, 25 St Stephen's Green, Dublin 2, Ireland
(a division of Penguin Books Ltd)
Penguin Books Ltd, 80 Strand, London WC2R ORL, England
Penguin Group (USA) Inc., 375 Hudson Street, New York, New York 10014, USA
Penguin Group (Australia), 250 Camberwell Road, Camberwell, Victoria 3124, Australia
(a division of Pearson Australia Group Pty Ltd)
Penguin Group (Canada), 90 Eglinton Avenue East, Suite 700, Toronto, Ontario, Canada M4P 2Y3
(a division of Pearson Penguin Canada Inc.)
Penguin Books India Pvt Ltd, 11 Community Centre, Panchsheel Park, New Delhi – 110 017, India
Penguin Group (NZ), 67 Apollo Drive, Rosedale, Auckland 0632, New Zealand
(a division of Pearson New Zealand Ltd)
Penguin Books (South Africa) (Pty) Ltd, Block D, Rosebank Office Park, 181 Jan Smuts Avenue,
Parktown North, Gauteng 2193, South Africa

Penguin Books Ltd, Registered Offices: 80 Strand, London WC2R ORL, England

www.penguin.com

First published 2012
001

Copyright © Niamh Greene, 2012

The moral right of the author has been asserted

Set in 13.5/16pt Garamond MT Std
Typeset by Palimpsest Book Production Limited, Falkirk, Stirlingshire
Printed in Great Britain by Clays Ltd, St Ives plc

A CIP catalogue record for this book is available from the British Library

ISBN: 978–1–844–88261–8

www.greenpenguin.co.uk

ALWAYS LEARNING   PEARSON

Prologue

My heart constricts as the tiny scrap of paper tumbles into my palm. It can't be . . . can it? Slowly, hands trembling, I unfurl the crumpled edges and read the message.

Listen to your heart.

How could I have been so blind? It's from *her* – of course it is. It's been her all along. I just couldn't see it.

Closing my fist around the note, I hold it tight, feeling it warm against my skin, as if her hand is somehow in mine.

I know what I have to do now, what she wants me to do, and there's no going back.

Chapter One

OK, Frankie, just focus – you can do this. You're a profes-sional. You broker deals and negotiate shark-infested business waters every day of the week. Helping your own mother organize a small party to celebrate forty years of happy marriage should be child's play. All you have to do is work through the list, item by item. It's not rocket science.

'So, do you think I should contact people in advance to ask them about the seafood or not?' Mum ponders, her voice interrupting my thoughts. She's sitting opposite me, at the other side of the scrubbed-pine kitchen table, tapping her lucky ballpoint pen against her cheek as she thinks aloud.

'No, I don't think so, Mum,' I say lightly. The key is to sound unworried or she might go off at the deep end and lose the run of herself altogether.

'But what if someone's allergic?' she asks, her forehead creasing with anxiety. 'That would be a disaster. And now that Jenny's expecting it could be dangerous.'

My brother Eric and his wife Jenny have recently announced that they're expecting their first baby and Mum has barely been able to contain her excitement – I swear she already knows every chapter of *What to Expect When You're Expecting* off by heart.

'Well, if people are allergic to it, they won't eat it, will they?' I reason. 'And Jenny can have something else – it's not like she won't have enough to choose from.' I glance pointedly at the caterer's menu that lies on the table between us: there's chicken, beef, a multitude of vegetarian options, six different desserts (but not crème brûlée because Mum's terrified it will curdle) and four different wines. My mother is leaving no stone unturned or option unexplored in the quest to pull off the function of the year.

'Yes, but do you have to actually eat something you're sensitive to to have a reaction? People who are allergic to peanuts just have to touch one and they could die! What if a guest who has a deadly allergy to seafood brushes against some by accident – you know, at the buffet?' She pauses and squints into the middle distance as if she's visualizing this very scenario in her mind's eye. 'Or there could be some sort of spoon mishap – like a server from the prawns could end up in the salad! Oh, my God – that would ruin everything!'

'Mum, I don't think you have anything to worry about, I swear,' I say, trying desperately to keep my cool and not leap from the table and sprint round the kitchen, screaming hysterically with frustration. Honestly, this party is turning into a complete nightmare. It was only supposed to be a small gathering to celebrate Mum and Dad's ruby wedding anniversary so how has it come to this – discussions about the likelihood of guests accidentally dive-bombing the Marie Rose prawns or the lobster platter and having to be resuscitated beside the salad bar?

Mum is anxiously chewing her lip, clearly not listening to a word I say. 'You know what people are like, Frankie – some will deliberately try to find fault. I wouldn't put it past your aunt Maureen to go into antapalactic shock on purpose.'

'She'd never do that.' I sigh. 'And it's "anaphylactic", Mum.'

'Oh yes she would,' she replies grimly. 'She told everyone she took a funny turn after Dan and Joyce's do – she swore the crab sticks were off. Poor Joyce was mortified. She avoided people for weeks afterwards – *weeks*!'

In fairness, Mum is right about Aunt Maureen – she's a total cow who devotes herself to making everyone else's life as miserable as possible, but I don't want to get into that now – it would only delay things even more and the clock is already against me. As it is, I have approximately fifteen minutes to get out of here if I have any chance of making it all the way to the other side of the city by eight for Antonia West's book launch – and there are still a million things on Mum's list to discuss.

'I don't want people to have any excuse to complain, Frankie,' she goes on, her voice getting wobbly and emotional. 'I want everything to be perfect.'

I take a deep breath. Being married for forty years *is* a huge achievement and I know this party means a lot to her. So, even though it's driving me crazy, I have to do my best to help.

'Well, what does Dad think about the seafood?' I ask, sneaking a quick glance at my watch. Fourteen minutes. I have to leave in fourteen minutes to get to the book launch in time. Antonia will never forgive me if I'm late – I am her agent, after all: she's entitled to expect me to turn up.

'Oh, you know what your dad's like,' Mum says, a definite tinge of bitterness in her voice. 'He says he doesn't mind – he says *I* should decide.'

'Well, then,' I say. 'Let's decide.'

'Ah, yes. But he said that about Bali too, didn't he? He said he didn't care about *that* either. When we were booking he said it didn't matter that it might be forty degrees in the shade. But when we got there, who had to listen to him for two full weeks griping on about that heat rash in his privates? Me! Those two weeks felt like a lifetime, Frankie.'

Oh, God. We're going round in circles. That Bali trip was easily ten years ago. I'm going to be here all night at this rate.

If I don't get a move on I'll definitely miss the speeches and if that happens then Antonia will go into a massive strop. And I can't say I'd blame her. She's my top author, one of the very few who came with me when I left Withers and Cole to set up on my own. The least I can do is be supportive.

'Look, why don't we ask the caterers to exclude seafood, then?' I say. 'Better safe than sorry, right? Now, let's pin down numbers – have you got a final figure?'

Thirteen minutes. Hurry up, hurry up.

'Well, yes,' she concedes, still a little huffy about Bali but clearly willing to forget about it temporarily to discuss her beloved guest list – the one she's been fine-tuning for weeks now. 'I've managed to pare it down to a hundred and eighty-nine. My only worry is the marquee. Do you think it'll be big enough? There's nothing worse than being hemmed in – and I don't want the guests to feel like they've been jammed into some flimsy garden tent like squashed sardines –'

'*A hundred and eighty-nine?*' I squeak. 'When did it get so big?'

'Well, I can't go leaving out people, Francesca,' she says, immediately defensive. 'Besides, Dan and Joyce had almost two hundred at theirs.'

'It's not a competition, Mum,' I say, knowing full well that that's exactly what it is. My mother is very close to her brother Dan and his wife Joyce but she's secretly been dying to get one up on Joyce for donkey's years and she won't be out-done.

'Of course it's not a competition!' she says, definitely huffy now. 'Anyway, we have completely different styles – I mean, for a start, I'm definitely *not* having a piñata. Grown adults beating a stuffed giraffe with a stick and then scrabbling around on the floor for cheap and nasty sweets is *not* my idea of an elegant evening.'

'I think it was supposed to be a llama or something actually,' I say, a vision of that night appearing immediately in my head. I don't think I'll ever forget it – the sight of hordes of tipsy senior citizens drinking margaritas and dancing in sombreros is likely to stay etched on my memory for ever.

'What?' Mum says irritably.

'The piñata. I think it was supposed to be a llama, not a giraffe. It was a Mexican theme, remember?'

'How could I forget? Those tortilla chips gave your father terrible indigestion for days afterwards. Anyway, the point is I don't care if that piñata was a dinosaur. I want my party to be classy – and remembered for the *right* reasons.'

'What's this about a llama?' a voice says, and I look up to see my father coming through the back door. Behind him, my two brothers – Eric and Martin – are manhandling a monstrous box between them, edging it through the frame with some difficulty and lots of dramatic groaning.

'What is that?' Mum splutters, her jaw dropping.

'It's the Flame Grill 700,' Dad replies, gesturing at it with his arms like it's some grand prize on a game show and he's the token curvy blonde in the miniskirt trying to sex it up. He's clearly delighted with himself. 'Martin had a friend of a friend who was getting rid of them. It was too good an opportunity to pass up – I got it for half nothing!'

With a final grunt, my two brothers heave the enormous box through the door and leave it next to Mum's beloved pine dresser, where photos of the three of us in our navy polyester school jumpers, with gummy smiles and scraped knees, are proudly displayed side by side.

'It's September. Barbecue season is over,' Mum says, stony-faced.

'Well, that's why it was such a bargain. And I thought it might come in handy for the party,' Dad explains.

'We are not having a barbecue at our fortieth wedding anniversary celebration.' Mum's voice is a funny strangled sob.

'It's only an option,' he replies, patting the box fondly. 'Just in case.'

'In case what?' she asks, her right eye twitching now.

'In case we run out of food – we can throw a few steaks on this thing.'

'Oh, God.' Mum's head is in her hands. 'Frankie, talk to him, will you?'

'Dad, you're having caterers, remember? We're not going to run out of food,' I say, smiling at him, hoping to defuse the situation. If World War Three breaks out I'll never be able to escape. Twelve minutes.

'I only wanted to help,' he says, looking a bit wounded.

'If you want to help you can put that thing in the garage where it belongs,' Mum says.

There's a small silence as they survey each other and the rest of us hold our breath.

'I was trying to surprise you, if you must know.' Dad sniffs. 'But if you don't want it, that's fine. Come on, boys, let's get this thing outside again.'

'Gimme a minute, will you, Dad? That yoke's heavy,' Martin gasps, collapsing into the chair beside me.

'Yeah. I'm bollixed too,' Eric agrees.

'Right,' Dad says, scowling at them both. 'Well, I'd better make some room in the garage then.'

The minute he's gone, Eric pipes up: 'Any chance of some grub, Ma?' He gives her his best boyish grin.

Mum jumps to attention and my heart sinks. Now she'll be waiting on this pair hand and foot and I'll be even further delayed. I glance at my watch. Eleven minutes. Crap.

'Of course, love,' she's saying. 'You must be starving, lugging that thing around. I don't know what your dad was thinking of!'

'What's on?' Eric asks nonchalantly, as if he's in some high-street deli and can just order the daily special.

Mum already has her head stuck in the fridge. 'Turkey? Coleslaw? I could make you a nice sandwich,' her disembodied voice says.

'Are there any chips going?' Eric asks.

'Of course, pet!' she replies, clearly in her element now. There's nothing she likes more than to cook for her 'boys'.

'Go on so, count me in,' Eric says, as if she's twisted his arm.

'Me too,' Martin agrees.

'So, sis,' Eric turns to me, 'to what do we owe the pleasure?'

I stick out my tongue at him, almost automatically. What is it about being in the company of my brothers that makes me feel like a fourteen-year-old again?

'Yeah, what are you doing in the suburbs, Frankie?' Martin smirks. 'Is it some sort of special occasion?'

'Very funny,' I reply. 'I was just leaving, actually.'

'What?' Mum's head is out of the fridge like lightning.

'Yeah, Mum. I have a work thing to get to, sorry. I meant to tell you earlier.'

There – I've said it. Hopefully, now her sons are here, she'll be distracted enough to let me off the hook without too much palaver.

'But we haven't finished the list yet!' she protests. 'We're not even halfway through.'

'What list?' Eric asks.

'For the party. Your sister is helping me with the final details. Or she was.' She gives me an injured look.

'Oh, yeah, the party,' Martin says, like he's just remembered. 'I meant to talk to you about that, Ma.'

9

'Martin, please don't tell me you can't come – I gave you the date months ago!' she wails.

'Actually, I was going to ask you if I can bring someone,' he replies casually.

There's a millisecond pause before she reacts. 'Of course you can, love!' she squeaks, beaming at him, barely concealing her excitement at this news. 'We've plenty of room – the more the merrier!'

'Great,' he says, kicking off his shoes.

I can see that Mum is about to spontaneously combust with curiosity – Martin hasn't dated anyone since he broke up with 'Honor the guard', her of the hefty shoulders and unusual-verging-on-freakish thick neck, and it's clear she's dying to know all the juicy details. But she also knows that if she presses him she'll get nowhere because prising information from him is like getting blood from a stone – it always has been. Even when we were kids he'd clam up about the simplest things. Silent but deadly – that's Martin when he wants to be cagey.

'Well, Frankie,' Eric asks, turning to me, 'are *you* bringing anyone to the party of the year?'

It's now suddenly so quiet that you could probably hear a pin drop on the twenty-five-year-old kitchen lino – the one I remember being fitted by two men in blue boiler-suits when I was little. All three of them are looking at me. Mum is practically holding her breath, I can tell.

'Why don't you mind your own business, brother dear?' I say, smiling tightly at him. He's done that on purpose, the smug married git, I could bet my life on it.

'Would you like me to set you up on a blind date?' he asks, all innocence. 'Mikey Grant still asks after you – I only met him the other day.'

'Ah, little Mikey.' Mum sighs fondly. 'He's a lovely fellow.'

'Mum, I am not bringing Mikey Grant to your party, thanks all the same.'

'There's nothing wrong with him, Francesca,' she says, her head bobbing. 'He's a very nice chap. He does everything for his mother.'

There's a definite undercurrent there, but I ignore it. 'Mum. He's four foot eleven.'

'Don't be so sizeist, Francesca,' Martin laughs.

'Yeah – good things come in small parcels.' Eric is snorting.

'Shut up, knob-head,' I say, glaring at him.

'It would be nice to have someone to bring, though,' Mum says. 'Eric will have Jenny and now Martin has someone too . . .'

Why is it always like this? Despite all I've achieved in my career, no matter how high I climb or how hard I graft, all my family ever want to know about is my love life. Like a man should be the thing that defines me. Like we're living in the eighteenth century. They don't value what I achieve in work. I don't think they would care less if I bagged the next J. K. Rowling or was crowned literary agent of the year. It seems that they just want to see me settle down and have babies. It's been even worse since Jenny got pregnant – I love babies as much as the next person, but that doesn't mean I want to hear my biological clock ticking like a time bomb every time I pop in for a cuppa with Mum.

This is exactly why I've never told them about my relationship – about Gary. It'd be far too complicated for them to process. They just wouldn't understand. Plus, they'd have me married off and pregnant in a second.

'There must be *someone* you could drag along,' Martin says, smirking at me.

'I'm far too busy for all that, Martin.' My hands are itching to smack him.

'Ah, yes, and how *is* the Rowley Agency going?' he says. 'Made your first million yet?'

'Not yet,' I reply sweetly. 'Any day now, though.'

That's a big fat lie, of course. The truth is, I'm struggling. Really struggling. But it's not like you can just start a business from scratch and expect it to go without a hitch, is it? There are bound to be little hiccups along the way. Like constantly exceeding your overdraft limit, or missing your rent payments. My head starts to buzz, as it always does when I think about the mess I'm in: the agency is in trouble – serious trouble. I can't let my family know that, though – not ever – and they won't have to because I'm going to fix it before anyone can find out the truth.

'Good, good,' Martin says. 'And Con Air is going great too – just in case you're wondering. The name's really worked – despite what some people thought.'

Martin set up an air-conditioning business a few years ago, and even though the company has what I think is possibly the stupidest name in history, he's actually managed to become quite successful.

'I'm delighted to hear that blowing on people is so lucrative,' I say, checking my text messages again. I really have to get out of here.

'Do you ever leave that thing behind?' Martin asks.

'I need it,' I say. 'It's called being available.'

'You're addicted to it,' Eric says.

'Yeah, it's not a BlackBerry, it's a CrackBerry!' Martin guffaws, and they both fall around the place laughing.

'What's so funny?' Mum says, reappearing from the larder with the deep-fat fryer.

'Mum, I hate to break it to you, but I seriously think these two morons were swapped with my real brothers at birth,' I say.

'We think Frankie is addicted to her BlackBerry – it's a CrackBerry, geddit? Like crack cocaine?' Eric is wiping tears of laughter from his eyes.

'Eh?' Mum looks completely confused.

'Mum.' I wave my phone at her. 'They're teasing me. They reckon I spend so much time with this – which, by the way, is an iPhone, you idiots – that it's a full-blown addiction. Isn't that right, boys?'

My brothers grin happily, delighted with their wit.

'Oh, you two are such jokers.' Mum chuckles, getting down the oil from the cupboard. 'But, Frankie, they have a point – you never let that phone out of your hand.'

'I run my own business – I have to be contactable twenty-four/seven, remember?' I argue.

No matter how often I explain this I don't think she'll ever grasp it properly. Yes, my iPhone is important – OK, vital – in my life, but there's nothing wrong with that.

'Well, it wouldn't kill you to put it away once in a while,' she goes on. 'Give yourself a break. Work isn't the be-all and end-all, you know.'

Except it is to me. Right on cue my phone buzzes. It's Helen, my assistant – a.k.a. the worst PA in Ireland – telling me that Antonia wants to know where I am. *Crap.* Out of the corner of my eye I see my brothers exchange another look with Mum as I punch in my reply: a lie telling her I'm almost there.

'Mum, I really have to go,' I say, pushing back my chair and grabbing my bag. 'I'll call you tomorrow, OK? Tell Dad I said goodbye.'

'Don't you want some chips, love?' Mum asks. 'Or some nice coleslaw? I made it this morning.'

'No, thanks. I'm fine.' I peck her on the cheek.

'All the more for us,' Eric and Martin say in unison and gleefully high-five each other.

'You two are a right pair of tossers, do you know that?' I sigh.

'Ah, now, blood is thicker than water,' Martin says.

'Yeah, you love us really!' Eric whoops.

I'd rather love you from a distance, I think, as I gallop out of the door, checking my messages as I run.

Chapter Two

The next morning I'm sitting at my desk, giving myself the same pep talk I do every day. You can do this, Frankie. You can make this agency a success. You have the skills, you have the ambition. All you have to do is banish the doubts that you made a stupid, fatal mistake in leaving your old job to set up on your own. Push away the fear that if you don't get some more high earners soon then the agency will be finished before it's really begun and your reputation will be in tatters. Mr Morris, the bank manager, is *not* coming to haul you away to some undisclosed secret location where they dump all the big fat failures. You have to focus on success. *Success.*

I try to visualize myself in a luxurious office, fielding frantic calls from Hollywood producers all baying for the rights to my authors' work. It's so close I can almost smell the exotic scent of fresh lilies and see the imported leather-top desk that will straddle one corner. I'll have floor-to-ceiling windows. A view. A decent assistant. It'll be amazing.

But then, out of nowhere, an image of Bruce Makin, senior partner at Withers and Cole and my former boss, floats into my mind. Dammit. Will I ever be able to shake him? It's bad enough having to read that they're going from strength to strength since they merged with that New York super-agency. I don't want him in my head space too. But, try as I might to push it away, that last morning in my old office plays in my mind's eye, just as it has a hundred times before.

'You're making a mistake, Francesca,' Makin said. 'Just hang on a little longer. Resigning like this is madness.'

'So you *will* make me a partner, then?' I eyeballed him.

'Of course we will,' he replied carefully. 'When the time is right.'

When the time was right: I knew what that meant. The New York merger had changed everything: all the goal posts had shifted, and the chances of me becoming a full partner in Withers and Cole in the near future were now slim to none. The Americans wanted two spots on the board, which left me in the cold. After years of loyalty to the firm, waiting in line for that precious partnership, I'd been shafted big-time. I either had to put up and shut up, try to get another job elsewhere and start the slow climb to the top again from scratch or strike out on my own. I thought about nothing else for weeks on end, tossing and turning late into the night, calculating how it would play out and if I could pull it off.

If I left, taking my most successful authors with me, I could work independently and have no one to answer to. That was the crux of it. The backstabbing and the endless political games would be over and I'd be free to concentrate on simply providing an excellent service to my clients. The Rowley Agency would be a bespoke boutique set-up: all I needed was a small office and an assistant. I had the contacts. I didn't need Withers and Cole. I could do it on my own – couldn't I? Yes, it would be a huge gamble, but if it paid off . . .

'Just wait a little longer and it'll all work out,' Makin said, when I told him I'd made up my mind to leave.

'Will it?' I replied. 'Or will I still be waiting three years from now for you and the boys in New York to get off the fence?'

'You know how it works.' He looked away from me then, clearly not wanting to meet my eye.

'Yes. I do. I know *exactly* how it works,' I said, my resolve strengthening. I had nothing to lose, not really.

Now, cradling my second cup of coffee of the day, I try to bat away the sensation that the walls in my tiny airless office are closing in on me. You can't turn a corner in here without meeting yourself coming the other way, as my granny would have said, and the rent is crippling me, but the address is good, which counts for a lot. Or so I keep telling myself. Just like I keep telling myself that in the end it will be worth all the sleepless nights, the stress, the uncertainty. When the Rowley Agency takes off properly, all of that will be a distant memory.

There's no point in dwelling on whether I made the right decision or not – it's too late for that. I just have to get on with it. No point in crying that, when push had come to shove, most of my big authors didn't come with me. They had all promised to come, of course – they all loved the idea when I first called them in secret to put it to them. But then, one by one, most of them backed out, too scared to take a chance on a new venture in a downturn, especially one that wouldn't have an international media arm and a huge foreign-rights department for quite some time. Only Antonia had taken the plunge, along with a couple of smaller mid-market authors. But that's OK, because her new novel is going to be massive and I'll find more bestselling stars soon. So, it's all fine. Totally fine. I just have to hold my nerve.

Taking a sip of coffee, I glance at the clock. There's still no sign of Helen – a.k.a. the worst PA in Ireland – because, of course, she's late. Helen's not a bad person but she is a very bad assistant. The kind who loses precious manuscripts, forgets to pass on important messages, screws up appointments, paints her nails at her desk, never makes me coffee . . .

If Helen wasn't Antonia's niece – and she didn't work for less than peanuts – I would have fired her ages ago. I need someone organized and precise: someone who knows not to ask the senior editor at Transit Publishing what his honest-to-God opinion was when Mariah Carey named her twins Moroccan and Monroe, or whatever it is they're called, or a past Booker nominee what he thought about the rumour that Rihanna was seeing Chris Brown again. I need someone . . . more like me.

'Hi, boss! Isn't it a beautiful morning?'

And here she is. Only twenty-five minutes late – not too bad, by her standards. A grinning Helen enters the office, her ruby-red shoulder-length hair bouncing cheerfully round her face as she walks. Her hair wasn't that colour at Antonia's book launch last night but, then, Helen is practically addicted to hair dye: a change of colour is as essential to her look as a neat, professional bob is to mine.

'Whaddya think?' She does a little twirl for me and I take it in. Not too hideous. A little too Cheryl circa *X Factor 2010* maybe, but definitely not as bad as the blonde with pink streaks she showcased last month.

'Yes, um, lovely,' I lie.

'I think red is such a happy colour, don't you?' she says. 'Sorry I'm late, by the way. Dave says I'm lucky you're so understanding.'

Dave is Helen's boyfriend. The one she spends so much time on the phone to that she forgets to answer most of my calls.

'It's all his fault, actually. He brought me breakfast in bed and we just lost track of time . . . you know how it is.' She shrugs off her coat, unveiling her super-long limbs, encased in slick black leggings. God, she's young. And skinny. And loved-up.

'That was nice of him,' I murmur. *Pity he wouldn't do it on someone else's time.*

'Yeah – he's so good like that,' she says. The pride in her voice is unmistakable as she flings her coat towards her chair, missing by a mile, and perches herself on the edge of my desk, her potent perfume assaulting my nostrils. It's sickly sweet and cloying – probably one of those awful celebrity-endorsed scents she's so keen on. She gave me a bottle of 'Britney' for Christmas – it's still shoved at the back of my bathroom cabinet. How anyone could think I like that stuff when all I wear is Chanel No. 5 is beyond me. 'Do you think Aunt Antonia was happy with how it went last night?' she asks now, twisting her hair into a knot on top of her head.

'Yeah, I think so,' I reply. 'There was a great turnout and the press came, which is the main thing.'

'God, I was *soooo* relieved when they turned up, weren't you? I thought she'd have a canary if they didn't!'

'It *was* looking a little hairy there for a while,' I admit.

Antonia knows it takes more than good writing to sell a book: publicity is key, now more than ever. If a few photographers hadn't turned up it would have been disastrous.

'Now we just have to hope that the book sells through, right?' she goes on.

'That's right,' I reply, smiling at her use of publishing lingo. 'We have to cross everything. And then some.'

'I'm sure it will, though. Even the title is brilliant – *The Edge of Love*. It makes you just want to pick it up and get stuck in, doesn't it?'

'It *is* fantastic,' I say. 'This is definitely her best yet – she's really moved things up a gear.'

Mind you, that might not be enough. The market is the toughest I've ever known it: everyone's sales are suffering, even the bestsellers. If Antonia's new novel bombs, I don't know what I'll do. Things are shaky enough as they are. But I'm not going to think about that because if I do I may have a nervous breakdown – I'm going to focus on the positive instead.

'Thank God it's Friday, right? I'm exhausted!' Helen sighs dramatically now, as if she's been slaving down a coal mine all week instead of making a cack-handed job of working for me. 'Have you anything nice planned for the weekend?'

She looks at me expectantly, waiting for me to divulge all the fascinating details, and for a second, I consider lying to her. I'm seeing Gary tonight, yes, but I'll probably spend the rest of my weekend reading the unsolicited manuscripts that get sent to me by the sackload, catching up on some emails and figuring out how to save my business. But I can't admit that to Helen. So I'll just be vague instead. 'No, nothing special,' I say. 'You?'

'Oh, yes!' she chirps, her dimples dimpling at me. She's so cheery all the time – it's almost exhausting. Even when she's making a total mess of everything she's still relentlessly happy. 'I'm going to the circus!'

'The *circus*?'

'Yeah – I just *love* the circus, don't you? Those cute little horses are my favourites – what do you call them again?'

'Shetland ponies?'

'Yes! Oh, they're *sooooo* adorable, aren't they? You could nearly put one in your handbag.' Her kohl-rimmed eyes are gleaming with excitement.

'Are you bringing your nieces?' I ask. Helen has half a dozen identikit nieces – and photos of each and every one are proudly displayed in an assortment of Daffy Duck and Mickey Mouse photo frames on her cluttered desk. Sometimes when I turn around quickly I swear I catch one of them watching me.

'The girls have already been. I'm going with Dave,' she replies, beaming at me.

'You and Dave are going alone to the circus?'

'Yes!' Her eyes go a bit misty. 'It'll be *soooo* romantic . . .'

'Romantic? But isn't the circus for . . . kids?' The last time I went I must have been about six. Possibly younger. I clearly remember eating too much candyfloss and throwing up on my brothers in the back seat of the car on the way home.

'Oh, no, Francesca! The circus is for everyone. You really should go – I have a discount voucher somewhere, if you want it.' She gestures over her shoulder to where her leopard-print bag lies by her desk, half its contents strewn across the floor.

'Er, no, that's OK, thanks. I have a lot on,' I say. And going to the circus is a childish waste of time.

'Honestly, you should! You'd love it – it's just magical!'

Helen loves anything even vaguely 'magical' – it's very unnerving. In fact she's a little like a child at Christmas all year round, which some people find sweet but I find really bloody irritating. The world is not a magical place: it's dog-eat-dog and the sooner she realizes that the better.

'Why don't we run through what's on today?' I say, swiftly changing the subject. I know from bitter experience that if I don't nip this sort of going-nowhere-fast conversation in the bud it could continue for ages and I'm far too busy for all this magical malarkey.

'OK,' she says, tottering over to her desk and retrieving the black book where all my appointments are written in her almost illegible handwriting, so I can cross-check them against the entries in my iPhone diary.

'You have to talk to Penguin about Barry Evan's latest jacket, then you have a conference call with those Italian publishers at twelve –'

Helen's desk phone rings, interrupting her. Instead of ignoring it for an age like she usually does, she jumps and, with a we're-in-this-together smile, springs off my desk, leaps across to her own and scoops up her phone in one swift movement.

'The Rowley Agency, good morning, how can I help you?'

she rattles off. 'Uh-huh, uh-huh. Can you hold for just one moment, please?

'It's Mr Morris at the bank,' she whispers to me, clasping the phone against her chest to muffle our conversation instead of simply putting him on hold properly, like I've asked her to do a million times. 'He wants a quick word?'

I shake my head and make a violent cutting motion across my neck.

'You don't want to talk to him?' she whispers, her eyes wide.

Oh, for fuck's sake.

'Tell him I'm in a meeting,' I whisper back, trying to keep my temper.

'OK,' she mouths in reply, nodding furiously. 'Ms Rowley is in a meeting right now. Can I please take a message? Uh-huh, uh-huh . . .'

I watch, feeling sick, as she makes detailed notes in her jotter – the one with a photo of her and Dave on the cover, holding hands and smiling giddily at each other.

'That was Mr Morris,' she says, stating the very obvious as she hangs up.

'So I gathered.'

There's no real point in being sarcastic because it goes straight over her head, but I find I can't help it.

'He wants you to call him on his personal number. He says it's urgent.'

His personal number. My heart plummets to my toes. That's not good. In fact, it's probably terrible.

Helen is watching me carefully, a fearful look on her face, so I work my features into a convincing nothing-to-worry-about expression. There's no way I'm telling her just how bad things are. For one thing she'd go into full-on headless-chicken mode and I couldn't handle it. For another, she might tell Antonia, and if *she* gets wind of it she could get nervous and run straight back into the waiting arms of Withers and Cole. And that would leave me completely screwed. I'd be the laughing stock of the entire industry: *Francesca Rowley – in business for less than a wet week and already losing her authors.* I can see the piece in *Books Today.* If word gets out that the agency is floundering I'm a dead duck in the water – a joke. I cannot let that happen. *I will not let that happen.*

'Is everything OK?' she asks nervously, her nose twitching like that of an anxious bunny rabbit in a pet-shop window.

'Yes, fine. He probably just wants to invite me to another of those boring corporate events,' I say coolly. 'I'll call him back later. Now, what else is on today?'

With a sigh of relief that there's some sort of reasonable explanation for his call, which doesn't involve cutting jobs or murdering kittens, Helen begins to read from the diary again, but this time I'm barely listening. My head is throbbing and my throat is dry. Bank managers don't just leave their personal numbers for no good reason. It's not like he wants to invite me to dinner, hold my hand across the table and tell me what a good job I'm doing, how he's behind me all the way, cheering me on with pom-poms.

And then there's the rent. I haven't told a soul, least of all Mr Morris, but I had a letter from the landlord's solicitor last week. If I don't come up with the back rent by the end of the month he's going to evict me – it said so in black type on cream vellum paper, which is pretty official, let's face it. There's no getting round it any more: I'm in deep water and, unless I get out of this mess soon, I'm going to drown.

Helen is still talking, her voice a distant drone in my consciousness, when out of the corner of my eye I spot a new text message: *Hey, Blue Eyes, can't wait to see you later. Gx*

Gary. I haven't seen him all week and he has no clue that

things are so bad because, so far, pride — maybe foolish pride — has stopped me telling him all the gory details. He would probably be horrified if he knew that my landlord was threatening to evict me or that I'm down to my last few euro. *I'm* horrified. Because even though I know I've been doing my very best, working my hardest, it still feels like it's all my fault. I've dropped the ball somewhere along the way. I must have done for things to have come to this.

Maybe now the time has come to confide in Gary, tell him the whole story, how difficult things really are. It will probably kill me to admit it, say it out loud, but I don't know if I can keep my secret any longer. I have to tell *someone*.

I listen half-heartedly as Helen talks on, freeing her ruby-red hair from its chignon and flipping it back over her shoulder as she does. God knows I can't confide in her. The worst PA in Ireland would definitely crack under the pressure if she knew the truth. The girl loves candyfloss and Shetland ponies, for God's sake — she can't cope with real-world problems. I can't tell my family either: Mum and Dad have enough going on, what with fretting over the party, and my brothers might find it funny. No, Gary is the one I have to talk to — not that I hold out much hope that he can help. Because I have a horrible feeling in the pit of my stomach that it might be too late for that. I need a miracle to keep this show on the road. A miracle. I just don't know where I'm going to find one.

Chapter Three

The thing between Gary and me began at a publishing convention just after I'd left Withers and Cole and set up on my own. I was sitting in a crowded hotel conference room, listening to the keynote address: 'The End of Publishing As We Know It'. The speaker – a jowly middle-aged man, with enormous sweat patches seeping through the underarms of his pale blue shirt and an unfortunate habit of sniffing loudly after almost every sentence – had walked us through the publishing landscape as he saw it in ten years' time, painting a very grim picture. He claimed that the technological changes facing the industry would make publishers *and* agents obsolete very soon. According to him, in the bleak future, which was fast approaching, authors would simply publish their books online and physical books would be consigned to history. A slightly controversial stance, maybe, but he sounded pretty persuasive and it was extremely depressing: if the few authors who'd followed me wouldn't need me in a decade's time, what would I do?

His presentation certainly didn't make for happy listening – especially because, although I was trying to be upbeat about my brand-new venture, I was already suffering from terrible regret wobbles. Why had I ever thought I could make my own agency a success? Why hadn't I stayed put? What had possessed me to set up alone in this economic climate? Was I completely insane?

I was wondering how I could slip out unnoticed before I lost the will to live altogether when I got Gary Elverson's text: *This guy makes me want to slit my wrists.*

I burst out laughing, tickled to get such an irreverent text from the legendary MD of Proud Publishing. Thing was, I'd been thinking exactly the same thing. *Me too*, I replied, smiling conspiratorially down the row to where he sat, four seats away, smirking at me.

Want to escape? he texted back.

That was how we ended up in the hotel bar, sharing a bottle of wine. It was probably the first proper conversation we'd ever had. I'd met him professionally over the years, of course – when I'd worked with Withers and Cole – but during any of the occasional meetings we'd had he'd always been aloof, standoffish. Last I'd heard he was going through a messy separation and getting over it by working twelve-hour days. I could definitely relate to that – work was my refuge too.

'So, do you think the publishing industry is doomed, Francesca?' he'd asked, leaning back in his seat and observing me carefully with those steel-grey eyes. It was also probably the first time I'd noticed how unusual their colour was. Like rainclouds whipping together in a stormy sky.

'No, not at all,' I'd replied.

'Which is why you set up on your own?'

'Exactly.'

'It was a very brave move, though, wasn't it? Leaving an international agency in this climate?'

'Brave or stupid.' I'd laughed. 'But I felt the time was right.'

Or, at least, I had when I'd left. Now I wasn't so sure.

'So, you have hope that all will be right with the book world? The industry isn't doomed?' he'd asked, swirling his wine glass, the golden liquid sloshing gently, and smiling at me. It was definitely the first time I'd noticed his smile, the way his mouth curved lazily at the edges, his eyes crinkled and one brow lifted, just a fraction. A bit James Bond. Not Pierce Brosnan. More Sean Connery.

I cleared my throat before I answered. He was MD of Proud, after all. I had to pick my words carefully, make sure I didn't ruffle any feathers. Remain professional, even if the wine was going straight to my head. 'You should have had that buffet breakfast, Frankie,' I remember thinking.

'It's not doomed, no,' I replied. 'But I do think that we need to move with the times.'

'You like ebooks, then?'

'It's not a case of liking or disliking.' I shrugged. 'They're here – that's the reality.'

'I prefer good old-fashioned paper,' he said, his eyes on mine. 'I like the feel of the pages between my fingers, the heat of the words under my skin. Reading is a . . . sensual pleasure. How can a digital screen even compare?'

And right then, without me even knowing how, the air between us filled with electricity and I realized for the first time just how attractive Gary Elverson was. He had presence. Charisma. And the most amazing eyes. *Eyes that saw into my soul.* If I'd read it in a manuscript I would have laughed at the cliché – but it was true.

'Where are you working from?' he'd asked, as my head began to spin. I couldn't actually *fancy* him, could I?

'I'm still searching for the right space,' I'd replied, sipping my drink, trying not to betray even the remotest sliver of the unease I was feeling – the fluttering in my stomach that was refusing to go away.

'There's a vacant office in the basement of our building,' he'd said. 'It's small, but it might suit you. I can give you the landlord's card, if you like.'

And so I'd accepted the card graciously and left, making my excuses. Sleeping with the MD of one of the best publishing houses in Europe was not going to happen. But still. There had been something. Something that I'd tried very hard to block out when I moved into the office he'd recommended. Every time I met him in the lobby of my new building and remembered the heat between us in that hotel bar, I looked away and tried to forget.

And then came the fire drill.

'Oh, my God! Fire! *FIRE!*' My new assistant Helen had bounded into the tiny office when the alarm had started to shriek on that rainy Wednesday afternoon. It was her first week on the job and I'd already known she wasn't going to work out. She was far too damn perky. And she kept calling me 'boss' in a joking, over-familiar way. If Antonia West hadn't insisted I give her a chance I would never have hired her.

'It's just a drill, Helen,' I'd replied, shutting down my PC and cursing silently. A fire drill was the last thing I needed: I was snowed under with work and I couldn't afford to waste even half an hour while heads were counted on the street to satisfy Health and Safety.

'What if it's not?' she'd panicked, clasping her hands together, her eyes wide, her blonde (as it was then) hair askew. 'What if it's the real thing? Oh, my God, what if we're *trapped*? We can't use the lifts – the stairwells could be filled with smoke . . .' How could she be so clueless? She'd worked in an office environment before – her CV said so. Although by then I was already beginning to think her CV was a complete fabrication. So far, the only thing I knew she could do for sure was juggle – she'd given me a demonstration with three of the glittery gel pens she was so fond of. But answering phones, filing, photocopying – all of those simple office concepts – seemed alien to her.

We'd trooped up the stairs from the basement and outside, where the rain was driving mercilessly down in sheets and gangs of people were huddled together, trying to shelter close to the grey building. The smokers were the only ones pleased, revelling in another fag break, a fog of nicotine hanging over them like a virtual umbrella.

Somehow I found myself standing beside him.

'Are you behind this stunt? Having a fire drill in the rain?' I'd asked, smiling. Just for something to say, really. To kill the embarrassed silence between us.

'See the lengths I have to go to to get you alone?' he'd shot back.

And that was it. Kaboom.

We had to be discreet, of course. After all, we worked in the same industry and knew the same people – there would have been talk. And, besides, there was his very difficult ex-wife to consider: Gary was convinced if she found out about us before the divorce settlement was agreed she'd imply that we'd been an item before they'd broken up – and *that* would make things messier and more acrimonious than they already were.

Her name is Caroline and she's a lawyer with her own small practice, which clearly gives her the upper hand in proceedings. She's petite and wiry, all lithe limbs and not an ounce of fat. I get the impression that she doesn't do fat – she doesn't do unnecessary extras. Like her hair, for example: no tumbling luscious locks for her but a gamine pixie crop that she's allowed to go a wonderfully glamorous silver. She wears black polo necks and tailored trousers, Louise Kennedy probably, that hug her non-existent boy hips and she has little diamond studs in her neat, close-to-her-head ears. A gift from Gary in their happier days, more than likely – or perhaps she bought them for herself after winning some high-profile case. She looks a little like Audrey Hepburn – maybe it's the large, knowing eyes. Not that I have ever met her – but I read the *Independent*'s profile at least a dozen times when I Googled her – which of course I couldn't resist doing. The headline was 'Law's Lady in Waiting', and the article described how Caroline Elverson, barrister at law, had made a name for herself championing the poor and under-represented, like some modern-day Robin Hood. Except she's not at all charitable when it comes to Gary – quite the opposite. She's already accused him of being unfaithful during their marriage – a ploy to get more alimony, he says, which is the lowest thing I've ever heard, especially as they have two teenage boys to think about.

So, here we are and still no one knows about Gary and me yet. It's not that we're hiding exactly – but we don't want to invite gossip either. People don't need to know about our personal lives; we want to remain professional. And, in fact, we've managed to remain so utterly professional that no one has ever suspected a thing. We never email each other, unless it's work related. Definitely no smutty stuff, not even when we pass each other in the lobby and he gives me one of those looks. It's as if somehow we both realize without acknowledging it that if our secret was out it would impact on our lives and careers in ways we're not quite ready for. Besides, while it's a little strange not telling a soul that we're together, it also suits me in a way: the last thing I need is for my family – specifically my mother – to get over-excited and start planning a big white wedding.

'I had such a shit day,' Gary says now, loosening the red tie round his neck and yawning into his hand. He's so handsome in his dark suit, his hair peppered with grey at the temples. We're in his favourite Italian restaurant, Cruzo's, on the coast. I would have preferred to eat somewhere more casual closer to town – trekking all the way out of the city seems like such hard work – but Gary loves the fine-dining experience so here we are. As I look around me, I can't help feeling that one of the reasons we always come here is precisely because it's so far from town and therefore the chance of bumping into anyone we know is probably remote, but I bat away that notion. It's silly to think like that. Gary just wants to treat me to a special meal, that's all, so why do I have to go and question his motives?

'Did you? What happened?' I ask, trying to sound sympathetic. Really, I'm choking back the urge to get in first and tell him all my woes – I'm going to be thrown out of my office, and the bank manager is so desperate to talk to me that he's left me his personal phone number. Things couldn't be much worse.

'We had a partners' meeting. God, it was fucking miserable. And, of course, April O'Reilly kicking the bucket didn't help,' he says.

My head jerks up. *What* did he just say? 'April O'Reilly *died*?' I splutter.

'Yeah. She had a massive coronary at her desk this morning – can you fucking believe it? Still, not a bad way to go, I suppose. She probably never knew what hit her.'

My hand flies involuntarily to my mouth. April O'Reilly was a senior agent with Withers and Cole. She was a proper legend in the industry, with a fierce reputation. Never afraid to say what she thought, she was gutsy and a straight shooter. She was also one of my favourites – and one of the few who had come to see me when I tendered my notice. I'll always remember her stalking into my office, waving a bottle of her favourite Californian merlot, her face like thunder.

'Bastards, all of 'em,' she'd announced loudly, as I'd tried to keep a stiff upper lip and not wail at the injustice of being backed into a corner and having to leave a job I loved. 'You're better off out of it, Frankie. Now let's get pissed.' Then she'd lit a cigarette, ignoring the no-smoking signs as she always did, and we'd proceeded to get tipsy on the firm's time. I hadn't really seen her since – but I'd never forgotten her kindness that day.

'Oh, my God. I can't believe it,' I say now. 'Poor April. Poor, poor April.'

Gary clicks his fingers to get the wine list. I see the waiter flinch and I cringe inside. I really wish he wouldn't do that – he doesn't mean it, not really, but it can come across as so rude. 'I know. I was only talking to her yesterday. It's insane,' he says.

'You were?'

'Yeah, about Ian Cartwright. I've been trying to get him to write a sequel to *Field of Memories* – the ten-year anniversary is coming up. April was helping me to persuade him.'

Ian Cartwright: of course – April was his agent. Ian's first novel was considered a modern classic in the vein of J. D. Salinger, but he hasn't written anything since. Last I heard he was holed up abroad somewhere, working on the next big thing. Over the years there've been articles in the press, journalists trying to track him down and interview him, but he's almost a recluse – as far as I know he's more or less disappeared. Now that the anniversary of *Field of Memories* is coming up, though, it's the perfect time for his publishers to cash in, and Gary is obviously hoping he'll lay another golden egg.

'I just don't know what the fuck I'm going to do now,' Gary goes on. 'I was counting on April to come through for me, Frankie. I need a big money-spinner this year – everyone's breathing down my damn neck.'

'They are?' I say, a little taken aback. This is the first I've heard of it. Seems like I'm not the only one keeping professional secrets.

'Yeah. We're seriously down on last year – my arse is on

the line if I don't pull off something big. Ian was my secret weapon – I've been in discussions with April for *months*. And now she's dead. I mean, Christ Almighty, what are the fucking chances?'

I wince a little at his tactlessness – after all, April has just passed away. But I can see where he's coming from too: a deal is a deal. It's a very tricky situation.

'Had Ian agreed to it? The sequel?' I ask.

'Not exactly – the man is as stubborn as a damn mule. But April thought he might have been coming round . . .' He rakes his fingers through his hair – his signature move when he's upset.

'You can fix it, Gary.'

'No, I can't. I'm fucked. By the time he gets himself a new agent and I start negotiations all over again it'll be too late. The anniversary will have passed – and that's another missed opportunity. The whole thing is a fucking nightmare.'

'I'm sure there's some sort of solution,' I say, reaching for his hand.

'Like what? The heavens open and an angel flies down to my rescue?'

I physically recoil at the sharpness in his voice.

He sighs heavily. 'I'm sorry, Frankie. I shouldn't have snapped at you. This Ian Cartwright thing is just the last straw . . . Caroline's been on my case all week about the boys. They're both acting up terribly at the moment and I'm worried . . . I'm afraid I'm not very good company tonight.'

'That's OK,' I reply. I have to at least try to be understanding. Of course he's stressed: work troubles, a difficult ex-wife, two gangly teenage boys clamouring for his attention, both of whom are now 'acting up' apparently. I don't know what that entails or what it means – but it certainly doesn't sound good.

'Anyway. How's your week been?' he asks.

'Oh, fine,' I say. 'Let's get something to drink, shall we?' There's no way I can tell him my problems now, is there? I mean, I can't add to his woes: he has enough on his plate already.

'That's the best idea I've heard all day.' He smiles at me and takes my hand in his again as he peruses the wine list the waiter placed between us.

Maybe after we've had a few glasses of wine the time will be right to tell him. We'll both be far more relaxed then. I don't know why I'm so nervous about it actually – it's not like he's going to judge me. After all, he has plenty of experience with this kind of thing – he'll advise me. He might even be able to help. All I have to do is tell him. I just need a drink first.

Just then Gary's phone starts to buzz and, frowning, he clocks the number. 'What the hell does she want now?' he growls. 'She never leaves me alone!'

Great. It's Caroline. His ex. Just what I need.

'Talk to her,' I say, immediately deciding this is the best course of action. If he doesn't take her call then he'll be on tenterhooks all night, wondering what she wanted. Better for him to talk to her straight away and get it over and done with.

'Why should I? She just wants to bust my balls as usual,' he snarls.

'But what if it's important? What if it's about the boys?' I say. 'Take it. I don't mind, honestly.'

The phone is still ringing. She's not giving up.

'You're sure?' Gary asks.

'Of course.' I smile at him. 'No problem. We have all night.'

With a grunt, he pushes himself up from the table and stalks away, the phone clamped to his ear, his forehead creased – with worry or anger I can't be sure. I watch him go, my heart sinking. This isn't exactly how I imagined our evening together.

'Would Madam care to order some wine?' I hear the waiter ask, and I jump. He's just appeared at my shoulder out of nowhere.

'Em, yes, we'll have the Californian merlot, please,' I say, quickly deciding without even looking at the menu. I'll toast poor April's memory with her favourite tipple. It's the least I can do.

'Excellent, madam,' he replies. He looks at me then, and for an instant I see sympathy in his eyes. Oh God, maybe he thinks I've been jilted or something.

'He'll be back in a minute,' I explain. 'He just had some . . . business to attend to.'

'Of course.' The waiter makes a small jerky movement with his head, which manages to make me feel even worse. 'Would you like me to bring the wine immediately?'

'Yes, please,' I say.

There's no point in speculating how long Gary's call will take. He could be gone for ages and I can't wait that long. No, I need a drink – and fast.

Chapter Four

Three hours later I'm snuggled in the crook of Gary's arm in his enormous king-size bed. Outside, the rain is beating rhythmically against the vast windows of his luxurious apartment building but in here a fire is glowing in the grate and his favourite Cole Porter CD is humming in the background. It's bliss. In fact, if it wasn't for the pounding in my temples and the horrible sense of doom crushing my skull, I could almost forget my troubles.

I'm half drifting off to sleep when my phone rings and I struggle upright to peer at the caller ID. It's Antonia. What can she want so late? Yes, she's one of my most high-maintenance clients – even if behind all her histrionics she's just incredibly insecure and a little lonely – but it's almost midnight and that's odd, even for her.

I pause. I want to let her go to voicemail, but then again, the last time I didn't take her call immediately she went into a downward spiral of anxiety. Besides, the number-one golden rule of being a good literary agent is to treat each client as if they're your only one. I should abide by my own rules, even if I have a sinking feeling that she's not calling to congratulate me on what a stellar job I'm doing for her. Especially at this time of night.

And then it comes to me. *Helen.* Helen must have told her about Mr Morris – that he's so desperate to talk to me he's left me his personal phone number. Shit. If Antonia gets spooked, I may as well jack it all in now. She's my only decent earner – I have to keep her happy.

'Hi, Antonia! Is everything OK?' I quickly accept the call and try to inject warmth into my voice.

'Francesca!' she wails down the line. 'Have you heard the awful news?'

I try to think what the awful news could be this time. Official first-week sales figures for her new book aren't out yet, so it can't be that. Maybe she got a bad review on Amazon – the last time that happened she almost had a full-scale nervous breakdown. Or it could be about April: they knew each other well enough and, depending on her state of mind, Antonia could take the news of her death badly.

'It's the festival!' she goes on, her voice increasing in pitch and volume in my ear. Beside me, Gary winces as he tabs through emails on his phone, his half-moon glasses perched low on his nose as he reclines against his pillow.

'The festival? Which festival?' I ask, rolling my eyes at him. Literary festivals are ten a penny – who knows which she's talking about?

'The City Book Festival, of course – it's on next month,' she replies.

Aha. *Now* I know what this is about. The planned schedule of events for the City Book Festival went live on the website tonight and she's obviously been on there, cyber stalking.

'Oh, yes, that!' I say brightly. 'What's the matter?'

'Well, I haven't been asked to contribute!' she huffs. 'No one has even *called* me! Don't they *know* I have a new book to promote?'

'I don't think that's the –' I start. But she interrupts me.

'I mean, why haven't I been invited to be on the panel for the commercial-fiction workshop at the very least?' she wails. 'Are they excluding me on purpose?'

I can visualize her now, pouting, her trademark honey-blonde tresses frizzing in anxiety as she speaks. Antonia is lovely but she's also paranoid. Extremely paranoid. No matter how many novels she sells or how well she does in worldwide translations, a part of her always believes that the entire book industry is conspiring to destroy her career. 'Of course not,' I say soothingly. Or as soothingly as I can while trying not to point out to her that it's very late, and while I do try to be available to listen to her, perhaps she's overstepping the mark just a little.

'They're trying to push me out, aren't they?' she says, sniffing, and I can almost feel her hysteria building.

The second rule of agenting is always to sound interested and engaged with your client, even in the most difficult of circumstances. And this counts as difficult. 'I'm sure it's not deliberate, honestly,' I say, as I fish about for the right thing to reassure her and get her off the phone. 'The committee probably just felt they had to give some new writers a chance this year . . .'

'Like who?' She's instantly suspicious and I could kick myself for taking this tack. She doesn't like to be reminded that there are new writers out there – writers who might somehow outshine or, worse, outsell her, given half a chance.

'You *were* on the panel last year, Antonia,' I remind her gently.

'Two years ago. I was on the panel two years ago.' Her voice is flat.

Shit. Two years ago. I could have sworn it was only last year.

'Well, um, I suppose the organizing committee can't be seen to have favourites – and you're everyone's favourite, you know that.'

'Really?' She sounds a little mollified by this.

'Of course! Secretly they want you on that commercial-fiction panel every year, but they can't be seen to admit that – you can imagine how other authors would kick up if they knew the truth. They have to be seen to be non-biased.' I'm warming to my theme now – I sound quite convincing, even to my own ears.

'Hmm . . . maybe,' she replies.

'There's no "maybe" about it,' I say. Miraculously, this might actually be working – I'm starting to think she might believe me. If I'm lucky I'll be able to wind up this conversation in the next twenty seconds and then I can go back to Gary, the fire and the Cole Porter CD.

'Well, what about the Book Awards? Am I going to be shortlisted this year?' Her voice goes up a notch again.

Crap. I should have known she wouldn't let me off the hook that easily. She wasn't included in last year's Book Awards shortlist – and she hasn't let me forget it since. If she's not on this year's there'll be hell to pay.

'It's a sure thing!' I say, crossing the fingers on my left hand quickly.

'Well, I hope so – I did follow you, Francesca. Not everyone did.'

Her tone is suddenly dark and laden with meaning, and I can't help but wince. Antonia also never lets me forget that she followed me from Withers and Cole. In fact, she likes to remind me of it as often as she possibly can.

'This will be your year for sure, Antonia. I've already heard *The Edge of Love* is selling really strongly,' I say.

This is a teeny white lie because I haven't had any news on initial sales yet, but she doesn't need to know that.

'You have?' Her voice wavers, and I hear the raw nerves. This is what her call is really about: she's afraid the book will bomb. No, she's terrified it will.

'Absolutely! It's flying off the shelves. Now, let's chat in the morning, OK?'

'OK,' she says reluctantly. 'I'll be at my desk.'

'Perfect!' I reply brightly, then hang up, lie back against the pillow and exhale, feeling completely drained.

'Everything OK, babe?' Gary asks, idly caressing my neck while still checking messages on his phone.

'That was Antonia – she's in a bit of a flap.'

'So I gathered. You're very good at smoothing those ruffled feathers of hers, I must say.'

'I've had a lot of practice.' I sigh. 'I swear she's getting worse. If her new one doesn't go well, I don't know what I'll do . . .'

Talk about understatement of the year. After a quick calculation of my finances this afternoon, I now know that the situation is even worse than I'd previously thought – if that's possible. I'm really down to the wire and I've no idea how I'm going to pay the outstanding utilities bills as well as the back rent. I'm in a hole, a deep, black hole.

'Hmm . . .' he replies – and I realize that he's probably only half listening to me. 'It'll do well surely. You've had some good pre-emptive bids in from overseas, haven't you?'

'There's lots in the pipeline, but the contracts take so long to process – you know what it's like,' I say.

This is it: my opportunity to discuss my situation with him. I just have to work my way up to saying it out loud. Tell him the truth, Frankie. Admitting you're in trouble is the first step, right?

'Yeah, I know what you mean . . .' he says distractedly, one eye still on his phone. He's definitely only half listening to me. But I have my phone in my hand, too, so I can't exactly judge.

'I need to find another star,' I say, almost to myself.

Building my stable of authors is my only hope. But it looks like there's a fat chance of that happening any time soon, judging by the quality of the manuscripts I've read recently. Besides, even if I was to find someone great, persuading a publisher to take a punt on an unknown is getting harder and harder. In this market, they're sticking with what they know, not taking risks. I'm stuck – well and truly stuck.

'You'll give me first look if you find someone special, won't you?' He grins at me, giving me his full attention for a second.

'And why would I do that?'

'Because you know I'm the best publisher in town. And there'd be something in it for you, of course . . .'

'Are you bribing me, Mr Elverson?'

'I'll do what it takes, Ms Rowley.'

'Well, if I do find someone great I'll have to go with the best offer on the table, you know that.'

'I can offer you whatever you like,' he says, his hand moving from my neck downwards. And then he stops abruptly, pulls away and suddenly sits bolt upright. 'Jesus Christ! I've just had a fucking brilliant idea! Why didn't I think of it sooner? It's perfect!' His eyes are shining, excitement pumping from every pore.

'Can you speak in English, please?' I laugh.

'April has croaked it, right? And that means Ian Cartwright is now in the market for a new agent.'

'I guess so,' I say, wincing at his choice of words. Poor April.

'And that new agent could be you, Frankie! Fuck me – it's *genius*!'

'*Me*? But Withers and Cole will never let that happen, Gary! Bruce Makin will ring-fence all April's clients, you know that.'

Bruce Makin might come across as amiable enough but I know what he's really like. It was him who persuaded most of my clients to stay when I left, and it'll be the same now that April is dead. No one will poach her writers, not if he has anything to do with it.

'But Makin won't see it coming, will he? Not if we're quick,' Gary says.

'What are you talking about?'

'You could go over there, talk to Ian and convince him you're April's natural successor. The old bird loved you – everyone knows that. Yeah, and then you could get him to agree to that sequel before Makin knows what's happening. It's fucking genius, Frankie!'

He punches the air, his face alight, and my mind is racing now. Ian Cartwright is still a massive name. If he was to sign with me, especially if he agreed to a sequel, then the possibilities would be endless. It could be the solution to all my problems. The public would eat up another *Field of Memories* – they've been clamouring for it for years, sending emails to his website, writing him pleading letters – and with the anniversary coming up, the timing is perfect. He's the ultimate cash cow.

'Hasn't he always refused to do a sequel, though?' I ask, twisting myself round to face him, thinking quickly.

'Well, yes. But maybe he just needs . . . handling. And you can be very persuasive, Ms Rowley.'

'Flattery will get you nowhere.' I laugh. It's ridiculous – a crazy idea. And yet there's something bubbling in my chest . . . I think it might be hope.

'It's true, though,' he goes on. 'There's no one better than you at this sort of thing. Why don't you fly over there, bat those gorgeous eyelashes at him and see what he says? It would knock his socks off – he'd never be able to resist you in the flesh.'

'Are you suggesting I use my womanly wiles to get what I want?'

'Not at all.' Under the sheets, his hand is moving up my leg. 'But can you imagine if you did it? It would be a huge coup. Can't you see Makin's face? The Withers and Cole partners would be furious! It'd be priceless.'

He's right. It would be sweet revenge if it worked. They shafted me – and this is my chance to shaft them back. Plus it would help Gary out and solve all my financial problems, all in one fell swoop. It could be the perfect solution. It's almost too easy.

'And if it works with Ian, the sky's the limit, Frankie.' His fingers are caressing my inner thigh now. 'April's list was one of the best in the business, and her clients will be feeling adrift now she's dead. If Ian goes with you, more will follow, sure as night follows day.'

My mind is whirring, working overtime. He's right again. If I somehow managed to persuade Ian to sign with me, others would follow. Part of me feels weak with excitement at the thought, even if another part feels guilty for even thinking like this when poor April is barely cold. Her body might still be at her desk – they could be awaiting post-mortem results or something for all I know. An image of her, fag in mouth, phone clamped to her ear, rigor mortis setting in, pops into my head.

'You could do it, I know you could,' Gary whispers, as he nuzzles my neck.

'It's a nice idea,' I admit. 'But Ian Cartwright is virtually a recluse, you know that. He'd never agree to see me – why would he? I'm no one to him.'

I shouldn't get all excited about nothing – this is a pipe-dream, nothing more. Besides, I can't just stroll in and snag Ian for myself: that's not how it works. April was just one agent in a very large team at Withers and Cole: Makin will be on high alert and they'll all be guarding Ian with their lives in case anyone tries to nab him at this vulnerable time. And, really, poaching a client is not the done thing. You don't just take another agency's author . . . unless that author approaches you first, of course. Then all bets are off.

'You underestimate yourself, Frankie,' he says. 'You could do it, I know you could.' His eyes are locked on mine now and I see the intensity blazing there. He means it – he really means it. 'Just think about it,' he says. 'That's all I ask.'

'OK,' I agree, smiling at his boyish enthusiasm. 'I'll think about it.'

'You drive me wild, Blue Eyes, you know that . . .'

He moves closer to me, his body moulding to mine. Then his hand is travelling higher – and I forget all about Antonia and Ian Cartwright and the bank and everything else.

Chapter Five

It's Monday morning and I'm working my way through the piles of unopened post on my desk when Mum rings. I missed two calls from her yesterday so I know I have to pick up now or risk her arriving at my door with a party checklist in hand. And that's the last thing I need, what with every-thing else that's going on.

'Hi, Mum.'

'Frankie! Where have you been? I've been trying to get you for *days*!'

Ah, gross exaggeration – her calling card of choice.

'Sorry, I haven't had a chance to get back to you – things have been hectic, you know how it is.'

'You work too hard.'

There it is – the note of disapproval in her voice that's always omnipresent when my career is mentioned. I know she means well and she worries for me, but it's very wearing. 'Mum. Let's not get into this again, OK?'

'OK. But you can't let work take over – there's more to life, Frankie.'

'Yes, I know. So, what's going on?'

I have to distract her – get her talking about the party, although if I hear another word in the ongoing debate about mocktails versus cocktails I might scream.

'Well, I don't know where to begin,' she says.

That's not good. She always knows where to begin.

'Just tell me.'

She sighs melodramatically and I brace myself.

'I'm cancelling the whole thing.'

'*What?*'

'I've made up my mind. Don't try to talk me out of it.'

'But why? What's happened now?'

'Your aunt Maureen rang me today.'

Oh, God. The dreaded Maureen.

'Do you know what she told me?' she goes on.

I brace myself. Aunt Maureen is a grade-A bitch who'll say anything to get a reaction.

'What?'

'She told me that Donald and Catherine are getting divorced.'

'Donald and Catherine from the catering company?'

OK. So that's not exactly great news, considering they're supposed to be cooking and serving all the food for the party together.

'Yes! Maureen was at a wedding last week when Catherine emptied an entire tureen of tomato and basil soup over Donald's head right in front of everyone! She said it was bedlam. "All hell broke loose" – those were her exact words.'

I scrabble round for something positive to say. At least they're still working together – that's better than nothing, isn't it? But I can't say so – I have a feeling it mightn't go down well.

'Look, Mum, don't let Maureen get to you – that story probably isn't even true,' I say instead.

'I bet it is – that Donald is a rogue, everyone knows it,' she wails. 'Poor Catherine's been putting up with him for years. I really should have gone somewhere else for the food, but I couldn't, could I? Not when I know them both so well.'

'I'm sure it'll be fine, honestly,' I say, silently cursing Maureen. 'They're professionals – they won't let it affect your night.'

'But what if something kicks off at the party, Frankie? What if they create some kind of a scene like they did at that wedding? I'm worried sick.'

'They won't, don't worry.'

I hope.

'Well, we're not having soup, I suppose. That's a plus,' she says.

'Exactly. Look on the bright side. So – how's Dad?' I'm almost afraid to ask.

'He's fine,' she replies tightly. 'Of course, he would be – he's left everything up to me to organize. I don't know why I ever started this, if I'm honest.'

'Because you wanted to celebrate.'

'Celebrate? We'll be having a divorce party soon – maybe we could go halves with Catherine and Donald. Your father might be all for it.'

'Why? What's going on?'

'He doesn't like the band apparently. There. Now you know.'

'The band? What's wrong with the band?'

It's a Frank Sinatra tribute act, for goodness' sake – he can hardly object to Frank Sinatra, can he?

'Well, it's not the band *per se*. It's Andrew Stevens. That's what it's all about.'

'Who's Andrew Stevens when he's at home?'

'The lead singer.'

'And what's he got to do with it?'

'Nothing. Only he might have had a little crush on me when we were younger. Your father thinks he still does – it's so silly.'

'Why does Dad think that, Mum? That this Andrew still likes you, I mean?'

'Well, we saw them last night in the golf-club bar – the

47

band, I mean. They were doing a lovely set for Maurice Galvin's seventieth – they went down ever so well. *Everyone* was up dancing. Even Jean Baldwin – and you know what her hip is like.'

She's rambling – I'm never going to get to the bottom of this.

'Did something happen, though?' I ask. 'With him and Dad?'

There's a slight pause.

'Your father says Andrew was flirting with me.'

'And was he?'

'He might have winked at me once. Twice, tops! But it's all part of the act, Francesca, it meant nothing.'

Oh, for God's sake. Dad's jealous because the oldest swinger in town is making eyes at my mother. This is crazy.

'I know it probably didn't mean anything – but, then, I suppose Dad might not see it that way,' I say.

'But he's blowing the whole thing out of proportion! He says we have to cancel Andrew and get someone else! Where am I going to find another act at such short notice? It's impossible and he knows it. I'm starting to think he never wanted this party at all.' Mum dissolves into great big sobs, loudly blowing her nose down the line.

'Ah, now,' I say helplessly.

'It's all getting too much for me, Frankie. I'm not sure I can cope,' she cries. 'Can you come over tonight?'

Oh, God. There's no way I want to go over there tonight and be piggy in the middle – I have to get out of it.

'I'm really sorry, Mum, I'm not sure I can.' A wave of guilt crashes over me as I speak. I probably qualify for the Worst Daughter in the World Award.

'Why not? Do you have something on? A date?'

For a split second I hear hope in her voice. All she wants

is for me to find true love, like the princesses in those fairy-tales she used to read to me when I was little and we'd cuddle up in bed together as the wind howled outside. Thing is, I figured out those stories were fantasy when I was about eight. And now is not the time to tell her about Gary. 'No, nothing like that. There's been an emergency at work – something's cropped up,' I explain.

'Oh.'

There it is, right on cue. The crushing disappointment.

'Anyway, Mum, the party isn't for another few weeks – can't it wait?'

'Right. Well, don't mind me. I'll just soldier on. Maybe I could put the radio on at the party instead of having a band and hope for the best. Your father would probably *love* that.'

She hangs up abruptly and I'm left holding the phone, the dialling tone ringing in my ear. It *is* all getting too much for her, that's the problem. It was only supposed to be a small affair and she's practically living on her nerves because of it. And now Dad's freaking out too – it's very unlike him to act like this. And, of course, there's no sign of Eric or Martin – they're good for lugging boxes and eating all my parents' grub, but where are they when it comes to this sort of thing? Nowhere to be found.

A surge of annoyance erupts in me. Why should I keep standing for this? Why do my brothers get away with everything? I'm not an only child, after all – I can't be expected to deal with all this on my own.

I punch in Martin's mobile number and wait impatiently as it rings. I'll start with him and then I'll call Eric. I'll tell them they have to start rowing in more. Just because I'm the only girl in the family doesn't give them licence to abuse my good nature.

'Con Air, here to cool you,' I hear Martin say.

For God's sake – it has to be the stupidest catchphrase in corporate history. 'Martin, it's Frankie.'

'Hiya, sis, whassup?'

Martin likes to talk like he's down with the kids, when he clearly isn't and hasn't been for at least two decades.

'I'll tell you what's up, will I? Mum's been on the phone to me again about this bloody party and I've just about had enough of it.'

'OK, OK, don't get your knickers in a twist,' he says, in the condescending way he does that makes my blood boil.

'It's not funny, Martin! I have enough to be doing without dealing with all this crap as well – it's high time you and Eric helped out.'

'We are helping out!'

'What have you done exactly?'

'I helped Dad get that barbecue – they were in very high demand, you know. I had to really pull in some favours to get it for him.'

'They don't need a fucking barbecue,' I growl, just about ready to strangle him. 'They need proper help.'

'Like what?'

'Well, they might need to get a new band now because Dad's decided he doesn't like the one Mum booked.'

'Ah, yeah, the Frank Sinatra band – they would be boring in fairness.'

'They would not be boring – Mum wants a classy do, Martin.'

'I think they should get a DJ myself – and a shots bar. Or we could get those drinking hats for everyone – the ones with the straws. They'd be deadly!'

His voice sounds crackly and distant and then the line goes dead. Great. I wouldn't put it past him to pretend to hit a black spot and hang up on purpose – I've seen him do it

before when he wants to wriggle out of a tricky conversation. If I call back now I'll really explode. Better to wait for a
while, get on with some of the paperwork cluttering my desk
and talk to him later when I'm feeling calmer.

Taking a deep breath, I slit open the first envelope in my
hand and unfold the letter within. Suddenly it's as if I'm
looking down on myself as I read – the words are dancing in
front of my eyes, my throat is closing with fear. It's from Mr
Morris: '. . . unable to contact you . . . overdraft facility to be
withdrawn . . . no option but to close your account.' Oh, my
God.

They're closing my bank account. Can they do that? Can
they really do that? I can't operate without a bank account –
the business won't function. My head is spinning and my
heart is hammering in my chest as the reality of the situation
hits me full force between the eyes. All my worst nightmares
have been realized. Not only am I going to be evicted, but
now the bank has turned its back on me too. With no premises and not even a bank account to its name, my agency is
doomed. Properly doomed.

I close my eyes and try to battle the panic that threatens to
engulf me. There must be something I can do – there has to
be. I have to *think*.

Suddenly an image of Gary pops into my head. Gary and
our conversation about Ian Cartwright. If I got Ian on board,
persuaded him to write that sequel to *Field of Memories*, maybe
I could get out of this. If I could show Mr Morris I'm back
in the game he'd have to give me more time, wouldn't he?

It's a long shot, a very long shot, but if it worked, it could
solve everything . . .

In a daze, I punch in Gary's number and listen as it rings.

'Francesca.'

'I've been thinking. About Ian Cartwright.'

'And?'

'And . . . there might be something in it.'

'What changed your mind?'

'I just think it's too good an opportunity to turn down.'

And I don't have anything left to lose.

'I knew you wouldn't be able to resist!' he whoops jubilantly. 'This is brilliant!'

'So. I'm thinking I'll just give him a call – you know, have an off-the-record conversation,' I say.

'That won't work. He never answers his damn phone. Besides, you need to make an impact – speak to him in person. If I was you I'd get over there pronto, meet him and then charm him like you've never charmed anyone before.'

I can hear the excitement in his voice. 'I can't do that, Gary. What about the office?' What's he thinking of? I can't simply fly to San Francisco at such short notice. Helen would never cope without me. Never. She can barely cope when I'm here, let alone if I was five thousand miles away. I can only imagine what would happen – total and utter chaos, that's what. Besides, I've never even met Ian Cartwright – so, thinking about it, why would he even agree to see and talk to me?

'You'll have your phone, won't you? You can work remotely. If you're quick, no one need even know you're gone.' Gary's voice is urgent in my ear.

That's sort of true. My iPhone is my office – I would be totally contactable twenty-four/seven, like I always am. And I could rearrange any meetings: there's nothing too urgent in the next few days now that Antonia's book is safely launched. I could do it. I could take a chance. And imagine if it actually worked. Just imagine.

The elephant in the room, of course, is the cost. How can I afford the air fare? Unless . . . unless I use the company credit card. That's not at its absolute limit yet. Almost, but not quite. I shouldn't, should I?

'Do you really think this will work, Gary?' I say instead.

'I believe in you.' His voice is low, as if he's trying not to be overheard. 'You can do it, I know you can. Think how much you have to gain. How much *we* have to gain. We're going places, Frankie – we're going places together. This could make us, *both* of us.'

He's right. If I pulled it off, it would solve everything – it's the quickest, easiest solution to all my problems. And it might be the only one.

Helen strolls in as I'm hanging up, having made my decision, for better or worse. 'Everything OK, boss?' she chirps, flinging her bag on the floor as usual.

Right. This is it. Show-time.

'I have to go to San Francisco,' I reply, straining to keep my voice steady and not betray my nerves to her. 'It's all very last-minute – there's an . . . issue I have to deal with.'

'Oh, my God! I *love* San Francisco!' she squeals. 'Did I ever tell you I spent a summer there when I was a student? We had a place near Fisherman's Wharf – it was amazing! There's so much to see and do – you're gonna *love* it!'

'I'm not sure I'll have time for sightseeing,' I say. 'I'm going to be very busy.'

'But you just have to see the sea lions – they are *sooooo* cute! And the chowder – you have to taste it! Don't go to the touristy restaurants, though. I can give you the name of some brilliant places where all the locals go.'

'First things first, Helen,' I say, my mind working overtime. 'I need you to book me a flight.'

'Of course! No problem. Business class?'

I pause for a second. Business class makes sense – it *is* a very long way to the west coast of America and I need to have my wits about me when I get there and not be too exhausted to think straight. But I know I can't possibly afford a premier seat. When I travelled for Withers and Cole someone else was paying – I don't have a travel budget any more. I don't have any sort of budget any more.

'Economy,' I reply. 'And I need to get out there ASAP.'

'ASAP. Right. I understand.' She nods energetically. 'Maybe you'll be lucky and get upgraded to Business – that almost happened to me once. Did I ever tell you that story?'

'No.'

And I don't want to hear it now.

'Oh, yeah, I was so close. I mean I'd just love to get one of those special seats – you know, the ones that go flat so you can sleep in complete comfort? And they have these cool private pods now too. Cheryl loves those. It was in *Grazia*. She gets massages when she flies to LA. And she can have all this gourmet food – she probably doesn't even eat half of –'

'Helen!' I bark.

The dreamy expression in her eyes vanishes as she snaps back to reality. 'Yes?'

'I need you to focus. Do you understand me?'

'Of course,' she replies earnestly.

'This trip is important. Very important.'

'Wow!' Her eyes widen. 'Is it, like . . . critical?'

I think about Ian – what I have to lose if I don't get this right. What I have to gain if I pull it off. 'You could say that, yes.'

'Why? What's happening?' Her voice lowers. 'Or can you not tell me?'

'It's confidential for now, OK?' Last thing I need is her blabbing this news to everyone who calls when I'm away. Or to Antonia.

'Right.' She nods solemnly, as if this is life or death, which it sort of is.

'I'm going to need you to keep on top of things here. You have to step up.'

'Of course I will! You can rely on me, you know that,' she says.

That's just the problem – I know nothing of the sort.

'We'll be in different time zones. You'll have to make allowances,' I say.

'Boss, if anything urgent crops up, night or day, you can call me. I'll be here for you, I promise. I'll be on red alert. Nothing will get by me. I'll be a ninja!'

She waves her hands around in karate-chopping fashion and I close my eyes for a second as she babbles on, panic engulfing me.

Stay calm – you can still keep on top of everything. You'll have your phone – you'll be totally contactable. No one need know you're gone. Just get over there and get Ian on board.

I take the company credit card from my wallet and hand it to her. I can't afford this trip, I know that, but if I don't want my beloved fledgling agency to crash and burn before it even gets off the ground then this is what it's going to take. Because I can't afford to fail either. Not now. Not after everything.

'Right,' I say, drawing breath. 'Helen, this is what I need you to do.'

Chapter Six

'You're going *where*?' Mum gasps down the line. I can almost picture her standing in the kitchen, one hand clasped dramatically to her bosom.

'To San Francisco, Mum.'

'But what about the party? What am I going to do?'

'The party isn't for ages yet. We've plenty of time. I'll help you when I get back, I promise.' Helen has booked a return flight for next week, but I might be back earlier, depending on how it goes. The flexible ticket cost more, of course, but I'm trying not to think about the added expense.

'You always say that,' she grumbles.

'Mum. I have to go. It's work. I can't get out of it. Now, I spoke to Martin yesterday – why don't you give him a call? He can help with the band.'

'But Martin's far too busy, Frankie – he has enough to do running his own business.'

Eh? So do I! I bite my lip to stop myself snapping at her. There's one rule for my brothers and another for me and there always has been since we were little. 'Look, Mum, I have to go – we're just about to take off. I'll call you soon, OK?'

'But –'

I tap the red button before she can say any more, lean back against the headrest and exhale. I've only just boarded the flight – I'm wedged into a tiny seat with zero leg-room in Economy – and my calf is already cramping. I'll be lucky if I don't get a thrombosis. The only plus is that at least there's no one sitting beside me – no award-winning small-talker to make the journey even worse. That's a bonus. In fact, thinking about it, maybe this journey won't be so bad. I'll be able to spread my things on to the next seat and then I can get a pillow and lean against the window. I might even be able to snooze a little, if I pull up the arm rest. Maybe it won't be as awful as I imagine. OK, so I have a teeny seat in Economy, but at least I'm not trapped beside someone really irritating who wants to chat the entire way from Dublin to San Francisco. Now *that* would be hell.

'Twenty-three B? Ah, yes, here it is! Hello there!' a loud voice booms.

Oh, crap.

I look up, my heart sinking, to see a plump woman of about fifty beaming down at me. She has 'small-talker' written all over her fair, freckly complexion. I can spot one a mile off. And it's worse. She's wearing a bright green T-shirt with a shamrock on the front picked out in glitter and a green baseball cap jammed on her auburn hair that reads 'Proud to be Irish' at the front. There's glitter on that too. I know what this means: she's an American who, from her attire, has been over to 'research her roots'. In approximately five minutes she'll be pumping me for information about her ancestors. This is just my bloody luck.

'I guess I have to stow my stuff up here, right?' She surveys the overhead locker doubtfully, then heaves her carry-on bag upwards with a grunt. Her breasts are so enormous I almost have to move backwards against the window so I'm not enveloped in them.

'Gosh, I just hate flying, don't you?' she pants, wedging herself into the seat next to me with some difficulty.

I get a flash of her underwear as she manoeuvres her way in and even that's green. She's hardcore. I'm doomed.

'I mean, you read about it all the time in the papers,' she goes on, not waiting for me to reply. 'Planes dropping from the sky and then . . . *kaboom*! Lordy, it makes me sweat!' She wriggles about trying to fasten her seatbelt, which strains round her extremely ample hips, then fans her face dramatically with the emergency-instructions card.

I know the rules in situations like this. Don't talk back to the small-talkers. Say nothing. Maintain a stony silence because engaging on any level will mean getting sucked into unwanted conversation. But I can't do that – because it would be really, really rude. I know what I'll do – I'll just quickly acknowledge that she's here, so she won't be offended, and then I'll go back to ignoring her.

I smile half-heartedly in her direction. There. No need to be impolite or hurt her feelings. But she'll get the message: *I am not going to talk to you, lady.*

I go back to my phone again and begin scrolling through messages, hoping she'll get the hint and talk to someone else. This wouldn't be happening to me if I was in Business. Up there people know not to talk to each other – anyway, they're probably far too busy to chat, what with all the free biscuits, warmed blankets and aromatherapy oils. That's where I should be, stretched out in comfort, watching five different sorts of movies, sheltered from the lunatics back here. *Next time, next time, next time.*

'Lordy, these seats are getting smaller! Or maybe I'm getting bigger! Ha-ha-ha!' The American is still chuckling – she's not getting the message. This is bad. This means she has no boundaries. She's the worst type of small-talker – she'll talk into thin air if needs must.

A voice in my head begins to babble double time, offering advice: Pretend to be mute, Frankie. Pretend to be in a coma, if you have to. Otherwise you'll be forced to chat to this woman for at least ten hours. Think about it. Think about the consequences of replying to her. OK, so you might appear rude but surely that's better than striking up a conversation. It might seem harmless at first but it won't be so harmless endless hours from now when you're tearing out your hair or hiding in the toilets just to get some peace and quiet.

'They are small,' I concede, kicking myself for giving in and replying. I need to start listening to my inner voice, not ignoring it! Responding to her was a big mistake: I now have no one to blame but myself for what happens next. I should have pretended that I don't speak English.

'I'm glad it's not just me.' She grins at me, clearly delighted I'm chatting back. 'I've put on fifteen pounds since I've been here, eating too many of those dang chips you got! What d'you call 'em? They're in a red and white bag.'

'Tayto?'

'That's it! Tayto! They are *sooooo gooooood*! I'm shipping some home.'

I nod silently, then pretend to be engrossed in a text so I don't have to answer.

'You're addicted to that, I guess.' She jerks her head towards my phone. 'My daddy was never without his either – he was never parted from it, never! That thing was always in his hand! He was a real techie, that's what he used to call himself.'

I smile politely again, hoping she can read my mind, which is saying something like: 'OK, this conversation is over now. We've done the pleasantries. Please go away.'

I have to do something because the phone gag's obviously not working. Maybe if I just pretend to busy myself with my in-flight magazine, she'll get the hint and we can go back to being complete strangers. Which means, by definition, we won't be talking to each other.

I put my phone into my lap and pick up the magazine, which features a cheerful-looking couple, brightly coloured cocktails before them, on the cover, and burrow my head in an article about travelling by donkey through Greece. Who knew you could do that? More importantly, who would want to do it?

'Gosh – where are my manners? My name's Rosie – what's yours?'

She's just not taking no for an answer. She is going to strike up a conversation with me if it kills her. Or me.

'Frankie,' I mutter. God, I wish I could be blatantly rude. Tell her I'm sorry but I don't want to talk to her. It's nothing personal, but we obviously have nothing in common so can we sit in blissful silence? Please?

'Frankie? Like, a boy's name? That's so cute!'

'Well, it's Francesca, actually, but my friends call me Frankie.'

And you are not a friend so please take the hint and leave me alone.

'You don't mind me calling you "Frankie", do you? I know we're not exactly friends yet, but I guess we will be by the time we get to San Francisco, right? I just know when I'm going to be friends with someone. It's in the eyes. I can always tell – always! I'm never wrong.'

Her blue eyes, framed by long auburn lashes, clamp on mine and I find I can't look away. 'You're not?'

'Oh, no! I once met a lovely lady on a flight to Los Angeles – Maria, her name was. I knew right off we were gonna be best friends, and guess what, Frankie?'

'What?' My voice is just a whisper. I'm afraid to ask.

'We still are best friends twenty years later! We swap homes and everything! She lives in Texas – where I'm from. So it was, like, Fate. Isn't that amazing?'

'Amazing,' I parrot.

OK. Frankie, under no circumstances are you to swap

addresses with this lunatic. No matter what she says. Otherwise she'll be turning up on your doorstep next year for her annual European vacation.

'Yup, it was Fate, all right! Do you believe in Fate?'

The man in front of us turns to check us out and Rosie gives him a massive wink as I make pleading eyes at him. He's reading Ian Cartwright's *Field of Memories* – maybe it's a sign that everything's going to be OK. Either that or this trip is going to be the biggest mistake of my life.

'I'm not sure . . .' I mutter.

'Oh, but you must – I mean, here *you* are, a friend from the land of my ancestors sitting right here. If that's not Fate I don't know what is.'

Half the passengers on the plane are from the land of your ancestors, you crazy woman, I want to say. We *are* in Dublin. But I don't. Instead I wonder would it be Fate if I locked myself in the toilet for the duration of this flight? I know it's probably illegal but, heck, I'm almost willing to take the chance.

'Would you like some gum? I've got, like, a stash.' She produces a packet from her handbag and pops a tab into her mouth, offering one to me too.

I shake my head. At least I didn't speak out loud. That's progress. And, even though I'd quite like some gum, I know that accepting snacks is a big no-no. She'll take it as the green light that I'm open to chatting to her for the next gazillion hours. I should have brought some sleeping pills. Then I could have popped one and passed out, woken fresh and ready for battle on the other side.

'So, do you fly much?' she asks now, chewing happily.

'Not really,' I murmur, keeping my eyes glued to the picture of the donkey in the article. He looks like I feel: hopelessly despondent.

'Me neither. My daddy used to say that if the Almighty'd intended us to fly, he'd have given us wings. Amen to that!'

Oh, God. Maybe she's some sort of religious freak or in a cult. She might want to convert me. She could be trying to brainwash me, right this minute! *Don't look in her eyes!* my inner voice screams.

Why does this always happen to me? *Why?* Is it too late to ask to move? I crane my neck and try to catch the stewardess's eye as she saunters down the aisle in her navy polyester uniform, making sure that everyone is fastened in safely with luggage stowed securely above their heads. There has to be a spare seat somewhere else. Up there – beside that screaming baby maybe. OK, so it might cry for ten hours straight but I can handle that. In fact, I'll volunteer to help. I've no experience with infants, of course, but I'm sure its mother will be grateful – she's already looking hassled . . .

'Don't look so nervous, Frankie!' Rosie interrupts my thoughts once more.

'Nervous? I'm not nervous,' I whimper. No. I'm terrified.

'Sure you are. I know what you're thinking!' She giggles.

'You do?'

'Oh, Lord, yes! You're thinking I'm crazy. A crazy American. Right?'

Tick.

'No, of course not,' I mumble.

'Now, Frankie, don't lie to me!' She chuckles, shaking her head, the green hat bobbing.

'I'm not.' *Oh yes I am.*

'All you Irish are so cute! Look at you, denying it! Well, let me tell you something . . .' She leans in so close to me I can smell the menthol on her breath. 'You're only half right! You wanna know why?'

Not really, no.

'Well, I'll tell you! I'm only half American – because the rest of me is Irish! I'm a Kelly from Waterford!' She dissolves into hysterical laughter at her own little joke and I smile at her, gritting my teeth.

'Great,' I mutter.

'Yep, my great-great-great-granddad took the *Dunbrody* ship from New Ross town to America during the Great Famine. Now here I am, all these years later, tracing my heritage. Isn't that awesome?'

'Awesome,' I repeat hollowly.

'He had nothing, you know, when he left. But he made it to New York and then he met my great-great-great-grandma at a dance in Queens and they travelled down south together. They were happily married for fifty-four years.'

Suddenly her eyes are filling with tears and I don't know where to look. I can't handle this.

'I'm sorry.' She sniffs. 'That gets me real fired up. You must think I'm nuts for real. I'll stop talking now.' She pats her face with a hanky she pulls from her bag.

The relief is enormous. Finally! Finally she's going to stop talking and I can relax. But then I glance at her and I feel bad. She looks genuinely upset. She's almost properly crying. Now I feel really guilty. 'Are you OK?' I say, unable to help myself.

'Oh, yes.' She smiles weakly at me. 'It's just that my daddy would have loved to see the Old Country. He was so proud of his Irish roots.'

'He's passed away?'

'Yes.' She blows her nose loudly. 'Last year. He lived in Houston all his life – that's where I grew up.' The man in front turns to look at her again, despair in his eyes. We haven't even taxied on to the runway yet.

'Where do you live now?' I ask. I can't help it – she looks so sad.

'In Sausalito. Just across the bay from San Francisco. It's real nice, but sometimes I miss Texas, y'know.'

'They must be very different,' I say.

'Yup. They sure are. So, where are you from, Frankie?'

'Dublin.'

'I love Dublin!' She brightens visibly. 'Do you know the Dublin Kellys?'

'Well, Dublin is a pretty big place,' I reply.

'Yes, of course it is. I can be such a dumb-ass!' She throws her head back and guffaws loudly, all trace of tears now gone. 'Do you know the Kellys of Waterford, then?'

'Er, no. I don't. I don't know any Kellys, actually.'

'You don't? Wow! And you're from here! Isn't that amazing?'

'I suppose it is.' Except it's not. Not really.

There's a small silence.

'Can I ask you something? If you don't mind?'

I brace myself for another outlandish question. Do I know her second cousin twice removed, perhaps?

'Would you hold my hand for takeoff and landing?' Her eyes are glued on mine once more.

'Hold your hand?' Is she kidding?

'Yes. Just for takeoff and landing – they're the worst bits. I just can't stand it when the plane wobbles, you know. I get kind of insane!'

Kind of insane?

'I sure would appreciate it.' Her gaze is still fixed on my face.

I gape at her, trying frantically to say something, anything. And then my phone beeps in my lap. Saved by the bell. 'Excuse me,' I murmur. 'I just have to, ah, check my messages.' A text from Helen pops up: *Everything under control here boss!*

64

Helen. Right this second she's being me at a booksellers' event. All I can hope is that she's not making a show of us both.

'Ma'am, you need to put away your mobile phone, please.'

I lift my head when I hear the stewardess's voice, snapping back to the present. This is my chance. Rosie is fiddling with her handbag. I just have to ask to be moved. Maybe a seat has opened up in Business. Maybe it's not too late. I'm wearing my best Prada jacket, after all, the one I treated myself to when I worked with Withers and Cole and had a healthy bank balance. I'll fit right in.

Turning off my phone quickly and shoving it back into my bag to show the stewardess how nice I can be, I try my most charming smile. The more co-operative you are, the higher chance there is of being moved – I know that. OK, so that tactic didn't work at check-in when I tried to be my most enchanting as I enquired politely if there was any way I could be upgraded. The girl's face was blank when she told me that Business Class was full and there was nothing she could do. But maybe a seat has become free: business people often double book so it's totally possible. It's now or never.

'Excuse me, could you . . .' I start. 'Would it be possible –'

But I don't have the chance to finish because Rosie interrupts me: 'Has the captain said a prayer, or done a meditation maybe?' she says to the stewardess, her face anxious.

'I'm not sure,' she replies, patently startled. *Is this woman a terrorist?* is written all over her face.

'Well, could you give him this, please? If you don't mind? It's just a little meditation – I'd sure be more at ease if you did.' Rosie produces a piece of paper that she presses into the stewardess's hand.

The woman's face is working overtime. She almost looks like she's trying to decide whether or not to pepper-spray her. But then she scans the note quickly, smiles and slips it into her apron. 'Sure I will,' she says at last. 'And try not to worry – you'll be perfectly safe here with us.' She looks at me, her smile fading, her expression stern once more. 'Phone away? Good. Now you ladies just relax and enjoy the flight!'

Then she's gone and so is my moment to escape. Relax and enjoy the flight? Easy for her to say. She's not trapped beside a real live lunatic.

'Ladies and gentlemen, we will be departing in less than one minute. Please make sure you have all items of luggage stowed safely either in the overhead compartments or under the seats in front of you. We hope you have a very pleasant journey. Cabin crew, cross-check for departure.'

As the announcement is made, Rosie grabs my hand, gripping it tightly and crushing the bones so hard that I wince. 'This is it!' she cries. 'Will you hold my hand, Frankie? Please!'

'Em, I'm not sure that will . . .'

But it's no use. She squeezes my fingers in a vice-like grip, panic in her eyes. 'Oh, Lordy,' she bleats. 'What if we crash?'

'We're not going to crash,' I reassure her. Jesus, I can't feel my fingers any more. That's it. I want to get off. I can take the next flight. Tomorrow, maybe. But it's too late for that – the plane is already hurtling down the runway. I'm trapped. Trapped beside a crazy woman who's holding my hand so tightly that I'm sure she's doing permanent nerve damage. There's no going back now.

Chapter Seven

Nearly twelve hours of hell later, I'm almost at the top of a very long line that snakes half way across the Immigration hall. I'm cross-eyed with exhaustion, not having slept one solitary wink during the flight. Unlike Rosie who, once she recovered from her hysterical episode during takeoff, had snoozed happily on my shoulder for at least three hours straight, snoring on and off and occasionally muttering, 'Oh, Lordy,' in her sleep. When she *was* awake she talked the entire time, even after I'd plugged in my earphones and tried to watch the movie. She just wouldn't get the message – kept digging me in the ribs, laughing loudly at the antics on screen, giving a running commentary throughout, as the man in front turned round and glared at her a dozen times. But she didn't seem to notice him, just like she didn't seem to notice that I was desperate for some blessed silence. Instead, once the movie was over, she pulled out a folder of details about her Irish ancestors and insisted on naming and describing each one while I gritted my teeth and tried not to scream. And then I had to endure the landing – she held my hand so tightly, her eyes clamped shut, that I'm half convinced she shattered a bone. It's still throbbing. At least once we'd disembarked I lost her.

'Next!' the female Immigration official calls gruffly and I step forward, passport in hand. I immediately feel overwhelmed with irrational guilt, just like I always do when I have to go through Customs or Immigration, which is ridiculous. I've done nothing wrong. There's nothing to be nervous about: I am a legitimate business traveller. I am not a terrorist. I'm not carrying illegal contraband in my knickers. I packed all my cases myself.

Except . . . what if someone intercepted my bags? What if someone stashed cocaine in my handbag and I never saw? It happened to Bridget Jones and she was thrown into a Thai jail for weeks and Mark Darcy had to come and rescue her . . . I shake my head and try to get a grip. This is not some movie, based on a bestselling novel. This is real life. All I have to do is maintain eye contact and smile – that way, the nice Immigration woman will know I'm not lying and she won't have to strip-search me or check out my body cavities, or anything like that.

'You're here on business?' she asks, glaring at me, open hostility on her face.

Wow, her forearms are big. Huge. Can she be on steroids? Maybe that's a perk of the job – maybe they all sprinkle a sachet of the funny stuff over their bagels every morning, just in case they need extra-terrestrial strength to deal with the scumbags. I have to show her, beyond doubt, that I am in no way a scumbag.

'Yup. Yes, I am. Business. Big business!' I say cheerfully. Crap. Where did that come from? What am I talking about? Big business? I'm not here to host a convention on greenhouse gas emissions or a worldwide initiative to reduce weapons of mass destruction. *Oh, no.* Now I have the word 'weapons' in my head. She can tell, I know by the expression on her face, that I'm thinking about bombs right this second.

'Big business, ma'am?' she says acidly.

Is it my imagination or is she staring into my eyes just a little too intently? Like she's trying to read my soul? And her massive forearms – they're sort of flexing ominously, glinting under the fluorescent lights. I start to sweat, a trickle rolling down the back of my neck and between my shoulder blades. And this Prada jacket is dry-clean only. Shit. 'Well, not big business exactly,' I backtrack. 'Just business. I'm an agent. A *literary* agent, I mean, not the other kind, obviously, ha-ha-ha . . .'

Dear God. I'm going to be arrested for impersonating an FBI agent. That's, like, the worst crime ever – a federal or capital offence or something. Something terrible anyway. Why is she tapping on her screen? Is she checking I'm not on some master list of terrorists?

'You see, there's an author,' I babble on. 'I have to get him . . . um . . . to write this book.'

'Uh-huh.' She's staring at me again. One of her pupils is dilated but the other isn't. What does that mean? Is one of her eyes bionic, maybe? Does she have some special sort of chip implanted in it to separate the terrorists from the civilians?

'He's a big name – he's only ever written the one book, but it was a modern classic, a masterpiece . . .' My mouth is now working without me meaning it to.

'A masterpiece, huh?' She studies my passport as if her life depends on it. Or mine.

Oh, God, this is terrible. She thinks I'm some sort of literary snob. She certainly doesn't look like a big reader. She probably only reads specialist military magazines or books on guns. Oh, God. Now the word 'gun' is in my head too. OK. I'll just explain quickly, so she'll know I'm not any sort of risk . . . But what if she thinks I'm talking down to her – like she's some sort of uneducated loser? She won't take kindly to that.

From the corner of my eye I see Rosie, in her green 'Proud to be Irish' hat, hand her passport to another official, get it stamped and breeze away, pulling her carry-on grey wheelie-case with a green shamrock ribbon looped through the handle. She looks suddenly authoritative, business-like, as if she knows exactly what she's doing. How can that be right? She was a babbling bag of nerves all the way here and now she looks like she could be the one chairing an international symposium on greenhouse emissions. I make a concerted effort to pull myself together. I'm a successful businesswoman, for goodness' sake. I'm well travelled: this sort of thing shouldn't faze me. I'm cool. Cool as a breeze. Cool as a . . . cucumber.

But the sweat is seeping out of my underarms into the silk lining of my Prada jacket. It'll be ruined, absolutely ruined – but, hey, I'm not going to need a Prada jacket in prison, am I? I'll have a nice boiler-suit to wear.

Suddenly, with a grunt, the official stamps my passport and hands it back – she's looking past me. She's lost interest. I'm not going to get any of my cavities searched after all.

Quashing the urge to whoop with relief, I scurry away, my heart pounding. I really need to get a grip on this whole Customs and Immigration phobia thing. I'm a professional: I deal with crises every day of my working life, so why do I fall to pieces like that every time, work myself into a sweaty panic?

Shaking off my Prada jacket and wrapping it round my waist, I start to weave my way through the throngs towards Baggage Reclaim. I need to pick up my stuff, grab a cab and get to the hotel. There's no time to waste. My first task is to go straight to the address Gary gave me and talk to Ian.

I've already tried to contact him, leaving multiple messages on his machine, but there's been no word back from him as yet. I'm hoping that while I've been on the flight he's called me back, or maybe called the office – Helen is under strict instructions to contact me immediately if he gets in touch. In fact, I'm sure to have missed lots of messages during the long flight – and I'm already itching to start catching up.

'Lordy, those Immigration people are *soooo* intense!' Out of nowhere, Rosie is somehow at my elbow, her wheelie-case clattering along behind her.

'I guess they have to be,' I mutter.

'Yours sure looked scary,' she says, giggling.

'Scary?' I laugh, as if I wasn't the least bit intimidated. I don't want her to know that I was quite rattled. 'Not at all. We were just having a chat, actually.'

'You're such a joker, Frankie!' She punches me playfully on the arm and I flinch. She's fond of doing this and my arms will have the bruises to prove it – she hit me excitedly on the flight when she came across a funny passage in the book she was reading and when the in-flight movie made her crack up. She's uncannily strong.

'Now, don't you go running off before we swap numbers, ya hear? Where's your phone? I can input mine for you.'

'Why don't you just scribble it down on some paper?' I say, not meeting her eye. That way I can lose it, accidentally on purpose.

'You must think I'm dumb!' she hollers, punching me playfully once more. I've never been sure what a holler is until now – but I know that was one. 'You'll lose that piece of paper. Now, gimme your phone and I'll put in my number.'

There's no getting away with it.

'OK,' I say. I don't want to be rude – Rosie is a little over the top, but she's quite nice, really. A bit in your face, for sure – but warm, cheerful. *Insane*. And it can't be easy travelling overseas to trace your heritage, especially when you know your dead father would have loved to be there too. A fleeting image of Mum and Dad pops into my head – they'd be horrified if I was rude to this sweet, if overbearing, lady. I may be a grown woman but they still expect me to mind my manners and behave myself in public, even with complete strangers. I once sent back a steak because it was overdone and Mum was scandalized.

'That's not how we raised you, Francesca,' she gasped, shocked that I'd actually asked for what I wanted the way I wanted it. Then she apologized to the waiter when he returned, carrying my new steak, and proceeded to tell him that I'd always been picky and had refused to touch a carrot until I was ten.

Yep, I have to behave myself and be nice – it's Eric and Martin they let away with blue murder. When Eric was eighteen he practically got into fisticuffs with a traffic warden over a parking ticket, but instead of punishing him Mum and Dad had started up a petition to get him off the fine – all the neighbours had signed it. And, really, Eric was totally in the wrong and they knew it.

I rummage resentfully in my bag as I think about that, searching for my phone. I'd been sure to obey the big signs in Immigration, not to power it up until we got to Baggage Reclaim. The last thing I wanted to do was draw more attention to myself. But now that I want it I can't put my hand on it. I squat down, bag balancing on my lap, to take a better look. After what seems like minutes of searching through every interior pocket, I finally realize it's not there. My phone is gone. *My phone is gone.* Frantically, I spill the contents of my bag all over the floor, willing it to appear, my heart palpitating. It has to be there – *it has to be.* There are my lipsticks, my Kindle, my wallet, my antiseptic hand gel, my keys. *But no phone.* Then I remember: there's a small tear in the lining of my bag – it must have fallen through it. I turn the bag inside out, desperate now, heart pounding, patting it all over, hoping desperately to come across the tell-tale rectangular shape. But it's not in there. It's not anywhere. I must have left it behind. But I couldn't have, could I? Unless it fell out of my bag when I was gathering up my stuff. Oh, my God.

I leap up. I have to get back on the plane. I have to go back and search. I can't be in a strange city with no phone, no contacts . . . My mind starts to race, my legs almost buckling beneath me as the consequences hit me full force. I can't function without my phone. I rely on it for everything – I need it back!

'Are you OK, honey?' Rosie asks. 'You've gone white as a sheet.'

'It's my phone,' I say hoarsely. 'I've lost it.'

'Oh, my.' She grimaces, her eyebrows knitting together. 'That's terrible. Do you think you left it on the plane?'

'I must have.'

How? I had it on my lap . . . it must have fallen off, under the seat . . .

'I guess it could have fallen out – it could be under the seat,' she says, echoing my thoughts.

'Will they let me go back?' I ask wildly, looking around for someone to appear and tell me it's going to be OK, that they'll get it back to me straight away. But even as I ask I know there's no chance of that happening. They'll never let me get back on the plane – it's protocol. If I even attempted to go back they'd probably lock me up and throw away the key.

'Gosh, no,' Rosie confirms. 'Not a chance. You'll have to go to the airline desk, honey – fill out a form, I guess. They'll get your phone back to you, don't worry – the cleaners will hand it in.'

'Do you think it'll take long?' I ask, my heart lifting with hope. Maybe this isn't so bad. Maybe I just have to do the paperwork and I'll get my phone back by the end of the day.

73

'Maybe a day or two? Though it could be longer. I left my purse on a flight once and it took me three weeks to get it back.'

'*Three weeks?*' I suddenly feel very sick.

'Yeah, they said it'd got lost in the Lost and Found, if you can believe that,' she snorts. 'But I was lucky. My friend Harvey left his PC on a flight once and he *never* got it back – not ever! He was so mad he . . .' Her voice trails away as she clocks my expression. 'But that won't happen to you, sugar,' she soothes. 'You'll probably have it back by tomorrow. The day after, latest!'

'I can't wait that long!' I howl. 'I need that phone today, right now!'

'The world won't stop turning just because you've lost your phone, sweetie.'

'You don't understand – my entire life is on it! This is a *disaster*!'

My notes, my calendar, all my contacts . . . I'm panicking properly now as the implications come flooding at me.

'I know you might think that now,' she says, patting my arm, the one she bruised earlier with her playful punching, 'but you're only here for a few days, right? All you have to do is rent a holiday phone – there's a place in the arrivals hall. Loads of people do it when they're overseas.'

Of course – I can rent a phone for now. My mind begins to whirr. It's still a disaster, but maybe it's not catastrophic. I'll probably get my own phone back by tomorrow and I do have Helen at home – she'll field calls in the office and let me know if anything urgent crops up. It's all I need, another drama like this, but I'm just going to have to cope somehow.

Two hours later I'm in my hotel room on the phone to Helen. 'So, you'll email me all the contacts I need?'

'Of course, boss.'

I wish she'd stop calling me 'boss', as if she works in some newspaper office in the 1950s. But I won't get into that now – it'll only distract her and I need her to focus on the task at hand, which is, even without my own phone, making sure I'm contactable twenty-four/seven. I've gone through my handbag a million times since I got here to check that it's definitely gone. I can't shake the feeling that it's just out of reach, that I'll put my hand on it any second if I search hard enough. But it's never there. I've lost it on that plane somewhere – left it behind – probably throbbing with texts and missed calls. It's pure anguish being without it like this. I may as well have left a part of me behind.

'You definitely have my temporary number?' I say. I've already given it to her twice, but experience has taught me always to triple check.

There's a rustling in the background as she goes through her notes. Then there's a pause. A significant pause. *Oh, God, this just gets worse and worse.*

'Yes . . . I do!' she confirms at last. 'I have everything right here in black and white, boss. It's all in hand.'

I'm battling the urge to scream at the top of my lungs. Losing my temper won't help anyone, least of all Helen. The key is to keep calm – if she senses that I can barely contain my anxiety about this it will rub off on her. Like the time I thought I'd lost the precious home number of one of the most influential editors in the business and, instead of trawling through every piece of paper on her desk to find it as quickly and efficiently as possible, she burst into tears. *I* had to get *her* a hot chocolate with extra marshmallows to calm her down once we eventually located it. Listening to her babble on now about how everything will be fine and I'm not to worry about anything, I rub my throbbing temples and try to relax. I have to trust her. I have no choice. She's going to email me all my contact numbers so I have them to hand and, anyway, according to the airline, I should have my own phone back within forty-eight hours, less if I'm lucky, which I'm hoping I will be. Until then the phone I rented at the airport will just have to do.

Hanging up, I roll my neck and shoulders, trying to shake off the stress, and look around my pleasant executive hotel suite. Helen may have screwed up a million times since she first started working with me but getting this room at the bargain price she did was brilliant. Granted, the only thing vaguely executive about the 'suite' seems to be a sofa in the corner, a small sign reminding me that Wi-Fi is available and a note on my pillow telling me that the business centre on the third floor has free coffee and donuts. Still, the hotel itself, or what I saw of it as I walked from the reception desk to my room, is beautiful – all art-deco design and gleaming marble surfaces.

I didn't see much of San Francisco from the cab coming into the city as I was too frantic about my phone, but there's plenty of time for that. First I have to find Ian – that's my top priority.

A wave of tiredness hits me, but I try not to give in to it. Everyone knows that the only way to deal with jet lag is to block it out and keep going. All I want to do is curl up in bed but I can't think about that now, not even when I can feel the soft hotel mattress beneath me, beckoning me to lie down just for a second. I probably wouldn't be so damn tired if it wasn't for Rosie, gabbling non-stop on the flight. She saved her number on my temporary phone before we parted ways, insisting that I had to call her so we could meet for coffee or brunch and a 'chat'. I promised I would, not wanting to offend her, but secretly I have no intention of ever seeing her again. You don't keep in touch with strangers you meet on planes: it just doesn't happen. Especially not people you have absolutely nothing in common with.

My hired phone buzzes just then and I grab it. It could be Helen – maybe there's been some word of Ian. *At Coit Tower. I miss you so much it hurts. I feel like my heart is breaking.* Coit Tower? Where the hell is Coit Tower? The Northside? Why is Helen texting me about some tower? This is typical of her ditziness. God, she's useless.

And then I spot the digits. It's not Helen. It seems to be an American number. And, now I come to think of it, I'm sure there's a Coit Tower here in the city, isn't there? It's near North Beach, the Italian district – I read something about it in the in-flight magazine on the plane. The tower is some sort of commemoration to the fire fighters of San Francisco.

I look at the message again and try to figure it out. I don't know anyone in the city who could be texting me – unless it's Rosie. But Rosie saved her number in this phone, with a picture of herself, so I know it's not her. Besides, she went back to her home in Sausalito from the airport, not to visit some tower. I sit puzzling about it for a second or two until it comes to me: obviously this message is for someone else. It's been sent to me by mistake. That explains it.

Putting the phone on the bedside locker, I flop back on the bed and let my head settle on the crisp cotton pillow. Maybe I'll lie down, just for a second. I'm not going to fall asleep, though. That would be totally feeble. I'll just rest my eyes – there's no harm in that, just for a little while. Then I'll go and find Ian and save the day. Simple.

Chapter Eight

'Excuse me?'

I smile as I call to the little boy cycling carefully round the cu-de-sac, his red bike wobbling beneath him. I know I don't look exactly dangerous, but his parents probably spend half their lives warning him not to speak to strangers and I don't want to scare him.

His Converse-clad heels skid on the ground as he comes to a stop in front of me. 'Yeah?' He squints at me from underneath his Ben 10 helmet, cornflower blue eyes peeping out from under a mop of blond hair. He's an all-American kid, that's for sure.

'I don't suppose you know who lives in there, do you?' I ask, gesturing to what I hope is Ian Cartwright's house. I can't see the building itself – only the top of the roof – because it's surrounded by very high whitewashed walls. There's a small key pad at the black-painted gate, but no number. The cabbie who dropped me off said this is the right address, but before I ring that bell I want to make doubly sure.

'Yeah. A man does,' the little boy replies, and I spy the cute gap between his teeth. 'I don't know his name, but he's real mean.'

'He is?' It must be Ian – he does have a contrary reputation, after all. I shield my eyes from the morning sun and squint at the gate. Maybe I should try phoning him again before I ring the bell. But he might just ignore my call, like he seems to have ignored all the others, and I've really wasted enough time as it is. The ten-minute nap I intended to take in my hotel room turned into a three-hour sleep. The last thing I remember was allowing my eyelids to droop and then I woke up feeling drugged, fuzzy and very confused. I'm quite sure I would have slept even longer, but the buzz of a text roused me.

It took me a minute to come to and then I grabbed my phone in a panic when I remembered where I was and saw how long I'd been asleep. What if someone had been trying to contact me urgently and couldn't? But once I'd read the text I relaxed – it was just another message that wasn't meant for me, sent in error again: *Life is so unfair my darling. All I want is for you to be here with me.*

Again, I had no clue who it was from – it was bizarre and it was starting to get annoying.

'Are *you* mean?' the little boy asks now, eyeing me a little suspiciously.

'No, of course not.' I smile at him again.

'You talk funny.'

'Well, that's because I'm from Ireland. Do you know where Ireland is?'

'In Minnesota?'

'No.' I laugh. 'It's in Europe. Close to England. You know England, right? Manchester United? Liverpool FC?'

'What are they?'

'Football clubs. I mean soccer clubs.'

'I play baseball.' He shrugs. 'You dress funny too.'

I look down at my dark navy suit. Maybe I do seem a little formal, in comparison to his sneakers, green T-shirt and yellow shorts.

'Yup. Are you a lawyer? My dad's a lawyer.'

'No, I'm a literary agent,' I reply.

'What does that mean?' he asks, his head cocked to one side, like a cute spaniel puppy's.

'I help writers get their books published.'

'Is he a writer, the mean man?'

'Yes, he is.'

His brow crinkles as he considers this information. 'I like Harry Potter,' he says at last. 'Do you know him?'

'Well, not personally.' I grin.

'Hmm.' He shrugs again and cycles carefully away.

I buzz the intercom, crossing the fingers on my other hand as I do. Ian's going to get the shock of his life when he finds out I'm here: I just hope he reacts well and doesn't fly into a rage or something – he's supposed to be extremely difficult.

'Yes?'

The voice is faint as it crackles through the monitor. Hard to tell if it's male or female. 'Hello? Is that Ian Cartwright?'

'We don't want any.'

There's a clatter and the line goes dead. Damn. He obviously thought I was selling something. I'll have to try again. My stomach clenching with anxiety, I buzz once more.

'I told you,' the voice bellows this time, 'I don't want any.'

'I'm not selling anything!' I say quickly. 'It's Francesca Rowley from Dublin, Ian. I'm here to talk to you.'

There's a silence, and for a second I'm not sure he hasn't hung up again.

'Who?' the voice crackles.

'Francesca from the Rowley Agency. I used to work with Withers and Cole? I don't know if you got my messages. I was wondering if I could have a minute of your time.'

There's another silence. Then the door buzzes and the gate swings open under my hand. He's letting me in. He's actually letting me in! I take a deep breath as I walk through, my heart hammering. This is it. My big chance. I can't mess up.

As I pick my way along the flagstone path through a small

overgrown garden to the front door, I try to decide what my approach should be. Unfortunately, Ian doesn't sound very receptive – obviously he has a difficult reputation for a reason. That said, he hasn't told me to go away. So there is a tiny chink of hope – a chink I'm going to try to use to my very best advantage.

The black door, paint peeling, is ajar when I reach it so I tentatively stick my head around it. 'Hello?' I call.

There's no reply so I step over the threshold into a cream and red tiled hall. The walls are painted a warm yellow, and large Aztec-style tapestries are dotted here and there. Books are piled haphazardly all over the place, looking as if they could topple at any second. But there's no sign of anyone.

'Hello?' I call again.

'What do you want?' someone asks. The voice is deep, gravelly and extremely unfriendly.

At the top of the stairs, his face like thunder, is the man I presume to be Ian Cartwright. I'm presuming because he looks nothing like the author photograph from the jacket of *Field of Memories*, although that doesn't mean much. Author photographs are generally unrealistic, usually highly stylized and airbrushed. Besides, it's ten years since that book was published – he's bound to have changed.

'Em, hello there.' I clear my throat and step forward into the shaft of light that's streaming through a stained-glass window behind him. 'My name is Francesca Rowley – I have a literary agency in Dublin. Like I said, I, ah, used to work with Withers and Cole.'

'What do you want?' he growls again.

'Um, well, I did leave you some messages to explain. Did you get them?' I say.

'My assistant is . . . away,' he mutters, almost inaudibly. 'He deals with all that stuff.'

So he hasn't been ignoring my messages, he just doesn't know about them. That's a start. 'Well, do you think I could have a word?' I ask tentatively.

'Why? You're just a vulture, aren't you?'

'Em, sorry?' What does that mean? This is definitely not going to be straightforward.

'A vulture. I knew they'd start to circle once April died.' He glares at me. 'Here to pick over the corpse of my career, are you?'

'It's not like that,' I protest. Except it sort of is.

'Isn't it?' he sneers. 'The poor woman is barely cold in her grave and here you are.'

'I just want to talk to you,' I begin. This is definitely not going to be straightforward.

'Well, *I* don't want to talk to *you*. Now, please close the door on the way out.'

With that, he turns away to go back where he'd come from. I can't let that happen – I have to capitalize on the fact that he let me in. If I go now he'll never answer the door to me again, I know that for sure.

'I brought you some of these from Ireland,' I say, whipping out a box of Barry's teabags. 'And these.' I produce some Kimberley biscuits too.

'Kimberley biscuits?' he asks.

I may be wrong, but I think his eyes light up for a millisecond.

'Yes – I remember hearing somewhere that you liked them. That you miss them, being away.' I pause, trying not to let my nerves show. Let him take it all in.

He walks down a couple of steps, observing me keenly. 'Humph,' he grunts, obviously deeply suspicious. 'So you thought some Irish biscuits would butter me up, is that it?'

'What? No!' I bluster.

'I'm not stupid, young lady. I know why you're here.'

'You do?' Of course he does – he's not stupid.

'Oh, yes – I've been expecting this. They'll all be coming out of the woodwork soon, bearing gifts like the Trojan Horse.'

His eyes are hard, glittering in the half-light. I have to persuade him just to hear me out – even five minutes of his time will work in my favour.

'Look,' I say, 'why don't you point me in the direction of the kettle, and I'll make us some tea? These bad boys are just waiting to be eaten.'

I wave the Kimberleys at him and I can tell by his expression that he's wavering. His eyes are already devouring the biscuits.

'The kitchen's that way, but I can't vouch for its hygiene. The cleaner is gone as well,' he says unwillingly, after what seems an eternity.

'That's fine. I'm not picky,' I reply, silently congratulating myself on this small victory. Maybe a cup of the famous Irish Barry's tea and some of his favourite biscuits will thaw him. It's definitely worth a shot.

'So, how long have you been living over here?' I ask, as I pour hot, golden tea into a stained cup I rinsed under the grimy tap.

He hadn't been joking about the state of the kitchen – every available surface is strewn with household debris, books, crockery, cutlery, even clothes. The sink is full to overflowing with dirty dishes and the floor definitely needs a good wash. There's a faint smell too – something in here stinks. But I'm trying to ignore all that and concentrate on my charm offensive.

'Eight years,' he replies, his mouth full of crumbly biscuit.

He's eaten three already, relishing every morsel. Those biscuits were a great idea – I have to hand it to Helen: she was the one who suggested they might break the ice. At the time I thought it was one of her stupider notions, but I'm grateful now.

'Why here? San Francisco, I mean.' I ask this even though I already know the answer – he moved here to try to find his voice again, away from the pressure of home. That's the story doing the rounds back in Ireland anyway.

'I did some research in San Francisco for a book, years ago. The area's intrigued me since then, I guess. So when the time came for a change, I thought of here . . .' He shrugs.

'A novel set in San Francisco? Sounds great,' I say.

'It wasn't fit to be published, believe me. I never even finished it – it was just another dead end.' His tone is instantly tense and I curse myself for saying something so stupid, reminding him of something he'd obviously prefer to forget. It's well known that, over the years, Ian has started and never finished any number of projects.

'Right. Well, that kind of thing happens all the time, doesn't it?' I say, trying to lift the dark mood that's suddenly descended.

'To me more than most,' he replies wryly, and I think I see a flicker of humour in his eyes.

'I'm sure it was very good,' I say.

'No, it was total rubbish. An infantile story about a middle-class kid who came to San Francisco to join a hippie commune . . . awful stuff.'

'Of course – the hippies! San Francisco's famous for them, isn't it?' I ask, hoping he'll open up and the conversation will keep going.

'Most people agree the movement started here, yes. Then it spread across the States, through Canada and into parts of Europe.'

'They were considered really radical, weren't they, in their day?' I say. Good, he's talking. Now I just have to keep the chit-chat going.

'People were shocked by their alternative lifestyle, yes. Drugs played a large part in that, of course.'

Another wry smile – I know I didn't imagine that one. 'Where did they all come from? I mean, why did they flock here in particular?'

'They came from all over, searching for what they thought they wanted – a lot of them were from wealthy middle-class families, actually.'

'I can't imagine leaving the privilege of wealth to live in a commune.' Why would anyone want to do that?

'That's what I was trying to explore in the book – why someone would want to throw away a life of leisure for something so different. I can understand why many of the older generation believed that these young kids were spoiled and wasting their lives, but from my research I know that the hippies genuinely believed in this way of life. No one was going to get in the way of their dreams.'

'Dreams of doing LSD all day?'

He laughs properly then, and I'm surprised by how his stubbly face lights up. 'Maybe it wouldn't be so bad. We all have our drugs of choice.' He reaches for another biscuit. 'I spent a lot of time down in Haight-Ashbury, researching. That's where the movement was centred,' he goes on, as if he's almost lost in thought. 'I met some very interesting characters.'

'I'd say.' I smile. 'Maybe I should take a tour.'

'You should. Back when the tours of the district first started it was said that it was the only foreign tour within the continental limits of the United States. Isn't that funny? The hippies were so different that the conservative middle classes couldn't relate to them and saw them as aliens.'

'That must have been quite something – tons of middle-class people bussed in to see all these hippies living alternatively.'

'Well, yes. They basically took over Haight-Ashbury for a few years in the mid-sixties. There are two parks down there – the Golden Gate and Buena Vista – where they used to hold free concerts and festivals to celebrate LSD. And there were anti-war rallies too, of course.'

'Wow, it all sounds fascinating. San Francisco seems like a great city, although I haven't seen much of it yet. I can't wait to explore.' I smile at him. *Please like me.*

'Yes, it is,' he agrees, a hint of passion in his voice, and I feel the atmosphere thaw by another degree.

'So, what else do you recommend I see, while I'm here? I know I have to get to Fisherman's Wharf and Alcatraz . . .'

'Go to Crissy Field,' he says, reaching for another biscuit. 'It's glorious there this time of year.'

'I've never heard of it,' I reply, intrigued by the way his face has just lit up.

'It was originally an airfield – part of the Presidio. It used to be just asphalt and debris, but there are more than a hundred thousand natural plants there now. It's a wonderful spot – I used to go there quite a lot to think before I wrote.'

He pauses, realizing what he's just said, and I do too. This is it – the opportunity, the in I've been waiting for to bring up his writing. I can't let it pass by. 'It sounds great,' I say carefully. 'So, speaking of books, as you know I'm a literary agent and I'd very much like –'

'Please don't.' He holds up a hand.

'I just want to explain –'

'I don't want any explanations. I just want to be left alone.'

'If you'd give me a minute . . .' That's all I need to do my pitch – one minute to tell him how much I admire his work, get him to consider signing with me.

86

'I'd like you to leave, please.' He makes to stand abruptly.

'What?' I'm flabbergasted. How did that happen? I'd thought things were going quite well. OK, so maybe there was a whiff of awkwardness, but weren't we bonding? There was tea and biscuits and all the chat about the hippies. I haven't even had a chance to talk about my proposal yet.

'Please leave. Go.'

'I'm sorry if you've misunderstood me, Ian. I'm just trying to –'

'I've heard enough,' he interrupts me crisply. 'Thank you for the biscuits.'

And then he walks out of the filthy kitchen, not even glancing over his shoulder as he goes, and I'm left, open-mouthed and speechless, behind him.

Chapter Nine

'He didn't go for it, then?' Gary asks, and I can hear the disappointment in his voice.

'He was a little frosty,' I reply. That doesn't actually come close to describing my disastrous meeting with Ian Cartwright, but it's all I'm willing to admit to right now.

'So you don't think he's interested in signing with you?'

'Well, we didn't get to that,' I say, 'but my gut feeling is that he's open to the possibility.' I mentally cross my fingers behind my back. My gut feeling is telling me almost the opposite but there's no point in saying as much. Not yet.

'So the door might be open?' Gary asks.

'Yes. I'd say so.' *Unlike the door he slammed behind me when he practically threw me out.*

'Where do we go from here?' he asks now. I can almost see him running his hands anxiously through his hair, five thousand miles away.

'I'm going to take him for lunch,' I say, plucking the idea out of thin air. The truth is, I haven't decided on a tactic yet, but lunch seems as good as any. Ian definitely likes his food so I need to use that information to my advantage.

'Are you?' Gary sounds instantly more upbeat.

'Yes. I'm thinking about a picnic in Crissy Field.'

'A picnic?' He's incredulous.

'He told me he used to like to go there to think,' I explain. 'So an outing there might just tip things in my favour.' It sounds faintly ridiculous in this context, I'll admit.

'OK, great. Well, do whatever it takes, Frankie – you know that.'

'I just need a little time to work my magic,' I reply. Trouble is, I'm not sure I have any magic left in me and my time is running out: the clock is against me in more ways than one.

'That's what I like about you, Blue Eyes. You're a tough cookie – you never give up.'

'That's me!' I say, trying to sound confident. Instinctively, I know that Gary doesn't want to hear that I don't know if I'll be able to pull this off – he just wants results. He was completely uninterested in my lost-phone story, barely listening when I told him about mad Irish-American Rosie and my nightmare journey. In fact, I couldn't help feeling he was only being polite as I rambled on about it all, just waiting until he could quiz me about Ian. Like he couldn't care less what had happened. Like he hadn't given me a second thought since I'd left. But, then, this is just as big a deal for Gary as it is for me: he needs to ensure that Ian's next novel is a bestseller – his neck is on the line. So this isn't personal – it's business. That's the problem, though: in our relationship the lines between personal and professional can get blurred – and that can make things very complicated.

Finishing my conversation with him and hanging up, I look out of the window from where I sit in Macy's coffee shop on the third floor and watch as the crowds bustle by on the pavement below. I'd come in on the spur of the moment, asking the cab driver to pull over and let me out when I'd spotted the world-famous store, with its immediately recognizable logo, on the opposite side of Union Square as we were crawling past Tiffany's. My plan was to browse for a while, keep my mind off Ian and our meeting, before I headed back to the hotel and tried to formulate a strategy for moving forward. But after only twenty minutes of rummaging through designer handbags, the desire for a serious coffee had driven me here. The small café, nestled beside the huge windows that give a bird's eye view of the square, seemed like a great spot to sit and think for a while.

Now, as I watch the traffic snaking round the streets below, it strikes me how much this place reminds me of a trip that Gary and I took to New York. The Big Apple has a totally different vibe from laid-back San Francisco, which, from what I've been able to see, feels quite compact. New York was amazing, though, and whizzing round in yellow cabs driven by sweaty, aggressive drivers, with Gary beside me, I felt like I'd stepped straight into a movie set.

The trip was business – a publishing conference – but we skipped some of the more boring lectures and explored the city together. We walked hand in hand through the crowded streets, stopping at art galleries and coffee shops in Greenwich Village, wandering aimlessly through Central Park, eating hot dogs on street corners. I didn't think it could get any better, until on the last night Gary said he had a surprise for me.

'Isn't this amazing?' he'd whispered, nuzzling my neck, as we stood on the viewing deck of the Empire State Building, marvelling at the city below us, twinkling under the lights.

'It really is,' I'd replied. I honestly felt just like Meg Ryan in *Sleepless in Seattle* and Gary was my Tom Hanks, minus the cute kid with the backpack.

I'd let my head rest on his shoulder, breathing in his musky scent, his strong arms wrapped round me, the soft cashmere wool of his coat scratching pleasantly against my cheek, wondering if this might be perfect after all. OK, so he'd been badly bruised by a painful and messy marital separation, but things were going great between us. We had a real connection. It had moved on from just a physical attraction: we really enjoyed each other's company. We liked to bicker together over the *Irish Times* crossword, we loved the same books, we had the same interests. We were well matched. It had already occurred to me more than once that this might be it. OK, so he had baggage and there were his kids to consider – two lanky teenage boys I hadn't met. Even the thought of them scared me: I knew nothing about spotty, hormonal teenagers and they were bound to hate me. But I also knew I was willing to try to make it work for Gary's sake. And so, as I snuggled closer, the freezing New York air biting my cheeks, I was thinking, 'This really could be the start of something great.'

And then, in the blink of an eye, he was pushing me from him, panic all over his face.

'What is it?' I asked, startled. What had happened? Had I done something wrong?

'I don't fucking believe it,' he hissed, his eyes darting anxiously around. 'It's Veronica Bell.'

'Who?' I was totally confused. Who the hell was Veronica Bell? The name meant nothing to me.

'She knows Caroline.' Gary's voice was shaking – actually shaking.

I looked over my shoulder and immediately knew who he was talking about. A skinny blonde in a very expensive black suede knee-length coat and fox-fur hat was approaching, her arm linked through that of a much shorter, rounder man, wearing a grey trilby, a plaid scarf wrapped tightly round his wobbling jowls.

'They can't see us together,' Gary said, his eyes wild.

'Why not?'

What was wrong with him? We were being discreet, yes, but that was mainly to protect our privacy at work. Sharing the same building, we didn't want everyone watching us – it made sense, at least for the moment. But we weren't at work now – we were in another country altogether. So what was the problem?

'I'll explain later. You have to hide,' he hissed.

'What do you want me to do? Jump over the edge?' I asked, almost giggling. He wasn't serious, surely.

'Frankie. Please.' His gaze was glued to the blonde and her companion. They were bearing down on us. We had maybe ten seconds before we were seen.

He was serious. Deadly serious.

I'd walked away from him then, my head spinning, pulling my own hat further down, just in case they recognized me too, even though I knew they wouldn't. Why should they? I was no one, it seemed.

I heard, from a few yards away, their delight at seeing him. 'Gary? What are you doing here?' the woman exclaimed, embracing him enthusiastically.

'Just business, Veronica,' he replied smoothly, kissing her on both cheeks.

'So you're alone?' She peered around her, as if she was checking for a companion.

'Yes, all alone,' Gary replied, shaking the man's hand warmly, then slapping him on the back for good measure.

'Sure you're not here on a dirty weekend, you old dog?' The man smirked.

'No fear. Once bitten, twice shy. Ha-ha!' Gary laughed, and the couple joined in.

I'd felt sick as I watched and listened from a safe distance. Was this how it was always going to be? This cloak-and-dagger dance? Was this what I'd signed up for?

'I'm sorry about all that,' he'd explained later that night as he speared a succulent tiger prawn at dinner. 'I just don't want Caroline to know about us yet – she'd use it as ammunition against me. You have no idea what she's really like.'

'It's OK,' I'd said, feigning indifference. Inside I was badly stung, of course, but there was no way I was going to make a fuss about it. It wasn't as if I'd wanted a great declaration of love from him. And yet ... there was a bad taste in my mouth. Until then I'd been happy not to go public because we both valued our privacy. But I was wary now. He'd literally shoved me to one side earlier that day – was that what I really wanted?

'You're not cross, darling?' he'd asked.

'Of course not.' But I didn't meet his eye – I found that I couldn't.

'You wouldn't want certain people to know about us either, would you?'

'Maybe not,' I admitted. 'But . . .'

'Well, it's the same thing. Caroline is trying to take me to the cleaner's – you know that. And more idle talk about our divorce is the last thing I need. Just bear with me a little longer, Frankie. Everything will be sorted properly soon.'

'But you *are* going to tell her about me?' The question was out before I could stop it, accompanied by a whiny, needy voice I didn't recognize.

'Of course.' He'd reached for my hand, his eyes suddenly filled with hurt. 'You don't actually think I've been lying to you, do you, Blue Eyes? I'm going to tell everyone just how much you mean to me when all this is done.'

'And what about the boys? Shouldn't I meet them?' I was feeling marginally better. He wasn't lying to me – why would he do that? Maybe I was being paranoid.

'I think it's best to keep them out of it for now, don't you? It'll all happen in good time – it's just complicated at the moment, Frankie. Like I said.'

I don't see what's so complicated about it, I'd wanted to reply, the clear consommé before me untouched, getting colder by the second. I hated consommé and had no idea why I'd ordered it. It looked like something Mum would pour down the sink. But that didn't really matter any more because I'd lost my appetite. And very suddenly I wanted to tell Mum all about it.

'Now, try one of these. They're divine.' He'd offered me a prawn and obediently I opened my mouth and chewed, wondering how something so expensive could taste like cardboard. Meanwhile, a picture of Mum's sad, disappointed face floated across the bowl in front of me.

I rub my eyes with my knuckles now, bringing me back to the present. No point in moping over all that. Another coffee. That's what I need.

'What'll you have?' The bespectacled teenage barista behind the counter smiles widely at me as I approach him. His sleeves are rolled up to the elbows, green apron tied securely round his waist.

'I'll have another decaff skinny latte, please,' I reply, smiling back at him. Everyone seems so friendly in this city.

Earlier, two assistants in the handbag department on the lower ground floor asked me if they could help as I was browsing. When I said I was just looking, they'd told me to have a good day as if they really meant it. It's so refreshing.

'We call that the "Why Bother?"' The barista grins.

'"Why Bother?"' I try to think what he might mean.

'No caffeine and non-fat milk in a coffee?' He laughs. 'Where's the fun in that?'

'You're right.' I giggle, his mischievous grin infectious. 'I'll have a grande mocha instead. Double shot, please.'

'Woo-hoo!'

'And I'll have a blueberry muffin as well, while I'm at it,' I add.

'Now that's what I call living on the edge!'

'Well, I am jet-lagged. I need the sugar hit to keep awake.'

'Yeah, yeah, that's what they all say.'

I sit down at my window table again, sip the delicious hot coffee and watch everyone bustle about below. I'm almost able to forget what a failure the meeting was, how badly it went. *How I'm so screwed.*

I have to talk Ian round. There's no other option. I'll give him time to cool off and then I'll take him to Crissy Field – ply him with food and drink, work my magic. There's nothing else for it.

My phone beeps just as I'm practising what to say in my head. *I dreamed about you last night. We were on Baker Beach, and you were wearing that red dress you love. I miss you so much.* It's another mystery text – that's so weird. They're so personal too, which makes me feel very uncomfortable. My fingers hover over the keypad. Maybe I should reply, let whoever is sending the messages know that their texts aren't getting to the right person. After all, they might be expecting a response.

But before I can, my phone suddenly shudders into life, a familiar face flashing at me. It's Rosie. I don't believe it – she's actually calling me. She said she would, of course – but I never thought she'd really go ahead and do it! What am I going to do now? Can I just ignore it? After all, I don't want to meet her again, even if she does think we have some sort of connection. *Because* she thinks we have some sort of connection. Eventually, after what seems like an eternity, it stops and I breathe a sigh of relief. Good. She's given up. But then it starts again – she's calling back. Heads are beginning to turn in the café and I know I have to answer. I have no choice.

'Hey, Frankie, honey! How you doin', doll?' Rosie chirps, her voice unmistakable when I pick up.

'I'm good, thanks, Rosie,' I reply. Maybe she just wants to see that I've settled in – that's probably it.

'I bet you didn't think you'd hear from me ever again, am I right?'

'Em . . .' Something like that.

'Us Kellys keep our promises, honey! And I can't have you all lonesome, now, can I?'

'Er . . .'

'So, what do you think of our foggy city so far?'

'It's lovely.'

My mind is working overtime, coming up with excuses. If she asks to meet I'll tell her I'm caught up with meetings and business stuff. That'll put her off.

'So I guess, right about now, you're trying to rustle up some excuse why we shouldn't meet, right?' she says, a laugh in her voice.

Oh, my God! Either I said that out loud or she can read my mind. 'Not at all,' I exclaim – possibly overenthusiastically to make it sound totally realistic.

'Well, that's good! Because I was thinking we could hook up tomorrow.'

'Tomorrow? I'm not sure that would work. Let me just check . . .'

'. . . your schedule?' she finishes my sentence for me. 'Sure! I'll wait.'

There's a pause, during which I know she can hear my guilty conscience lecturing me. *She's only trying to be kind,* it hollers. *She's only trying to be welcoming.*

'Em,' I say eventually. 'It looks like tomorrow morning is free.'

'It *is*? Why, that's just peachy!'

'Yep.' Peachy. Shit.

'So, why don't you take the ferry to Sausalito and we can spend the morning together? Easy-peasy, lemon-squeezy. OK, honey?'

'The ferry?'

'Yep – that's the best way. You could hire a car, drive across the Golden Gate Bridge, but the ferry is so fun and there's such a pretty view of the city too. You'll love it!'

'Um, OK,' I agree.

'Great! So text me on this number when you're leaving and I'll pick you up at the pier, OK, honey? My place is only a few minutes away. Can't wait!'

'Me too,' I mumble, trying to sound like I mean it. I hang up, reassuring myself that Rosie is a nice person, trying to make a stranger feel welcome in a strange city. She's not a certifiable lunatic who wants to befriend me so she can murder me and then steal my liver.

At least, I hope she's not.

Besides, it'll pass a morning. I have to let Ian be for a little while – I don't want to crowd him. I can already tell that pushing him into something isn't going to work. I have to take the softly-softly approach. And talking about the hippie district really seemed to get him to open up – maybe my visiting Sausalito will create some common ground between us, give us something else to chat about. And when he's relaxed, I'll convince him that I'm his ticket to success and we're going to have a wonderful future together. Easy-peasy, lemon-squeezy.

Chapter Ten

'I'm *sooo* glad you made it, sweetie!' Rosie flings her arms around me as if I'm her long-lost sister and hugs me tight.

Despite my reservations, I find myself smiling back at her – it *is* sort of nice to see a familiar face again. And, after spending all those hours at close quarters with her on an international flight, her face is more than familiar – it's practically etched on my brain, never to be forgotten.

Today, though, she's not wearing her 'Begorra' Irish outfit. There's no sign of the green T-shirt or hat. Instead, her golden-red curls are swept back off her freckled face and into a high ponytail, her ample bosom and womanly curves accentuated to their best by a floaty white linen dress to the ankles. Up her arms are stacked dozens of jangly beaten-silver bangles, some with tiny blue beads. There are simple tan leather sandals on her feet, and her toenails are painted pale pink. She looks almost . . . normal. In fact, she looks really great, beautiful even. And her bone structure is amazing – I hadn't noticed that before.

'Hi, Rosie.' I hug her back as she keeps her arms wrapped round me. She's so cheerful and good-natured, it's hard not to feel warm towards her now, even if I did spend a long flight almost hating every fibre of her body.

'Had a little trouble recognizing me, huh?' She grins.

'You do look a little . . . different,' I begin carefully.

'Like completely and utterly?'

'Well, yes,' I admit.

'You didn't think I wore that green tourist stuff all the time, did you?' She laughs.

'No, of course not!' I lie. *Um, yes, I did.*

'I'm just joshing ya.' She guffaws. 'Course you did, cos I didn't say otherwise. I was wearing all that as a little joke – met a second cousin of mine, just before I got on the flight and thought it'd give him a kick. I was even wearing green drawers!'

She dissolves into giggles again and I laugh along. She was wearing all that stuff for a *joke*?

'I'm sorry about the taking-off and landing thing,' she says, suddenly serious. 'I hope that didn't freak you out – I get kinda crazy on planes.'

'That's OK,' I reassure her. 'My hand is nearly better now.'

She throws her head back and laughs again. 'You sure are a ticket, Frankie! So . . . whaddya think of little old Sausalito?'

'It's so pretty!' I say, peering about me. 'And the boat trip was great.' I'd sat on deck for the short trip from the city across the bay to Marin County, feeling the sun warm on my face as the seagulls wheeled overhead. It really was lovely.

'I know! Isn't the ferry the cutest thing? Now, come on, we'll get going. I made us lemonade back at mine – let's not keep it waiting.' She links my arm and leads me away from the pier.

'We don't have to go back to your house, Rosie,' I say. 'We can just grab something in town if you prefer.'

'No way.' She shakes her head, grinning. 'I want you to see my little nest. I think you're gonna like it. Jump in!'

She swings open the passenger door of a white pick-up truck with a large shamrock stencilled on the side, and I hesitate. Isn't this how people meet their grisly end? Getting into cars with total strangers? But then I see Rosie's smiling face and take in the 'Irish and Proud' stickers on the window. She's harmless, I know it. Eccentric definitely, but an axe murderer? Probably not.

'This is Dolly,' she says, patting the door. 'I gave her an Irish makeover recently – do you like it?'

'It's certainly . . . unusual,' I reply.

'Oh, I know you probably hate it – it's a little silly but, hey, it makes me smile, don't it, Dolly?'

'Why do you call your truck Dolly?' I ask, squinting at her in the sunlight.

'After Miss Dolly Parton, of course – the patron saint of us gals with girls!'

'Gals with girls?'

She shakes her bosom at me and chuckles. 'You can't miss these ladies, can you? Now, come on, that lemonade'll be a-spoilin'!'

I clamber inside, noticing for the first time a tiny leprechaun swinging from the rear-view mirror. This must be the only leprechaun-decorated pickup in California.

'So, how's your work going?' Rosie asks, as she starts the ignition and the truck judders into life. 'You're a literary agent, right?'

I try to think how she knows this – I can't remember sharing any personal information with her on the flight. In fact, I was really careful not to, in case she Googled me, tried to track me down and forcibly swap houses with me or something.

'You told me about your job when you lost your phone, remember?' she prompts me. 'Said you were here to meet an author?' There's a smile playing round her lips, like she knows exactly why I never said anything before then.

'Oh, yes, of course,' I reply, slightly embarrassed. I'd been so cautious with her and she'd known why all along.

'So, things are going well? With this mysterious author of yours?'

'Yep, all going to plan,' I reply, almost automatically. Never admit to any failing in public: that's my failsafe setting.

'Well, that's just sweet, possum! It would have been a real shame to travel all this way and things not work out.'

It strikes me that this, ironically, is exactly what's happening. Nothing is working out the way I planned it to. I haven't been able to get Ian onside so far – in fact it seems he wants nothing at all to do with me. Apart from trying to talk him round, I don't have many other options, and if he refuses to meet me again, this entire trip has been a waste of time and money. I feel really despairing when I think about it.

For some bizarre reason, I suddenly decide to tell Rosie the truth. We barely know each other, after all – it's not like it really matters.

'Actually, it's not going that well, if I'm honest,' I admit. It's a relief to say it out loud.

'Oh. Bummer! How come?' She flicks me a sympathetic look as she reverses out of her parking spot.

'That author I told you about wasn't exactly welcoming.'

'You're fishin' but he ain't bitin', huh?'

'Something like that – our meeting didn't go too well.'

I watch the fluorescent-green leprechaun swing round the rear-view mirror. She bought that in Duty Free, I'd bet my life on it.

'Well, maybe a day off will give you just the inspiration you need to see the problem from a new angle,' she says cheerily. 'It ain't over till the fat lady sings, doll.'

'I hope so.' *Because if I can't come up with a solution quickly I'm in serious trouble.*

'Hey, has the airline got your cell phone back to you yet?' she asks.

The truck swerves a little as she turns to talk to me and I grip the edge of my seat, my nerves jangling. I still can't get used to the fact that we're driving on the wrong side of the road – it feels so strange, as if every car hurtling in our direction is destined to plough right into us.

'Not yet. I called them again and they said they'd get back

to me ASAP, but so far there's been nothing.' I've been trying not to think about it – the rented mobile is OK so far, but being without my beloved iPhone is incredibly painful. I still can't believe I was so stupid as to lose it.

'That sounds familiar.' She tuts. 'Remember I told you about my purse? But your new cell is working out OK, right?'

'It'll have to do for now, I suppose.'

'Maybe losing your cell was a blessing in disguise, huh? All those text messages, everyone wanting a piece of you – it must be kinda restful not to have to be available to everyone all the time.'

'I guess so,' I say, feeling doubtful. The truth is, I still feel like I'm missing my right arm, not having it with me. But there's very little I can do about that, until the airline get it back to me. Then I remember the mystery texts I've received and realize that I never replied to tell the message senders they had the wrong number.

'Actually, I've been getting strange texts since I arrived,' I say, as Rosie swings right on to a small side-road and we bump along, the tiny leprechaun dancing like an energetic Michael Flatley in front of our eyes.

'Like what? Pervy?' She glances at me again, her eyes narrowing. I wish she wouldn't take her eyes off the road – I'm freaked out enough as it is – but I don't know how to tell her.

'No, not pervy,' I say. 'Just someone sending me messages by mistake, that's all. I'm going to text back, tell them I'm not who they think I am. You know, in case they're expecting a reply.'

'That's kind of you.' Rosie smiles, and suddenly I feel stupidly bashful.

'Not really,' I say. 'Anyone would do the same.'

'No, not everyone. Lots of people would just ignore the messages, like it wasn't their problem. You're a kind soul, Frankie – I knew it the minute I saw you.'

For some insane reason, I suddenly feel stupidly weepy. Obviously the jet lag is setting in, but my eyes are now so blurry that I can't see the keys on my phone.

'Here we are!' Without warning, Rosie steps on the brake, and I see what appears to be hundreds of houseboats before us in a series of docks.

She can't possibly mean ... 'You live here?' I ask, dropping the phone into my lap.

'On a houseboat! Yes! Do you love it?' Her face glows with delight.

'Wow!' I breathe. It really is a spectacular sight, so many different floating homes of all shapes, colours and sizes glittering on the water. 'You never said anything!'

'I wanted to surprise you. I just love the reaction on people's faces when they see it for the first time. Isn't that silly of me? Now, come on, I can't wait to show it to you properly.'

She springs out of the truck, slamming the door behind her, and I do the same. I've never been on a houseboat before and these are all so pretty, their painted exteriors welcoming and attractive.

'The community has been here for years,' Rosie explains, as we traipse through an unlocked gate on to a dock. 'Lots of boats were abandoned after the decommissioning of the Marin shipyards at the end of World War Two and ended up here. It was a real mess for a long time.'

'But it's so great now. What happened?' I ask, enthralled. There are so many different types of boat, some quite modest, yes, but others obviously very high spec. A real mixture.

'Well, so many anchor-outs came that it created real problems with sanitation,' she says. 'Plus the area became a real mish-mash. There were tons of improvised floating homes – from the beautiful to the downright dangerous. And they say that the mix of people living here was the same . . . There was even a murder once.'

'Really?' I can't imagine that this place would ever have been shabby or ill cared-for as we stroll past sweet-smelling potted plants and flowers, their scent wafting towards me.

'It's true. After the murder the officials clamped down and made all the remaining boats come into harbours. At least then they could be linked to sewer lines because before you could get the smell at low tide all the way from Highway 101.'

'Yuck!' I say, wrinkling my nose. 'That must have been gross.'

'I bet it was!'

'It's so beautiful now,' I say, as we pass a man sitting by an easel, looking out at the water, brush in hand, wearing an expression of intense concentration.

Rosie follows my gaze. 'Yep, it sure is. And I don't mean to brag, but the people who live here are just swell – there are a lot of artists.' She waves to the man on the deck and he waves back, breaking into a grin.

'So how did you end up here?' I ask, intrigued. I don't even know what Rosie does for a living, come to think of it. I was so intent on not revealing anything much about myself that I never really asked her about herself.

'I inherited it. And, boy, am I glad I did – it's my favourite place in the whole wide world.'

'Are you an artist too?' I ask, not wanting to pry, but curious now.

'I wish!' She grins. 'No, I do love to paint, but I suck at it. And, to answer your question, I'm between jobs right now.'

I bite my lip, a little embarrassed that I've put her on the spot like this. No wonder she's never elaborated about her work. Her trip to Ireland was either her last hurrah or a once in a lifetime journey she saved very hard for. She probably has to live on this boat – maybe it's the only thing she can afford. I feel awkward now for even bringing it up.

'Well, here we are. My little palace!' she says proudly. Her face is ecstatic as we stop in front of a houseboat that's painted a pale green. I should have guessed.

'Isn't she pretty?' Rosie smiles at me. 'I had her repainted recently – my favourite shade, as you can see.'

'She's lovely,' I agree, as we step on board.

'Actually, technically, she is a he.'

'I thought boats were usually female. Like cars?' It had always struck me as a stupid sexist rule.

'You're right. They are. But I called this one Kenny, so I guess it's a boy!'

'Kenny? After . . . ?' I think I can guess.

'After Kenny Rogers, of course. "Islands in the Stream" with Dolly is my favourite song of all time!'

'And, of course, we're on water so . . .'

'So it fits perfectly, right? Now take a load off and let me get this drink for you – my throat is drier than the Sahara at sun-up!'

'Tell me more about these texts, honey,' Rosie says, pouring me some lemonade a while later. She's already given me a complete guided tour of the houseboat that she calls home, and while it's a little too compact for my taste, I can see why she loves it.

'There's not much to tell,' I say, taking a sip of the ice-cold liquid. It really is the most amazing lemonade I've ever tasted. Sweet, but with a perfectly bitter tang that gives it just enough bite.

'Oh, sure there is! I love a good mystery,' Rosie urges.

'They're not that mysterious. Just texts sent to me that are obviously meant for someone else. Actually, now that you've reminded me again, I'm going to reply right now.'

I fish out the phone and find another text waiting. *I don't know how to do this any more. It's not getting any easier.*

I read it out loud.

'What does *that* mean?' Rosie asks.

'I dunno.' I shrug, then send a response to say they have the wrong number.

'At least now whoever it is won't be wondering why no one is replying,' Rosie says.

'Yeah, I may have saved a beautiful relationship. Who knows?' I smile. 'There were a couple of numbers, though – I should probably contact them all.' But before I can my phone starts to ring – and, bizarrely, it's the number I've just texted flashing on the screen.

I peer at it, confused. Why on earth would a complete stranger want to talk to me?

'Maybe they want to thank you,' Rosie suggests. 'For letting them know about the mix-up?'

That would never happen at home. Unless maybe you were drunk and doing it for a dare.

The phone is still ringing and, I have to admit, I'm kind of intrigued now. What harm could it do to answer? Probably none.

'Francesca Rowley speaking,' I say, accepting the call.

'Who the hell are you and how did you get this number?' a voice growls back.

'*Excuse* me?' I gasp.

'I said, who the hell are you and how did you get this number?' the man shouts, fury in his voice.

'Listen here, I don't know who you are, but how dare you speak to me like that?' I manage to splutter back.

'This isn't your number!' he yells. 'It doesn't belong to you, it belongs to Aimee. Now you tell me how you got it, right this instant!'

'Get lost!' I say. Then I hang up hastily and throw the phone on to the low table between Rosie and me. I'm shaking and my heart is racing. Rosie's eyes are wide as she watches me.

'Did you hear what he said?' I ask, aghast.

'I sure did! What the hell is going on? Who's Aimee?'

'I don't know, but there's no way I'm taking another call from him to find out.'

I watch as the phone starts to buzz again, hopping angrily around the small coffee-table, like it's in a complete rage.

Rosie's face is grim. 'Don't worry, honey,' she says, her lips thin with annoyance. 'I'll handle this.' She lifts the phone to her ear. 'I don't know who you are, mister, but you call this number again and we'll be calling the cops, y'all understand?'

I strain to hear what the man is saying in response, but I can't.

'You can stop right there,' Rosie says, shaking her head vehemently. 'I don't care what cock-and-bull story you tell me, you have seriously insulted my friend Francesca. She was only trying to help you.'

There's more talking from the other end. Rosie listens, her face working overtime. She says very little, just frowns every now and again. What is going on?

'Well?' I demand, when she hangs up. 'What did he say?'

'Well, his name is John Bonner apparently and he lives in the city. He kept saying this was Aimee's number and you shouldn't have it. It was all kinds of weird.'

'Jesus!' I whistle, then take another long, cool drink of lemonade to calm myself. That guy has properly freaked me out.

'Funny thing is, I think he was pretty harmless behind it

all.' Rosie shakes her head again, wispy tendrils of her hair escaping from the sides.

'Harmless? He sounded like a complete nut, Rosie!' Doesn't she remember the yelling?

'Yeees . . . But I'm sensing he's actually an OK guy. He was just riled, is all. I don't understand it.' She shakes her head, baffled.

'Rosie, the guy is a basket case. I mean, who *does* that?'

'I dunno – but I think there's more to this than meets the eye.'

'Why? What else did he say?'

'Not very much – just that there had definitely been some sort of mix-up and he had to sort it out. He kept babbling about this Aimee. He sure was mighty vexed. But there was something about him, Frankie. I can't put my finger on it, but I almost felt a . . . connection.'

'I'm not sure that's necessarily a good thing,' I reply.

'Aha! But I felt a connection with you too,' she said. 'And you're not a crazy so how do you explain that? Besides, I know this John sounded like he was one sandwich short of a picnic, but I think there's an honest-to-goodness explanation for his behaviour.'

'Like what? He's been let out of a medical facility for the weekend?' I say, quite pleased with my witty quip, then instantly worried that I might be right.

'I'm telling you,' she goes on, 'that guy might sound crazy, but there's something more to this . . .'

Oh, for God's sake. If I have to listen to her harp on about karma and the cosmos and all that stuff, I'll lose it. She's already been going on about Fate intervening, how the two of us were destined to meet on that flight and be friends.

'Yes, there is a reasonable explanation, Rosie,' I say. 'The world is full of nutters.' *And you might be one of them.* I don't say that aloud obviously.

'No . . . That phone, or at least that number, must belong to this Aimee . . . so how did you end up with it? Aren't you just itchin' to find out what it's all about?'

'Not really.'

'Oh, I am! It's something good – I can feel it in my bones.'

'Well, if it's all the same to you, Rosie,' I say, 'I'm going to leave your bones out of it. Now, can we add something a little stronger to this lemonade? My nerves are bloody shot.'

Chapter Eleven

'It's so pretty here, Ian,' I say, spreading on the grass the green and red plaid wool blanket I bought in Macy's this morning. I thought it would be a nice touch, along with the old-fashioned wicker basket stuffed full of goodies chosen with care for our picnic in Crissy Field. Hopefully, all this effort will pay off and I'll get through to him. Considering that the last time I saw him he practically threw me out of his house, I'm quite pleased we've got this far. In fact, part of me can't believe he even agreed to see me again. Not that I'm asking him why he eventually did. I'm simply grabbing opportunity by the scruff of the neck and going for it.

'Why can't we sit at one of the tables?' he asks, scowling at me as I smooth out the rug. 'I don't want to sit on the ground like a child.'

We're at the West Bluffs picnic area near Fort Point and, of course, there are wooden picnic tables dotted everywhere – I hadn't thought there would be. There are restrooms too, and BBQ pits, and allocated parking. It's all extremely organized. 'Much better idea!' I agree brightly, mentally kicking myself. 'Honestly, what was I thinking, bringing this old thing?'

I shove the very expensive picnic blanket back in the basket, cursing silently. Of course I can't return it now, because I pulled the tags off just before I collected Ian. More money down the drain. But at least he seemed to like the swish town car. Not that I would know – he's said practically nothing since I picked him up. Still, I'm glad I splashed out to make an impression. A cab was far too low key, not special or exclusive enough, so I organized a fancy Cadillac through the hotel concierge. My company credit card is definitely fit to burst, yes, but I think it's worked – Ian might have said almost nothing on the way here, but I sense he was pleased all the same. He even nodded quite cordially to the driver when he got out – and now the car is parked not too far away, ready to spirit us home again when we're finished.

'You were right about this place. It's lovely, isn't it?' I go on, as he sits down and looks around.

'Yes, it is,' he says, his tone suddenly melancholy, almost wistful. 'I haven't been here for some time.' He gazes at the Golden Gate Bridge, which looms large before us – it's such an iconic image and now it's so close I can almost touch it. In the distance I can see the Marin Headlands and Angel Island – all pointed out to us by our friendly driver Pete as we parked. I know I should be drinking it in and committing it to memory but I'm so wound up that I can't enjoy it.

One thing I am enjoying is the sun warming my skin as I lay the food on the table. So much for the foggy San Francisco I've read about – I could cope with this sort of weather every day.

'So, Ian . . .' I pour him some juice and gather my courage '. . . I think you know why I asked you here today.' There's no point beating around the bush too much – I have to tackle it head on.

'I can guess,' he replies. 'You want to be my new April, right?'

I take a deep breath. Best to admit it. 'I would like to represent you, yes, that's true,' I say. 'I know you might be inclined to stay with Withers and Cole, even though April is gone, but I'm just asking you to consider me. My agency is small but I'm a very hard worker and I can promise you I'll devote lots of time and energy to your writing career. And, of course, I have an excellent working relationship with Proud Publishing so the transition would be seamless and trouble-free.'

'You want to be in my gang, is that it?'

'Well, yes, I'd be honoured.'

'Honoured, huh?' He snorts. 'April would laugh if she heard that. Be careful what you wish for, young lady.'

'Why do you say that? About April?' I ask. I can't help wanting to know.

'Because, my dear, she knew the awful truth about me. I'm a failure, a big fat failure. There – what do you think of that?' He stares at me, his expression stony.

'I really don't know why you'd say that.'

'I'll tell you, shall I?' he bites back, bitterness oozing from his every pore. 'Because everything I write is useless. Less than useless.'

Wow – his morale is seriously low. Why? OK, so he hasn't published anything since *Field of Memories* but that is considered a modern classic. Some authors would kill for his reputation . . . and his sales. His fans love him – whole websites are dedicated to him, for goodness' sake. *Field of Memories* is on college curriculums now – students have even done PhDs on his one great novel.

'I'm sure that's untrue, Ian,' I say hotly. 'You're an amazing talent – the themes you tackled in *Field of Memories* are universal! Love, death, despair – it was all there: the human condition in all its frailty.'

'No, it isn't untrue,' he barks fiercely. 'After that damn book, I lost the ability to write anything really worthwhile or special. I've lost count of the novels I've begun and then never finished. That's the sad, irrefutable truth. Do you still want to be my agent now?'

'Yes, I do,' I say. 'Of course I do! Every writer goes through difficulties. You're not alone in that regard.'

'Huh,' he grunts. 'At least you're not trying to railroad me into a bloody sequel, I suppose – that's something. April kept going on about it – until she died . . .'

Crap.

'Wouldn't you want to write one?' I ask, feeling a little sick.

'Oh, God, no! That bloody book cursed me! I wish I'd never written it and I certainly don't want to go back for more. I can't bear to even think about it.' He takes a slug of juice, his face thunderous. Then his eyes narrow as he looks at me again. 'Why do you want to know anyway?'

I take a deep breath. It's now or never. 'Well, I don't think a sequel would necessarily be a bad thing, to be honest.'

There's a silence as he stares at me, his pale eyes not shifting from my face. I begin to feel ever more uncomfortable. 'Why is that?' he says eventually.

'Well, it would copper-fasten your legacy for one thing,' I say.

'My *legacy*?'

Immediately I get the feeling this was the wrong thing to say. Most authors like the legacy talk – but Ian Cartwright isn't most authors. 'Yes . . . and your fans would love it! I know you get letters from people all over the world, asking what happened next to the characters in *Field of Memories*.'

'So, this legacy is nothing to do with the bottom line?' His voice is suddenly icy.

'The bottom line?' I repeat.

'Your profits?'

'Well, no,' I say, even more nervous now and desperate to hide it. 'Of course there's no denying that we'd all benefit if the novel was a success, including me. My agency is a commercial enterprise, after all – but my main concern has always been to nurture and develop the writing of my authors.'

'Why's that? To fill the publisher's coffers? And yours, for that matter?' he spits viciously. As reactions go, it's not a particularly good one.

'No. Like I said, to copper-fasten your –'

'Please don't talk to me about legacy,' he interrupts. 'It sickens me to my stomach.'

I start to unwrap the sourdough rolls I bought, a San Francisco speciality, and try to think of another angle to take. This one is clearly not working – I'll be lucky if he doesn't storm off and demand to be driven home.

'OK, if you don't want to write a sequel, what *do* you want to write?' I say. Maybe if I can get him talking we'll be able to figure out something – there has to be a way to solve this. There always is.

'That's the problem, isn't it?' he mutters, eyes downcast, face truculent.

'Why?' I probe. Honestly, dealing with writers is like dealing with toddlers. All cajoling and bribery – just like potty training must be.

He sighs heavily. 'I thought coming to San Francisco would help. It was only supposed to be for a few months, until I could get back in the groove. But here I am, eight years later. It's pathetic.'

I look around the beautiful park, the sun glittering across the water, the runners jogging on the path, people in small groups enjoying food and drink in the open air. 'It's not such a bad place to be, is it?' I can certainly think of worse – like my poky basement office in Dublin for one.

'No, I guess not,' he muses thoughtfully, looking at the historic bridge and smiling faintly. 'But it wasn't supposed to be for ever.'

'You're a truly gifted writer, Ian, you do know that?' I say softly, hoping to connect with him.

But his face suddenly twists. 'Listen, I don't need a piece of eye candy to butter me up or tell me what I'm worth, OK?' he explodes, eyes bulging.

Eye candy? *Eye candy?* How *dare* he call me that?

A silence hangs between us for a beat while I try to decide if that sexist remark has infuriated me enough to walk away from him. Although I may be just a teeny bit flattered that he thinks I'm attractive. Still, 'eye candy' is a derogatory term, and I'm not standing for it, no way.

'That remark was uncalled-for,' I say coldly, at last.

'Perhaps,' he mutters, avoiding my eye. 'I may be a little testy today.'

'Today?' I arch an eyebrow at him and decide to let it go. No point arguing with the talent. 'Here, have a roll. Maybe it'll improve your mood.'

'I don't suppose you have any more Kimberleys, do you?' he asks hopefully, suddenly deflated.

'No, I don't,' I reply. 'You gobbled the lot the other day. And after what you just said about me being eye candy, I'm not sure I'd give you any, even if I had.'

'I'm sorry.' His eyes drop. 'You're not just eye candy. You seem like a nice girl. Smart.'

Then he bites into his bread with relish, as if he hasn't eaten since we last met. Looking at him now, in proper daylight, he really is incredibly thin. I wonder does he eat properly? His house was pretty chaotic – it wouldn't surprise me if he forgot to half the time.

'Thank you for the compliment,' I reply. 'My parents would be pretty pleased with that description – nice and smart ticks two of their boxes. Now if only I'd get married I could polish off their to-do list for them!' I laugh at the absurdity of the situation. From eye candy to nice and smart in less than a minute – that's quite a turnaround.

'Aren't you married, then?' He gazes at my ring finger.

'Nope.' I waggle it at him. 'I'm an old maid.'

'Hardly.' He grins, taking another bite of his sourdough roll, as do I. They really are delicious. And the delicate Jarlsberg cheese and spicy sliced salami are divine. Something about eating in the open air always makes me feel even hungrier than usual.

'It's a fact,' I say. 'I've been left on the shelf.'

Well, there is the small matter of Gary. But I'd better not mention that. It might put a spanner in the works if he knew I was dating his publisher – he might believe there was a conflict of interest. Which there is, sort of.

'A girl like you, left on the shelf? I don't believe it. No way.'

'It's true, I'm afraid. Anyhow, I'm practically married to my job. I didn't become an agent just to make money, you know,' I say, surprising myself with the force of my conviction.

'No?' he mumbles, mouth full.

'Of course not. I mean, it's great if an author becomes successful, I won't deny it, but I have authors on my list who may never achieve any sort of fame or make any money. I want to represent them because I feel passionately about their writing and I want readers out there to experience their work. That's the most important thing.' I surprise myself again by realizing this is true.

He surveys me carefully as he chews, as if he's trying to make up his mind about me. 'That's what April used to say,' he replies at last. 'I really can't believe she's dead . . .'

Poor Ian. It sounds like he genuinely liked and respected April – he must be feeling so confused, abandoned, even.

In that moment I decide to take a risk. 'Look, Ian. I'll level with you. Gary Elverson asked me to talk to you – he thought we'd work well together.' I cross my fingers at this. It's almost true. No point in mentioning that both Gary and I have a lot to gain. That information would only muddy the waters – better to keep it simple and straightforward.

Ian looks at me carefully. 'Gary Elverson, huh? So, you and Gary are in bed together, is that it? He'll scratch your back, you'll scratch his?'

I grimace inside at this – it's too close for comfort. 'Of course not. It doesn't work like that. Gary just thought you and I would be a good fit. He knows I'm a huge fan of yours.'

'Are you sure about that?' he asks, his face disbelieving.

'Of course I'm sure,' I say, hoping I sound sincere. It's mostly true anyway. It's not like I'm lying – not technically. 'I'm here to help you, but only if you want. Now that April is gone you'll need a new agent. That's a fact. I'm available and I'd love to work with you. That's all there is to it.'

'And the sequel?' He eyes me carefully.

I know that how I respond now will seal my fate. I have to be careful – very, very careful. 'Look,' I say, 'if you really don't want to do a sequel, no one is going to force you to. Tell you what, let's consider some of the other ideas you have – maybe I can help you with those.' I feel a little bad, bluffing like this, because of course I'm not telling the truth. What I'm doing is trying a little reverse psychology. Maybe it's enough that I've planted the idea of a sequel in Ian's head. I don't want to push him too much on it, because if I do he'll never go for it. Maybe if we talk about some of his other ideas he'll come back to the sequel himself, once he sees how much there is going for the idea. Reverse psychology may not be the best angle to work, but I've had to do it plenty of times to cajole authors and at this stage I'm left with very few options. If I keep pressuring him, I know instinctively that he'll run right back to his house behind the high, white-washed walls, lock himself in and never take my calls again.

'I see. Well, that's a surprise, I must say,' he remarks now.

'Listen, Ian, I want to work with you, not against you,' I say smoothly, with a charming smile, slicing some more Jarlsberg and offering it to him. 'If you feel a sequel is not the right approach to take, then that's fine. We can brainstorm together.'

I feel quite confident as I say this that nothing will come of any 'brainstorming'. Ian has already told me he believes his new ideas won't set the world alight and that he can't finish what he starts. It stands to reason, then, that once we thrash it all out, he'll come round to my way of thinking. It may seem cruel, but it's for his own good: once his sales go through the roof and his star is back in the ascendant, he'll be thrilled. Anyway, it's not like I'll ignore any of his new ideas – if there's any spark in them, I'll happily help him work it through. There might even be something that we can use for the next book – after the sequel is written. Yes, this is going to work out just fine. I can feel it in my bones, as Rosie would say.

I'm busy congratulating myself silently when my phone buzzes and a text pops up. *Can we meet? I need to speak to you. John Bonner.*

'I don't believe this!' I exclaim indignantly, forgetting for a second that Ian is beside me. 'The *nerve* of that guy!' If that lunatic thinks I'm going to agree to meet him, he must be certifiable. I'm not even going to reply.

'What is it?' Ian asks.

'Oh, some nutcase, nothing to worry about.' I don't want to get into the phone mix-up with Ian. We need to concentrate on work, not get sidetracked.

'You look pretty incensed for nothing. Come on, tell me. Is something the matter?' He looks worried, as if it might be something to do with him – as if there might be some massive conspiracy against him. I have to tell him about John Bonner or he'll get even more suspicious, start to think I'm plotting. Which I am, just a little.

'Everything's fine. I was getting texts on my cell that were meant for someone else, that's all. This is a temporary phone – I left mine on the plane. It's no big deal.'

'And this guy is a nutcase because?' He gestures to my phone.

'Because I texted him back to tell him about his mistake, and then he called me and went crazy, accused me of stealing the cell-phone number. He reckons it belongs to some girl – Aimee her name is.'

'What?' Ian perks up immediately.

'Can you believe his nerve?' I feel my rage building, almost instantly. 'And now he wants to meet me! Did you ever hear anything so stupid?' I'm absolutely furious again. After the abuse he gave me, now he wants to meet! What on earth makes him think I'd ever agree to that?

Unless . . . unless he plans to do me some sort of harm. He did sound out of his mind when I spoke to him – maybe I should inform the police. What he's doing could technically constitute stalking, thinking about it. What if he's somehow found out who I am or is even following me? I look around, trying to spot anyone who might be paying us too much attention, but everyone looks innocent enough. What has me thinking like this? Honestly, I need to get a grip. How could this person possibly know who I am? I'm just overreacting that's all, letting my imagination run away with me.

Suddenly I'm aware that Ian is staring at me, his eyes bright, a grin spreading from ear to ear. 'You *have* to meet him,' he says.

'You are joking, Ian.' I laugh humourlessly. 'I have no

intention of meeting him, ever.' I peel off a piece of salami and wedge it between two slices of sourdough bread. I'm anger-eating now – I know that – but I can't help it. This John Bonner person pushes all my buttons.

'But you have to – this is perfect!' Ian says.

'Perfect? Perfect for what?' What *is* he on about? Is everyone in this town crazy or what?

'You said you'd be happy to work on some new novel ideas me with me, right?'

Dammit. I knew I shouldn't have said that – there's a fine line between encouragement and delusion. 'Well, yes, I did,' I admit.

But I didn't really mean it. What I meant was for him to sign with me and then agree to my plan of writing a sequel.

Ian is on his feet now, pacing back and forth. 'This is the story I've been waiting for!' he says, real urgency and excitement in his voice.

Er, excuse me? Are you completely insane? 'I'm not following you, Ian, I'm sorry,' I say.

His eyes are gleaming. 'A woman gets texts meant for someone else – all the confusion, the intrigue . . . And the endless possibilities – it's a brilliant hook!'

Oh, for God's sake. He cannot be serious. I immediately rearrange my face to my nice-try-but-no-cigar expression. 'Ian, I don't think that's a very good idea,' I start. Be tactful. Tactful but firm. I'm used to this – my authors get crazy ideas all the time, ideas I bat out of the ballpark before they can ever get too attached to them.

'Why not?' He swivels to look at me.

'Because it's too outlandish for a start. Your readers –'

'It's *not* outlandish! It's happening to you right now! It probably happens all the time but we don't hear about it! All you have to do is meet him, find out what this is all about –

get me the inside track. I just need a few more details – who this guy is, who the texts were meant for – what was her name? Aimee?'

Crap. He's all lit up like a Christmas tree, which means his imagination has gone into overdrive – I'd recognize that look anywhere: the look of a writer who's been hit by what he believes is the next big idea. If I deflate him utterly, he'll turn against me and I'll have no hope of ever convincing him to join me or write a sequel. My mind is working overtime to find a way out of this. Maybe if I agree to a quick meeting with John Bonner, just to keep Ian happy and onside, demonstrate that I'm willing to go the extra mile . . . That might work. He'll start to trust me, sign with me – and I'll talk sense into him later. It's a little sneaky, yes, but sneakiness is part of this job. It's for his own good, after all: I have his best interests at heart.

'OK, Ian, if that's what you really, really want, I'll do it for you.' I sigh, as if I'm giving in, just to make it sound more authentic.

'You will?' Ian almost claps his hands with glee.

'Of course.' I smile benevolently at him. 'Like I said, I'm here to help.'

'Thank you, Francesca!'

He does a jig of joy in front of me and I feel a little bad. He's really into this idea. But I push the guilt away: as his agent – OK, his almost agent – I know best. He'll thank me in the end. 'That's OK,' I say magnanimously. 'Anything to help.'

'Fantastic!' he goes on, apparently overjoyed. 'I can't wait to get working on this story!'

'Honestly, don't mention it.' I smile, like the Duchess of Cambridge in a high-street dress that's destined to sell out in seconds, might to a small child. But in my head, I'm already decorating my dream corner office with a gigantic oak table. Or maybe mahogany. And there'll be fresh flowers in crystal vases . . . lots and lots of flowers . . .

Chapter Twelve

I can't quite believe I'm doing this. I've actually agreed to rendezvous with a stranger, some random person who could be a complete and utter lunatic, just to appease an author. It seemed like a good idea yesterday, but now, sitting in this little café on one corner of Washington Square Park in the North Beach district of the city, waiting to meet John Bonner in the flesh, I know it's possibly the stupidest plan I've ever had. The delicious coffee and the pecan amaretto finger – a speciality, according to the beautiful doe-eyed waitress with the endless legs – might possibly be the last meal I ever have. When I'm missing, presumed dead, and they do a *CSI: Crime Scene Investigation* here and discover my fingerprints all over this cup, my lipstick on the rim, one weary San Francisco cop will say to his partner, 'What a stupid broad,' and he'll nod sagely and agree before they tuck into their 'donuts'. And they'll be right. About the stupid bit at least. Because I'm not quite sure what a broad is, or whether I fit the criteria. I think I might have to be wearing shoulder pads and smoking cigarettes to be one. But stupid – yes, definitely. I tick that box, at least today.

Granted, I've pulled some pretty silly stunts in my time to make my writers and publishers feel loved, but this has got to be right up there with the best. Sending lavish baskets of fruit, enormous bouquets, magnums of champagne on publication day – even that time I bombarded an editor with her favourite Percy Pigs for two full weeks until she agreed to read a manuscript that I knew she would love – they all pale into insignificance now. This is quite possibly the stupidest thing I've ever done and if my job, possibly my entire career, wasn't on the line, there's no way I'd be here now, sitting in a small, run-down café in North Beach waiting to meet a man who's already verbally attacked me for no reason.

Who knows what he'll say or do when we meet? He ranted down the phone at me – what if he does the same here, or worse? I have no idea what he's capable of. He could be a hardened criminal – he might have done time. He might think nothing of cutting me to ribbons right here in public. Why didn't I Google him before I turned up? What was I thinking? John Bonner, the North Beach killer. It has quite a ring to it.

I push the thought away, panic fluttering in my stomach. There's no need to let my imagination run riot. I just have to meet this guy briefly so I can tell Ian I did. Five minutes, ten, tops, get the background to this mysterious story, and then I'll be out of here as fast as my feet can carry me. *Before he has a chance to slash me to pieces, gut me like a fish.*

'Excuse me, are you Francesca?'

A shadow falls across my small table and I look up. A tall man with a strong Roman nose, deep-set black eyes and olive skin is standing by my table, his face tense and unsmiling. He's broad-shouldered, Italian-looking, dressed in a grey T-shirt with a Berkeley University logo and faded jeans, his thick black hair curling slightly at the collar. He doesn't look altogether friendly but he doesn't look like a serial killer either, but then most serial killers don't, do they? It's not as if they go round with a bell hung from their neck, letting everyone know they like Chianti with the liver of their victims. They look like ordinary people – they blend in. And therefore I still intend to be extremely careful.

'John?' I query.

'Yes,' he confirms formally. 'Thank you for meeting me. I know this must seem strange to you.'

Strange to me? This scenario would be strange to *anyone*.

I nod, and indicate with a tiny head movement that he should sit. I'm determined not to engage in unnecessary pleasantries with this man. Get the bones of his story for Ian, that's all I have to do. *And then persuade Ian that it's a pointless waste of time and he needs to get writing that sequel pronto.*

'Another coffee?' he asks stiffly, twisting around to catch the waitress's eye.

What? And you'll lace it with Rohypnol? I want to shoot back.

'No, thanks, I'm fine with this,' I say, deliberately injecting my voice with ice. No point in being overly warm – I'm not here to make friends.

I stir my cup of now-cold coffee, still half full. I'll make sure to keep it near me, just in case he tries to slip anything into it, get me unconscious and drag me to his waiting van. That might be hard for him to pull off in a coffee shop, of course, but who knows what tricks he has up his sleeve? I can't be too careful. In my head I can hear Mum warning me never to accept lifts from strangers or take drinks from men I don't know.

'I'll have an espresso, please,' he tells the same doe-eyed waitress, who approaches, her notepad ready to take his order.

'Sure.' She smiles at him, as if he's not the North Beach Killer but just a regular nice guy. Of course, she could be in on this too. I eye the remains of the pecan amaretto finger she gave me with new unease. Maybe I shouldn't have gobbled it. It may be sprinkled with sedative.

'You're not American?' John Bonner settles his unsmiling stare on me. He's not hostile – not exactly. But it's close.

'No,' I reply shortly, staring right back, bristling at his

rudeness. How dare he be so brusque? I'm the one who took the time out of my hectic schedule to meet him here. He could at least act a little more grateful.

He raises his eyebrows, just a fraction, probably surprised that I won't elaborate. But I have no intention of telling him where I'm from exactly – I'm not disclosing any personal details that he doesn't need to know.

'I'm here for work,' I add primly. That's enough information for him to chew on.

'So your phone – your number – it's . . . temporary?' he asks.

I try to decide whether or not confirming this is a good idea. But I sort of have to tell him the truth – there's no point in denying it.

'Yes,' I say. 'I hired the phone when I got here. My own phone is . . . indisposed.' I'm not going to admit that I lost it on the flight – that's none of his business. Besides, it sounds kind of scatty and that is not the impression I want to give him.

Something like relief crosses his face and his body sags a fraction, his tense shoulders relaxing. 'That explains it,' he mutters, almost to himself.

'Explains what?' I ask. I still have no idea where this is headed. But if I'm to do my job properly and come up with information for Ian, I need to get to the bottom of the mystery.

'You should never have had that number,' he says grimly, sitting bolt upright again. His expression is hard and cold once more, all traces of relief, or whatever it was, gone.

'The telephone company gave it to me,' I reply, prickling at his tone. 'I didn't request it specially. I didn't ask for this number, just to annoy you.'

I'm being deliberately sarcastic to needle him. But if it's

working he doesn't show it. Instead he ignores my mocking tone and continues, his eyes blazing now, 'They shouldn't have. It's a mistake. That number belongs to Aimee and I – I mean she needs it back,' he says.

The nerve of him! Who the hell is Aimee anyway? If I didn't have to do this, I'd happily tip the remains of my cold coffee over this guy's head and storm out. But I faithfully promised Ian I'd get some more background and I'm not in the habit of breaking my promises.

'Look, I don't know what's going on,' I start, 'but, in my experience, a telephone company can't just take someone's number and reassign it without there being some sort of logical explanation. If she didn't pay her bills and they took back her number, then redeployed it, that's not exactly my problem.'

There. That'll force him to explain. I've definitely hit a nerve – I can tell because his face is working overtime.

'They made a mistake. You should never have had that number,' he repeats.

My hackles rise. We're going round in circles and so far I've absolutely no information about the mysterious Aimee to pass on to Ian. It's all I can do to keep my temper and not fly off the handle. 'OK, they made a mistake. But what do you expect me to do about it?' I ask, trying another tack.

'You have to give me that phone.' He says it as if it's the most natural thing in the world. Like I'm just going to hand it over, no questions asked.

'Are you insane?' I laugh, unable to stop myself. But I stop laughing when I see the serious look in his eyes. Suddenly I feel a little nervous. What if he is some sort of violent lunatic? What if the last person who refused him is floating in the bay, missing vital organs or limbs or both? Could I be about to go and sleep with the fish? I swallow nervously, then make a valiant attempt to look brave. This guy has never met me before – for all he knows I could be an award-winning karate champion, able to knock him out with a flick of my finger. Not that that would do much good if he has half a dozen knives secreted about his person. Or a few henchmen sitting in a getaway car outside. But still, I have to hold my nerve.

'I need that number back and this is the only way,' he replies, his voice like ice.

That was *definitely* a threat. I'm quaking inside now and suddenly I wish I had some back-up. The café is almost deserted except for the waitress and a blonde woman in the corner, cradling a cappuccino and reading the *San Francisco Chronicle*. Why didn't I let Rosie come with me? She was thrilled when I told her I'd decided to meet John Bonner – and she was dying to tag along. But I didn't allow her to. The truth is, I didn't want her to know that this is all to do with Ian – I wanted to keep that part of the story to myself and I was afraid I might let something slip. Still, it was stupid to come here alone. Now my instincts are telling me to leave, walk away. But something inside is also telling me not to give up.

'And what do you expect me to do in the meantime?' I hear myself say. I sound impressive – and surprisingly tough, despite my nerves. 'Do you want me to go without a phone altogether?'

'No.' He looks a little startled, as if he hasn't thought this part through. 'I'll – I'll organize a phone for you.'

'You'll organize a phone for me?' I repeat, gaining more confidence now. 'What does that mean?'

'It means I'll get you another one,' he replies, and his tone is so dismissive, so ambivalent, that I feel like reaching across the table and smacking him hard in the face. This is absolutely ludicrous. And I'm not going to stand for it, even if he is some sort of a gangster.

'Well, if you think I'm going to hand this phone over to you just like that, you've got another think coming!' I huff, sounding uncannily like my mother on the very odd occasion she's lost her temper with my dad. 'I signed a contract with the phone company for one thing. What are you going to do about that?'

'I'll figure it out,' he says blandly, his eyes not leaving my face.

'And what do you expect me to tell my office and my clients?' I ask, incredulous. But he just shrugs his shoulders, as if he couldn't care less about these mundane details. 'Ah, so you don't care about that,' I say, trying not to lose my temper altogether.

'I'm sorry for the inconvenience,' he says tightly. 'I'm willing to pay you, of course, by way of compensation.'

He pulls his wallet from his pocket and begins peeling out twenty-dollar notes.

I can't believe it – this guy is actually paying me to hand this phone over. Which means that he's desperate. There's definitely something very fishy going on – probably highly illegal. And I'm right in the middle of it.

'There's five hundred dollars,' he says, pushing the cash across the table to me. *Five hundred dollars?* That would buy the gorgeous Marc Jacobs bag I saw on sale in Macy's. I could wander down there, right now, get them to wrap it up for me, and no one need ever be the wiser. I could just call the telephone company, tell them I lost the phone – silly me, stupid tourist. They have insurance for such things, after all. No big deal.

'What are you waiting for?' he says, as I sit looking at the money, stupefied.

That's enough for me to make up my mind. He's assuming I've already agreed. As if I can be bought off, no questions asked. Well, he can forget it!

'No.'

'Six hundred, then.' He opens his wallet again.

'I'm not giving you this phone.' My voice is so determined it surprises even me.

He stops counting money and his eyes narrow. 'You have Aimee's number,' he growls. 'And you're going to give it back to me.'

'I don't even know who this stupid Aimee is!' I explode. 'But whoever she is it's up to *her* to sort this mess out. Why are you doing her dirty work? Is she afraid to handle her affairs herself?' I'm taunting him now and, boy, does it feel good.

'How dare you?' He practically spits the words.

'How dare *I*?' I lean across the table towards him until we're almost nose to nose. 'How dare *you*? Just who do you think you are, making all these demands?' I can feel the eyes of the waitress and the woman in the corner on us, their expressions startled, but I don't care. This man has unbeliev-able gall, and he's not going to get away with speaking to me like that.

'I want that phone,' he insists, his black eyes still on me, grim determination shining from them.

I push myself up and away from the table, grabbing my bag with the phone inside it. 'Well, you're not getting it,' I snarl, shaking with rage now. He can't treat me like this. I don't care if he does have henchmen lying in wait to ambush me outside. Right now, I could take on half a dozen of them. And their sidekicks. Flinging one last hate-filled look in his direction, I stomp out of the coffee shop, my chin up, my head held high. That guy is an unbelievable arsehole, thinking he can just buy me like that. I'm not for sale and neither is this phone. He can't treat me like – like something on the sole of his shoe.

I stalk down the street, rage coursing through my veins. I showed him! I showed him I can't just be dismissed like that! Who does he think he is anyway? He can't walk all over me – no way. And then I remember Ian and my anger deflates. *Crap.* Ian. I was supposed to get information for him – unearth the true story. Thanks to John Bonner's arrogance, I have nothing. But then I pull myself together. It'll be OK. I'll be able to make up something plausible, fabricate a story: it won't be too difficult.

Maybe it's all for the best anyhow: if I come up with some lame explanation then Ian will realize that writing the sequel really is the way forward. Besides, I'm not being dishonest, not really, because there is nothing to this story – there's just some arrogant bully who thinks he can get whatever he wants. And I'm certainly not giving in to him.

Chapter Thirteen

'That's terrible, Frankie. I should never have encouraged you to meet him,' Rosie says unhappily, as we walk together through the city streets, climbing up and away from Union Square.

'It's OK,' I reassure her, feeling a pang of guilt that she's blaming herself in any way for what happened. After all, I had my own reasons for meeting John Bonner. But the more I think about it, the crosser I get. I was the one who put myself out. OK, so I only did it to get on Ian's good side, but John Bonner doesn't know that, does he? As far as he's concerned, I met him out of the goodness of my heart.

'I don't know why I thought it would be a good idea. There was something about his voice when we spoke ... He sounded so genuine.'

'Don't worry about it,' I say. Rosie has no idea that I only ever went along with it to keep Ian happy and I'm not going to tell her now – it would make everything far too complicated. Ian, and his plan to use this phone mix-up as a hook for his next novel, will have to stay my little secret.

'But you were so kind, Frankie, agreeing to see him when you're so busy. Lots of others would just have walked away,' she says now, looking at me as if I'm Mother Teresa. It makes me feel very uncomfortable, especially when I know I did it for my own reasons. I feel really sneaky, but I can't tell her the truth, can I? There's client confidentiality for one thing – Ian's writing plans are top secret. If Rosie found out, she might do something stupid – like post spoilers on the Internet. Unlikely, of course. Especially because I'm not sure she has an Internet connection on her houseboat. But still. Better not take any unnecessary chances. I am a professional, after all. People do entrust me with their careers – I have to honour that special bond. The only thing is, I do feel a little . . . seedy. I've lied to Rosie, and that makes me feel terribly awkward. It's ridiculous – I haven't even known her a wet week so why am I thinking that way? This is business, pure and simple. If Ian wanted information on that guy I had to try to get it for him, full stop.

So, I wasn't being seedy, not really. I was just on a fact-finding mission for a valued client – or a possible valued client. It's just like the time I arranged for Antonia West to intern at an advertising agency because she was setting her latest novel in one. It was research. Well, sort of. The point is, I was only trying to do my job. I need to get Ian to sign on the dotted line by whatever means possible – I have to secure my future.

'I was sure this mix-up meant something to him,' Rosie says now.

'Oh, it means something to him, all right. He's desperate to get his hands on the phone, or the number, that's for sure.'

'Why, though?' Rosie muses. '*Why* is he so desperate?'

'I don't know,' I reply. 'He wouldn't tell me.' And I sure as hell didn't ask him. Tosser.

'So he didn't even say who Aimee was?'

'No.' I wince a little as I remember how I yelled at him, demanding to know why she couldn't fight her own battles. He hadn't liked that. But it had served him right for being so rude. If he'd explained to me what it was about, made his case politely so to speak, I might have co-operated with him. After all, I'm getting my own phone back soon so we could probably have come to some sort of arrangement. But, no, he had to go and be all high-handed and dismissive – and then he'd tried to pay me, like I was some sort of charity case. The whole encounter has left me feeling dirty, used and extremely annoyed.

'It's all so strange,' Rosie muses. 'I just can't help wondering what it's about.'

'Well, I've stopped thinking about it,' I say.

'But what if you get another mystery text?' she asks. 'What will you do then?'

'Well, I haven't. Not so far. And if I do get one, I know exactly how I'm going to reply. And it's not going to be polite.'

'You sure are fixing for a fight,' she answers sadly.

'I can't abide bullies, Rosie,' I say fiercely. 'I just won't stand for that sort of behaviour.' I surprise myself with my strength of emotion – John Bonner really vexed me.

'I don't know why people have to be so ornery. He should've used a little honey, that's what my daddy used to say.'

'What does that mean?' I ask. Rosie's southern sayings aren't always exactly clear.

'It means that if he'd buttered you up some then he would have got what he wanted. Instead he got nothing and you got hot and bothered!'

'I guess his version of honey was offering me six hundred dollars,' I say crossly. 'The nerve of him!'

'He tried to *buy* the phone from you?'

'He practically forced the cash on me.' I feel outraged even thinking about it. 'The cheek of him – I was tempted to belt him, I can tell you.'

'Belt him?'

'Slap him,' I explain. 'I wanted to slap him.' Hard, all over his smug, passive-aggressive face.

'So you turned him down?'

'Of course I turned him down! I hate people who think they can buy their way out of any situation,' I fume, getting het up again. 'He thought if he gave me enough I'd have to do what he wanted – it was so insulting!' Thinking about it makes my blood boil. I'm glad I stormed out of there, dignity intact. There was no way I was taking money – possibly dirty money – from that creep.

'I guess you're right,' Rosie agrees. 'That was pretty insulting.'

But I can tell her response isn't exactly wholehearted. I glance sidelong at her, see that her cheeks are slightly flushed and feel guilty all over again. Rosie is quite obviously struggling for money – she lives on a tiny houseboat she inherited and she's between jobs. Six hundred dollars is a lot to her, and here I am rubbing her nose in it that I had that amount on the table and turned it down. Thinking about it, I could have found a million different ways to use it – designer handbags aside, it's not even a drop in the ocean of my business debt.

'So, where are we going?' I ask, to change the topic of conversation. I've barely been watching where we were walking but suddenly I notice that we could be in Hong Kong – we're surrounded by teeming crowds, heat, noise and smell.

'This is Stockton Street,' she explains, grinning at me. 'Most tourists go to Grant Avenue to see all the souvenir shops, but I want to show you the places only the locals know – the real Chinatown.'

'It's certainly very busy,' I reply. If this is the real Chinatown I'm not sure I'm going to enjoy it. The street is thronged with people, the pavements packed with fish markets, herbal-medicine stores and restaurants. Everywhere I look, shopkeepers are selling their wares, haggling loudly with customers, while poultry squawks in wire cages at their feet. Stacks of dry goods, bottled and canned ingredients, are piled outside every store. Along with fresh fruit and vegetables there's live seafood – I spot shrimp, crab, lobster all fighting for space in murky tanks, their claws clanking despairingly on the sides, making me want to run for cover. I don't want to see live shellfish clamouring to escape. I prefer to think of my seafood as having spent a nice happy life somewhere – with Nemo, perhaps, singing songs on the seabed – before it hits my plate.

'I come here all the time to shop,' Rosie is saying. 'It's the best place in the city to get meat and soup fixings.'

'Really?' I feel a little doubtful about this. What's wrong with a good old-fashioned supermarket? I sidestep a bin of what looks and smells like dried fish guts, trying not to gag as she continues.

'Oh, yes, you can get wonderful herbs to use in tonic soups and stews, and then there's the seafood – that's the best. You can even get fresh eels!'

'Eels?' I squeak. I feel my stomach roll. She can't be serious.

'Uh-huh.' She nods enthusiastically. 'My daddy used to cook 'em up real good with mashed fermented black beans and garlic. Yum!' She rubs her tummy, and I smile weakly at her. I can think of nothing more revolting. 'It can be a little overwhelming at first,' she says, 'but you'll get used to it. And there's so much to see and do! They say this is the biggest Asian community outside China.'

I already know that from reading my guide book, and really I should be grateful that Rosie is taking the time to show me a part of the city that many overseas visitors never see, but she's right – it is a little overwhelming: it's a teeming melting pot of activity and noise and steam. I've never seen anything like it before.

'Now, come this way.' She's all authority as she takes me by the arm and begins to barge confidently through the throng. 'I'm not here to stock up on groceries today. We're on a secret mission.'

I breathe a silent sigh of relief. At least I won't have to pick out the saddest lobster and take it home for dinner or shove some eels in a bag to boil up later. But a secret mission? What's that about? Could there be something worse in store? But what could be worse than live eels, wriggling in buckets, waiting to slither up my leg and wind themselves round my torso before ... Oh, God, I feel a little weak. Rosie is marching me down the street, past gaggles of people, all seemingly shouting happily enough at each other as they drive their deals. I have no idea where we're going – I just hang on to her for dear life as she weaves expertly in and out, dodging bodies, letting myself be guided. There's no point in arguing with her when she's like this – she can be fiercely determined. I know that already. Her grip is tight as we work our way through the crowd until we reach a door. There's no sign or bundles of materials or produce outside like at other doors. Rosie winks at me and knocks once. The door creaks open, as if by itself, and I peer inside.

'What is this place, Rosie?' I ask, my eyes adjusting to the dim interior.

'I'm taking you to meet two women who have the most amazing silks – you just have to see them!'

'Um, I'm not really a Chinese silks sort of person,' I reply. The last thing I need is a gaudy kimono or whatever the Chinese equivalent is. I already have bags of clothes I don't wear that I have to bring to the charity shop – if I ever get round to it. I certainly don't want any more. And there's no way on earth I'd ever wear anything tacky with a dragon on the back.

'Just wait and see.' She winks at me again, pushing me

gently over the threshold, her hand on my back. 'These are special.'

We're inside now and I can see that rolls of silk fabrics – reds, blues, jade greens – are stacked against the walls, all shining in the half-light. There are displays of embroidered purses and scarves draped across the counter in bundles and, to each side, the racks spill with Chinese silk jackets and shirts. Before us, as if they've appeared out of thin air, are two little old Asian ladies, both dressed in black tunics that reach almost to their knees, so sombre compared to the explosion of colour in the shop.

They bow to Rosie, then me, giving small smiles, gesturing that we should look at the displays.

'Aren't they amazing?' Rosie is stroking an orange jacket with a yellow and green design.

'Hand embroidered,' one old lady says, in a lilting, sing-song voice.

'Imagine the work that's gone into them,' Rosie says. 'They're just . . . exquisite! You have to try one, Frankie!'

'Um, they're not exactly my cup of . . .'

But then I glance at the little old ladies, both smiling and nodding at me, and at Rosie, her face shining with delight. She really believes she's sharing something special with me. 'OK,' I say, swallowing the urge to say I hate all this stuff. 'Let me take a look.'

I rake slowly through a rack of jackets and hum and hah over each one, pretending to deliberate between them.

'You like?' the taller little old lady asks, her eyes twinkling. She doesn't know I'm pretending, does she? No, that's silly, she couldn't.

'Oh, yes, they're lovely,' I say. And, actually, they are. I couldn't wear them in public obviously, but they're beauti-fully made – the detail in the stitching is incredible and the fabric is so soft. They're nothing like the polyester versions I've seen before. These are made of the best material, finely cut and finished.

'You try, you try,' the other little old lady says, smiling too.

'Um, no, it's fine,' I reply. I might have to buy something cheap and cheerful – Rosie will probably be gutted if I don't. But trying these things on would be too much like hard work, no matter how silky and luxurious they are. For a start I'm not sure if I'm wearing the right underwear – I'd probably need a camisole . . .

'No, no, you try, you try!' the old ladies cry in unison, more insistent now.

'Go on, Frankie!' Rosie urges. 'How will you know which suits you best if you don't?'

I want to tell her that it doesn't really matter what suits me best. Even if I had money to spend – which I don't – this sort of stuff is just not me. But then I see the expression of sheer joy on her face – she believes that I'm loving every moment of this. I can't disappoint her. I'll just have to choose the very cheapest and get rid of it later.

Before I know it, the two little old ladies have almost shoved me into a tiny changing room, yanking the curtain closed behind them. They may be tiny, but appearances are deceptive: they're strong as oxen. There's no getting out of it now. I tentatively try on the first jacket they shove through the curtain at me, a startling orange with yellow embroidery across the back and shoulders.

'You like?' The ladies yank back the curtain and survey me critically before I even have a chance to button it up properly or look at myself in the mirror. They begin to chatter excitedly to each other in what I presume is Mandarin as they stare at me. They both look intense as they talk, like they're really debating the pros and cons of what I've tried on. Hard to tell because I have no clue what they're saying, but their body language speaks volumes. And from it I can see that they don't particularly like this specimen on me. They're frowning a lot and pointing, their bony fingers jabbing the air as they chatter at high speed.

Then one giggles and the other joins in. Are they laughing at me? I don't look that bad, do I?

'No good,' the first one says. Then she plucks another from a rack close by and hands it to me. 'This one better.'

She shoves it into my hands – a purple one with green embroidery. It's the oldest trick in the book, of course – the hard sell. This one is probably even more expensive than the last. Before I know it, they've pulled the orange and yellow specimen from me and are spinning me round, tugging on the purple and green, not bothering with the changing room, clucking their tongues and muttering to each other. Occasionally they stop and break into peals of laughter.

'Look at the size of the arse on that!' one could be saying.

'Let's sell her the vilest thing in here!' the other one could be suggesting.

They yank at me, pulling the fabric this way and that until they're finally happy. Then they spin me to face the mirror and I actually gasp. The jacket is beautiful. The purple actually suits my skin tone, and the green accentuates the colour of my eyes.

'You like?' they say together.

'Yes, I like,' I say. I mean, I could never wear this in public – it would have to be strictly for lounging around – but still . . . it's lovely.

'Oooh! You look beautiful!' Rosie appears, holding a pair of pink silk slippers.

'Yes – good colour!' one lady clucks approvingly.

'Very nice!' the other agrees.

'It really suits you!' Rosie adds. 'Are you going to take it?' Her eager face is what does me in.

'Yes, I think I will,' I say. If I have to buy something, then this may as well be it. It actually makes me . . . glow a little. For something I'm never going to wear it looks pretty good. 'I'll take it,' I say to the two ladies. They nod and bow and babble excitedly to each other again. Before I know it, I'm out of the jacket and they're happily wrapping it for me in cute Chinese paper, red embossed with gold. 'How much is it?' I ask, pulling my purse from my bag. Probably twice the price of the first one I tried on, knowing my luck.

'One hundred dollar,' the first little old lady says.

I try to hide my surprise. That's not too bad, considering the quality. 'OK,' I say, handing her two fifty-dollar bills.

They frown.

'No, no. You haggle,' the second old lady says, shaking her head.

She can't be serious. But from the set of her wrinkled face I can tell she is.

'Go on, Frankie,' Rosie whispers, under her breath. 'You can't offend them.'

'Um, seventy dollars?' I offer tentatively.

They turn to each other, speaking fast, pistol-shot Mandarin again, as if they're debating whether or not to accept my offer. This is nuts. They already know I'm prepared to pay the full asking price – why are they keeping up this charade?

'Seventy-five dollar,' one says. 'Final offer.'

I look to Rosie. Is it OK to accept this? Should I haggle some more? But she nods at me. I'm done. 'OK,' I agree.

The ladies are beaming at me, accepting my money, giving me change. A deal has been struck and apparently they're delighted with the outcome.

Rosie goes through the exact same ritual with her slippers, obviously keen to get a good deal because of her financial situation, and at last we're leaving, waving goodbye as they bow and smile. We're just through the door when they rush after us, pressing a fortune cookie each into our hands.

I don't like fortune cookies, but I don't dare refuse. This could be part of the whole haggling thing. Instead I thank them both, then stumble into the sunlight and the crowds, the noise and smell assaulting me, Rosie by my side.

'Oooh, let's see what they say!' Rosie whoops. 'I love fortune cookies!' She cracks hers open immediately, uncurling the tiny message. '"Love lies round the corner,"' she reads, her face creasing in delight. 'Oh, my! How wonderful!' Then she glances round hopefully, as if a new lover is about to jump out from behind a bin of dried fish guts and ravish her here and now. 'Now open yours!' she urges, her cheeks flushed with excitement.

I crack the cookie and pluck out the curled-up piece of paper. '"Listen to your heart,"' I read.

'"Listen to your heart . . ."' Rosie repeats, taking the scrap of paper from me. She narrows her eyes, thinking hard. 'That sure is abstract. I wonder what it means?'

I look at her face, her frown of deep thought, and realize she's actually taking this seriously. I should have guessed – she's into all this stuff. 'I don't think it means anything, Rosie,' I say, automatically popping the cookie into my mouth and crunching. It's delicious – buttery and sweet – nothing like the ones I've tasted before.

'Everything means something, honey,' she says, her face serious. 'Now think!'

An image of Gary flickers into my mind's eye. Can the message mean that I should listen to my heart about him? And if it does, then what exactly is my heart trying to tell me?

'What is it?' Rosie probes immediately. 'You've thought of something, haven't you?'

'It's nothing!' I say. I don't believe in this mumbo-jumbo. As if a fortune cookie could actually tell me something profound about my life – these things are manufactured by the million in a sterile factory somewhere: they mean nothing. OK, so this one tastes homemade, but that's probably just my imagination working overtime. I'm hungry, that's all.

'Come on, Frankie! You *did* think of something, I know it! Please tell me!' she begs.

'I didn't, I swear,' I fib, shoving my neatly wrapped parcel into my bag as my phone starts to buzz with a new text in the depths somewhere. 'Now, come on, let's go and find some of that awesome dim sum you keep telling me about. My tummy is –' I stop mid-sentence as I see who the text is from. John Bonner.

'It's him, isn't it?' Rosie says gravely. 'What does it say?'

I turn the phone to her so she can see and she reads aloud: '"Please can we meet again so I can explain properly?" Oh, my gosh – what are you going to do?'

'I'm going to call the police,' I say, my voice as clear as a bell.

'The *police*?' Rosie sounds shocked.

'I told him I wanted nothing more to do with him, and yet here he is, contacting me again. He can't be allowed to get away with it – he's practically harassing me.'

'But will they take you seriously? The police?'

There's a beat of silence between us as we think about this.

'Why wouldn't they? I have the evidence right here!' I wave the phone at her. 'Plus he was so rude to me in the café. That's threatening behaviour.'

'Hmm. I don't think that does count as threatening behaviour, sugar,' she says.

'Yes, it does!' I disagree hotly. Or if it doesn't, it should.

'Did he actually physically threaten you?' she asks.

No, is technically the answer to that. But he was aggressive – extremely aggressive. 'Not exactly,' I admit. 'But he did have a threatening air about him.'

'A threatening *air*?' Rosie says doubtfully.

'Yeah. I could see it – it was in his eyes.'

'He looked at you kinda funny – is that what you're trying to say, Frankie?' She giggles, then quickly turns it into a cough when she sees my face.

'Well, yes. But it was more than that. He was angry.'

'I don't think being angry is a criminal offence either. Not last time I checked. And neither is sending texts,' she says.

'Well, they should be!' I say. But I feel a little disappointed. She's probably right – if I go to the police with this, they'll just laugh at me. They might even accuse me of time wasting.

'*I* think you should meet him again,' Rosie says firmly.

'You are joking! You said earlier you were sorry you ever encouraged me!'

'I know that,' she admits. 'But I'm not usually wrong about people, Frankie, and this guy – John – he's not a bad person. I *feel* it.'

'I'm not listening to you.' I shove the phone back in my bag, and start to walk away from her, pushing my way grimly through the crowds.

'Oh, come on!' she pleads, trotting behind me. 'Don't you want to know what this is all about?'

'Nope. I really don't.' I continue walking. I'm not going to listen to her, no way.

'I don't believe you!' Rosie cries. 'You must want to know! How could you not? He said he wants to explain everything properly – you should give him the chance. You should *listen to your heart*.' She emphasizes the last four words.

My head snaps up. 'You can't be serious.'

'I'm deadly serious,' she replies. 'That's what the fortune cookie meant. You're destined to meet John Bonner again and find out the truth.'

'You're nuts,' I say.

'It's been said before. But that doesn't mean I'm wrong. Besides, I happen to know for a fact that you would relish the chance to have him grovel at your feet. Am I right?'

'Rosie, this is not an episode of *Jerry Springer*.'

'I know!' she whoops. 'It's better! Come on, Frankie, what d'ya say? Give him another chance, pretty please? If you don't you'll never know the truth behind it all – and that will doggone kill me!'

'I don't need to know the truth behind it,' I say firmly, but inside I'm wavering, just a fraction. It's the grovelling thing that's done it – Rosie's right, I would relish that.

'How can you not want to know?' Rosie howls. 'Aren't you just a teeny bit curious? And he's so persistent – there *has* to be more to it.'

'Persistent? Persistent is a stain on a white shirt that won't come out!' I mutter. But she's right. Maybe I am curious. Just a teeny bit. And then I think about Ian, how I managed to get none of the information he wanted. He won't be pleased – he was expecting some big saga that would inspire him. I can't tell him I stormed out of the coffee shop, still knowing nothing. That definitely wouldn't help my quest to get him onside. And finding out the truth – banal as it probably is – will be easier than trying to concoct a story. Maybe I could just meet this guy one more time. It might be worth it if it gets me off the hook with Ian.

'Oh, all right,' I hear myself say reluctantly. 'I'll do it – I must be nuts too.'

'Yay! I knew you'd see sense!' She does a little dance of joy. 'Come with me!' She tugs happily at my sleeve.

'Where are we going now?' I groan.

'You said you're hungry, right? Well, you're going to have the best doggone dim sum you ever tasted!'

Chapter Fourteen

When I walk into the small café in North Beach the next day, the doe-eyed waitress with the endless legs does a double-take. Well, she raises one of her bushy eyebrows in my direction, but it's enough to let me know that she recognizes me, that she hasn't forgotten the little drama that went down here. Of course, her reaction is probably to be expected. After all, last time I was here I did sort of storm off after having what could have been construed as a screaming match with a total stranger. Not that any of it was my fault, mind. It was all John Bonner's and when I see him I'll . . .

'Francesca?' I hear his voice before I spot him sitting at a table near the window. Same grey T-shirt. Same faded jeans. But his expression is different. As he stands, the better for me to see him, I can tell that he's nervous. Good. He *should* be nervous. He should be quaking in his boots because I am in no mood for tolerating any attitude today. If he says even one thing I don't like then I'm out of here. Like a shot. And the bushy-browed waitress, who's now openly staring at us, can go take a running jump too. Honestly, hasn't she heard of tweezers? Or a customer's right to some privacy?

I take a seat opposite him, not saying a word or even look-ing at him properly. No way am I rushing in with small-talk to put him at ease. He persuaded me to come here again so he can do the talking. And he can start with an apology. An abject apology. On his knees would be good. Rosie reckoned I wanted some grovelling and she was right. I do.

'I'm sorry about the other day,' he starts.

Humph. So you should be, I want to say. And you should be sorry about wearing that T-shirt too – that's a crime against fashion. And a crime against hygiene, come to think of it. I'm sure it's the same one he had on before. Yuk. Yuk. Double yuk. But I say nothing. I just stare balefully at him.

'This . . . situation is delicate.' He shifts in his seat. 'And I haven't handled it very well.'

'You can say that again,' I remark coolly.

He grimaces a little. 'I deserve that, I know,' he says.

I just look at him and say nothing. Silence can work wonders in situations like these – and I know how to hold my nerve: I did it for years at Withers and Cole. Publishers would call, make a low-ball offer for a book – taking a chance – and I would just keep quiet. It's amazing how many of them crumbled and went on to offer more. People hate silence – it makes everyone uneasy. It's easier to do on the phone, of course. It's always trickier to pull off face to face. But, still, I'm going to be aloof at the very least, just to let him know how little I think of him.

'So,' he says hesitantly, 'I appreciate you agreeing to come back here and meet me again – I know you're probably busy.'

'Yes. And I don't have long.' I look pointedly at my watch. Get on with it, I want to say. But then I remember Ian and keep my tongue in check. I want to be reserved and distant, but I also want to get the bones of the story. And accept a little more grovelling while I'm at it.

'Would you like a coffee? Or tea, maybe? You're Irish, right?' he asks.

'Yep, I am. But coffee is fine.' Not everyone in Ireland drinks tea, you big eejit, I want to say. Just like not everyone lives on potatoes and cabbage either.

As if he can read my mind, he twists away in what I suspect is embarrassment and calls to the waitress. When he turns back to me, his cheeks are flushed. He's incredibly twitchy – fiddling with his spoon and napkin. Good, good, good. I'm glad this situation is making him anxious – it serves him right.

'What part of Ireland are you from?' he asks, looking at me but not quite meeting my eye.

'Dublin,' I reply. *Monosyllabic. Well done, Frankie. Keep it up.*

'Dublin's great,' he says.

'Yes. It is,' I say.

'I was there in 2009 for a work thing. We stayed in Balls-something?'

'Ballsbridge?'

'That was it. Really nice place, close to the train – what's that called again?'

'The Dart?'

'The Dart! I knew it rhymed with something . . .'

I find I almost want to laugh but I don't. It was a juvenile joke. Besides, I'm still far too annoyed for that. 'How . . . interesting,' I say instead, with just a hint of lofty sarcasm.

'I loved Ireland. The people were great, really welcoming, so friendly. I worked with an Irish guy once too – his name was Connor and he was absolutely . . .' He catches my eye then and seems suddenly embarrassed again, as if he's just remembered I'm not some friendly Irish girl he can reminisce with about his trip to the old country. He practically begged me to meet him here – we're not buddies. I could swear he blushes a little again as this registers once more in his mind.

'So. OK.' He clears his throat and moves the sugar shaker across the table, playing for time, searching for the right words. 'I guess I need to tell you why I asked you here.'

He's really, really nervous.

'Yes, you do,' I agree.

149

'This is awkward,' he says.

'Awkward just about covers it.'

'I'm sorry about the shouting thing here the other day. It was completely out of character. I was just . . . extremely upset.'

Again, I say nothing to this. I'm not going to forgive and forget so easily, and he needn't think that I am.

He sighs heavily, as if it's very painful for him to try to explain. Well, keep trying, Buster, I'm tempted to say.

'OK, let me start at the beginning.' He takes a breath. 'The thing is, when you texted me, to say, you know, that I had the wrong number, I was very . . . shocked.'

'I was only trying to help you,' I point out. 'I knew your message wasn't for me. I thought letting you know was the right thing to do.'

'It was. I appreciate it, honestly. It's just . . .'

'You were expecting this Aimee to reply?' I pre-empt him.

'That's right.' He lowers his eyes, fiddles with the sugar shaker some more.

'Well, obviously there's been some sort of mix-up,' I say. 'Like I said the other day, I hired this phone at the airport when I arrived – I lost my own in transit. So I'm afraid it's not my fault I got this number. It came with the handset – it's the telephone company's mistake. You, or your friend Aimee, need to talk to them about it.'

'I already have. I called them after we . . . met the other day.' He raises his eyes and looks at me and I'm shocked by the anguish I see there. 'They reassigned Aimee's number and she can't have it back.'

'I'm sorry but I don't see how this involves me,' I reply, still very confused. 'It's the telephone company that's at fault – the people there will have to organize something, a new number maybe.'

'That's the problem, she can't get a new one.'

I'm guessing this girl is in arrears with her bill or something and the telephone company is refusing to give her a new number until she settles up, none of which is my problem. I eye the clock. This conversation really isn't going anywhere. I'll make my excuses now, get over to Ian's and tell him there was nothing to it. The story really was a dead end – and now I can tell him that with my hand on my heart. 'Look, John, I'm not sure why you asked to meet me again,' I say slowly, 'but you either explain where you're going with all this or I have to go. You may think the Irish are friendly, but I can assure you, we don't appreciate being taken for fools.'

'I'm sorry.' He rests his forehead briefly in his hand, his face pained. 'I'm not making much sense.'

'No, you're not.' I'm giving him two more minutes. *Two more minutes and then I'm out of here.*

'The thing is, that number is extremely important. For me and for my family.'

'I don't see how I can help you,' I say, starting to feel impatient. 'Even if the telephone company agreed to give it to you, there's no possible way *I* would, at least not until I get my own phone back.'

'And when will that be?'

'Who knows?' I sigh. 'The airline can't seem to find the damn thing. But losing it has caused me enough aggravation without adding to the confusion.'

The phone still hasn't turned up – in spite of the airline's assurances – and I certainly don't want to call Helen again and give her another new number: she may have improved her PA skills but I don't know that she could cope with a second number change. And as for Gary – I don't want to tell him any of this: the only thing he wants to hear right now is that Ian Cartwright is on board and has agreed to pen a sequel to *Field of Memories*. Anything else is just an irritant.

'I can understand that,' John Bonner continues. 'But Aimee's number should never have been assigned to you in the first place. It was never supposed to happen like this . . .'

'OK.' I hold up my hand to silence him, my impatience finally boiling over. 'First things first. Who *is* this mysterious Aimee? Your wife? Your girlfriend? And why, may I ask, without you flipping out this time, isn't she doing her own dirty work?'

He smiles wanly, his eyes resting on mine. 'Aimee isn't my wife – she's my sister.'

'Your *sister?*' Wow, this guy is going to a lot of trouble for his sister – he must be Italian: they're so into family relationships. My God, maybe he is a criminal. Maybe he's a drug lord. His sister could be some sort of drugs mule . . . This number could be the contact for every low-life in the Bay Area. I am going to be swimming with the fish.

'Yes. She's my sister,' he continues. 'Or she was. Aimee is dead.'

'Dead?' I squeak.

She's dead?

'Unfortunately she was born with a congenital heart defect. She was in and out of hospital her whole life . . . and she died almost a year ago.' He nods at the waitress as she places our coffees on the table and I see their eyes meet, as if they know each other.

I say nothing, just sip my coffee and try to get my head round what he's just told me. Does this mean I have a dead girl's old phone number? Even if it's only temporary, it's still weird – and very, very creepy.

'I'm sorry,' I offer, because I don't know what else I can say. 'How old was she?'

'Twenty-two.'

'*Twenty-two?* How terrible!' I forget that this guy might be a mass murderer, that this could be some elaborate scam. If it is, he deserves an Oscar because the grief is quite clearly etched on his face now. In fact, I know for definite that he isn't lying. I can tell by the sadness in his eyes – this is a real story, although what it has to do with me, I still have no idea.

'Yeah, she was only a baby, really,' he goes on. 'Or I thought she was, I guess because there was a big age gap between us. But she had such grand plans for her life, you know? She struggled through school, because of her illness, but she never gave up – she'd even gotten a place at Berkeley.' He gestures to his grey T-shirt, with the college logo. 'She was going to study literature, she absolutely couldn't wait, but then her condition deteriorated . . . so she never made it in the end.'

So that's why he's wearing the T-shirt again. I feel a twinge of guilt for assuming he was an unhygienic moron. He obviously wears it for his sister, in her memory. How tragic, a young life just snuffed out like that.

'She liked to read?' I ask. Anyone who chooses to study literature at university must be a bookworm, I know that.

'It was her passion,' he replies. 'Jane Austen, Emily Dickinson, all that stuff. She couldn't wait to do it full time. She wanted to write eventually. But she said the first rule of writing well was to read lots first.'

'That's exactly what I always say!' I exclaim.

He looks at me inquisitively.

'Sorry, I'm a literary agent,' I explain. 'My job is to represent writers, get them published. I always tell prospective authors, "If you want to write, you have to read."'

'A literary agent, wow, that's amazing. Aimee would have loved to meet you, I bet. Reading was her world – when she was ill and couldn't do much else it was what kept her going.'

'She sounds like a great girl,' I say, genuinely feeling for him now, despite my best efforts to continue hating him.

'She was. When she was well she was the life and soul of the party, the first one to get up to dance, the last one to leave. That was Aimee.'

'A live wire?'

'Yeah! That's exactly what she was – she never stopped talking. The only time she ever shut up was when she was reading. Her nickname was Little Miss Chatterbox – she loved the Mr Men books when she was a kid. Anyway, when she died, there was suddenly this enormous silence. It was . . . unbearable.' He swallows hard, his eyes glittering with tears that I know he doesn't want to shed in front of a stranger.

'She obviously left a huge void,' I say softly.

'Yes, she did. She was the heart of our family and my mother hasn't exactly coped well with her death,' he goes on, his voice faltering. 'She idolized Aimee – we both did. So that's why we began to call her cell phone after she passed away.'

I've heard about this sort of thing before – relatives of dead family members continuing to call a person's voicemail long after they'd passed away to leave a message. Apparently some people can find it really comforting – like they're calling Heaven, contacting their loved one.

'I know it sounds stupid, but it made sense to us. We'd call, just to listen to her voice. For a second you could believe that she was still here . . .' He pauses to compose himself. 'And then we started texting too – when we were at her favourite place or we saw something we knew she'd get a kick out of. Or when we just wanted to let her know we missed her . . .'

I think about the texts I've read and suddenly it all makes sense. 'I can imagine that might help,' I say.

'You probably think we're nuts,' he says, smiling wryly.

'I think people can do nutty things when they're devastated,' I reply.

'Well, we've definitely done our fair share of nutty things, believe me.'

'I can understand now why you reacted like you did when I texted back,' I say.

He smiles again. 'I was so rude, and I'm really sorry. It was just a shock – we've been texting her cell for months now. To suddenly get a reply . . .'

'Must have freaked you out.' Now, finally, I understand where he's been coming from.

'You could say that. I thought you'd somehow stolen her number, that you were trying to maybe . . . impersonate her or something. Crazy, I know. I must have been out of my mind.'

'You got a huge shock – it's understandable,' I say. So that's why he was shouting at me on the phone.

'It's really kind of you to say so,' he mutters, looking out of the window. 'Anyway, I stupidly thought I could persuade you to give me the number back. I didn't even think to call the telephone company – how dumb am I?'

'I guess you weren't thinking straight.'

'You can say that again. But after we met, after I realized you'd genuinely been given Aimee's number, I *did* call them.'

'And?'

'And they told me they'd reassigned it and that was that.' He looks at me, utterly despondent.

'They didn't have to inform you first?' Even though I never met this girl, don't know a thing about her, really, I'm shocked.

'No. Apparently it's routine. It should have happened much earlier – but somehow it didn't until last week. Her account had been in some sort of limbo until then . . .'

'And there's nothing they can do now?' I ask.

'No. The account is officially closed, and so is access to her voicemail – it had to happen sooner or later. It's just bad timing, what with her anniversary coming up.'

'I'm sorry, John.' I'm at a loss for words. Of course he and his mother are still grieving for Aimee. And this won't help.

'The thing is, Francesca, I don't think my mom will take this news very well,' he says quietly. 'She's struggled terribly since Aimee died and these last few weeks, with this milestone coming, have been really difficult. It's like she refuses to accept that Aimee's really gone.'

'It must be impossible to accept losing a daughter – it's so unnatural, isn't it?' I say.

'That's exactly it. Parents are supposed to go first, that's what she keeps saying. She hasn't come to terms with it at all.'

'I can understand that – it must be so very hard to let go,' I muse.

'Yes, but she needs to. We'll never forget Aimee, of course not, but she'd be so pissed if she thought we weren't moving on in some way. If she could see us now, the mess we're in, she'd kick our asses! Especially mine.'

'Why yours?'

'Because before she passed away, she made me promise not to let Mom mope. She knew she was dying and she knew we'd be devastated, of course, but she really wanted us to keep living, keep enjoying life.'

'And your mother can't?'

He shakes his head. 'She's like a zombie. We have a small restaurant on the next block and she gets up and works all day, like she always did. But she's only going through the motions. The joy is gone. And I don't think it's ever coming back.'

'Which is not what Aimee wanted.'

'No. She gave me strict instructions. We were to clear out her room, donate her clothes and albums to her favourite charity store and try to get back to normal.'

'And I'm guessing you haven't managed to do that?'

'No.' His eyes are vacant. 'Her room is like a shrine. Nothing has been moved since she died. Mom won't let anyone touch her stuff or her clothes. Everything has fallen apart.'

'It's still early days, though. A year isn't a long time, not really.' I'm not sure what to say to him – words are probably meaningless in this situation.

'Sometimes it feels like for ever. And yet it seems like only yesterday since she was here . . .'

A silence falls between us then and I know I have to ask the question that's on my mind – that's been on my mind ever since he asked to see me again.

'So, John, you've told me the story. But, em, you still haven't told me exactly why you wanted to meet me.' I'm curious to get to the bottom of this once and for all, but I'm also very aware that I have to be careful how I broach it – this is a very emotionally charged scenario.

'I asked to meet you again because I wanted to apologize and explain. But I also wanted to beg a favour,' he says. His sad eyes are on my face and I find I can't look away from his gaze.

'A favour?' I brace myself – what's coming next?

'Yes. I can't tell Mom that she mustn't text Aimee any more, not right now. Once the anniversary has passed, I will. So,' he takes another deep breath, 'all I ask in the meantime is that you tolerate getting some strange text messages. Don't reply to any – just ignore them. Would that be OK?'

Phew – that's not so bad. In fact, it's nothing. Ignoring some odd text messages or calls would be no big deal, if it would save this woman more anguish in the run-up to her daughter's first anniversary. What skin would it be off my nose? None. Now that I know the truth behind John's behaviour it seems churlish to refuse him. In fact, I want to help because it sounds like they're going through agony. And Aimee sounds like exactly the kind of girl I could have been friends with if we'd ever met.

'That's fine, of course,' I agree, not even thinking twice.

He sighs heavily, as if a weight has been lifted from his shoulders. 'Thank you,' he says, his dark eyes still on mine. 'Thank you.'

'But what about Aimee's voicemail?' I ask, thinking about this complication. 'What if your mother calls it? Didn't you say it's been closed?'

'I'll tell Mom her voicemail box is full, not to call,' he says. 'That'll throw her off the scent for a while. I'll come clean once her anniversary has passed.'

'OK – good idea.' He's really thought this through.

'Thank you so much for this, Francesca. I really appreciate it. I know you don't have to be so kind, especially after I was so rude the other day.' He smiles crookedly at me.

'That's OK.' I smile back. 'I understand – you want to protect your mother. I'd do the same.'

Suddenly he gives a half-laugh and the sorrowful atmosphere is broken.

'What's so funny?'

'I was just thinking – if Aimee could see me now, I know what she'd call me.'

'What?'

'A loser. She'd tell me to march right up to Mom and just confess. That's what she would have done.'

'She was really gutsy, wasn't she?' The more I hear about her, the more I love the sound of this girl.

'You have no idea.' He's still laughing. 'If there's a heaven, she's looking down right now, telling me to get a life.' He glances at his watch, then drains his coffee, pushes back his chair and stands up. 'I've taken up enough of your time already,' he says, shaking my hand. 'I really appreciate you meeting me again – and I'm sorry to have intruded on your stay in the city like this, Francesca.'

'That's OK,' I smile, the air between us clear. 'I wish you all the best, honestly.' Then he's gone, the café door jangling behind him.

I take a minute to finish my coffee, mulling over the sad tale John told me, thinking about Aimee, what a tragedy it is that she had to die so young. How strange that Emily Dickinson was her favourite poet, just like me. And she loved Jane Austen, too, and wanted to write. I wonder what her style would have been like – what topics would she have tackled? Would she have been published one day? It's all irrelevant now, of course, the poor girl is dead, but it's kind of odd that, not only do I have her old phone number, I also have the same taste in literature. She wanted to be a writer and I'm a literary agent . . .

I nod to the bushy-browed waitress when she offers a coffee refill, trying to shrug off the strange feeling that this all means something. That's silly. People die every day. Phone numbers get reassigned every day too and it's just a coincidence that this girl and I share the same literary taste. Half the world likes Austen and Dickinson: that doesn't mean we're all connected by some strange cosmic force. Just because Aimee loved the same writers I do it doesn't mean we have some freaky link. It just means I've been spending far too much time with Rosie, who honestly seems to believe that everything means something. It's a good thing I know that this is most definitely not true. Some things mean precisely nothing.

Chapter Fifteen

'Lordy, isn't that the saddest thing you ever heard?'

I'm lying across my hotel bed, on the phone to Rosie, explaining the story to her. 'It really is,' I reply, sighing. 'It sounds like they just weren't able to do anything for Aimee in the end.'

'I guess her heart just kept getting weaker and weaker – it's tragic.'

'Yeah, it's awful,' I reply. 'She was so young too . . .' I haven't been able to get John Bonner and his sister out of my head since I met him. It was such a heartbreaking tale that I can't help thinking about it. Plus, knowing I have a dead girl's old phone number is the strangest feeling – it's almost like I've stepped into her life in some way. But I'm trying to keep those sorts of thoughts at bay because otherwise I'll get completely freaked out.

'So that's why John got such a shock when you replied to his message,' Rosie says.

'Yeah – he and his mother have been texting her all this time.'

'Isn't it strange what can give you comfort when someone dies?' Her voice is wistful. 'Like, it was so hard to go to Ireland without my dad, but I'm really glad I did. It was sort of bittersweet. It must have been the same for the Bonners.'

'I guess,' I reply, feeling bad for pigeonholing Rosie as a stupid Irish-American tourist when we first met. Yes, she's kooky and eccentric, but going back to her father's homeland was her way of being closer to him. Just like texting Aimee was the Bonners' way of being closer to her.

'You sure are being awesome about all this, Frankie,' she goes on.

'No, I'm not,' I mutter, a massive wave of guilt washing over me.

'Yes, you are. Not everyone would meet a complete stranger just cos he asked them to, you know. But you did – that was real sweet of you.'

'Not really. Besides, you did have to twist my arm, remember?'

I still haven't told Rosie my real motivation for meeting John – to keep Ian happy and onside. I was going to tell her, but somehow it sounded mean-spirited when I formed the words in my mind. Besides, she kept going on about karma and all that; I knew she might somehow disapprove. Not that I should worry about what she thinks, I hardly know her. But still.

'Come on, girl! Why do you have such a hard time admitting that you're a nice person?' she says now.

Maybe because I'm not, the voice in my head whispers. I'm in this for what I can get for myself – that's the truth. But, then, is there any point in feeling ashamed of that? Business is business, after all, even if all this does feel weird . . .

'I have to go, Rosie,' I say, eager now to end the conversation. 'I'm really tired – I think I need to take a nap.'

'OK, honey. I'll let you be – you sound bushed. Now don't be a stranger, ya hear?'

I hang up and rest my head on the pillow, my limbs weak, my head shattered. If I didn't recognize the symptoms of fierce jet lag then I would probably think I was dying of some rare tropical disease. I feel like I could sleep for a hundred years. My head is fuzzy, as if I'm swimming through treacle, and I can barely assimilate my thoughts into any coherent order without supreme effort. All I really want to do is curl up under the crisp cotton covers and float away into oblivion.

My phone rings again, just as I'm drifting off, and I decide not to answer. Whoever it is will call back if it's important. But then I open one bleary eye and recognize the number – it's Gary. He doesn't believe in jet lag: he thinks it's an excuse that the weak use to get out of working twelve-hour days, just like he thinks that exhaustion is a figment of your imagination. I have to pick up.

'Frankie?' His voice, smooth like chocolate in my ear, snaps me back to the present. It seems like such a long time ago that I last spoke to him – he sounds strange and unfamiliar.

'Hi, Gary,' I reply, trying to sound awake and alert.

'How are you?'

'I'm OK.' *Well, I have a dead girl's phone number and I can't shake the feeling that she's somehow looking down on me – but otherwise everything is hunky-dory.*

'Good. I was starting to worry when I didn't hear from you, babe. So . . . how are things going? With Ian?' There's a tiny note of impatience now. Gary doesn't suffer fools, especially when it comes to work.

'It's going all right,' I answer carefully. I have to tread with caution here. I've no intention of telling him I've been side-tracked by the Aimee story. Admitting that would bring nothing to the table. And, besides, I still feel massively on edge about the whole thing. I'm jumpy every time the phone beeps in case it's a message from her mother and I still can't shake the silly feeling that she sounds like someone I would have liked if I'd ever met her. The jet lag is clearly making me a little gaga.

'So, you've made progress?' he goes on, and I hear the suspicion in his tone. Damn him. He knows I'm bluffing. He always knows when I'm trying to keep something from him. My only advantage is that he's on the end of the telephone line, not here in person, looking me straight in the eye. The phone at least gives me some sort of refuge, even if it's only temporary. Gary is like a bloodhound – he can sniff out bullshit at thirty paces.

'I think we might be getting there,' I say.

'Meaning?'

'Meaning, like all men, he needs a little buttering up,' I quip, hoping to distract him with a little mild flirtation. Wrong, yes. But needs must – I'm not going to let Gary know that, far from jumping at the opportunity to sign with me or the idea of writing a sequel, Ian is hell-bent on pursuing a tale of mixed-up phone numbers.

'Buttering up, eh?' he says, and I hear the smile in his voice now, the impatience gone. 'You want to elaborate on that?'

'He just needs to get used to the idea, that's all,' I reply loftily. I can show no weakness, that's key. Gary hates it when people whine, claims it gives him hives.

'Hmm . . . as long as that's *all* you mean.' His voice is lower now. 'I don't want you using your charms on him the way you do on me.'

'Don't be ridiculous, Gary. Besides, Ian's almost old enough to be my father.' I laugh at the insinuation but inside I'm bristling. Does he actually think I flirt to get what I want? That would be incredibly insulting. And it's definitely not true.

'You might want a sugar-daddy, for all I know.'

'Sugar-daddies are highly overrated from what I hear,' I reply briskly. OK, he just wants to banter. He didn't mean to insult me, not really.

'Are they now?' he says.

'Yes. Apparently they have a habit of dying, often before they include you in their will.'

'And that would never do.' He chortles.

'No. Besides, I'm a professional, remember? I don't mix business and pleasure.'

'Except when it comes to me,' he replies, like lightning.

Something in me shifts uneasily, but before I can process it, Gary is talking again. 'I miss you,' he says huskily.

'You do?'

'Yes. What are you wearing?' His voice is even huskier now.

I know where this is headed: Paris. We were staying in a wonderful little hotel in the Latin Quarter. The room was tiny, like most Parisian hotel rooms are, but right in the centre, barely fitting between the four walls, there was a massive four-poster bed, a dozen luxuriously embroidered cushions scattered across the pale bedspread and silk curtains hanging elegantly all around. When we pulled them closed it was like we were in our own special world, just him and me, surrounded by the soft glow of light dappling through the dark yellow drapes. We spent most of the weekend there, only emerging to eat in the tiny bistros dotted on almost every street corner at night. During the day, we took croissants to bed, not caring that the crumbs went everywhere. We'd sip chilled champagne after we'd made love, laughing together as the bubbles fizzed and spilled on our naked skin, licking it off each other until we were breathless with desire. Then we'd have long hot soaks together in the claw-footed bath, washing away the crumbs, caressing each other's skin with bars of heavily scented handmade lavender soap.

On the final day he'd had to attend a meeting with some French publishers a few blocks away so I lazed one last morning in bed, pushing away thoughts that I should be out exploring, instead luxuriating in the sounds of the busy Parisian pavements as they drifted through the half-open sash window, knowing I was going back to a desk piled high with work.

When he called me to say he was delayed, would be another hour, and that he missed me, couldn't bear not to hear my voice, feel my touch, had to have me, that very instant, one thing led to another and it all got very heated.

But that was then. San Francisco is not Paris. In Paris hot phone sex is practically required. Here it just seems sleazy.

'Come on, tell me,' he wheedles. 'What are you wearing?'

'Um, nothing special,' I say, wanting to kill the conversation. I'll tell him I'm in my manky grey sweatpants. That'll put a halt to his gallop. He's only seen me in sweats once – when I had the flu and he'd called into my apartment with hot soup and a wilting bunch of chrysanthemums obviously bought from the petrol station. I remember the way his eyes travelled down my body as I lay sniffling into my hanky on the sofa – as if he was ever so slightly repulsed. He'd dropped off the soup and left pretty quickly, making his excuses, saying he had to go back to the office. For ages afterwards, I couldn't shake the notion that he hadn't been coming to see how I was or if I needed anything – he'd come over hoping for sex but just couldn't bear the pathetic sight of me, red-nosed and snuffling, my old tracksuit too small for me, grubby and the worse for wear.

'Are you wearing that skirt?' he breathes now.

'What skirt?'

'The one that's so sexy it makes me want to cup your arse and . . .'

OK, time to nip this in the bud before there's no turning back.

'No, I'm not.' I hear a strangled laugh. It appears to be coming from me. I have to change the topic, think of something else to chat about. The weather maybe? San Francisco

165

is supposed to be foggy all the time, isn't it? How come I haven't seen any? I like a good mist – there's something quite creepy about it that appeals to me.

'What's so funny?' he asks.

'Um, nothing. It's just that if you could see me now, you would definitely not think I was looking sexy, believe me,' I reply. I glance at my reflection in the mirror. My eyes are tiny slits – the result of overtiredness. My skin is dull, my hair needs a brush. I'm not even lying. I do look pretty awful – even without the manky sweatpants.

'I don't believe that,' he says. 'You're always sexy.'

'No, I'm not.' I laugh again but inside I feel very strange and I'm not sure why.

'Oh yes you are. Every meeting we ever have, all I want to do is –'

'Gary!' I warn him.

'What? It's true. You know it's true, Blue Eyes . . .'

My heart melts, just a fraction, as it always does when he calls me that. He came up with the nickname that weekend in Paris. Lying in bed, he'd taken my face in his hands and examined me so intently that I'd blushed under his gaze. I hadn't had time to sneak to the bathroom, apply a layer of tinted moisturizer, mascara and lip balm – my absolute minimum coverage.

'You have the most amazing eyes,' he'd said, between butterfly kisses on my lips, cheeks, nose.

'No, I don't.' I'd felt suddenly bashful, pulling the sheets up to cover my bare breasts. Silly, really, considering he'd already explored every inch of my body, even the inches I was self-conscious about, but I was feeling exposed and inexplicably shy.

'Yes, you do,' he'd murmured, his hand snaking slowly below the sheets again. 'They're so blue – they're gorgeous.'

'No, they're not!' I'd batted him away, covering my face

with my hands, not wanting him to see that the fine lines I'd been fighting for a few years had settled in for a long-term stay, bringing all their baggage with them.

'Yes, they are – you're Ol' Blue Eyes, just like your namesake.'

'Frank Sinatra?' I giggled, as he reached and tickled me under my ribs. 'You think I look like Frank Sinatra? I'm not sure that's such a compliment, thanks!'

'That's going to be my nickname for you now, my Frankie,' he went on, his hand moving ever downwards, caressing the inside of my thigh. 'Blue Eyes.'

And then we were kissing, lost in another moment, and I forgot about mascara and tinted moisturizer and under-eye bags and just about everything else.

'Tell me about your underwear,' he says softly now.

'Gary!'

'Go on. Describe your bra. Or are you even wearing one?'

I tug the hotel bathrobe around me. I'm not. But for some reason I don't want to tell him that. 'Of course I am,' I lie. There. That'll put him off.

'What colour is it?'

'Oh, just a grey, baggy old thing,' I say cheerily. 'Nothing to write home about. Hey, by the way, you haven't bumped into Helen recently, have you?'

Even though Helen makes it sound as though she's got everything under control every time we speak, I can't help feeling that she might have blown up the office and forgotten to tell me.

'Helen?' He sounds puzzled.

'My assistant? The worst PA in Ireland?'

'Oh, yes, her – well, I wouldn't call her the *worst*, would you?'

There – I've distracted him. Good. 'She's close! I'm

hoping she's not running the agency into the ground while I'm away.'

'She seems pretty capable actually,' he says, seemingly coming to from his phone sex fixation a little. 'I met her in the lift with Ivan Watters. We had quite a conversation – Ivan reckons she has a spark.'

'A spark?'

'Well, she does have something, Frankie – charisma, I suppose.'

Helen has charisma. Now I've officially heard it all.

'She even managed to get Ivan on *Tonight* with Vincent Browne – the old boy was thrilled.'

'She got Ivan Watters on TV?' I'm dumbfounded.

Ivan Watters, a former financial journalist who's written numerous non-fiction tomes on the economy, is a mutual client of mine and Gary's. He's one of the very few who came with me from Withers and Cole but his star has not been in the ascendant for quite some time – in fact, I've been worried that Proud won't offer him another deal after his latest effort sold fewer than a thousand copies.

'Yes, she did. He told her he couldn't understand why he finds it so hard to get on the box – you know what he's like – and she said she'd look into it for him. She called him back the next day with the slot – it was pretty fucking impressive, I have to say.'

Oh, my God. All Ivan ever wants is to be on TV – I've spent forever listening to him moan that he never gets airtime. And now Helen has him on *Tonight* with Vincent Browne – one of the hottest current-affairs shows in Ireland. How the hell did she manage that? *And why didn't she tell me about it? Did she forget?*

'Twenty minutes of prime time,' Gary goes on, sounding very pleased with himself. 'He did well – stuck to the point for once, got his oar in.'

I can't believe it – Ivan is known as the most long-winded person around. Why use ten words when a hundred would do? That's his credo. I can't imagine him making succinct points without winding himself up in knots like he does when he talks to just about everyone.

'He did?'

'Yep. She organized a quick session of media training to help him make the right impression – old Ivan was delighted!'

'Media training?'

Since when is Helen organizing media training? And, more to the point, who the hell is paying for it? It'd better not be me. The bank manager will have your guts for garters, Frankie, the little voice whispers in my head.

'She thought all Ivan needed was a confidence boost,' Gary goes on. 'She reckoned he always rambles because he's nervous. And she was right. He was great on *Browne* – even the producers were happy with him. They want him back again next month apparently.'

'That's fantastic,' I say. But inside I'm on high alert. How did this happen?

'It really was. She's a gem, Frankie – where did you find her?'

Helen? Helen is a gem? The same Helen who's always late, who never brings me coffee, who goes to the circus like a big child? *That* Helen? 'Um, she's Antonia's niece,' I reply.

'Well, you should hang on to her – give her a rise maybe,' he goes on. 'I wish I had someone like her – I'm up to my neck in it since Marian's been off.'

Marian is Gary's PA – the one I privately nicknamed the Rottweiler because she sits outside his office ready to rip people apart with her teeth.

'Marian's off?' I ask. I can't believe it – she never takes holidays. She can't be off for no good reason, though – maybe someone died. Although word on the street was that she scheduled her mother's death so that it wouldn't clash with the London Book Fair. What's going on back there? I've been away only a few days and already things are changing at lightning speed.

'Oh, she's having a hysterectomy, I think,' Gary says. 'Some emergency or other. I don't know why she couldn't have planned it better. I'm up to my tits in work.'

'Well, if it was an emergency, she wouldn't have been able to plan it, would she?' I say brightly, forcing myself to laugh. How tactless of him. Poor Marian. She's not my favourite person in the world, but a hysterectomy can't be fun, even if I do spend half my life wishing I never had to deal with another crampy period pain ever again.

'I suppose it couldn't be helped,' he says gloomily. 'Still, it's very inconvenient and she didn't organize cover before she left.'

Suddenly I'm overwhelmed by the urge to tell him not to be so bloody insensitive. He was exactly the same when he heard April had died – he only thought about how her death would impact on him.

'Ooops, I think I have another call coming in, Gary,' I say, hearing a beep on the line. 'It could be Ian. Can I call you back?'

'OK,' he says, like a child who can't have a lollipop, and I hang up quickly. Gary really can be incredibly self-centred and insensitive.

But aren't you just as bad? You didn't mourn April for long, did you? And what about Ian? Do you really have his best interests at heart or are you simply willing to do whatever it takes to succeed, no matter what? The voice in my ear is loud and clear now and I have to shake my head to get rid of it. What's wrong with me? I'm not self-centred: I'm just good at my job. I don't know why I'm thinking like that. I must be exhausted. The jet lag is killing me, that's why I'm feeling this way – disoriented and unsure of myself.

Checking my phone to see who I missed when I was talking to Gary, I spot a new text. *Another customer asked me for your favorite spaghetti sauce again today my darling. Don't they know that I'll never make it again now that you're gone? Can't they tell my life means nothing now?*

Oh, God. It's from Aimee's mother. The poor woman. She sounds like she's at her wit's end. I have no idea what the sauce is, but it seems that a customer asking for it has really touched a raw nerve. Grief works in the cruellest way: the small everyday things that remind you of a person are what can tip you over the edge. Like hearing a song on the radio or smelling a particular food. Shoving the phone into my bathrobe, I take a deep breath and pad into the en-suite bathroom. Right. I have to forget about Aimee and get ready to meet Ian. I'll have a shower, wash my hair, try to freshen up and get rid of this strange feeling.

Slipping the bathrobe from my shoulders, I step into the massive power shower and under the steaming spray. I have to wake up, shake off this weariness and the awful, gnawing feeling that being privy to someone's thoughts is really wrong.

But as the hot water streams over me I can't stop thinking about John Bonner. That overwhelmingly sad expression in his eyes when he spoke about his sister. And then there's her poor mother who's so devastated that she can't let go and keeps reaching out to her dead daughter through her cell phone. It's heartbreaking. Truly heartbreaking. I soap my skin fiercely, trying to wash away my unease, but try as I might, I just can't.

Chapter Sixteen

'She's *dead*? This just gets better and better!' Ian whoops with glee, as if I've told him he's won the lottery and can buy his own private island.

We're in his chaotic kitchen and he's sitting opposite me, notepad on his lap, jotting down Aimee's story and nodding enthusiastically as I regale him with the saga. I'm trying not to retch – the rank smell from the other day has intensified, and when I produced the box of pastries that I stopped to buy on Eleventh Avenue in a very expensive French patisserie, he couldn't find a clean plate to put them on. They're currently sitting in the box between us – I can't help thinking they're afraid to come out in case they catch something deadly.

'So, tell me more!' he exclaims, his eyes shining as if he's drunk on life, giddy with joy. There's no escaping it. Any which way I look at it, it seems that, unfortunately, Ian's not changing his mind about this harebrained scheme to write a story based on my phone mix-up. In fact, he seems more entrenched than ever, especially now he's learned that Aimee is dead and there's a proper tragedy to be exploited. I should have known this would happen.

'Well, apparently she passed away last year,' I say, feeling a twinge of discomfort but pushing it away. I have to be pragmatic: he is happy and that's a good start. I've given him what he wanted – information – and at the very least that's a brilliant way to butter him up, get him on my side, make him see that signing with me is the best idea he's ever had. Not that it is his idea but I want him to believe it is.

'So what you're saying is that, once she died, they used her old number as a way of communicating with her beyond the grave,' he says, scribbling furiously.

'Yes,' I confirm. 'They couldn't bear to let her go.' I feel a pang of sadness thinking about it, but I'm not going to linger on that now: I can't be distracted. I have to concentrate on the job at hand – reeling Ian in.

'Fascinating!' he mutters, writing this down too. 'What a remarkable insight into human behaviour – into how the psyche operates, don't you think?'

'I guess,' I say, keeping my voice nicely neutral. I'm gearing up to discuss the sequel next – but there's no point in rocking the boat before that. I have to keep everything on an even keel. If I rubbish his ideas outright it will probably make him even more intransigent so I must tread very carefully.

Ian is still talking: 'I mean, they know, they know, that she's never going to be able to reply to their messages yet they keep on doing it . . . What drives people to do that sort of thing?' It's like he's talking to himself.

'Grief?' I reply, even though I'm not sure he needs me to. 'They just couldn't face life without her – this was their way of hanging on to her for as long as possible.'

'Yes, of course, of course, of course . . . They're in shock, they barely know what they're doing . . .' he mutters, scribbling on.

I think about John's sad face, his exhausted expression. He's gone beyond shock now to acceptance, but from the sound of it, his mother is stuck, unable to move forward. The poor woman must be in pieces. I think about Mum and Dad – they'd be devastated if anything happened to any of us.

'This is exactly the sort of information I wanted!' Ian says now, his eyes shining. 'You're a genius, Francesca!'

I wince at the praise. I don't feel like a genius. The truth is, I feel kind of awful, passing all this sensitive information on to him, as if I'm somehow intruding on the Bonner family. But I have to get past that. This is business. Nothing more, nothing less.

'So, he wanted the phone, did he?' Ian goes on.

'Initially, yes, he did,' I say, remembering John's first outrageous rant – how he demanded I return the phone to him. I can understand that now I know what had happened – how he was trying to protect his mother from more pain.

'But you refused?' Ian probes. 'That was gutsy of you – I admire that.'

Oh, God. This isn't coming out right – he's misunderstanding me. 'Well, I didn't refuse exactly. We came to an agreement. I promised him I would just ignore any new messages from his mother and he's going to tell her the truth once Aimee's anniversary has passed . . .'

'Great!' Ian enthuses, his face working overtime. 'So you still have it, then?'

'Yes.' And there's no chance of me forgetting that – it makes me jump every time it buzzes and I check to see if there are any new texts for Aimee.

'And have you had any more? Messages, I mean . . .' Ian pauses, his expression hopeful now.

In a heartbeat I decide to lie. I realize instinctively that he'll want to know what they say, and now that I know the full story it doesn't seem right to share them, even if this *is* just business. I've already given Ian enough to get on with – and, anyway, this is just a ruse to get him onside: I have to start veering him away from it now.

'Nope,' I say. 'It's all been a storm in a teacup, really.'

'Far from it, Francesca, far from it,' Ian mutters, making

more notes, writing frantically in the margins of the page. 'Can't you see how great this story is? How it could touch so many people?'

He's right. It hits me like a bolt of lightning. This story could touch people – it's certainly affected me. It's so profoundly sad, yet Aimee's life seems to have been lived with such hope and vivacity – a powerful combination. But Ian can't write about it. Now that I know more, it feels very wrong for him to try to poach it. But that's irrelevant in the grand scheme of things: if I don't get him to agree to a sequel, this is all a waste of time. He has to write another *Field of Memories*. My future – and that of the Rowley Agency – depends on it. I begin to sweat as I think about it. If I don't pull this off, I'll be evicted from the office. The bank won't want to know me. I have to make it work.

'So he's going to tell the mother the truth, is he? Once the girl's anniversary has been and gone?' Ian says.

'Yeah – he thinks that would be best. Then he hopes she can move on.'

'Hmm . . .' Ian chews the top of his pen, looking off into the middle distance, a frown creasing his already lined forehead, as if he's not sure this is the right course of action. 'Well, I can work on that part later,' he mutters.

'Which part?' I ask, almost dreading the answer. Ian is properly fascinated by all the details – it's as if he's in another world, fantasizing about how the plot will work, how the structure will form.

'Oh, nothing,' he replies vaguely. 'Just mechanics.'

Oh, God. I have to stop this now, before it goes too far, before he has every chapter plotted, every character drawn.

But he's still talking: 'You can't deny it, Francesca.' He lifts his head, his expression ecstatic. 'Don't you think this will make a wonderful novel?'

'It does have something,' I say slowly. 'But, Ian, I'm still not sure it will work . . .'

'What do you mean?' he asks, immediately wary.

It's now or never. I have to let him down gently. He can't pursue this story – not in the way he wants to anyway. He has to write a sequel. It's what the public wants, it's what Gary needs and it's what I have to make happen.

'I just don't know if this kind of thing is what your readers will expect from you – they might be . . . confused,' I say. 'This sort of plot isn't exactly your signature style.'

'I'm sure my readers are extremely intelligent, Francesca. I think you underestimate them,' he says, his eyes cold. 'Besides, do I have a signature style?'

I sense he's getting defensive – not good. I change tack again. 'Of course your fans are intelligent. I just meant that, these days especially, readers like to know they can rely on their favourite authors to deliver what they want.'

This is a fact. More and more, during these dark recessionary times, with the books market seriously contracting, readers are only buying books they know they'll like. Fewer are taking chances, or changing direction in their reading. With purses tightening, many are only investing in authors they're sure they'll enjoy. For Ian to come back with a bang, readers need to know they'll be getting more or less what they want from him.

Ian's face darkens. 'So you want to dictate to me what I should write, is that it?'

'No, of course not. But the market is a complicated place right now, Ian. Everyone knows that. All these things have to be taken into consideration.'

I'm on tricky territory here. If Ian feels he's being strong-armed he'll never agree to write a sequel. He'll lock himself back into this house and become more of a recluse than he already is. Bang goes his shot at hitting the big-time again. *And bang goes my career, my beloved agency, dead in the water before it even had a chance.*

'The only thing that has to be taken into consideration, in my opinion, is the writing,' he says coldly. 'Will the writing stand up? But I'm only a writer, what do I know?' He glares at me.

Crap. This is all going horribly wrong. I have to pull it back before it's too late. I pause, pretending to think deeply. 'You know what?' I say, as if the idea has just occurred to me. 'I think there *is* a way that we might be able to do this. Just hear me out for a second.'

His face is still closed and cautious, but he leans towards me, just a fraction. I have an in. 'What if this was one of the back stories in your next novel?' I say.

'A back story?' he asks, clearly confused.

'Yeah, like – say, for example, you *were* to write a sequel to *Field of Memories*. This phone story could be interwoven in there, with one of the more minor characters maybe . . .'

Please let this work.

'One of the more minor characters?' His tone is icy. 'Francesca, I don't think we're on the same page here.'

Please, please, agree. I want a swanky office and a fancy imported desk. I want everyone to respect me. I want to pay my rent. I want to survive.

'We *are* on the same page, Ian,' I reassure him, feeling extremely wobbly but trying to hide it. 'Of course we are. I'm just trying to tease it out a little, that's all. I think the kernel of an idea is there. I'm just not sure it would work as a stand-alone novel.'

'You think the kernel is there?' His voice is cool. 'That's very interesting. I wonder what Makin will think of it.'

'Bruce Makin? From Withers and Cole?' I squawk, my throat closing round the words.

Shit, shit, shit.

'Yes.' Ian glances back at his notes. 'He's always been so encouraging.'

'You've spoken to him?' My voice sounds strangled.

I'm dead. My career is kaput. It's all over.

'Not yet. But he left me a message. The poor man is just devastated about April, of course.'

'Is he?'

The lying bastard – he never liked April and she *despised* him.

'Yes. He seems sure that April would have wanted me to stay with Withers and Cole. Quite sure, actually.' Ian eyes me knowingly, getting his message across, and I fight to control my feelings. So much for the Kimberley bloody biscuits! Would Bruce Makin cart them over here to make an impression? Would he lug a basket all the way from one side of the city to the other and lay on a lovely picnic in Crissy Field? No, he would not because Bruce Makin is a snake who only wants to protect his own interests now that his senior agent is six feet under and her clients are on the loose.

I clench and unclench my fists, trying not to let my feelings show, hoping to sound calm. I can't let Ian think I'm rattled by this revelation. Even if I am. Instead I have to play for time, while I try to decide which way to go with this. I need to discourage the contact with Withers and Cole, for sure. But I don't want Ian to think I'm that desperate for him to sign with me – he can't know he holds all the cards, has all the power. I need to get some balance back – and there's nothing as good for levelling the playing field as introducing a little doubt into the equation. It's time for some serious poker face.

I take a deep breath and clear my throat before I speak. 'Poor Bruce,' I say sympathetically. 'He really has had such a terrible year.'

Ian's head snaps up. 'A terrible year?'

I'm clawing back some ground. Good. 'Well, he's had a horrible time recently, you know, what with everything . . .'

I can almost see Ian's ears prick up. 'What do you mean?'

I really have his attention now. Excellent.

'Of course, you probably didn't hear, did you?' I grimace. 'April was always so discreet about these things – she wouldn't have wanted to blacken his name by telling you . . .' I'm quite a good actress – I'm even surprising myself.

'Telling me about what?' There's impatience in his voice now: he's getting agitated.

'I don't know if I should say, really. I mean, it could have been just rumour . . .'

'Rumour? What rumour?'

I pretend to pause, as if torn between confiding in Ian and not wanting to reveal too much. 'Well, I guess there's no harm in telling you – it's not like it's a big secret. The entire industry is buzzing with it,' I say at last, just as I think he might be about to scream.

'For God's sake, Francesca, just spit it out!' Ian barks.

'OK.' I hold up the palms of my hands, as if to admit defeat. 'Rumour has it that Makin is being sued.'

'Sued? By whom?'

'An author.'

'What? What happened?' Ian's face displays his shock. An author suing an agency is not exactly inspiring.

'Well, from what I gather, a writer sent him an idea and Makin rejected it, thought it was too out there.'

'So what? That happens all the time,' Ian says, confused.

'You're right. But then Makin passed the idea to another writer, encouraged him to go with it.'

'He poached another writer's idea?' He's aghast.

'Yes, so they say. Obviously, it's appalling behaviour if it's true . . .'

Ian's face is white, as if he can't quite believe it. Good, this is exactly what I want. The truth is, there were some rumours about a potential lawsuit against Withers and Cole – some unpublished hopeful author claiming he'd sent in an idea and that it had been passed on. Who knows what the real story is? But that's beside the point. I've achieved what I wanted to – I've planted the seed of doubt in Ian's head about Makin's ethics. An agent has to be supremely professional – and if Ian doesn't believe that Withers and Cole is beyond reproach then that'll definitely work in my favour.

'It could be complete rubbish,' Ian says now, rallying. 'People make false accusations all the time.'

Damn. That didn't last long.

'Yes, of course. There are two sides to every story,' I say. 'There has been a lot of talk, though. Then again, it could be just talk, of course – you know how these things can grow legs! Maybe there's nothing the matter.'

Ian's face is working overtime as he clearly tries to think what to say. Then he pushes his shoulders back and looks me straight in the eye. 'Enough about him. Let's get back to Aimee's story. I need some more details.'

It's a clear message. He might be willing to go with me. I'm just not sure what the catch is yet. 'Well, I think I've already told you everything,' I say, holding my nerve, waiting for his next move. Where will this go next?

'I need some more background,' he says, looking away. He doesn't want to meet my eye any more but I can't be sure why.

'Background?' I repeat.

'You need to meet them.'

'Who?' For a second I really don't know what he's talking about.

'The Bonner family, of course. You need to meet them

and report back to me. The mother especially – I'd like to know more about her.'

'You're not serious, Ian.'

'Of course I'm serious,' he says calmly. 'Why wouldn't I be? Now that you've connected nicely with . . .' he glances at his notes to confirm the name '. . . John, it shouldn't be too difficult to organize, should it?'

'We chatted,' I correct him. 'We didn't exactly connect.'

'Every conversation is a connection, Francesca, you know that,' he says, sounding uncannily like Rosie. 'I'm sure you'll find a way to make this work.'

'I'm not sure if that would be possible.'

Oh, fucking hell.

'I'm sure you can make it possible.' He smiles a loaded smile, and I hold his unblinking gaze.

It's vital to say the right thing now or I'll push him away for good. But what? This negotiation is one of the toughest I've ever done – it seems we're constantly one step forward, two steps back. Just when I think I'm making progress, getting him to see things my way, he wriggles out of my grasp. But I can't give up yet: I have to keep the lines of communication open. I won't give in. I can't.

'Ian, I did what you wanted. I met John, I got the story,' I say. 'You can't ask me to do much more.'

He gazes at me, his expression unreadable. 'OK.' He shrugs at last. 'If that's how you feel, I'll do it myself. Would you like me to call you a cab?'

He'll do it himself?

'Ian, you wouldn't,' I gasp. So much for my professional poker face.

His eyes are wide, innocent. 'Wouldn't I?' he asks. 'Why not?'

'Because it would be . . . unethical for one thing!' I bluster.

'Unethical? But, Francesca my dear, you've already acquired most of the information. Was that unethical too?' He cocks an eyebrow at me.

I can't believe he's taking this tack. The sly bastard. 'That's different,' I say.

'Really? Meeting the poor, grieving man just to pump him for information on my behalf wasn't unethical? Silly me!'

I can't believe he's turning this round on me. I clear my throat, search for the right words to say to get me out of this corner. 'Where are we going with this, Ian?' I ask. There's no way out: it's time to lay the cards on the table.

He pauses, looks me in the eye again. 'I might just sign with you, young lady.'

'You will?' I squeak, then clear my throat again to camouflage my excitement. Oh, my God. Oh, my *God*!

'I said I might.'

Might? Shit. Might is not good.

'Might?'

'Let's just say I'm warming to the idea.'

OK. This is progress. No mention of writing a sequel, but one thing at a time.

'There's only one condition.'

'What is it?' I hold my breath, afraid to hear his reply.

'Before I sign on the dotted line I want you to get me more information about the Bonners. That's the deal. Take it or leave it.' Then he reaches across with a fork that looks as if it's been used to clean out a cesspit and begins to dig into the box of fancy pastries. The ones that have probably finally exploded my business credit card.

'These are very good – not as nice as the Kimberleys, of course, but thank you for bringing them all the same. You really are most thoughtful,' he says, his mouth full.

I watch him munch and wonder, wordlessly, how I'm going to do this. Because if I don't, the chances of getting Ian Cartwright to come to the Rowley Agency will go up in smoke. I know that now for sure.

Chapter Seventeen

'Would you like a doggy bag?' the waiter asks, as I push away my plate.

'No, thanks. I honestly don't think I could fit in another bite,' I reply.

'Our job is done, then!' He grins at me as he clears my table.

I'm not kidding when I say I couldn't eat another bite: I've just comfort-eaten my way through an enormous burger and fries followed by a massive slice of Classic Cheesecake in the famous Cheesecake Factory on the top floor of Macy's on Union Square and I don't think I'll be eating again any time soon. I look around me now, feeling happily stuffed. The restaurant is dimly lit, dotted with art-deco lamps and black and white tiled floors. It's incredibly stylish. It's also packed with people, the air buzzing with talk as dozens of hungry customers wait to get a table.

It was Rosie who recommended this place: the way she spoke about it – as if it was the eighth wonder of the world – piqued my curiosity so I couldn't resist trying it out. I couldn't believe it when I discovered there are almost fifty varieties of cheesecake and desserts here. And that's alongside dozens of regular menu items too – burgers, chicken wings, tacos, fries. Rosie had told me that the enormous portions are legendary, even for the States, but I thought I'd die when a plate heaped with the most food I'd ever seen in my life was placed in front of me. But, miraculously, I've managed to chow my way through most of it.

Pushing my way through the doors and back on to the street now, I decide to go for a walk. The confines of my hotel room just don't appeal: I need some air – and the chance to digest my lunch and mull over what Ian wants me to do.

I walk briskly, my mind working overtime, not really taking in anything. It seems there's a Gap on every corner, with bright autumn knits in the window, or a Starbucks, with wonderful coffee aromas drifting on to the street. Before I know it I've gone further than I intended and I'm by the Stinking Rose Café on Columbus Avenue. I remember reading about this place in the magazine on the plane: it's a world-famous restaurant where everything has garlic in it – even the ice-cream. I can't imagine wanting to eat garlic ice-cream, but this is one of the most popular restaurants in the city and the queues can be blocks long.

I pass it, then continue along by the historic City Lights bookstore, and across Broadway, where the bars jostle for space with launderettes and liquor stores, the cars whizzing by at speed. I take a turn, then another, just following my nose, eager to get off the main thoroughfare and away from the noise and congestion. In a few minutes I'm in a much quieter area beside Washington Square Park in North Beach, by the café where I met John Bonner. I'm not sure how I've ended up here but it's so pleasant – like a small oasis in the city – that it seems the perfect place to stop and take a breather before I return to the hotel. In fact, it might be the ideal spot to gather my thoughts and try to decide what to do next. I'll have to call Gary at some stage, fill him in, but I want to delay that for as long as possible – get it all straight in my mind first, see if there's nothing more I can do to dissuade Ian from pursuing Aimee's story. Gary wants Ian signed with me and ready to do a sequel: this Aimee thing was never part of the plan and I have to find a way round it. For both our sakes.

I sit on a faded wooden bench with peeling green paint and try to think. Close by, a group of tiny old Chinese ladies are doing their t'ai chi – perhaps the two old ladies who sold me the silk jacket are in there somewhere: this place isn't far from Chinatown. It wouldn't surprise me – those two were as nimble as ninjas, the way they twirled me round that shop.

On the far side of the park, people lounging on the grass are overlooked by the shadow of an enormous church, its spire soaring into the sky. From the guidebook I flicked through in my hotel room I know that this is where Joe DiMaggio and Marilyn Monroe had their wedding photographs taken after they got married in City Hall. In another corner there's a playground where children are pushing each other energetically on the swings and scrambling up and down the slide. How easy everything is when you're a kid – the worst that can happen is that your best friend can go higher on the swing than you. If only the rest of life was so straightforward.

Sitting here now, the sun warming my face, I'm glad I stopped. The park is alive with activity and it's distracting me from the decisions I know I have to make. Ian wants me to get closer to the Bonner family, find out more about them and Aimee's death. He sees it as legitimate research. I, on the other hand, know that it's a very grey area. Researching a book is one thing; invading people's privacy is quite another. But Ian seems almost fixated on the Bonners – he truly believes that Aimee's story is the one he wants to tell, that this is his new big idea. If I refuse to co-operate he's already insinuated that he'll delay signing with me, maybe even stay with Withers and Cole, with Bruce Makin.

I close my eyes, listen to the background hum of noise, hoping my head will clear because, at the moment, it's all over the place. How am I going to keep Ian happy enough to sign with me? He wants me to meet John Bonner and his mother, and if I refuse he might walk away. I can't take that chance, not when I'm so close to what I want.

'Hello there!'

I open my eyes, blinking against the blinding sunlight. At first all I can make out is a shadowy figure hovering over me and I automatically grab for my bag. I probably stick out like a sore thumb here – maybe everyone can tell I'm a tourist. They may be queuing up to mug me. But as my vision adjusts I realize it's John Bonner, stopped astride a bicycle, smiling down at me. 'Oh, hello,' I reply, startled to see him when I wasn't expecting to.

Gosh, Rosie was right – she said this city was like a small town. I knew John's family had a restaurant around here somewhere but to bump into him now seems bizarre. Yet Dublin is exactly the same: you can't walk ten feet down Grafton Street without meeting someone you know.

'Sorry, did I startle you?' he asks, smiling at me.

'Yes, you did a little. I was just . . . resting my eyes.'

'Sure.' He grins. 'I like to do that sometimes too. So . . . what brings you back here?'

He can't possibly know what Ian wants me to do, but I can feel a tell-tale blush creeping up my neck all the same. 'Um, nothing,' I reply. 'I, um, strolled up from Union Square, just . . . exploring. Doing the tourist thing, you know.'

'That's quite a walk!'

'Well, I needed to work off my lunch,' I explain. 'I ate in the Cheesecake Factory.' It's a miracle I could walk after the feed I'd had in there. My waistband is still straining round my middle.

'Ah, the famous Cheesecake Factory,' he says. 'What was your verdict?'

'Well, the portions were huge.'

'They're known for their servings. You gotta be hungry.'

'You can say that again!' I laugh ruefully. 'I don't think I've ever eaten so much in my life.'

'And which cheesecake did you have, if you don't mind me asking?'

'The Classic,' I reply. 'It was delicious.'

'Aha! That tells me a lot,' he replies, his expression serious but his eyes twinkling a little.

'What does it tell you?'

'Haven't you heard?' he asks.

'Heard what?'

'There's an art to choosing cheesecake in there: the one you pick says a lot about who you are.'

'Yeah, right!' I guffaw.

'It's true!' he replies, wide-eyed. 'In fact, it's scientifically proven.'

'Scientifically proven? I don't think so.'

'Would I lie to you? A team of scientists sat down and meticulously cross-referenced people's cheesecake preferences against their personality traits. It made for a very interesting study.'

'OK.' I laugh. 'So what does choosing the Classic mean?'

'Well now,' he shifts on his bike, 'that's an interesting one. Most people would think that choosing the Classic means they're old school, right?'

'I guess.'

'Well, according to the study, it actually means they're party animals.'

'Party animals?' That so does not describe me. I can't remember the last real party I went to. In fact, Mum and Dad's fortieth wedding anniversary bash is the next one in my diary. Which reminds me: I really need to call home –

who knows what's going on back there or where the party planning is at?

'Yes,' John goes on. 'They're so partied out that by the time it comes to choosing cheesecake they just want the plainest one. It's the quiet ones who go for the out-there choices, like Red Velvet.'

'That's ridiculous!' I giggle.

'It's the truth,' he says solemnly.

There's a pause then, and we just smile at each other.

'So, you're just taking a load off, yeah?' he asks.

'Um, I'm not sure what that means, sorry,' I say.

'You're chilling out?'

'Oh, yep, I am. Just watching the world go by.'

'Like your authors? Don't they say that good writers have to be good people watchers?'

'That's true,' I say. 'Most of my authors say they could watch other people for hours. I have to admit, it is one of my favourite pastimes.'

'Mine too. Especially here.' He gestures at the park. 'It's a real melting pot. There are so many different characters.'

He's right. The age spectrum here is vast: there are babies being pushed by yummy mummies in baseball caps and sneakers round the perimeter, there are little old men playing chess on the grass, squabbling energetically, and there's everything in between.

'Have you ever done it?' He waves to the group of old Chinese ladies stretching and swaying in the sun, their wide-brimmed hats shading them from the warming rays.

'T'ai chi? No. But watching them, I'm thinking about taking it up – those ladies are rocking it.' Every single one of them is lean and lithe, bending with a supple quality I haven't had since I was a toddler. I don't think I could touch my toes if my life depended on it.

'It's cool, right? All those tiny movements – and they're so graceful and supple. I could do with taking it up too.' He sighs.

'You look in pretty good shape, though – surely cycling up all these San Francisco hills keeps you fit,' I say.

'You'd think so. But having a family restaurant doesn't exactly help, as you can probably see!' He pats his stomach ruefully, although I can't see even an inch of fat round his waist.

'Do you work there? In the restaurant?' I ask, shielding my eyes from the sun with my hand. He knows what I do, but when we met I never asked him what he does for a living.

'Occasionally,' he replies. 'But photography is the day job.'

'What sort of stuff do you do?'

'News mostly – I freelance for the *Chronicle*,' he replies.

'So no moody nude portraits, then?' I quip.

'Uh, no. Not exactly.' He looks at me a little strangely and I kick myself for saying something so stupid – what was I thinking? I really must be feeling guilty and nervous, letting my mouth run away with me like that.

'If you don't mind me asking, did you get any more texts, you know, from my mom?' he asks.

'I did, actually,' I say. 'It was about Aimee's favourite spaghetti sauce. I didn't reply obviously.' I'm not sure whether to elaborate about how sad the message was – does he need to know or would it make it even worse for him?

'Thanks,' he says, seeming embarrassed. 'I know this must be a real pain in the ass for you.'

'No, it's fine, honestly, I don't mind.'

We look at each other then, acknowledging that proper peace has been restored between us.

'So, your mother's special sauce is good, then?' I ask, to break the silence.

'All her sauces are legendary,' he says. 'She uses secret ingredients.'

'What are they?' I ask.

'Well, I could tell you, but then I'd have to kill you,' he says, grinning again. 'Mom won't tell a soul. There was a tomato one that was Aimee's favourite – she used to eat it all the time when she was well. And when she wasn't Mom would try to get her to have just a little, if she was feeling up to it. She hasn't made that one since Aimee died though. It's been off the menu.'

'I'm sorry, John.'

'Me too.' He looks at me, quite intently for a second or two, and suddenly I feel a little uncomfortable. Have I said something else stupid?

'Would you like to come?' he asks suddenly.

'Excuse me?'

'Would you like to come to the restaurant tonight? You've been so kind, you know, about the phone. I'd like to pay you back – my treat.' He leans against his bike and looks nervously at me, his smile unsure.

I can't believe it. This is my golden opportunity. Ian wants me to meet the family – and this is the perfect in. If I accept John's invitation, I can gather more information for Ian, maybe even get him to meet them eventually. But I'm unsure – isn't that a terrible invasion of their privacy? Something about it doesn't feel right.

Still, I'm curious. More than a little. And I have to eat. OK, I'm so stuffed after the Cheesecake Factory that I can barely move right now, but that will probably change soon enough.

'Of course, you might have plans,' John says, as I sit and ponder. 'It was a silly idea, sorry.'

'I don't have plans,' I say quickly. What harm can it do? One little dinner won't hurt, surely.

'Great!' He grins. 'It's called Carlo's and it's on Union at Stockton. Do you think you'll be able to find it?'

'Of course.'

'Great! Say seven o'clock?'

'Sounds good.'

'Oh, and you won't mention the phone thing when you're there, right?'

'Of course not. My lips are sealed,' I assure him.

'Great, thanks,' he says, and I recognize relief in his voice. 'I'd hate Mom to find out before Aimee's anniversary. Once that's over I can tell her everything.'

Suddenly I get it. He has his own agenda too. He wants to make sure I don't screw up – this free meal tonight is to remind me to co-operate, make sure I keep my side of the deal. Well, that's cool. I can go along with that. And at the same time I can suss out his background. Maybe I'll discover something awful about him or his mother – something that would persuade Ian not to pursue the story. Maybe they're actually vile, unpleasant people. Ian has certain standards – I'm sure something like that would turn him off the entire scenario. And turn him back on to writing just a sequel, maybe even a prequel too. Now, that's a really good idea – why didn't I think of it before?

'I'll reserve a table for you,' John says, and then he's pedalling away, weaving through the park, past the little old ladies as they stretch in the sun.

I lean back, close my eyes again. It's not weird that I've accepted this invitation. It's fine – I've done him a good turn and now he's returning the favour. That's all. And if I happen to find out anything while I'm there and then happen to relay that information to Ian, well, that's fine too.

Chapter Eighteen

At seven o'clock on the dot I walk through the red door of Carlo's. There's a gaggle of people standing in line at the reception desk and a leggy, dark-haired girl is working her way down the queue, taking everyone's details. At a second glance I see it's the waitress with the bushy eyebrows from the coffee shop on Washington Square. So she did know John.

'Welcome to Carlo's. Can I have your name, please?' she says, as she gets to me, barely glancing up from her notepad.

It looks like she doesn't recognize me, which is probably a good thing – she hasn't exactly seen me at my charming best.

'Um, Francesca Rowley,' I reply.

Her head snaps up immediately. 'Oh, yes. It's you,' she says, her voice flat.

'Yes, it's me,' I reply, flushing. I can hardly expect her to be friendly. I did scowl at her quite a lot – that's not exactly endearing behaviour.

'John told me to expect you,' she says, her tone clipped and frosty now. 'If you'd like to follow me?'

She takes off at speed, her glossy ponytail swinging, and I trot after her obediently. Wow – she's even more incredibly skinny from this angle, and her legs are all the way up to her armpits. I suddenly feel beyond dumpy in my too-tight jeans. I bet this girl never goes to the Cheesecake Factory. She probably exists on coffee.

'Hey, I thought you weren't able to reserve a table in this place?' I hear a disgruntled customer mutter loudly, glaring at me as I pass him in the line. 'Isn't it first come, first served?'

'Yeah. They're usually really strict about it,' his companion hisses in reply. 'She must be someone – a friend of the family, maybe.'

The haughty waitress doesn't even look over her shoulder at me as we weave our way through the already buzzing restaurant, past small tables with red and white checked tablecloths and candles in old wine bottles dripping wax down the sides. Couples and larger groups are sharing huge pizzas and enormous bowls of pasta, smothered in butter and Parmesan, amid the hum of noise, laughter and conversation.

'Am I skipping the line?' I ask her tentatively, as we step through another door. Those people back there were pretty pissed off that I seem to be getting special treatment. I don't want to be lynched during dinner – although, to be fair, what would they do? Attack me with an oversized pepper mill? But still the place is packed – Carlo's is clearly a very popular spot – and I don't want to be the most hated diner here, with customers spitting in my food as it passes them.

'We don't usually take bookings,' she says icily.

Am I imagining it or is she sort of sneering at me? 'Well, I can wait in line,' I say. 'I don't mind.'

'No, John gave special instructions for you.' That was a definite sneer! 'He reserved a table for you out here.'

We're through to a tiny courtyard, where dark green creeper climbs the walls and fairy lights drape prettily across the wooden pergola. With the lights twinkling and the candles glowing on the tables, it's really beautiful.

Out of the corner of my eye I can see her assess my reaction.

'If you'd prefer to sit indoors . . .?' she asks.

'No, this is perfect,' I reply. 'Thank you.'

'OK. Your waiter will be with you in just a second. Here's the menu.' She practically throws it at me as I sit down, then turns on her heel and is gone, leaving me feeling that either I have already made a terrible impression and she disapproves of me being here at all or she's having a spectacularly bad night. Maybe it's PMS. If it is then she needs to start taking industrial-strength evening primrose oil to improve her symptoms because, boy, is she touchy.

I open the menu, rearrange my sweater over my shoulders and try to relax as I gaze around me. It's like a secret garden – from the street you'd never even guess it was here. No wonder it's so popular – if the food is even half as good as the ambience, it'll be amazing.

'Good evening, madam.'

I look up to see John standing before me, a green apron with 'Carlo's' printed in white lettering round his waist. 'You're my . . . ?'

'Waiter for this evening? Yes,' he says, his face solemn.

'I thought you were a photographer?' I say, trying not to laugh at his deadpan expression. He did say he worked here occasionally, I remember that, but I didn't expect him to be serving me!

'I am by day. But tonight I'm Super-waiter.'

'Super-waiter?'

'Well, Mediocre-waiter, then. I've been roped in to do a few shifts – just keep your order simple and I won't mess up. Now, is your seat to your liking?'

'Very much so – it's lovely. Thank you for saving it for me.'

'You're very welcome. I told Martha to give you special treatment.'

I cringe a little inside but try not to let it show. Martha is obviously the sulky waitress who, by all accounts, hates me.

'She's the girl from the café right?' I ask. Unless she has an evil twin, perhaps.

'That's right. She's my cousin.'

'So she works here too?'

'Part time in both. Modelling is her main gig.'

'She's a model?' I squeak. So that explains the bushy eyebrows. All those girls are discouraged from plucking – I know that from watching *America's Next Top Model*. I should have guessed – she has the height, the long limbs, the wide-set eyes . . .

'Yep,' he replies, apparently blasé about her beauty. 'Now, let's get down to business – what would you like to drink?'

I glance at the extensive wine list and am unsure which to choose. Usually I'd give it lots of thought but tonight I just want to chill, not worry that I'm picking the most appropriate drink for my meal. 'Can you choose a white for me?' I ask.

'Of course.' He does a formal little bow. 'How about a glass of something from a local vineyard? Our sauvignon blanc is particularly good.'

'That sounds perfect,' I say.

'Certainly, madam.' Another formal bow. He's teasing me now. 'And to start? Some garlic bread, perhaps? It's the house specialty.'

'Great.' I grin, my stomach rumbling in anticipation. So much for me never wanting to eat again after the Cheesecake Factory, or existing on coffee like Martha probably does. I'm starving.

'Extra cheese?'

'Why not?' Who cares? My jeans are already too tight – in for a penny in for a kilo.

'Of course,' he replies solemnly. 'And now for the most

important decision of the night . . . your main course. What's
it to be?'

'I think I'll try the pasta carbonara, please. And can I have
that garlic bread on the side instead of as a starter?'

'Your wish is my command!' With a fleeting grin and a
comedic click of his heels, he's gone and I'm left watching
the couples around me. Because now that I've had the
chance to look around properly, I realize I'm the only person here alone. I'm surrounded by loved-up twosomes,
gazing sickeningly into each other's eyes: the romantic
ones obviously request the courtyard for its extra canoodle
factor. Good thing it's pretty dark or I'd feel a right goose-
berry.

Would it be nice if Gary was here now? Then we could
share a bowl of spaghetti and maybe end up in a sloppy
kiss, like something from a movie. Although, thinking
about it, Gary would never dream of coming to a place like
this – it would be far too downmarket for him. He likes
haute cuisine, the pricier the better. I don't think I've ever
seen him eat a pizza or plain old spaghetti. I've seen him
curl his lip at pasta that wasn't perfectly *al dente*, yes, but
that's as close as he's come. If we were in San Francisco
together I probably would never have eaten that divine
cheesecake either. Gary hates chain restaurants. He can be
a bit of a food snob, actually. He likes to think he's a proper
foodie – he'd certainly look down his nose at a good old-
fashioned family-run joint like this.

A vision of us in the New York restaurant on the night of
the Empire State building débâcle drifts into my mind. After
we'd discussed Caroline he'd tried to get me to share his tiger
prawns, a conciliatory gesture, but I hadn't the heart for it.
The awful incident when he'd shoved me to one side had
killed my appetite. When the waiter had arrived with the

main course – pan-fried sole for us both – I'd just pushed it round the plate.

'This is vile,' Gary had said disdainfully, poking at the fish with his fork.

'I'm sure it's fine.' My head was throbbing. The last thing I wanted was a drama. I was already worn out and I didn't need one of Gary's legendary strops.

'No, it's not,' he snapped, calling over the waiter with an impatient click of his fingers – like he had a habit of doing. 'The sole is undercooked,' he announced loudly. 'Are you try-ing to poison me?'

Heads began to turn, as he'd known they would. Gary didn't mind a scene – in fact, I'd often suspected he quite enjoyed one.

'Oh, I do apologize,' the waiter murmured. 'I don't know how . . .'

'And so you should apologize,' Gary snapped. 'It's ruined our evening – my friend couldn't even touch hers!' He pointed to my plate. It was untouched, just like he said, but not because it was underdone.

'I'm terribly sorry, madam,' the waiter said. 'Let me take that from you.'

'Actually . . .' But before I could explain that I hadn't tasted it, Gary was on his feet, flinging his napkin on to the table. 'Let's go, Francesca,' he declared dramatically.

'But, sir,' the waiter was horrified, 'please, let me get you a fresh dish. I'll talk to the chef – we can –'

'Too late,' Gary snarled. 'Our night is ruined. And if you're expecting me to pay for our starters then you're sorely mis-taken!'

He had almost pulled me to my feet, and I had followed him, mortified, from the restaurant. The poor waiter was speechless – he'd had no idea that it hadn't been the food that had ruined our night but Gary's revelation about his wife and his reluctance to commit to us. It had turned what was meant to be a romantic break in New York into something else entirely: a cheap and shabby interlude that had left me feeling used.

Now, with a jolt, I realize that that was the weekend when everything had changed between us. Watching the lovers around me in the candlelight I can't help but wonder: is what Gary and I have real? Do we really fit or is our relationship just a convenience?

'Here we go!' With a flourish, John presents me with my steaming bowl of pasta carbonara. The smell wafting towards me is divine and that, mingled with the sight of gooey, melting cheese dripping from the sumptuous garlic bread, is enough to make me want to groan with delight, despite my enormous lunch.

'This looks delicious!' I say. 'Thank you!'

'You're most welcome – and here's your wine.' He presents me with a glass of chilled sauvignon blanc. It's all I can do not to fall on it and gulp it back in one go. 'Enjoy!' He's off again at speed and I dig in, using the garlic bread to soak up the carbonara sauce, which is the best I've ever tasted. The wine is dry and crisp – absolutely divine. I'm enjoying myself so much that I almost forget about the whispering couples holding hands across the tables all around me.

'So, how did you like it?' John appears before me as I'm attempting to finish. I'm fighting a losing battle, though, because after my lunch this meal has got the better of me – I don't think I can force down another morsel.

'It was delicious,' I say, groaning and pushing the plate away. 'But I can't eat another bite!'

'Em, you have a little something . . .' He points to the

corner of my mouth and I quickly wipe it with my napkin, a great blob of creamy sauce coming off on the linen.

Great. That's really attractive – I've got carbonara dripping down my face – I must be a proper sight.

'Whoops! I was in such a hurry to eat it – it was really good,' I say.

'I'm glad you enjoyed it.'

'Is it always so busy in here?' I ask, hoping there's not a great wedge of garlic bread stuck somewhere in my teeth too.

'Mostly. My mom is sort of a legend round these parts. People come from all over the Bay Area to eat here.'

'And you don't even take bookings.'

'Nope. Mom decided that getting in line was the fairest way. She likes to keep it simple.'

'Who are you calling simple, son?' I hear someone say, and turn to see a small woman, glossy black hair in a neat chignon, apron round her waist, approach us.

John shoots me a warning look and I immediately know what he means: don't mention the phone. I give him a tiny wink to let him know I understand and he relaxes visibly. 'Mom, would I ever call you simple?' he asks, mock-serious.

'Not to my face!' She slaps him playfully, then turns to me, hand outstretched.

'Hello, I'm Anita, John's mother.' She smiles, the lines round her mouth deepening as she does, and I notice that she has the most amazing almond-coloured eyes. She's wearing a small silver cross round her neck and another chain with 'A' dangling from it.

'Hello, I'm Francesca,' I reply, feeling a little awkward. This is Aimee's mother – I'm face to face with a woman I know far more about than I probably should. I've read her texts and I know her story. But she has no idea.

'What a beautiful name.' She takes my hand between both of hers and sort of strokes it. Her skin is soft and her grip firm but friendly. 'I knew another Francesca once, years ago. People used to call her Frankie. She was a real sweetie – worked in a candy store on Chestnut Street. I used to love the gob-stoppers there when I was a kid – they were the best in the city.'

'Everyone calls me Frankie too,' I say shyly.

'I didn't know that –' John stops abruptly as Anita looks at him more sharply for a second, her eyes narrowing a fraction.

'You guys know each other?' she asks.

Shit.

'Um, not really,' I start.

'Frankie is a friend of Connor's, Mom,' John says, out of the blue.

'*Irish* Connor?' Anita exclaims.

Irish Connor? Who's he when he's at home? And then I remember – didn't John say he worked with a Connor once? This is clearly his way of trying to explain how we've met before.

'Yeah! Isn't it a small world!' John says, looking at me. *Co-operate*, his eyes plead.

'I thought you sounded Irish!' Anita is beaming at me. 'That boy! He broke my heart the summer he worked here – he ate us out of house and home! The customers loved him, though, didn't they, John?'

'They really did,' John agrees, in a slightly panicked tone.

'Yes, he sure had that Irish charm!' Anita goes on. 'So, how do you know Connor?'

'Oh, we . . . lived close to each other,' I ad lib. Phew – that was quite quick thinking.

'You're from the Aran Islands too? What an amazing coincidence!' Anita exclaims.

Oh, no – Connor is from the Aran Islands? I know next to nothing about these islands near Galway Bay, except that people who live there still speak Gaelic.

'Um, yes, I am,' I say. 'I moved away ages ago, though – years, really. I live in Dublin now.'

There. That'll put a stop to this conversation and we can move on to something else.

'The islands sound awesome!' Anita sighs, not taking the hint. 'I'd love to visit one day.'

'Er, yes, they're great,' I reply.

'So, which one are you from exactly?' she asks. 'Connor tried to explain it all to us, but I'm afraid I forget. My memory isn't what it used to be.'

Crap – of course there's more than one Aran Island. What are they called? I desperately try to recall any of my very limited geography. There's a couple of small ones and a big one – Inis Mór! That's it! I just hope that's the one Connor's from too.

'Inis Mór,' I try, wincing a little in case it's wrong.

'That's right!' She beams. 'How could I have forgotten?'

'Easily done.' I laugh, relieved. Phew. Glad we're off that topic.

'So, you grew up speaking Gaelic as well, did you?' she goes on.

'Um, yes, I did,' I reply. *Or I'd thought we were off it.*

'Connor tried to teach us all these Irish sayings when he was here – what was that one, John, about the fireplace?'

'I can't remember.' John is shifting from foot to foot, clearly appalled by the direction in which this conversation is going.

'Oh, you know it! Something about a fireplace . . . What was it again? It was about being homesick . . .'

It comes to me and I blurt it out: '"*Níl aon tinteán mar do thinteán féin*"?'

'That's the one!' Anita whoops. 'What does it mean exactly? Remind me again.'

'"There's no hearth like your own" – or "There's no place like home",' I explain, more of my school Irish flooding back to me. I learned so many of those phrases by heart to regurgitate during exams.

'Ah, yes,' she says happily. 'I love that saying. So, you're pretty far from your hearth, Frankie. What brings you to San Francisco?'

'Work,' I reply, feeling increasingly uneasy. This is way too close for comfort. I know I'm supposed to be gathering information for Ian – that's the only reason I'm here – but now that I've met Anita I feel really guilty about it. I have to do my best to ignore that emotion, though. I'm here to work, nothing more. There's no room for maudlin sentiment.

'Francesca is a literary agent,' John explains.

'Really?' Anita says. 'How fascinating! Who do you represent? Anyone we know?'

'Most of my authors are Irish,' I say. 'You wouldn't have heard of any of them, probably.'

'Oh, you Irish, you're so artistic! What is it about the Celts that makes them such good storytellers, do you think?' she asks.

It's a question I'm often asked. 'Well, there's lots of reasons I think – but some people say it goes back to the tradition of the *seanchaí*,' I reply.

'I remember that – Connor explained it to me. A *seanchaí* was a professional storyteller, isn't that right? He used to visit a house in the area and all the neighbours would gather round to hear him tell a tale.'

'That's right.' I nod. 'There's a wonderful storytelling tradition in Ireland – it's in our blood, I think.'

'Isn't that romantic, John?' Anita sighs.

'It sure is, Mom.' John smiles at her, and I can feel the love between them. Suddenly I remember that I really need to call Mum and ask how the party preparations are going, see if she's sorted out the band or if the caterers have finally killed each other. There's bound to have been loads of drama – and it serves my brothers right if they're stuck in the middle of it. Maybe when I get back they'll appreciate me a little more.

'So, are you eating alone this evening or is your husband somewhere here?' Anita's voice breaks into my thoughts.

'I'm not marri– I'm alone,' I say.

'Not married, eh? Isn't that interesting, John?' She cocks an eyebrow at him and he visibly cringes with embarrassment.

'Oh, honestly, I'm just kidding.' She laughs at his pained expression. 'Although who could blame him for having a crush on a beautiful girl like you?' She turns to me and winks.

'Mom!' he yelps.

'Oh, hush, son. Now, Frankie, you won't mind if I join you for a drink?' she asks.

'Mom, Frankie mightn't want to . . .' John's face is twisting with mortification again.

'Don't be silly,' she chides good-naturedly. 'Frankie and I know what we're about, don't we, Frankie? Now, I'm on my break and I don't have much time so hurry up! Can I sit down?'

'Of course,' I murmur.

I see alarm register on John's face before I reply but what else can I say? Get lost? I can't talk to you – I know all your secrets?

'John, I'll have a limoncello, please,' she says, sitting down opposite me with a sigh. 'My feet are killing me.'

'OK, Mom. I know better than to argue with you,' he says, at last. 'Frankie, what will you have?'

'I'm fine, thanks,' I reply. 'I honestly couldn't have another thing. Your food was delicious, Anita.'

'Thank you. I'm so glad you enjoyed it! So, how is Connor?' Anita asks, leaning back in her seat and smiling at me. 'We get a postcard every now and again from around the globe. He never seems to stay still.'

'Ah, yes. That's Connor, always roaming,' I joke, hoping she can't tell I have no clue who he is.

'And how do you like our city?' she asks.

'I love it,' I answer. That, at least, is true.

'Have you done all the tourist things yet?'

'Well, I went to Sausalito and Crissy Field,' I say.

'Very nice. How about Alcatraz?' she asks.

'No, not yet.' Although if Rosie has her way, I'll be there soon. She's dying to take me.

'Well, we'll have to rectify that. John will take you, won't you, honey?'

'Take you where?' John is back, setting the glass of limoncello in front of his mother.

'To Alcatraz. Frankie would like to go and you know it better than anyone. He's photographed it a million times so he knows all the best corners to visit,' she confides, her voice proud.

'Mom, I'm sure Frankie doesn't want to go to Alcatraz with me. She's a busy lady, you know.' John laughs nervously.

'I'm sure she'd love to,' Anita replies, grinning at him. 'Wouldn't you, Frankie?' She turns to me for a split second, but doesn't wait for me to answer before ploughing on: 'You can't come to San Francisco and not go to the Rock. It's unthinkable! And you two would get along just fine for a morning, wouldn't you?'

John rolls his eyes at me, then mouths, 'Sorry.' But his mother doesn't notice. 'It's a nice idea, Mom, but we'll never get tickets at this short notice,' he says. 'You know what it's like – tourist season is still going strong.' He's definitely trying to put her off the idea. But it seems that nothing is going to stop her.

'Aha!' Anita's eyes gleam. 'But that's exactly why it's even more important that you be the one to take her. We know the girl in the booking office.'

'Do we?' he asks, confused.

'Yes, we do! Juanita Rodriguez,' she replies, triumphant.

'The cook's niece,' John replies weakly.

'That's right. She told me she can get you tickets anytime and I have her number right here. I think you should go tomorrow.'

'*Mom*, Frankie might have something on for tomorrow,' John says.

'Do you?' She turns to me, her open face a question mark.

I try to think of a reasonable excuse as to why I can't go – I *am* here to work, after all, so I can't really be gadding about the city like a tourist – but something in Anita's eyes makes me demur. She thinks this is a welcoming thing to do, just like Rosie did when she invited me to Sausalito. Refusing would seem rude, and I don't want to insult her, do I?

And you can get more information for Ian, the little voice in my head says. *It makes total sense – go and pump John for more details. Ian will love you for it.*

I almost hate myself for thinking like this – but I can't afford to get all soppy and emotional now: Ian wants details and this is another chance to get them for him.

'I think I'm free,' I say at last.

'Well, then, it's all sorted. Let's drink to that!' Anita claps her hands together and raises her glass as John and I look at each other. Tomorrow it is.

Chapter Nineteen

I'm leaning on the wooden railings looking out over the water, watching the famous sea lions as they bask in the sun. I can't exactly see the attraction: they look like enormous balls of blubber, lying there, lazily soaking up the warm rays, grunting loudly, occasionally slipping into the water to cool off. I can't help feeling that at any minute they might pull out a six-pack of beer, crack open some peanuts and settle back to watch the footie. But it seems I'm in the minority because, all around me, tourists stand and watch, pointing out their favourites, the kids screeching with excitement.

'Can we take him home, Mom?' one little girl asks excitedly, tugging at her mother's trouser leg as she points out the biggest and ugliest of them all. The sea lion she wants has a hairy beard and the sort of face only his mother could love.

'I don't think so, honey,' the woman replies kindly, sharing a look with her husband that says, 'Isn't she the cutest thing?'

'Why not?' The little girl pouts. 'I can put him in my backpack – he'd fit.' She pirouettes to show the Dora the Explorer bag on her back, craning her head round to try to see it herself, and the mother and father laugh, as if it's the funniest thing they've ever heard. She really is very sweet, with her chubby cheeks and her brown hair in lopsided bunches. As they move away, I turn to watch, feeling a sudden sad pang. They're like something from a Gap ad, the perfect family unit, Mum, Dad, daughter, probably another on the way if the mother's rounded belly is anything to go by. Or maybe she just has that dreaded jelly belly – the same one I seem to have after all the American portions.

I shake my head to get rid of the stupid, soppy feeling that I'm missing out on something. So the little girl is cute, just like that little boy who lives near Ian, the one who asked if I knew Harry Potter, but kids aren't on my radar, not really. This is what my brother Eric and his pregnant wife Jenny have to look forward to, not me. Especially not if I'm with Gary. Because Gary doesn't want any more children: he's already made that crystal clear.

'I think it's great, you know,' he'd said to me out of nowhere one night, as we lay in bed together.

I was only half listening. In my head I was trying to figure out a way to persuade Antonia West's publishers to up her marketing budget. In Antonia's opinion – which she was never afraid to share with me, loudly and on rewind – they were operating on a wing and a prayer, hoping that some free PR would generate enough publicity to sell the book. But Antonia wasn't falling for that old chestnut. Radio adverts and lots of them – that was what she wanted and it was my job to figure out how to get them for her without everyone's nose being pushed out of joint.

'Hmm ... What's that?' I replied, darting a look in his direction. His chest was smooth and tanned – courtesy of a week in the Caribbean sun with his kids on their mid-term break. Caroline had gone too – they had made the effort to holiday together for the children's sake. It was Gary's peace offering to her – or that was what he'd told me. His effort to halt the war between them, he'd said. There was nothing else to it, I know that.

But when he'd been away I'd tortured myself with images of them enjoying hot, sweaty reconciliation sex after too many cocktails at the poolside bar. That was silly, of course

– they hadn't made love for years before they'd finally split. Caroline just wasn't interested – Gary had practically said so – and that side of their marriage had died soon after the kids were born. So why would they have wanted to reinvent the wheel on holiday? It was absurd. Or so I kept telling myself.

'I said I think it's great, you deciding not to have kids,' he'd gone on. 'It's brave – you're brave.'

Suddenly I was listening. Intently. Not having kids? Who said I wasn't having kids? I mean, not right that minute of course – I didn't want them immediately. But some time in the future, maybe. In a few years. I'd have to think long and hard about it first, of course – I'd need to get the business up and running properly, hire a really good nanny, all that stuff. But it wasn't like I'd ruled it out completely – the door was still open. I was still leaving it ajar, just in case.

Mum was dying for it to happen. OK, as far as she knew I wasn't even dating, but that didn't stop her pondering baby names or wondering if she'd like to be called 'Granny' or 'Nana'. 'Granny' sounded too old, she'd always felt that, but 'Nana' wasn't right either . . . My imaginary children could call her by her first name, of course, but Mum thought that sounded a little cold . . . The pointless arguments had gone on and on. And then Eric and Jenny had announced that they were expecting and it had all moved up a gear: a real, live grandchild was on the way so therefore licence had been given to talk of pretty much nothing else.

'Well, I haven't exactly decided about the kids thing yet,' I'd said, twisting in bed to look at Gary.

'Good one, Frankie!' He'd laughed, poking me in the ribs.

'Er, why are you laughing?' I'd asked, instantly aggrieved. Why did he think I was joking? Then it had come to me. *Did he think I'd make a bad mother?*

'Well, because you're not cut out for motherhood, of course,' he'd replied, grinning. 'I mean, can you imagine it?' He'd laughed again, as if even the very idea tickled him.

The thing was, now he'd said it, I could imagine it. Not very well – it was a little hazy round the edges, but still, I could. Yes, it would be scary – terrifying, probably. But that didn't mean I couldn't do it, right? Setting up the agency had been terrifying too – all those sleepless nights wondering if I could pull it off, if any of my clients would follow me, if I'd be struck down dead by the partners at Withers and Cole for having the audacity to leave. That had been proper stress. There was no possible way that having a baby could even come close to that sort of anxiety.

'I could do it if I wanted to,' I'd said coolly.

'Yeah, right – where would you put the child? In your briefcase under your desk?' He'd really guffawed then, his tanned belly shaking, his skin rippling.

'Caroline managed.' The words were out of my mouth before I could stop them. His wife juggled a successful career *and* kids – what made me so different?

'Caroline had lots of help when the boys were young,' he'd said, still smiling, but being a little more careful now. There was definite wariness in his eyes. 'And she could afford it, Frankie.'

'So will I – when the business is up and running,' I'd retorted, knowing I was on shaky ground but charging on all the same. Who knew when the business would, if ever, become profitable? Antonia was my only big client and my search to find new talent wasn't exactly going to plan – I still hadn't found my new big thing, not unless a book about a magic dinosaur was going to be the next *One Day*.

'Are you serious?' he'd asked.

'Why wouldn't I be?' I'd replied. Suddenly the conversation

was going places I wasn't sure I was prepared to visit, but I felt reckless, as if I didn't care.

'Frankie.' His voice was sombre as he struggled to sit up, pulling the sheet over him, his tanned belly disappearing from view. 'You do know I don't want any more children, right? You do know that? I've done the baby thing.' There was a tense silence as we surveyed each other.

'Relax,' I'd replied eventually, forcing myself to smile. This was all too dangerous, too close to the bone. 'The agency is my baby.'

I'd watched as the relief flooded his face and he drew me to him. 'You had me there for a second.' He'd chuckled, his face in my hair. 'I knew you weren't a baby person.' And then I'd closed my eyes and tried to push away the strange feeling that maybe I wasn't so sure about that any more.

My phone rings, interrupting my daydream, and Ian's number flashes on to my screen. Glancing at my watch, I reckon I have about five minutes to talk to him before John Bonner gets here.

'So, what do you have to report?' he asks immediately, clearly too excited even to attempt to engage in idle chit-chat.

'I went to their restaurant last night,' I reply, eyes darting about in case John should materialize out of thin air and feeling a little like a CIA operative. 'I met the mother – her name is Anita.' See how efficient I am? I want to say. See how I'd make you an excellent agent?

'Let me get my notebook!' he cries. There's rustling in the background as he scrambles to find paper – if he's in that filthy kitchen I dread to think what he has to search under.

'So, the mother is typically Italian, then?' Ian asks, back on the line, his voice alive with interest.

'Yes, I'd say so. She's quite fiery, but really warm and inclusive too,' I reply. I think about Anita, all gleaming black hair and large gestures, sitting at my table, chatting animatedly and sipping limoncello until her break was over. She was so open and friendly, but there was something in her eyes, a certain sadness, that has stayed with me.

'Right. And what about the father?' Ian asks, barely drawing breath he's so anxious to get to the nitty-gritty.

'I think he's been dead quite a long time – there's a picture of him at the reception desk. His name was Carlo, like the restaurant,' I say, describing what I'd spotted as I was leaving.

'Any pictures of the girl? Aimee?'

'Not that I could see.'

I had looked, I couldn't help myself, but I hadn't spotted any.

'And how did the mother seem to you? Emotionally, I mean.'

'It was hard to tell – she was very welcoming to me. She did seem a little tired, but she works incredibly hard – the place was packed.'

'I'll have to go there – get a feel for it all . . . What else did she say? Do you think she knows about the phone?'

'*Anita*,' I say, a wave of irritation washing over me all of a sudden.

'What?' Ian replies, obviously confused.

'Her name is Anita,' I repeat crossly. Ian seems so enthralled by the story that he's forgetting real people are involved – this is a real-life tragedy, not fiction, and I'm finding it harder and harder to disregard this, no matter how many times I tell myself it's just business.

'Yes, Anita, that's right,' he says, distracted. 'So, did she speak about her daughter?'

'No.'

Thankfully, she hadn't. It was bad enough that she'd sat and chatted to me like I was a long-lost friend – I felt so awful about it. And now I'm going on a boat trip with John. What made me agree to that? I'm regretting it already. I don't know this guy from Adam, yet here I am going on a day out with him. It's ludicrous. Yes, it's a good opportunity to pump him for information but, funnily enough, even though I mostly agreed to the trip to Alcatraz to get on Ian's good side, I haven't told him I'm going. I don't know why I've decided to hold back. After all, it would earn me Brownie points for sure. I'm doing exactly as Ian asked in gleaning information – so why am I reluctant to disclose what could ultimately help me nab him for the agency?

'I have to go, Ian,' I say, hanging up quickly as I spot John coming towards me, waving to catch my attention. If he hadn't already seen me I'd be very tempted to melt into the crowd and disappear. But it's too late to escape, too late to run for the hills. I stupidly agreed to this expedition and now I have to follow through.

As he walks over to me, I realize that he probably feels exactly the same. His mother practically forced him to take me to Alcatraz – it's not like it was his idea. He could hardly have refused when I was sitting in earshot. Oh, God, he's probably dreading this as much as I am – maybe even more. Perhaps I should come up with an excuse to get us out of this horribly awkward situation. Ian has enough information – I've already gone above and beyond the call of duty for him. If he doesn't sign with me then maybe it's just not meant to be.

'Hey there,' John says, as he approaches.

'Hi,' I say in return, suddenly feeling stupidly bashful. Maybe I'll just be upfront – tell him I know he was press-ganged into this and that he's under absolutely no obligation whatsoever to take me anywhere. He'll probably be hugely relieved. In fact, I know he will, just like I will be too.

'So, you all set?' he asks.

He's a good bluffer, I'll give him that. You could never tell from the expression on his face that he's dreading this. In fact, from the wide smile he's wearing, it's almost as if he's . . . looking forward to it. But I know that's not right: he's taking me to Alcatraz because he couldn't be rude. And maybe he still feels guilty about shouting at me when we first met, or thinks he's indebted to me for keeping the phone thing secret. Either way I just know he feels obliged to go through with this. The poor guy will be so relieved when I tell him he's off the hook.

'Listen, John, there's really no need . . .'

Just as I'm about to tell him, a tanned teenage girl wearing a baseball cap, a sleeveless Nirvana vest and denim cut-offs that are just about decent materializes out of nowhere and hands John tickets with a wink. She must have been watching out for him from the ticket booths. 'Hey, Juanita.' He gives her a quick hug. 'Thanks for these.'

'Sure thing, anytime! Tell your mom I said hi.'

'I will. Pizza on us next time you're in,' he replies.

'Cool!' With a high five, and a dazzling smile in my direction, she's gone, and we're left facing each other.

'Frankie, we don't have to do this if you don't want to,' he says. 'I completely understand if you want to take a raincheck.'

'You do?'

'Sure. You were totally railroaded into it. I'm really sorry about that – my mom can get . . . overly enthusiastic about things. She hasn't been like that recently, what with Aimee . . . but it's sort of her default setting.'

'Your mother is great – I can see why she's a legend in North Beach. But I was thinking *you* were railroaded into it. You don't have to go with me. I'm sure you have much better things to do,' I reply.

'Actually, I'd quite like to go, if that's OK. Mom was right — I probably have taken a million shots of the island, but I could always do with a few more.' He pats the black photographer's bag slung across his body and grins at me. 'Besides, she was right about one thing. If we don't use these tickets you might never see the Rock — they're like gold dust.'

He actually *wants* to go? I blink at him in the sunlight, unsure what to say. Going to the Rock with him might be incredibly awkward. We'll have to get the boat together, spend time on the island together . . .

'Em, we don't have to stay together once we get there — you can do your own thing, if you like. But it'd be a pity to waste the tickets . . .'

Why is it that everyone seems to be able to read my mind in this damn city? 'Don't be silly!' I say, giving a little tinkly laugh and hoping it doesn't sound too false. 'I'd love to go with you.'

He gives me another lopsided grin and I shove my sunglasses back on as we move towards the ferry. That way he won't be able to tell what I'm really thinking — or see the inexplicable buzz of excitement and anticipation I suddenly feel. Why is my tummy fluttering? What's wrong with me? I can't actually be looking forward to this . . . can I?

Chapter Twenty

One very chilly trip across the water later, we're disembarking on Alcatraz.

John has spent the entire voyage trying to scare me with creepy stories about the dangerous criminals who were once incarcerated here and, although I know he's probably only teasing me, I do feel oddly nervous. The island does look kind of sinister and creepy, even in broad daylight. I'm just glad Anita didn't get tickets for one of the night-time tours I've seen advertised on board – I'm not sure I could have handled that. 'Prepare to be freaked out,' he says solemnly, offering me a helping hand as we step on the pier.

I'm already plenty freaked out, I think, flinching as our hands touch, then trying to hide it by pretending to adjust my sunglasses. What's wrong with me today? Why am I so damn jittery? I can hear Rosie's voice in my head, telling me I'm 'as jumpy as a cricket in spring', as we begin the trek uphill past towering dilapidated buildings, paint peeling from their exteriors. It must be the ferry ride that's making me feel strange and giving me flutters in my stomach – I'll probably be fine in a minute. After all, we're back on dry land now so the butterflies will stop soon – or, at least, I hope they will. 'We're in luck,' John whispers to me, as we join the crowd gathered round a tour guide and find a spot to stand and listen. 'I know this guy – he's awesome.'

The guide – a young guy in a khaki jacket and cap – catches sight of us, nods at John, then stares with naked interest at me.

For a split second I can't help wondering how many other women John Bonner has brought here – how many others he's taken on the boat across the bay, regaling them with funny stories, but I firmly push away those thoughts. It's really none of my business what he does or with whom – it's not like we're long-lost friends: we barely know each other. We've been thrown together for the day, that's all, and if I'm smart I'll shake off this weird feeling, make the most of the opportunity and get as much information as I can for Ian. That's the main reason I'm here: to impress a potential client with my dogged determination. I have to remember that. Once I get round to telling Ian about this trip he'll be so impressed by my professional commitment he'll probably want to sign with me on the spot.

Clearing his throat, the guide clasps his hands in front of him and begins to speak. 'Hello, ladies and gentlemen, and welcome to Alcatraz. The island is, of course, most famous for the twenty-nine years it operated as a US Federal penitentiary but it's also been a lot more than that. Today I'm going to dig a little deeper into the Rock's history!'

There's an excited murmur among the crowd, who are obviously here to be entertained and expect a show.

'What did he say?' an elderly woman in a blue dress beside us bellows at John.

'He said we're going to dig a little deeper,' John replies kindly.

'Dig deeper? Who's digging deeper?' she says, confused. 'I'm not digging anywhere.'

'No, not you, him,' John tries to explain.

'Eh?'

'Tell you what, why don't we get you closer so you can hear better?' he suggests, and escorts her through the crowd, guiding her by the elbow.

'Thank you, dear,' she says, laying a hand on his arm in a gesture of gratitude as he finds her a perfect spot for her at the front.

I smile at him as he makes his way back to me. That was a really kind thing to do, take care of an old lady like that. I can't help thinking that Gary would never help a pensioner in a million years. In fact, I've always had the distinct impression that old people get on his nerves, maybe because I've heard him swear more than once at slow, unsure elderly drivers in traffic. I'm not sure that it ever occurred to him that he'll be old himself one day and might need assistance. But, then, Gary has a unique take on the world and how it works. Would he feel even the tiniest bit jealous that I'm spending the day with another man, for example? It's not like there's anything between me and John, but he is a very charming, good-looking guy. Would Gary care that I'm here with him? I doubt it – in fact, I'm sure that, like me, he'd probably see it as a way of expediting the deal with him. He might even encourage me to flirt with John to get what I want. I push away those thoughts too. It isn't the time or place to be thinking like this: I need to concentrate on the matter at hand.

In front of me, the guide is continuing his monologue, telling the crowd that, as well as being a prison for many years, the Rock was also the birthplace of the American Indian Red Power movement. He's just getting into his stride when a bald man with glasses interrupts him.

'Al Capone was here, right?' he asks, clearly dying to get to the good stuff. 'I mean, that's the only reason we came.'

The guide grins easily at him, obviously used to putting up with interruptions. 'Yes, sir, you're right. Alphonse Capone was incarcerated here – he arrived in 1934.'

'They say he ran rackets from his cell,' the bald guy goes on bossily, like he's the authority on the subject.

'Racket? What racket?' the old lady whom John helped asks, fiddling with her hearing aid. 'I can't hear a damn thing.'

'Not a racket, ma'am, *rackets* – as in criminal activity,' the guide tells her, speaking slowly and clearly so she can understand him.

'So did he? Run rackets?' the bald guy asks excitedly. 'I heard he bought off the guards!'

'Well, that has never been verified,' the guide says, 'but he was the subject of intense media attention while he was on the Rock, that's for sure. In the end, though, he was only here for four and a half years.'

'What happened to him?' John calls out, in a deadpan voice, although something in the way he asks tells me he might already know the answer.

The guide pauses, clearly for dramatic effect. 'Well, sir,' he replies, an impish glint in his eye, 'he eventually developed syphillis symptoms so he was transferred to the Federal Correctional Institution at Terminal Island in Los Angeles.'

'Syphillis? Did he say syphillis?' the old lady says, to no one in particular.

'Yes, ma'am, I did,' the guide replies. 'But Al Capone wasn't the only infamous prisoner to spend time on the Rock. Robert Stroud, the so-called Birdman of Alcatraz, was also here, although, contrary to popular belief, he wasn't actually allowed to keep birds.'

'What? No birds?' a few people say to each other, disappointment in their voices.

'I knew that!' the bald man in the glasses says loudly, nodding triumphantly at his companions – at a guess his long-suffering wife and teenage daughter. 'It was just a myth!'

'There are many myths about this great and mysterious island,' the guide goes on, smiling tolerantly at him again, but the truth is that no one can tell the Alcatraz tale like the men who actually lived it. I recommend you all take the Cell House Audio Tour. That way you can hear the voices of the correctional officers and inmates who lived here. You'll be able to learn about both sides of life in the island prison and, believe me, it's spine-tingling stuff.'

'Will it tell us about the escape attempts?' the bald guy asks. 'I heard three guys once swam all the way across to the mainland. Is that true?'

'Well, it's true that in 1962 the Anglin brothers and Frank Morris attempted to escape from the island by chiselling their way out of their cells, yes. They left papier-mâché dummies in their beds to fool the guards – they even decorated their dummies' heads with stolen human hair from the barber shop to make them look more realistic. They had constructed an inflatable raft from raincoats to try to cross to the mainland, but it's believed they drowned in the cold, unforgiving waters of the bay.'

'Aha! But their bodies were never found, were they?' the bald guy says.

I see his daughter roll her eyes. The poor girl – I remember exactly what it's like to be a teenager embarrassed by your father in public. Thinking about Dad, I feel a proper twinge of guilt that I haven't called home to see how the party preparations are going. I can only hope he and Mum aren't at each other's throats.

'No, they never were,' the guide admits.

'Aha! So those guys could be living the high life in Vegas right now for all we know!' the bald guy whoops, and his wife and daughter back away from him, just a fraction.

'Vegas?' the little old lady in blue bellows. 'Who's going to Vegas?'

*

An hour later, John and I are sitting in the prison's outdoor recreation area.

'OK, so maybe that *was* a little creepy,' I say. We listened to the audio tour as we visited the cell house and, I have to admit, hearing real-life inmates describe their time here – how they survived riots, food rations and solitary confinement – was spine-tingling, just like the guide had promised.

'Told you so.' John grins at me. 'It gets me every time!'

'So . . . how do you know the guide?' I ask, curiosity getting the better of me.

'He used to go out with Aimee,' he replies quietly, fiddling with the camera in his hands. 'He took her to his prom, actually. They were a cute pair.'

'Oh, I say, kicking myself. I wish I'd never brought up the subject now that I see the fresh pain in his eyes – but what were the chances that Aimee was the connection between them?

'Actually . . . I have a photo of her from that night here. Do you want to see?'

I have no time to reply before he flips the camera round to me and, in an instant, I'm looking straight into a young girl's dark eyes. It's Aimee – exactly as I imagined her. She's wearing a gorgeous red dress that flares at the waist, and at her neck is a chain with the letter A, just like the one Anita has. Her glossy black hair tumbles round her shoulders and she's grinning into the camera, her skin glowing and her expressive brown eyes dancing with mischief, just like her brother's sometimes do. As I look at her, I can almost feel how full of joy and life she was. 'She was very beautiful,' I say at last.

'Yep, she was,' he says quietly, giving a barely audible sigh. 'Now, come on, I want to show you something. It was one of Aimee's favourite places here – I think you'll like it.' He pulls me to my feet and leads me down a path away from the yard.

'Where are we going?' I ask, as we walk.

'To the only gardens that most prisoners could see during their time here,' John says, as we round a corner and come upon some terraces. 'An inmate called Elliot Michener created this place with garbage scraps and seed packets from the staff back in the 1940s,' he explains. 'He even built the greenhouse and birdbath with salvaged materials – all to give the prisoners one bright spot in their day.'

'I need someone like him to make something of my garden,' I say ruefully, thinking of the pathetic patch of decking I have back home, with the pots of dead or withering plants.

'Yeah.' John laughs. 'Me too.'

'You're not a gardener, then?'

'I like to photograph roses, not water them,' he replies, beginning to take shots of the scene before us.

'These gardens must have been like a slice of heaven for the prisoners. They're such a great contrast to the prison.' I sigh, imagining what it must have been like all those years ago.

'Yeah, they must have softened the place a little for everyone – officers, their families and the prisoners.'

'I didn't think of that,' I muse. 'Families once lived here too. How weird must that have been?'

'Aimee used to say that she'd transport our family over here sometimes.' He laughs. 'She always reckoned we wouldn't survive five minutes.'

'There's a reality show in that,' I say. '*Family on the Rock* – I can see it now.'

He chuckles. 'She'd have loved it.' A shadow crosses his face, but then he composes himself. 'Now stand there and smile,' he commands. 'I need to get your picture.'

'No, thanks,' I say, shying away. 'I'm the most unphotogenic person in the world.'

And I hate having my photo taken.

'I don't believe a word of that,' he says.

'It's true, believe me. Every photo that has ever been taken of me is awful – worse than awful.'

'Oh, come on! That's a lie! What about your prom – or what do they call it in Ireland?'

'They call it a debs, and even the photo taken at that was a complete disaster.'

'I don't believe you! Every girl looks gorgeous on their prom night.'

'I didn't.' I shake my head. 'I had chicken pox.'

'At your prom?' He grins, eyes wide.

'Well, I was recovering,' I say. 'The scabs were getting nice and crusty.' Mum had dabbed every pockmark with calamine lotion for days beforehand, but it didn't really work. She'd been flabbergasted when I'd suddenly developed the spots – she was sure I'd had chicken pox at the same time as Eric and Martin when we were little. I wasn't surprised, though – it was just my luck to get it twice.

'You had *scabs*?' He grimaces.

'All over. My mother tried to tell me that people would barely notice, you know, because the lights would be down low.'

'But they did?'

'Oh, yeah, they did. I was the talk of the night. Even more so when my date dumped me halfway through the first slow set and then snogged my so-called best friend.'

'Ouch – that is rough.' John winces.

'You have no idea. He didn't even stick around for the official photos – so there's just a sad snap of me and my spots. Not pretty.'

Mum insists on keeping it on top of the piano, though – and my darling brothers love to remind me it's there every time we're at home together.

'That kind of experience could really scar you for life,' he says sympathetically. 'No pun intended.'

'It did – I haven't been able to listen to "Careless Whisper" ever since.'

I make a joke of it, like I always do when I tell this story, but the truth is that inside I'm smarting when I think about that awful night. At the time I pretended it didn't bother me, but I was devastated. Having the then love of my life tell me I looked like Frankenstein was bad enough but catching him kissing my best friend in the cloakroom was heartbreaking. I pretended I didn't care, even though it just about killed me, but the experience was a valuable life lesson: fairy tales are fantasy and never come true.

'Did you get revenge?' John asks, and with a bang I'm back in the present.

'Not really. My brothers wanted to give him a wedgie, but I told them not to,' I answer.

'Wow, remind me never to get on the wrong side of you – your brothers sound very protective,' he says, and gives a little whistle.

'I guess they did come in handy back then. I'm not sure they'd do it for me now, though.'

'Why? Aren't you guys close?' he asks.

'Not especially,' I admit. 'We don't see much of each other, these days.'

'I don't think you have to see much of each other to be close,' John muses. 'I mean, if you have each other's backs when it counts, that's the important thing.'

I think about my family, none of whom I've spoken to since I got here, and feel a pang. 'I suppose,' I reply. 'But the sort of relationship you had with your sister – with Aimee – that was special. That doesn't just happen every day.'

'Yeah, Aimee was special,' he replies. 'But that doesn't

mean we didn't have our ups and downs. We had our stuff too.'

I'm surprised to hear this – so far it's sounded as if everything was perfect between them.

'Sure we did. She was headstrong – she'd never listen to anyone. Least of all me. And I kept poking my nose in – that didn't help.'

'Like when?' I ask.

'Well, when she wasn't well I wanted her to slow down a little – you know, conserve her energy – but she wouldn't. She didn't want to miss a second . . .'

'It sounds like she was determined to fit in a lot of living,' I say gently.

'You're right.' He smiles at me. 'She said life was too short for sitting around, waiting. "You get busy living or you get busy dying" – that was her catchphrase.'

'Isn't that from a movie?' I ask.

'Yep. *The Shawshank Redemption*. It was one of her favourites. Anyway, we had lots of arguments about it. In the end, though, I realized I had to respect her wishes. She wanted to do everything and I had to let her, even though I was scared for her.'

'You "had her back"?' I say.

'I tried to,' he says softly. And suddenly there's something in the way he looks at me, something different, and my stomach lurches.

'So, you want to take my photo?' I say quickly, to break the awkward silence. I'm imagining the way he's looking at me, of course I am. He's emotional talking about his sister – and I'm probably still jet lagged. That moment was in my mind.

'Well, I have to,' he says, grinning easily again.

The look in his eyes is gone. I was imagining it. Of course I was. 'You have to?' I ask.

'Of course. Mom will want picture-perfect proof that we made this trip. Don't think she won't.'

'She will not!' I protest.

'She will too, just you wait and see.' He lifts the camera to his face again. 'Now just relax and say "cheese".'

I do as I'm told – lean back against the Rock and smile. And as he snaps, I realize I don't even have to fake it.

Chapter Twenty-one

'I can't believe you've already been to Alcatraz!' Rosie wails, her face scrunching up like that of a very cross toddler who can't get what she wants. If she wasn't already sitting down in one of the velvet-upholstered oversized Queen Anne chairs, I get the feeling she'd be stamping her feet.

We're sitting in the lobby of my hotel where I had been working quietly until she showed up with tickets for the Rock that she'd scored from some friend of a friend. Breaking it to her that I'd just been wasn't easy. As far as Rosie's concerned, she's my unofficial guide to the city – she wants to show me everything during my short stay – and she's not happy that I've been to a tourist hot spot without her.

'I'm sorry, Rosie,' I say, 'but John's mother insisted we go – she was the one who organized the tickets for us. I couldn't really refuse. It would have been rude.'

Rosie's jaw drops. '*Whaaat?* You went with John? Aimee's John?'

Um, didn't I mention that part? 'Er, yes,' I confirm. 'I did.'

'Well, now, honey, this is one story I'd pay to hear.' She settles back in her chair. 'So please do tell.'

I fidget under her piercing gaze. 'There's not much to tell, honestly,' I say.

'Uh-huh. I'm listening,' she replies, raising her eyebrows.

I know she won't settle for anything but the long version. 'OK. Well, I bumped into John in Washington Square Park and he invited me to dinner in the family restaurant to thank me for keeping shtum about the phone . . .'

'Hmm. You just bumped into him, huh?' she says, like she doesn't believe a word.

'Yeah. It was weird, actually, because I was just sitting on a park bench and he cycled by and spotted me. You were right – this city really *is* like a small town.'

'Uh-huh. There you were – there he was. I get it. So, what happened next?'

'Well, I went to the restaurant. It's a lovely little place called Carlo's. They don't take reservations and the queue was almost round the block, but John had left special instructions so I got a table straight away.'

Rosie's eyebrows rise even higher. 'Special instructions? Oh, my!'

'Stop that.' I flap her innuendo away. 'It was all perfectly innocent. I had a wonderful meal in the courtyard –'

'There's a courtyard?'

'Yes, it's absolutely gorgeous – all draped with fairy lights . . .'

'Sounds incredibly romantic.'

'It was – I mean there were lots of couples there, doing the whole smoochy thing, you know.'

'I can just imagine,' she purrs. 'And then what happened?'

'Well, then his mother – Anita – was on her break from the kitchen and he introduced me to her.'

'So early in the relationship?' she says archly.

'Shut up, Rosie, or I won't tell you the rest.' Threats are the only things that work with her.

'OK.' She holds up her hands, laughing. 'So what happened next?'

'Well, Anita suggested that John take me to Alcatraz because the cook's niece could get us tickets. I couldn't really get out of it.'

'The cook's niece? This is just like an episode from *As the World Turns*,' she says.

'What do you mean?'

'Oh, nothing. Sounds very interesting, is all.' She lifts her coffee cup to her lips and smiles knowingly at me.

'Don't be silly,' I rebuff her crossly. 'And stop teasing me.'

'Well, I can't help it, girl! You bump into John in the park and before you know it you're having a meal with his family and going to see the Rock together . . . It's all *very* cosy.'

'It's not like that!'

'Isn't it?' She looks at me innocently. 'My daddy used to say, "If it looks like it and smells like it, it probably is it."'

'Well, this is *not* it, OK?'

'OK, OK. Well, I can't say I ain't disappointed because I am. I thought *I* was your friend here . . .'

'You are!' I smile. 'Tell, you what, we can do something else together, my treat. I didn't see it properly, though – and it could be fun.' Part of me can't believe that I'm trying to keep on Rosie's good side. It's not like we're going to be best friends for ever. But I don't want to hurt her feelings. She's been really sweet to me the entire time I've been here and, in spite of myself, I'm now very fond of her.

'Let me think on it,' she says. 'Don't worry, I'll come up with somethin'! Now, how's work going?'

'I'm hoping to wrap it up soon,' I say. 'We're almost there. Actually my client's going to be here any minute.' I strain my neck to look towards the revolving doors – Ian is already twenty minutes late for our meeting, even though I sent a town car to fetch him and bring him here.

Rosie's head swivels round, searching for him. 'Oh, can I meet him? I'd love to meet a real, live writer.'

'He's not exactly the friendly type, Rosie.' And that's an understatement.

'But you managed to bring him to water and make him

drink too.' She grins at me, as if she'd always known I'd pull it off.

'I think we're there, yes,' I say. I'm almost reluctant to say it in case I jinx it. But Ian has no excuse not to sign with me now, right? I've played ball. I've proved to him that I'm on his side. Now all I have to do is get him to sign on the dotted line and then agree to write the sequel and the deal is done. I'm so close I can almost taste it.

'I guess your office must miss you, huh?' Rosie wonders.

A picture of Helen, ruby-red hair extensions swinging round her shoulders, pops into my head.

'But that's the blessing of the Internet,' Rosie goes on. 'You can always be in touch, even if you don't have your own cell phone.'

'Yeah.' I glance at my watch. 'Em, I don't mean to be rude, Rosie, but can we talk later.'

I'd had to lure Ian into the city with promises of juicy gossip about the Bonners, but it definitely beats his crummy kitchen, that's for sure – I really don't want to visit that dump again unless I absolutely have to. Plus sending the town car to pick him up meant he couldn't exactly refuse to meet me here. More expense but it'll be worth it.

'Well, isn't that just charming?' Rosie drawls, a smile in her voice. 'You're not ashamed to be seen with me, now, are you?'

'Don't be silly!' I say.

'Well, why can't you introduce me? I won't embarrass you, I promise.'

'Look, it's just that he can be a little testy,' I begin. 'He's cranky and sort of unsociable and . . .'

Too late, I see Rosie's eyebrows shoot up to her hairline in warning.

Shit. He's behind me.

'I wouldn't describe myself as testy, Francesca,' Ian Cartwright says. 'Slightly challenging, maybe.'

I have to brazen it out. No point trying to backtrack now. Instead, I inject as much charm as I can into my smile and stand to say hello. 'Ian! How are you?'

'Oh, I'm just fine, Francesca,' he says drily.

Behind me I hear Rosie snort with laughter. 'She didn't mean it – she was just trying to scare me off, is all,' she says.

'So that's why she was painting me as the big bad monster.'

'I think so! I'm Rosie Kelly, Frankie's mad Texan friend.' Rosie extends her hand like a Southern belle and Ian stoops to kiss it, like a Southern gentleman.

'Delighted to meet you, my dear. I'm Ian Cartwright – her contrary old client. Well, potential client, isn't that right, Frankie?'

'Em, yes. Rosie was just leaving, weren't you?' I say firmly, giving Rosie a no-nonsense look that says scram.

'Yes, ma'am.' Rosie sighs, gathering her things together.

'Please don't leave on my account,' Ian says.

'No, that's OK. I know y'all need your privacy,' she demurs.

'Not at all!' He tuts. 'I insist you stay. Now, won't you have another drink? Iced tea, perhaps?'

'Oh, I *love* iced tea! And I am so dry I could spit cotton,' Rosie proclaims, shooting me a triumphant glance.

'How charming.' Ian smiles genially. 'We can share a pitcher.'

Shit. They've clicked.

Thirty minutes later they're still gabbing to each other and I haven't been able to get a word in edgeways.

'So when I finally got to Waterford I was loster than two rabbits,' Rosie says now, after a long and complicated road-trip story. 'You Irish don't believe in road signs, do y'all?'

'Loster than two rabbits?' Ian asks me, clearly baffled.

'Really lost.' I'm used to deciphering Rosie's sayings by now.

'Ah, yes, I see. Well, I have to say, Rosie, your stories are absolutely enthralling,' Ian breathes. 'Tracing your family history like that is so admirable – it must have taken you years.'

'Well, it did.' Rosie says modestly. 'But Daddy had a lot of the information. He was so fired up by it that he put in all the leg work.'

'So, let me get this right,' Ian says. 'Your great-great-great-grandfather took the boat to America in 1845? Just as the Famine was beginning, then.'

'That's right. He was on the *Dunbrody*.'

'Ah, yes,' Ian says. 'I visited it in New Ross once – it's a remarkable reconstruction.'

'Isn't it wonderful?' Rosie claps her hands with glee. 'You get to go below deck and imagine what life must have been like for the voyage.'

'Pretty grim conditions,' Ian says. 'The *Dunbrody* wasn't as bad as the coffin ships, it was very well run, but trying to survive on corn rations for six to eight weeks must have been hellish.'

'My daddy always said those who survived were made of strong stuff,' Rosie says proudly.

'Well, he was right about that. Many didn't survive the journey. Your relative was one of the lucky ones – the *Dunbrody* was far better run than most by all accounts.'

'Yes – he made it to New York and met his sweetheart in Queens. Then they travelled down south together and here I am!'

'That's amazing. From the south-east of Ireland all the way to Texas,' Ian says, leaning forward, his brow furrowed with interest. 'How did your father get all that information?'

'Anything he couldn't find in the library I helped him source online. You know how wonderful the Internet is – you can find almost everything there,' Rosie replies.

'I don't use it all that much,' Ian laments, looking suddenly sorrowful.

'Why ever not?' Rosie asks, clearly astounded by this.

'Well, I'm rather hopeless at all that sort of stuff – I'm a technophobe, I believe they call it.'

'Nonsense! There's nothing to it,' she says. 'I could show you in a second!'

'You could?' he says doubtfully.

'Of *course* I could!' She smiles. 'But I'm confused – if you don't use the Internet then how do you manage to do research?'

Ian looks at me, guilt on his face, and I look away, feeling guilty too. What would Rosie think if she knew exactly how he was researching his new idea?

'I manage,' he says vaguely, lowering his eyes.

'Well, I can help you out anytime,' Rosie says happily. 'I'm quite good on the computer. I did a course a few years ago.'

'You did?' Ian asks admiringly.

'Oh, yes. I don't like to be left behind, Ian – you have to keep in touch with what's happening in the world, that's what I say. It's important to keep up to date, don't you agree?'

'I suppose you're right,' he says. 'I'm not very good like that, though. Do you know I don't even use the computer to write? I still use longhand.'

Rosie gasps with disbelief. 'But a PC would be so much easier! So much faster too!'

'I know it probably would but . . . I can't type,' he admits sheepishly.

233

'*What?*' Rosie can't believe this either.

'It's true. I never learned. Silly, really.' He looks like a little kid – vulnerable and unsure of himself.

'Well, I'll teach you, honey!' Rosie volunteers.

'I couldn't ask you to –' he begins.

'Now, hush up, it's no trouble. I'd like to help you. You can dedicate your next novel to me, if you like, as a thank-you!' She bursts into peals of laughter at this idea.

I can tell from the way Ian's face is working that he doesn't know quite what to make of Rosie's offer, but then, amazingly, he smiles broadly. 'OK,' he says. 'You're on!'

They grin at each other as I try to take this in. In less than an hour they've become bosom buddies. What is it about Rosie that makes her so irresistible? When we first met I vowed to get rid of her as fast as possible – and now here we are and she's teaching Ian Cartwright to type. It's like something from a badly written manuscript that I would throw on to the thanks-but-no-thanks pile.

'I think this calls for champagne!' Ian says now.

'Champagne?' I choke. 'It's not even noon.' And champagne is not in my budget – not until he's signed on the dotted line.

'Well, I'm feeling lighthearted,' he says, beaming. 'I'd like to make a toast to life.'

'How exciting!' Rosie giggles, her cheeks pinking with pleasure. 'I'm glad I stayed.'

'So am I, my dear.' Ian chuckles. 'So am I!'

'But, um, Ian, we have to discuss work,' I interrupt lamely.

'What's to discuss?' he says. 'I'm signing with you. We can drink to that too.'

'You are?' I squeak.

At last! He's agreed! I've done it – *I've done it!*

'Yes, it's all decided. We're a team, aren't we?' he says.

'Of course we are!' I reply, in shock but trying to hide it. 'We're a team! Yay!' I'm not too sure where that 'yay' came from but I hope I sounded suitably thrilled.

'Oh, how *exciting*!' Rosie trills. 'Congratulations, y'all!'

'It *is* exciting, isn't it?' Ian says. 'This is a fresh start for me – a new direction.'

Hang on. My jubilant mental cartwheels skid to a halt in my brain. What does he mean, 'a new direction'?

'A new direction? Is it really?' Rosie's eyes are shining as she looks at him.

'Yes. I've been really inspired recently, Rosie – and it's all thanks to this woman.' He gestures at me.

'That is *so* sweet! Isn't that just the sweetest thing, Frankie?' Rosie says.

'Um, yes,' I say. But inwardly I'm on alert because I know exactly where this is headed.

'People have been trying to box me in for years,' Ian goes on. 'I'm only seeing that now.'

'What do you mean?' she asks.

This is like manna from heaven for Rosie – she's lapping it up.

'Well, my old agent, April, she never had vision. I probably shouldn't say that – she died recently – but it's true. Now, Francesca here, she has it.'

If anyone else was saying this I'd probably be crying with gratitude and joy. But instead I'm feeling a little sick and extremely nervous: he's talking about Aimee's story, I know it.

'I think you're right!' Rosie is saying. 'I knew Frankie was special from the moment we met on the plane.'

'You met on a plane?' Ian forgets about his visionary speech for a second.

'Yes! On the flight from Dublin to San Francisco – Frankie

doesn't like to admit it, but it was Fate. We sat together and the rest is history!'

'You believe in Fate?' Ian asks her.

'Of course! Don't you?'

Ian ponders this for a second before he answers. 'Yes, I think I do. This new story I want to work on has a huge element of Fate in it, actually, doesn't it, Francesca?'

'Em, yes,' I reply, trying to think on my feet. He is talking about Aimee's story – that's crystal clear. He has no intention of writing a sequel and I have no idea how I'm going to persuade him to do just that. He might be signing with me, but if I can't get him to deliver what Gary wants – what I need – then what's the point? My mind is working overtime. There has to be a way around it, there has to be. My entire future rests on it.

'So what is this story?' Rosie asks. 'I'm intrigued!'

'Well, I don't want to say too much in case I jinx it, but it's something special – something really special. I haven't been so excited about writing in years!' He's gazing at her, his eyes shining.

'Well, bless your cotton socks, honey,' she purrs, as he pours some more iced tea into her tall glass and hands it to her, beckoning the waitress over to order champagne.

If only she knew what that new story was, she might think differently. Rosie has no idea Ian is talking about Aimee and she mightn't take too kindly to it if she did know. She feels really protective of Aimee's sad tale – if she ever found out I was trying to befriend the Bonner family simply to feed information to Ian . . .

'Ian, I know this might sound kinda crazy, seeing as we just met an' all, but would you like to go to Alcatraz with me?' Rosie asks out of the blue.

'Alcatraz?' Ian looks a little shell-shocked.

'Yes. I have two tickets for a sailing this afternoon,' she says. 'I was going to take Frankie, but she's already been.'

'Well . . . I'd be honoured to accompany you, Rosie,' he says, a little bashfully.

'You would?' She claps her hands together.

'Of course.'

What the hell is going on? That's enough for me – I have to get away, even for a few minutes. 'I think I'll go and freshen up,' I murmur, excusing myself. But they barely notice me leave, they're so busy chatting. Luckily they're talking about the Rock, and Ian doesn't seem to be divulging any more information so, hopefully, Rosie won't put two and two together and my cover won't be blown. She thinks I'm a nice person. If she knew what I was really like – how I've manipulated this whole situation just to get what I want . . .

God, what a mess. How did I ever get myself into this – and how am I going to get myself out? I'm not this person, am I? This deceitful liar?

I'm walking towards the Ladies, my heart heavy, when my phone buzzes with a new text message. *I can't believe it's almost been a year my darling. I wish you could come back to us.*

It's from Anita. The poor woman, she's been putting on such a brave face, but behind it she's heartbroken. If I didn't know Aimee's story I never would have guessed that Anita was grieving. She hides her pain very carefully. Another text pops in almost straight away. *I miss you so much, but it won't be long now my darling. I'll see you very soon.*

'I'll see you very soon'? What does that mean? How can she be going to see Aimee soon? Unless . . . My hand shakes as it comes to me. Oh, my God. Can Anita be planning to take her own life?

Oh, no – that can't be true, can it? She seemed so cheerful the other night in the restaurant, so eager to sit and chat, so full of life. I'd almost thought John had been exaggerating her grief. But now I know that the truth is far different. He's right: she hasn't moved on at all. And she might never be going to because, according to this text, she's planning to end it all and no one knows except me. My head is spinning now as the reality of the situation hits me. I can't just stand back, carry on and pretend I know nothing. Anita's in a black place – she needs help. And I have to do something about it.

Chapter Twenty-two

'I can't believe it.' John is clearly shocked.

We're sitting opposite each other at a small table in Carlo's. The restaurant is deserted – closed for the afternoon before the evening shift begins – and I've just told him about his mother's last message.

'I didn't know whether to tell you or not,' I say, feeling awful, 'but I thought it was better that you know.'

He looks at me, his eyes despairing. 'I'm really glad you did. Thanks, Frankie. And I'm so sorry you've been caught up in this – you must think we're crazy.'

'I think grief can do crazy things to people,' I reply softly. The poor guy looks so shaken and unsure. I feel terrible.

'I knew she was up and down emotionally,' John goes on, 'but I never thought she'd even consider this. It just didn't enter my mind.'

'Maybe she's not considering it, not really,' I suggest tentatively. But even as I say it, I'm not convinced.

'What if she is?'

I sit in silence, unable to answer. I have no experience of this sort of thing, no clue what to say.

'I don't know what to do,' he goes on, his head bowed.

'I guess you should try and talk to her,' I suggest.

'I wouldn't know where to start.' He puts his head in his hands. 'Oh, God, this is a total nightmare. And when she finds out about Aimee's phone, it'll tip her over the edge.'

I reach across to comfort him and stroke his arm. As I do, he raises his eyes to mine and a jolt of electricity runs between us. *I know you*, my inner voice whispers. He reaches for my hand and I for his.

'Frankie, I —' he begins.

'Hello there!'

We jump as we both hear Anita's voice. Please, *please*, let her not have heard us talking about her.

'What are you doing here?' she calls, smiling broadly as she bustles towards me, arms outstretched in welcome.

'Hi, Anita, I just popped in to thank John for taking me to Alcatraz,' I say weakly, my cheeks burning. Is it because I've read her private messages or because of the moment John and I just had? I can't be sure.

'That was so nice of you! Wasn't it, John?' she says.

'It was.' John's smile is strained. I can see he's searching his mother's face, looking for evidence of suicidal thoughts.

If there are any I can't see them. She looks tired, as she did before, with blue smudges under her eyes, but otherwise there's no clue as to her inner turmoil. She's hiding it very well.

'What did you make of the Rock, Frankie? Isn't it just wonderful?' She hugs me warmly and the unmistakable scent of jasmine and patchouli envelops me.

'It really is,' I agree, hugging her back. 'I'm so glad I went.'

'I knew you would be. See, John? Your old mother is right about these things.' She grins at us both, and I feel like a traitor. I know this woman's secret thoughts and I shouldn't. I should have got rid of the damn phone ages ago – it's wrong to be privy to someone's inner pain. It's like spying on their darkest secrets, the stuff they'd never share with another soul, least of all a complete stranger, as I am to Anita.

'I thought you were taking the afternoon off to rest, Mom,' John says.

'Oh, rest schmest.' She rolls her eyes.

'You need to take it easy. You're pushing yourself too hard.'

I see the anxiety in his face, the fear that Anita is so grief-stricken behind the cheerful façade that she's on the verge of doing something stupid.

'Silly boy,' she says, waving his concerns away. 'I'm fine – as strong as an ox. Now, Frankie, since you're here, do you fancy helping an old lady in the kitchen?'

I look at John, who's now wearing an expression of exasperation. This was never part of my plan, but maybe it would help to keep her mind off things. Maybe it'll cheer her up, distract her from other thoughts. Although she certainly looks as if nothing's wrong. Is this what people on the edge look like? Completely normal?

'Em, sure,' I reply. If it makes her feel better, it's the least I can do – and maybe it'll make me feel a bit better too. I may have done some questionable things, like ingratiating myself with this family to get what I want, but I'm not like that, not really. Maybe helping Anita in the kitchen will convince me of that.

Anita is beaming at me. 'That's wonderful! Come with me!'

'Mom –' John is still looking very doubtful.

'Oh, don't fuss, son,' she says. 'I want to show Frankie how to make pasta, that's all. Every girl should know how to make pasta, am I right?'

'I guess so.' I smile at her.

'You'll thank me, believe me. Off you go, John. We don't need your help.' She herds him out of the way and frog-marches me to the kitchen.

'Now, Frankie, don't look so scared,' Anita says, as I pull an apron over my head.

She's right: I am a little scared. I'm not good in the kitchen.

Not unless you count having a close personal relationship with the microwave good, that is.

Gary thinks it's sweet that I'm a hopeless cook. *But that could be because he likes to lord his foodie superiority over you.* The thought pops unbidden into my mind and I can't help smiling – maybe I'll learn something today that I can use with Gary in the future: he might even be impressed.

'Everyone should make pasta at least once in their lifetime,' Anita goes on, almost dreamily. 'It's very rewarding. There's something magical about turning flour, oil and eggs into a delicious dough with your own hands.'

'Magical? Really?' I don't like the sound of this much – it makes me feel a little nervous. Maybe I should just ask her how to make a decent pizza.

'Oh, yes. But it does take practice. You'll get better as you go along, so you need to persevere if it doesn't go exactly the way you'd like it to first time, OK?'

'OK,' I say, although I'm now starting to seriously doubt there will ever be a next time. I can't see myself doing this at home alone. Why would I when I could run to the corner shop and buy some organic spaghetti handmade by someone else? I keep this to myself, though – the last thing I want to do is hurt Anita's feelings.

'Good.' She nods approvingly. 'I always told my kids there's no such thing as failure – failure is only a try. And God loves a trier.'

'I like that idea. It takes the pressure off.'

'There's no pressure at all. It's so simple. All we need is some strong flour, two tablespoons of virgin olive oil and four eggs. Isn't that easy?' She wipes down the countertop before she begins.

'Everything must be spotlessly clean, but I'm sure you know that already. Now, we're going to sieve the flour from a height on to the surface, OK?' She takes my hands in hers as she shows me how to do this and I watch as the flour falls prettily through the sieve, building a little white mountain.

'Now make a hole in the centre, like this, then put in the four eggs and pour in the oil. See how easy it is?'

It does seem pretty easy, but I imagine that Anita makes almost everything in her kitchen look simple – she moves around the space with such lightness and delight in her work.

'Gently beat the eggs with a fork.'

I give this a go, immediately remembering why I gave up home economics in first year. I'm all thumbs.

Anita takes my hands in hers again. 'Do smaller circular motions with the fork, Frankie,' she explains. 'You want to break up the egg yolks, combine them with the oil, then slowly draw in the flour from the edges. See?'

And suddenly I do. I'm in a rhythm now. 'This is really . . .'

'Comforting?' she suggests. 'I know. It's one of my favourite things to do. Even more so since . . .' She trails off, as if she feels she's said too much, her face twisting. She'd been going to say something about Aimee, I know it. I hold my breath, hoping she'll confide in me. I want to help her, make her feel better in some small way, I really truly do. But she clears her throat and composes herself quickly, and the moment passes.

'Now, let's see. Yes, very good, Frankie. I think we're almost done. It's important only to take in as much flour as you need to make a soft dough – if it's nicely pliable and is forming a ball, don't use any more.'

'How's this?' I ask, peering at my efforts. Miraculously, it doesn't look too terrible.

'Pretty perfect! It's quite humid today so I think that's enough.'

'What's the humidity got to do with it?'

'Well, the weather can affect the flour – if it's drier you may need less. That's why making pasta is so satisfying – you're relying on touch and feel to make it. And it changes day by day.'

I'd never thought of it like that. I'd never taken the time to think about it at all, to be honest. The closest I've ever come to making pasta up until now has been watching Jamie Oliver from the comfort of my sofa, a glass of red in one hand, a bag of Kettle chips in the other.

'Now you have to knead the dough until it's smooth and forms one piece. Push it out with both hands and turn it over on itself – that's right. You need it to get round and smooth and slightly shiny.'

I attack the dough vigorously, eager now to see it take shape. She laughs as she watches. 'Don't pummel the life out of it, Frankie. Enjoy the process.'

'Sorry,' I mutter.

'That's OK. It's not like pastry – you can't overwork it – but treat it with some TLC all the same. This part takes time. Once you're done we'll cut the dough in half to make two balls and let it sit for an hour or so, covered with a dry tea-towel or clingfilm.'

'Why?'

'It'll be tired after all that kneading and it'll need to rest. And so will you,' she replies. 'Once it's ready we'll use the machine to cut it. Keep going, just a little longer.'

I don't want to admit it, but I'm pretty tired already. My arms ache, and so do my shoulders. Making pasta is tough work.

'You're doing great,' Anita encourages me.

I wipe some flour from my nose and redouble my efforts, frowning, my tongue creeping out of my mouth as it always does when I really concentrate.

'You look just like Aimee,' Anita says, her voice wistful, as if she's almost forgotten I'm there. 'She always did that tongue thing when she was concentrating.'

I hold my breath. Maybe she will confide in me. After all, this is the first time she's mentioned Aimee.

'Who's Aimee?' I ask tentatively, feeling like a complete traitor again. I have to pretend I don't know who she is – I can't muck this up.

'My daughter,' she replies, so softly I have to strain to hear. 'She died last year. She was the love of my life.'

'I'm so sorry, Anita,' I say. I don't know how to comfort her, whether or not to hug her, but I want her to know how much I can feel her pain. She hides it well most of the time, but I can see it clearly now, etched all over her face, and my heart aches for her.

'Thank you,' she whispers, her eyes filling with tears before she wipes them away roughly with her apron. 'She loved to make pasta – I taught her how to do it when she was a little girl. She made the best dough – she had magic fingers, I used to tell her.'

'She must have inherited them from you.'

Anita inhales sharply. 'That's what she used to say. Every single time.'

'Did she?'

'Yes. And then she'd say that if she had to inherit something she was glad it was my magic fingers and not my massive butt!'

We both burst into laughter together.

'She sounds so funny,' I say.

'She was. She really was.' Her face is sombre now, the laughter gone. She takes a deep breath and shakes her head a little, as if to bat away the painful memories. 'Now, you're almost finished. Well done. Let's have a glass of wine to celebrate. We deserve it.'

She reaches above my head and takes down two large glasses, and I know that this part of our conversation is over

– she has no intention of telling me any more about Aimee: the subject is far too painful.

'This is really good!' John enthuses, forking some pasta into his mouth.

'Isn't it?' Anita beams at me, and I smile back. 'Frankie has Italian hands.'

'I don't know about that,' I say, blushing. Secretly, though, I'm pretty amazed that the dish has turned out so well. After we'd let it rest we'd fed it through the pasta machine, and then I'd watched in amazement as it had turned out perfectly. I'm not saying I could do it again, not without Anita to guide me, but I know I want to try.

'Do you eat much Italian food, back in Ireland?' she asks, heaping some more pasta on to her plate and smothering it with fresh Parmesan.

'A bit,' I reply, thinking of the exclusive Italian restaurant on the coast that Gary likes to take me to. But their food, although good, is nothing like this. In Cruzo's they serve rare truffles and charge an arm and a leg for them. They don't serve steaming buckets of pasta with creamy sauce, or red wine in a stone jug, like here.

'The wine is delicious,' I murmur.

'I'm glad you like it,' Anita says, pouring more into my glass. 'It's from a vineyard in Napa, owned by the Neiland family. We've been getting our wine from them for years now, haven't we, John?'

'For as long as I can remember,' John replies. 'I'm going up there tomorrow, actually, to collect some stock.'

'Isn't Roberto coming down?' she asks.

'No, he called me yesterday – there's a problem with his truck so it's off the road again.'

'Honestly, that damn truck, they need to get it put down.'

Anita rolls her eyes. 'Anyway, Napa is so beautiful, Frankie, you'll have to visit before you go home. When do you think that'll be?'

Two pairs of eyes are suddenly on me.

'In a couple of days,' I say, feeling a sudden pang when I think about leaving. Silly, really. I have my life to get back to, after all – I can't stay over here for ever. In fact, I'm supposed to be at home already but I got Helen to change my departure date so I could spend more time with Ian – there was no way I was going back until I'd pinned down the contract. It cost extra, of course – more money down the drain if this doesn't work.

'So soon? Oh, no, you won't have time to go to Napa, will you? That's such a shame.' Anita sounds disappointed.

'Maybe not,' I reply, smiling at her. 'Next time.'

'Unless . . .' Anita's face lights up.

'Mom . . .' John's voice is warning.

'Let's go with John tomorrow, Frankie. It'll be such fun!' she exclaims, her eyes bright.

I look from her to John, flabbergasted. How do I deal with this invitation? 'I'm not sure I have time, Anita . . .'

'Oh, come on! Make the time – live a little!'

'It would be a good opportunity to see the Valley,' John says slowly. 'If you'd like to?'

There it is – that look. The look we shared earlier.

'We can take a picnic.' Anita's off. 'Some bread, olives, pesto – let me make a list.' With that, she takes off at speed, muttering to herself about food.

'Please don't feel you have to, Frankie,' John says, as we watch her retreating back. 'I don't want you to feel obliged to go.'

'Your mother seems to really like the idea,' I say, for some reason not wanting to meet his eyes properly. Why do I feel so stupidly shy all of a sudden? It's ridiculous.

'Well, she does love Napa but this is the first time she's wanted to go there in over a year.' He shakes his head in wonder. 'I can't quite believe it, actually.'

The unspoken hangs between us: this is the first time she's wanted to go there since Aimee died. How can I refuse Anita, knowing this? She's been so welcoming and kind to me. If a day in Napa is what she wants, if it goes any way to help heal the pain in her heart, then that's what I'll give her. It might take her mind off the dark thoughts I know she's been having. And it'll definitely make me feel better about the spying I've done.

And you could spend more time with John.

Why am I thinking like that? It's crazy. There's nothing between me and John. And yet the idea of being in his company again makes me feel warm inside. 'Well, let's go, then,' I find myself saying.

'Really?'

Am I imagining it or have his eyes lit up a little?

'Yes. Really. But there's someone else I need to invite as well. Is that OK?'

'Of course,' he replies. 'We have plenty of room.'

'OK, I'm in,' I say. 'Napa, here we come.' And then we're standing grinning at each other and, no matter how hard I try, I can't wipe the smile off my face.

Chapter Twenty-three

'Thanks for inviting me, Frankie.' Rosie squeezes my hand as we sit in the back seat of John's car on the way to Napa.

'Well, I had to – I knew my life wouldn't be worth living if I didn't,' I joke.

'You got that right.' She punches my arm and I barely wince. I must be getting used to it.

'So, you two girls met on the flight over here from Dublin?' Anita, in the front seat, twists to face us.

'We sure did!' Rosie confirms enthusiastically. 'Frankie didn't want me to sit beside her at first, but I wheedled my way in there.'

'That's not true!' I protest.

'Oh, sure it is, girl. You thought I was one fat American tourist sent to torture you – you was cuter than a box full of puppies.'

Oh, my God. She'd known all along. 'I did not think that, Rosie,' I reply, but I can't stop my cheeks reddening under her gaze.

'Ah, she's blushing!' Anita cheers.

'I knew exactly what she was thinking, Anita, but she came round to me in the end. She couldn't resist the Rosie love! Isn't that right, girlfriend?'

Anita and John burst into laughter.

'Oh, ha-ha!' I mutter. 'What is this? Make Fun of the Irish Girl Day?'

'Ah, honey, I'm just joshing. You know I love ya really!' She grins.

'Frankie told me you live on a houseboat, Rosie,' Anita says. 'How amazing!'

'Yeah, I love it. You're very welcome to stop by and visit any time,' Rosie replies warmly.

'I'd like to,' Anita says. 'Sausalito is one of the most gorgeous spots on this earth. When John's dad and I were dating we'd take the ferry across there all the time and picnic by the water . . .'

'I didn't know that, Mom,' John pipes up, his eyes darting to her for a second.

'There's a lot you don't know about me, son!'

'Ooooh . . . a woman of mystery!' Rosie calls.

'I have my secrets,' Anita says loftily.

'Let me guess . . . Hey, don't tell me you were a hippie back in the sixties!'

'Now, that'd be telling.' Anita laughs.

'And you ain't gonna?' Rosie giggles.

'Mom was never a hippie,' John says confidently. 'If she was I would have heard all about it by now. Now, Frankie, hold on to your hat, we're coming up to the Golden Gate Bridge.'

Our eyes meet in the rear-view mirror and I find myself grinning goofily at him, like a starstruck teenager. He looks incredibly handsome today, in a denim shirt rolled up to the elbows, and I'm finding it harder and harder to take my eyes off him or to ignore how I feel every time I'm in his company. Gary and all the crazy subterfuge involved in getting Ian on board seem like a million miles and another lifetime away.

'Oh, isn't it just gorgeous?' Rosie breathes, as the enormous red structure looms into view. 'It doesn't matter how often I see it, it's still magical up close.'

She's right. I've already seen the bridge from a few different angles, the ferries to Sausalito and Alcatraz, and from Crissy Field too, but actually driving over it is sensational, like stepping into history almost.

'It's breathtaking,' I gasp, as John whizzes through the toll-booth and I look out through the red railings to the water beyond, the enormous suspension bridge soaring high above us.

'Isn't it?' he calls back, catching my eye in the rear-view mirror again. 'I never get tired of it.'

'John knows all about the bridge,' Anita says proudly. 'He did a project on it in the third grade and got a special blue ribbon.'

'Mom!' he yelps, mortified. 'Do you have to tell them all my embarrassing secrets?'

'What, honey? You did! I was so proud of you, my little pumpkin.' Anita turns and winks at us. 'He was *so* cute. His hair had this little cow lick – I could never get it to sit straight.'

'OK, so now it's Make Fun of the Only Male in the Vehicle Day, is that it?' John says drily, keeping his eyes on the road straight ahead.

'Oh, come on, sweetie, you were adorable. I still remember when he won that ribbon, girls – he was so happy! Of course, he totally deserved it – the project was amazing, the details he had in there about the bridge. He spent weeks poring over his encyclopedias, didn't you, honey?'

'Tell us about the bridge, John,' Rosie begs. 'Please!'

'Nuh-huh, no way.' He shakes his head.

'Oh, pretty please with a cherry on top,' Rosie wheedles. 'For Frankie? She is a tourist, after all.'

John glances at me again so I widen my eyes and pout for effect. 'Oh, for goodness' sake . . . all right.' He sighs.

'Excellent!' Rosie claps while Anita and I cheer.

John takes a deep breath. 'OK. So, back in the day, there

were lots of people who wanted a bridge to connect San Francisco to Marin County. San Francisco was the largest city in the United States still mainly served by ferries, and it was thought that its growth rate was below average because it didn't have a permanent link with other communities around the bay.'

'But the experts said that a bridge wouldn't work, right, John?' Anita interrupts.

'Yes, Mom, that's what I recall from my third-grade project.'

'Which was a masterpiece! Did I mention that?' Anita adds, grinning widely at Rosie and me.

'Thank you. So, where was I? OK . . . There were lots of people who said that a bridge couldn't be built across the strait because of the strong tides and treacherous currents – and there were the winds and blinding fogs.'

'Didn't it all get very political too, honey?' Anita asks.

'It sure did. Everyone had to put in their opinion. The navy was fearful that an accident or even attempted sabotage could hamper access to one of its main harbours and the Department of War was worried that a bridge would inter-fere with ship traffic. The Southern Pacific Railroad didn't want it to go ahead because it would have been direct com-petition to its ferry fleet and, meanwhile, the unions demanded that local workers get the construction jobs. It was a complete mess.'

'It's a wonder the dang thing ever got built!' Rosie says.

'You're right,' John agrees. 'I don't know how they all came to some sort of agreement but I do know that work finally began on January 5th, 1933. A guy called Strauss was chief engineer but he wasn't very experienced with the proposed cable-suspension model so his design wasn't accepted.'

'What happened then?' Anita prompts him.

'Well, other experts took responsibility for a lot of the engineering and architecture and a man called Leon Moisseiff came up with the final design. It works here, thankfully, but another bridge he designed later using the same principle actually collapsed in a strong wind soon after it was completed.'

'Em, should I be nervous?' I pipe up from the back.

'Don't worry, the Golden Gate is perfectly safe, Frankie.' Anita reassures me. 'John, don't scare them, for goodness' sake!'

'Sorry, ladies.' He grins. 'That was probably too much information.'

'So what happened to the other guy, Strauss?' Rosie asks.

'Well, he remained head of the project and he oversaw the construction – there's even a brick from his college, the University of Cincinnati, in there somewhere.'

'I never knew that,' Anita says.

'You mustn't have read my project all the way through, Mom,' John jokes, and she slaps his arm affectionately. 'Another thing I remember about Strauss, though, was that he insisted on safety netting. That made a big impression on me when I was back in third grade.'

'I can't imagine working so far up in the sky.' Rosie shudders. 'It's a long way to fall. Heights scare me sideways – up there I'd be as nervous as a long-tailed cat in a room full of rocking-chairs!'

'I wouldn't blame you, Rosie,' John says, after we've all stopped giggling at Rosie's Southern expression. 'Quite a few workers died while the bridge was being built but the netting saved many men's lives – they used to call themselves members of the Halfway to Hell Club.'

'Honey, you are just incredible at remembering all that detail!' Anita marvels.

'I love the red colour,' I say, gazing out at the bridge.

'Aha! It's not red, though,' John says.

'It's not?' I ask.

'No, the colour is actually called international orange.'

'It was originally used as a sealant for the bridge, wasn't it?' Anita says.

'Yep. It should really be silver or grey but the locals loved the orange and it's been like that ever since. Actually, the Navy wanted it to be painted with black and yellow stripes to make sure passing ships would see it.'

'Can you imagine?' Rosie calls. 'A bumble-bee bridge!'

'Tell us about when the bridge was opened, John,' Anita instructs him.

'I can't remember that part,' he says, his eyes twinkling, clearly teasing.

'Oh yes you can,' Anita chides. 'Now hurry up!'

'OK, OK! Let me think. It was finished by April 1937, I think, about one point three million dollars under budget, which was pretty neat for such a massive project. The day before vehicle traffic was allowed to cross, they say about two hundred thousand people walked or roller-skated over.'

'I sure would have loved to be there!' Rosie says.

'Me too,' Anita agrees. 'Wasn't there some sort of song or poem, honey?'

'Yes, Mom. A song, "There's a Silver Moon on the Golden Gate", was chosen to commemorate the event and Strauss wrote a poem called "The Mighty Task is Done".'

'Ah, yes, I remember now,' Anita says. 'I must have heard about it during the fiftieth-anniversary celebration.' She turns to us. 'They closed the bridge to traffic again and allowed only pedestrians to cross in celebration, just like they had in 1937.'

'Except this time close to a million people arrived,' John says.

'That's right,' Anita goers on. 'There were real problems with crowd control and the bridge got congested – it couldn't take the weight.'

'What happened?' I ask, not sure I want to hear the answer – at least, not until we reach the other side.

'Well, the centre span of the bridge flattened out under the weight,' Anita says.

'Oh, Lordy!' Rosie says. 'Was anyone hurt?'

'No, thankfully,' Anita replies. 'The bridge is designed specially to flex that way under heavy loads.'

We're speeding along the highway now, the scenery passing in a blur, and before I know it we're driving through a pair of beautiful wrought-iron gates and pulling to a stop outside a low stone ranch, with a porch wrapped round it.

'Oh, wow!' Rosie squeals, as we all clamber from the car. 'This is amazing!'

'Isn't it?' Anita smiles, shielding her eyes from the midday sun. 'It's been run by the Neiland family for generations. Here comes Roberto now.'

A small man, his skin a deep copper, is approaching. 'Anita! What a lovely surprise – I'm so glad you came!' he says, as he draws near.

'Well, I had to,' Anita teases. 'Your damn truck is off the road again.'

He hugs her warmly, his face creasing into a million wrinkles as he grins. 'No, it's not. I only said that to lure you up here.'

'You're such an old flirt!' She giggles girlishly, and I sense the chemistry between them.

'Less of the old,' he retorts, pulling a face, although he must be seventy if he's a day. 'Now, who are these lovely ladies?' he asks, still beaming.

'This is Francesca,' Anita introduces me, 'and this is Rosie. They're friends of ours.'

'I'm Roberto Neiland.' He shakes our hands, then claps John on the back. 'And any friend of Anita's is a friend of mine. Come on, follow me and I'll show you around.'

He links arms with Anita and they amble off together, chattering happily. Rosie, John and I start after them.

'Well, aren't they like two peas in a comfy pod?' Rosie whistles.

'Roberto's always had a thing for Mom,' John explains.

'He sure is sweet on her,' Rosie says. 'And I get a feeling it's mutual.'

'I'm not sure about that,' John replies. 'Mom hasn't dated anyone since Dad died when we were kids. Not that Roberto hasn't tried.'

'Maybe she needs a little encouragement,' Rosie suggests.

'Rosie, maybe we should just leave them to it,' I say. I know what encouragement Rosie is planning and it entails sticking her nose in where it's probably not wanted.

Rosie turns to me, a misty, faraway look in her eyes. 'Anita and Roberto could be destined to be together, Frankie. They just haven't realized it yet.'

'Pah,' I grunt. 'That's a load of baloney.'

'How can you say that?' Rosie is appalled.

'Because all that "destiny" stuff is dreamed up by greeting-card manufacturers to make profits,' I say. 'And I don't buy into that crap.'

'Wash your mouth out, Francesca Rowley!' Rosie gasps. 'John – you believe in Fate, don't you?'

'I'm keeping out of this.' John laughs.

'You can't,' Rosie argues. 'You either believe in Fate or you don't, so which is it?' Her hands are on her hips now, her feet planted squarely on the ground.

'OK, OK. I believe in Fate. There – are you happy now?' He smiles at her and she beams back at him, mollified.

'You're a sensible boy!'

'You bullied him into it,' I mutter.

'I did not,' she crows. 'John knows what's what – and you will too.'

'What does that mean?' Sometimes Rosie makes no sense whatsoever.

'It means, honey, that you might not believe in Fate, but that doesn't mean Fate won't believe in you!'

'That's straight from a Hallmark card, isn't it?' I say.

Rosie looks offended. 'No, it is *not*! It's straight from my heart.' She pouts.

'Oh, for God's sake, come on,' I reply. 'I need a drink.'

I feel Rosie's and John's eyes on me as I march away towards the vineyard and, hopefully, a nice glass of red. We're here to look round, see how a proper vineyard works, not get into a far-fetched discussion about Fate and what's meant to be or not meant to be. That sort of conversation is for the pages of romance novels. It has no place in real life – and thinking any other way can only lead to trouble.

I try to convince myself of this as I walk towards the house, my heart pounding. But the terrifying truth is that I'm starting to think that something has led me here, something that no amount of rational reasoning can explain. And the thought scares me to pieces.

Chapter Twenty-four

'So y'all don't press the grapes with your feet?' Rosie asks, disappointment all over her freckled face.

'Not any more,' Roberto replies, his green eyes twinkling at her. 'It's all machines these days. Sorry.'

'Darn it! I'd imagined everyone squishing round in a great big vat of mush.'

'Well, we could organize it for you, if you really wanted to try,' Roberto says.

'Nah, checking out my size elevens would turn everyone off this delicious tasting.' She wriggles her toes at us. 'It'd be safer for me to keep 'em under wraps.'

'This is delicious,' I say, taking another sip of the red wine that Roberto has poured for us.

We're sitting under the shade of a large leafy tree in the cobbled courtyard, after a tour of the winery and the cellars. It's an impressive production, especially for a small, family-run operation.

'I'm glad you like it, Francesca,' Roberto replies, darting a look at Anita as she takes a sip, as if to check her reaction.

'Is this a new cuvée?' she asks, seemingly surprised. 'I don't think I've tried it before.'

'What's a cuvée?' Rosie whispers to John, who's reclining in a wicker seat beside her.

'It means a blend – most wines are a mixture of a few grapes,' he explains.

'It is new,' Roberto says. 'We've been working on it for a while now. You like it, Anita?'

'Very much. What are you calling it?'

'I have something in mind but I'm not sure yet. I have to think some more.'

'It's very good,' John says approvingly, sniffing and then swirling the wine round his glass like I've seen professionals do on TV. 'Are you in production with this yet? I think it would work well in the restaurant.'

'Not yet.' Roberto shakes his head. 'But soon.'

'Stop playing hard to get, Roberto!' Anita chides him and he takes her hand in his, stroking it gently.

'You, *bella*, are the only one playing hard to get,' he says.

She slaps his hand away, blushing. 'You're incorrigible.'

'When it comes to you, yes, I am,' he replies softly, and I see the adoration on his lined face.

'Honestly, Rosie, talk to him, will you?' Anita pleads.

'I'm sorry, Anita, but it's the cutest thing.' Rosie sighs, and I know she's thinking about Fate again. How these two are destined to be together and all that pie-in-the-sky stuff.

'See?' Roberto raises one shaggy eyebrow at Anita. 'Rosie thinks I'm cute.'

'Rosie is far too polite to tell you what she really thinks.' Anita laughs. 'Which is that you're a silly old man.'

'You make me feel silly, I can't deny it.' He beats his breast theatrically.

'Oh, Lordy, I wish a man would talk about me like that,' Rosie says. 'Just once.'

'I've been devoted to this woman for twenty years, Rosie,' Roberto says to us. 'Twenty years of unrequited love! Can you believe it?'

Can she believe it? *I* can't believe it! Twenty years of unrequited passion? That's devotion.

'And all this time . . .' Rosie looks to Anita, who's pretending to be busy examining her wine so she won't have to be involved in the discussion.

'. . . she has rebuffed me,' he confirms sadly. 'I'm doomed to die of a broken heart.'

'Oh, stop being so dramatic, Roberto,' Anita says. 'Honestly!'

'Rosie, Frankie,' he implores us, 'do *you* think I'm being dramatic?'

'*I* don't!' Rosie replies firmly, before I can answer. 'Now tell us more – where did you first meet?'

'She appeared here like a vision one summer's day,' he begins. 'I'll never forget it.'

'I came on business,' Anita interjects firmly. 'A friend had recommended the winery, and I wanted to check it out for myself.'

'I remember the second she walked through the door – my world stopped spinning.' Roberto sighs.

'Oh, for goodness' sake.' Anita giggles, her cheeks pink again. 'Don't listen to him!'

'It's true!' Roberto protests. 'But she didn't notice me.'

'Please take all this with a grain of salt, ladies,' Anita insists. 'Roberto likes to spin a yarn – he always has.'

'It's no yarn,' he answers. 'This is a true story! Anita broke my heart a million times over, never even giving me a second look. But still I wait. I will wait until the end of time.'

'Don't give up, Roberto,' John tells him. 'I think you may finally be getting to her.'

'He is not!' Anita says. 'Besides, this is all nonsense and I'm far too busy to be doing with any of it.'

'Too busy for love?' Roberto holds his hands aloft.

'Yes,' Anita replies.

'It's impossible, John,' Roberto says sadly. 'Your mother has no time for me – she never will.'

'Never say never, my friend,' John replies, pouring him another glass of wine.

'Yes, Roberto, don't give up,' Rosie says. 'If it's meant to be it will be.'

Roberto shoots Anita a look, as if contemplating whether or not to continue in this vein, then seems to decide against it. 'Let's change the subject,' he says. 'So, how is business at the best restaurant in the city?'

'Not bad,' John replies. 'We're not going to make a million bucks any time soon, but we're ticking over.'

'More than ticking over from what I hear,' Rosie comments. 'Frankie says it's the place to go.'

'There was a line down the street when I was there,' I confirm, nodding at her. 'People were queuing round the block.'

'You'll have to come for dinner soon, Rosie,' Anita says. 'And we won't make you wait in line – we'll give you a special table.'

'That sounds great – I'd love to!' Rosie is thrilled with this invitation, I can tell.

'It's all about who you know,' Anita goes on, smiling at her. 'We gave Frankie a nice spot in the courtyard, didn't we, John? Because she knew Connor?'

'Who's Connor?' Rosie looks at me, her eyes questioning, and I cringe inside. Damn, I was hoping Anita would forget about that connection.

'He's the reason Frankie came to see us in the first place,' Anita replies. 'She grew up on Inis Mór with a guy who waited tables for us one summer. He was a rogue – a lovable rogue, I should say.'

'What's Inis Mór?' Roberto asks Anita, sipping his wine.

'It's an island off the west coast of Ireland,' she replies. 'They speak Gaelic there. Frankie's first language isn't even English – isn't that amazing?'

'Amazing!' Roberto agrees, and I feel Rosie's eyes on me. I'll have to explain it to her later – honestly, this is all getting so complicated it's making my head spin.

'So, Anita,' Roberto is swirling the wine in his glass and watches her carefully, 'have you thought any more about the cookbook?'

A shadow passes over Anita's face as I heave a sigh of relief inside. Thankfully, the subject has been changed and I can forget about the Aran Islands. 'What cookbook?' I ask, anxious to ensure that talk steers away from Connor, the lovable rogue I supposedly grew up with.

'I've been trying to persuade Anita to write a cookbook for years,' Roberto says. 'It's just one more thing she ignores.'

'I do not ignore you,' Anita huffs, frowning.

'Yes, you do!' he replies. 'A Carlo's cookbook would be fantastic! People would queue up to learn more about your recipes, Anita, you know it!'

'Just like they queue up round the block to taste her food,' I say.

'Exactly!' he replies. 'I'm glad someone is on my wavelength.'

'Frankie is a literary agent,' John explains, 'so she knows about these things.'

He smiles at me and my heart expands a little. Crap. I like him. It hits me like a bolt from the blue. I like him a lot.

'A literary agent? Wow! Do you know anyone famous?' Roberto asks.

'Her clients are mostly Irish,' Anita says. 'You wouldn't know them. Isn't that right, Frankie?'

'Actually,' I start, 'I do know a few famous people.'

'You do?' Anita turns to me, surprise on her face.

'Well, yes. They're not clients, of course, but I have met some stars over the years.' Shut up, Frankie – why are you doing this? You don't need to prove yourself to anyone. Then I feel John looking at me with interest and I stupidly decide to press on. Why? Who am I trying to impress? With a start I realize it's *him*.

'Like who, Frankie?' Roberto is in like lightning.

'Oh, yes, do tell us, Frankie!' Anita claps her hands happily.

'Well, J. K. Rowling, for one,' I say.

Jesus. I do not know J. K. Rowling. I wish I did, but I *so* don't. What the hell am I saying?

'Oh, my *goodness*!' Rosie gasps. 'The Harry Potter woman? You never said a word! How do you know *her*?'

'Oh, well,' I reply vaguely, feeling bad that I'm lying to Rosie, 'we've met at literary events, that sort of thing . . .'

That part is sort of true. I have seen her in the flesh, across a crowded publishing event. OK, so we were never actually introduced as such – she was surrounded by hordes of people – but I did get a glimpse of her shoulder. And a lovely toned shoulder it was too. Besides, Gary has met her so that's like one degree of separation. Thinking about it now, I 'almost know' loads of celebrities through Gary. He knows everyone.

'What's she like in real life?' Anita clamours. 'Is she all mysterious?'

'She's lovely,' I say. 'Very . . . down to earth.'

'Wow!' Anita exclaims. 'Imagine being so hugely successful and still down to earth . . .'

'Who else do you know?' Roberto asks excitedly, leaning in to me.

'Em. David Nicholls. You know, *One Day*?' Christ Almighty. What did I have to go and say *that* for?

'You do not know him,' he says.

He's right, of course. I don't. But Gary does. Therefore so do I. Sort of. 'Yep, he's very nice,' I lie, my mouth still running away with me. 'But of course Dan Brown is one of my absolute favourites.'

'You know Dan Brown?' John is incredulous.

'Oh, yes.' I smile serenely at him. 'Dan and I go way back.' *Liar, liar, pants on fire.*

'That's amazing, Frankie,' Anita says. 'We had no idea you were so well connected.'

I shrug humbly, as if I'm indifferent to it all. But really I'm kicking myself – what the hell has come over me, making up stuff like this and stupidly trying to impress John? I need to get a grip. And I definitely need to get everyone talking about something else.

'It must be such an interesting job,' Roberto adds.

'Yes, it is,' I reply. *More interesting than usual, these days, for sure.* 'Now tell us more about this cookbook idea, Roberto,' I say, keen to get everyone's attention off me. 'It sounds fantastic.'

Roberto shoots Anita a look, as if trying to gauge whether or not he should proceed before he speaks. 'Well, people are always asking Anita for her recipes, right?'

'That *is* true, Mom,' John agrees, as Anita rolls her eyes.

'So, I think she should publish a book of her favourites – it would be a bestseller.'

'And a fantastic advertisement for the restaurant too,' I muse. It's actually a great idea.

'I don't want to give people my recipes,' Anita says firmly. 'They're family secrets – they've been passed on from generation to generation.'

'Well, you don't have to give them everything, Anita,' Roberto goes on. 'You could just do a selection. Keep your favourites for your eyes only.'

'That might work, Mom,' John says, turning to his mother.

'No,' Anita replies. She's firm about it.

'But, like Frankie says, it would be great advertising,' John says.

'We don't need advertising. Word of mouth has got us where we are today and it will keep us going.'

'But, Mom, you're not getting any younger . . .'

'Thank you very much for reminding me of that, son.' Her eyes are suddenly like flint.

'What I mean is, this book could be your retirement fund. It makes sense,' he says.

'It would be your legacy,' Roberto puts in. 'People know good food. And Anita and her family make good food. They always have.' He turns to Rosie and me, almost looking for our agreement.

'I'm not doing it. You can't persuade me,' Anita says stubbornly.

'I think it's a peachy idea,' Rosie says. 'Maybe you should reconsider, Anita.'

Anita shakes her head vehemently. 'Nope. Never gonna happen. Now, let's move on.'

'But, everyone would love it!' Roberto isn't giving up. 'Your secret-recipe tomato sauce alone . . .'

Suddenly there's a tense silence. Anita's face is white. 'Excuse me.' She pushes her chair away from the table and takes off, not saying another word.

'I'm such a putz!' Roberto groans, putting his head in his hands as Anita disappears around the corner.

'What is it?' Rosie asks, confused. 'Why is Anita so upset?'

'That was a sauce my sister Aimee loved,' John explains. 'Mom hasn't made it since she died last year – it's been off the menu.'

'And I had to bring it up,' Roberto moans. 'I'm sorry, John.' His eyes are miserable when he raises his head.

'It's OK,' John says. 'You didn't mean any harm, I know

that. Besides, it was good – we should have it back. The customers loved it – they're constantly asking for it. But I guess Mom just can't face it.'

'She's finding it very hard,' Roberto observes despondently.

John looks at me. Only we two know how hard she's really finding it. 'She's struggling, yes. And now the anniversary is bringing it all back.'

'Anniversaries are the worst,' Rosie says quietly. 'Especially the first few.'

'Shall I go after her?' Roberto says, his face ashen.

'No, I'll go.' Rosie is up. 'I'll talk to her.' She goes after Anita and suddenly Roberto, too, is on his feet.

'Excuse me,' he says hoarsely. 'I have to check on something . . .' He dashes in the other direction, but not before I spot that his eyes are filled with tears.

John and I look at each other. What had been a wonderful day has turned into a disaster.

'Poor guy. He'll beat himself up about this for sure.'

'Yeah.' I watch his retreating back. 'He seems to care about your mother a lot.'

'He really does,' John replies. 'He wasn't kidding about all that stuff – he adores her. He'd do anything for her.'

'But she doesn't feel the same way?' I ask, not sure if I'm prying too much.

'Oh, she does,' he says, his eyes resting on mine, 'but she'll never do anything about it.'

'Why not?' I stare back at him. His irises are the exact colour of chocolate. I hadn't noticed that before.

'Because she'll always stay loyal to my father,' John says. 'She thinks starting another relationship would be some sort of betrayal.'

'Even though it's been . . .'

'So long? Yes. That's the way her mind works. She won't budge, no matter what we say. Even Aimee tried to talk her round.'

From the little I know of Aimee I can imagine her sticking her oar in – she wasn't one to keep quiet when something was on her mind apparently.

'She did?'

'Oh, yeah. They had a big argument about it the week before she died. Aimee told Mom to stop being such a stubborn ass and marry Roberto.'

I stifle a giggle – what a way with words! 'And what did Anita say?'

'She told Aimee to butt out. Then Aimee said she'd be butting out permanently soon enough.'

'Yikes. I bet that went down like a lead balloon.'

'It did. But Aimee was determined not to shy away from the reality of the situation, even if the rest of us weren't.'

'She sounds so strong,' I murmur.

'She really was. She had her dark days, like when she found out there was no more that could be done. But she just got on with it. I can't believe it's been a year – it's insane . . .'

My bag beeps and we jump. Even before I fish out my phone I know it's a text from Anita. *No one understands how much I miss you my darling. How can they?*

I pass it to John. 'What can we do to help her?' I say, feeling truly awful. Poor Anita is in pieces.

'I'm not sure,' he replies. 'She's stuck and she can't move forward.'

'But she'll have to?' I ask, already knowing the answer.

'Yes.' His voice is weary. 'Sooner or later, she'll have to face the truth – that Aimee is gone and she's not coming back.'

'And what about the other text?' I can barely force myself

to bring it up, but the text Anita wrote about seeing Aimee soon still weighs heavily on my mind.

'I don't think she meant it,' John says, as if he can't get to grips with the idea that his mother might be harbouring suicidal thoughts. 'She couldn't have.'

But I can tell by the expression on his face that even he's not sure if he quite believes this. And the trouble is, neither do I.

Chapter Twenty-five

'I can't believe we have Ian Cartwright as a client!' Helen squeals down the line from Dublin. 'That is so cool!'

I'm sitting in the back of a cab on the way to Ian's house, his contract with the Rowley Agency safely tucked into my briefcase. Today he will make our working relationship official – we'll be a team. There are still formalities to conclude with Withers and Cole, who have no clue yet that he's defecting, and the biggest issue of all – the sequel – to deal with but I can look after that once Ian has signed on the dotted line with me. That's my game plan for now. Get him to sign, then worry about the rest later. It's not perfect, but at the moment it seems to be my only option. And at least it's heading in the right direction: this is a very significant step towards what Gary and I want. I have to keep reminding myself of that because for some reason I'm not as thrilled about it as I thought I would be. I should be over the moon – so why do I feel flat?

'Helen, you have to keep this to yourself, OK?' I remind her, as the cab whizzes down Eleventh Avenue, the cloying scent of the lemon air freshener swinging from the rear-view mirror making me feel sick. I'd take one of Rosie's little dancing leprechauns over that any day, I realize, with a little shock.

'I won't breathe a word, boss,' Helen says seriously. 'You don't have to tell me that.'

Of course I do – if I don't, who knows what she'll let slip? This is a small industry and word leaks out very quickly: the last thing I need is for it all to go pear-shaped at the final hour. As far as I know, Bruce Makin has no idea I'm poaching Ian – he's probably been busy dealing with April's other clients. But if he hears the chances are that he'll get the first flight over and try to outmanoeuvre me. There's no way I'm going to let that happen. Not now.

I haven't even confirmed all this with Gary yet – I want the contract signed, sealed and delivered before I do.

'OK. Anything else I need to know about?' I ask her.

'Well, you're not going to believe it but . . .'

My stomach clenches. What can it be? Has the landlord been round? Has Mr Morris turned up from the bank?

'. . . your old phone arrived here today.'

'My phone? How did *that* happen?' It was supposed to be delivered to my hotel – although it's been gone so long I was starting to lose hope it would ever turn up.

'I don't know,' Helen says. 'But Harriet says this sort of mix-up happens all the time.'

'Who's Harriet, Helen?' I interrupt her. She always does this – presumes I know everyone she's ever spoken to, however briefly.

'Oh, sorry. She's one of the girls who works in the airline's Lost and Found. She's such a sweetheart – her dog Scrappy was knocked down last week and the driver didn't even stop! Isn't that terrible? The poor girl has been through hell. I told her about the time that Snoopy was a puppy and got run over by a van. He was *so* lucky – he just had a few cuts and bruises – but poor Scrappy has two fractured legs. *Two!* Can you believe that?'

Helen has apparently forged a close enough relationship with an airline representative over the phone for them to have been sharing information about each other's dogs. Only she could do something like that. Not that I should be surprised. Helen is the type to befriend everyone – she's the only person I know who doesn't hang up on cold callers selling insurance. She and Harriet are probably already Facebook friends.

'So, my phone is?' I prompt her. I don't want to know any more about Harriet or her dog – I have enough to worry about.

'Sorry, yes. Your phone is here – it got sent back by mistake. It's on your desk right now.'

Finally. I'm finally getting it back. My whole life is on that phone. My old life anyway – it seems as if so much has happened since I lost it. It's like a lifetime ago.

'Is there anything else you need?' she goes on.

I'm just about to ask her how she managed to get Ivan Watters on TV when the taxi stops. There's no time for that now – I'm here.

'No, I'm fine,' I say. 'I'll talk to you soon.' Then I hang up and steel myself for one last push.

I hop from foot to foot as I ring Ian's bell, the pavement scorching beneath my feet. This must be a proper Indian summer, because, after a chilly start to the day, the sun is high in the sky and it's hotter than blue blazes, as Rosie would say. There's no sign of the little boy on the red bike I met the first time I was here – his mother is probably keeping him in the shade, safe from sunstroke or heat rash or any number of other deadly ailments I'm going to get if Ian doesn't open the damn door soon.

I try to keep calm as I wait for him to answer. I can't go in there like a bull in a china shop: I have to be cool and unruffled. Ian's already agreed to come with me – all I have to do is make it official. And when he agrees to a sequel I'll be in clover – I can negotiate TV and movie deals, get translations round the world . . .

The future of the Rowley Agency will be secure – I can hardly believe that the success I've always wanted is at my fingertips. And where Ian goes, others will follow, I'm sure. Former clients of April will probably flock to my door. I'll need to get more staff, bigger premises, that corner office . . . Part of me can hardly wait to get back to Dublin and set the wheels in motion. Yet I'll be strangely sad to leave this city too. For one thing, I'll miss Rosie, in a funny sort of way. I was so eager to get rid of her when we first met and yet now I'm . . . fond of her. And there's Anita: I've been tossing and turning all night thinking about her and the painful messages she's been sending to her daughter. How will I ever be able to forget her? And then there's John. My stomach flips when I think about him, but I push the feeling away. I have to stop thinking like this – none of it has anything to do with me, not really. I was caught up in it, and now the time has come to get back to reality. I have other clients to see, other deals to make. Yes, Helen has surprised me with her efficiency while I've been away, but the office needs me. My other clients need me. I can't stay in San Francisco for ever, even if the city has captured my imagination, just a little, and Aimee's story has got under my skin.

Another image of John's dark eyes pops into my head and I bat it away with force. Our meeting was just a coincidence, and the time has come for me to leave, get back to normality.

I'm wrapping this up today. No distractions, no time-wasting. Just results. I push back my shoulders and adjust my stance. I mean business. No more nice guy, no more excuses. All I have to do is get the contract signed and then I can get back to my real life. And it's not a moment too soon.

I balance the bottle of champagne I brought with me under my arm and ring the bell again. Ian would probably prefer some Kimberley biscuits, but champagne will have to do for today.

Where is he? Honestly, it's not like he doesn't know I'm coming. I peer through the gate for any sign of life and as I do so, it finally buzzes open. As I step through and look around, it seems that the garden's become even wilder since the last time I was here, if that's possible – it's like a mini jungle now.

The front door is on the latch and, as I step into the tiled hall, I get a whiff of something burning.

'Ian?' I call, retching on the acrid smell. What on earth is that stench?

'In here!' Ian calls from the kitchen.

He's at the stove, glaring balefully at a blackened pot, his face red and sweaty.

'What was that?' I ask, gesturing to the smoking pan. It's unrecognizable as anything even remotely edible.

'Lunch,' he replies. 'At least, it was supposed to be. It's ruined.'

'I think it might be,' I agree, peering into the pan. I still have no idea what it was originally and I'm not going to ask again in case he tries to persuade me it's safe to eat. I look around the kitchen, counters strewn with dirty plates and pots – it's a mess. Even worse than before.

Then, out of the corner of my eye, I see a battered cereal box move. Cereal boxes don't move of their own accord but this definitely is – and, worse, there's a rustling sound. As I watch, transfixed, I see a tiny furry grey head emerge from the top of the packet and I screech, suddenly beyond petrified.

'What's wrong?' Ian looks round, alarmed.

'There's a mouse. In there.' My hand shakes as I point to the cereal box. If there's one, there's bound to be more. There could be an entire mouse family shacked up in here, breeding squirmy pink babies under my feet as I speak. It's enough to make me want to run screaming out of the door as fast as my shaking legs can carry me. But Ian doesn't look in the least perturbed. In fact, he's smiling.

'Ah, that's just Shergar,' he says. 'He's harmless.' He goes back to poking the black mess with a fork.

'Excuse me?' Did he just call a rodent Shergar? The only Shergar I've ever heard of was a famous Irish racehorse that was stolen back in the 1980s and never recovered.

'He's harmless, honestly. He won't touch you.'

'You have a mouse as a pet?'

'He's not exactly a pet,' Ian corrects me. 'Not in the traditional sense of the word. We co-exist.'

'So he roams around as he pleases, is that what you mean?'

'Well, yeah.' Ian cocks his head to one side as if considering the ramifications of this for the first time.

'Don't you think that might be unhygienic, Ian?' My stomach is heaving at the thought.

'He leaves me alone, I leave him alone.' He shrugs. 'We've come to an understanding, you see.'

'You've come to an understanding with a mouse?' I have officially heard it all.

'Yes. Mice are very amiable creatures – they live and let live, I find. Shergar more than most.'

I watch as Shergar pokes his head out of the cereal box again, his little nose snuffling, as if he's deciding where to forage next. It's enough to make my skin crawl. 'Let me get this straight, instead of calling the exterminators or even setting a trap, you just let him be?'

'That about sums it up.' Ian nods.

'So he scurries round your kitchen, helping himself to whatever he likes, doing his poops wherever he wants, and you just work around him?'

'Well, he mostly sticks to cereal. And I don't like cereal.'

'Don't you care that his poops are probably everywhere?'

'They're called droppings,' he corrects me.

'Ian, this is possibly the most surreal conversation I've ever had,' I say. 'Putting the mouse aside for a second, which I am loath to do, you really need to get some help, because if this lot doesn't get washed up soon you won't have a plate to eat off.' The words tumble out of my mouth before I can stop them. I've tiptoed round his slovenly ways since we first met – but, honestly, it's gone far enough.

He looks around the kitchen, as if he's seeing the chaos for the first time. 'You might have a point. I suppose it's sort of built up – I'm a bit hopeless at this sort of thing,' he says helplessly.

'That is putting it mildly, honey. A baby in a stroller could do a better job,' a voice behind us says, and I turn on my heel to see Rosie standing in the doorway, arms folded across her ample bosom.

'Rosie! What are *you* doing here?' I say.

'Teaching this poor fool about the computer, of course,' she replies, as if it's not the weirdest thing in the world that we're all here together. 'I'm a lady who keeps my promises. Although if he keeps on being so ornery I might just have to skedaddle.' She throws Ian, who is standing shamefaced by the sink, the burned pot in his hands, a knowing look.

'I may have expressed a morsel of . . . frustration with the process,' he says to me, by way of explanation.

'He called the computer a fucking fuckwit,' Rosie says sternly. But her eyes are twinkling.

'I did say sorry.' Ian bows his head, looking thoroughly ashamed of himself.

'And so you should!' she lectures. 'I do not tolerate cussing.'

'I know. And I'm afraid I've burned lunch,' he replies.

'I can see that,' Rosie replies. 'Lordy, Ian. What *was* that? It looks as ugly as homemade sin.'

'I was making a Spanish omelette but it went wrong.'

'You had the gas on too high, you silly man. And you're supposed to put it under the broiler at the end to cook the top.'

'The broiler?' Ian looks bewildered.

'Yes, the broiler.' Rosie points out the grill to him. 'Haven't you never used it before?'

'Um, I'm not sure . . .' Ian replies doubtfully.

'Oh, my gosh, you are dumber than a mule!'

'I'm sorry.' Ian is downcast. 'I have some bread – maybe we could toast it . . .'

I am not eating anything that's been prepared in this kitchen. No way.

'I don't know how you haven't starved,' Rosie remarks. 'Come on, let's go out for lunch instead.'

'Out?' Ian looks a little fearful.

'Yes, out!' Rosie replies. 'Where do you think, Frankie? The Cheesecake Factory?'

I can almost feel the contract in my briefcase, burning a hole through the leather. I don't want to go to the Cheesecake Factory - even if the idea of it makes my mouth water. I just want this contract signed.

'The Cheesecake Factory?' Ian sniffs disdainfully. 'I don't think so!'

'Oh, Ian, don't be such a snob!' Rosie chides.

'I'm not a snob. I just hate cheesecake,' he mutters. 'It gives me indigestion.'

'Well, what tickles your fancy, then?'

'Maybe pasta?'

'OK. Get your jacket and we'll decide where to go, OK?'

He toddles off obediently and her eyes narrow as she

thinks. 'Hey! I've just had a great idea!' she says excitedly.

'You have?' I ask.

'Yes! Let's go to Carlo's!'

My head jerks up of its own accord. '*What?*'

'Yeah! Ian would like pasta and I'd kill for a good pizza – it'd be perfect, don't ya think?'

Er, no, I don't think. 'It's all the way across the city, though,' I say. *And I really don't want to go there – not with Ian.*

'At least we know it's safe to eat there.' She looks round the kitchen, her nose wrinkling in distaste. 'And . . . wouldn't you like to see John again?'

As she says this, I feel a ridiculous flush creeping up my neck.

'Francesca, are you *blushing?*'

'No, I'm not!' I protest. 'I'm just warm, that's all. Isn't it hot today?' I pull at my collar.

'If you say so.' She laughs as if she doesn't believe me. 'Well, I think John is mighty fine – and you two would be just sweet together.'

'Rosie, there's nothing going on between us,' I say, feeling very sweaty now. The last time I blushed like this was when I was dumped halfway through the first slow set on the debs dance-floor. I was so hot I thought I'd spontaneously combust to 'Careless Whisper'.

'Not yet,' she says, giggling once more. 'There's nothing going on between you *yet*. "Listen to your heart", remember?'

'You don't honestly think that a fortune cookie can tell my future, do you?' I ask.

'Mine came true, didn't it? "Love lies round the corner," it said.'

At that instant Ian trundles in, an oatmeal linen jacket slung over his arm. 'So, have you decided?' he asks.

'Yes – we're going to Carlo's,' Rosie replies, smiling at me

277

as I register what she just said. She's fallen for Ian – that's what she means. I can't say I'm surprised – they're perfect for each other. Anyone can see that.

'Carlo's?' Ian perks up. 'Isn't that –'

'The little restaurant I told you about? Yes, it is!' I interrupt, trying to shut him up. Rosie can't find out that I've been reporting back to him about Aimee's story. She'd never understand.

His eyes widen a fraction and then he nods at me, as if he understands where I'm coming from. *Don't mention this in front of Rosie.*

'Oh, you've heard about it too?' Rosie says. 'Great! Anita said I could drop by any time – and this is the perfect opportunity.'

'And Anita is?' Ian asks, his eyes darting from me to Rosie now. He already knows exactly who Anita is, of course, but he's not letting on.

'She's the owner. It's the saddest thing – her daughter Aimee died last year and she's just devastated.' Rosie's eyes fill with tears.

'That's awful.' Ian looks at me again. 'But how do you know this, Rosie?'

'Oh, didn't Frankie tell you?' Rosie glances my way. 'She's become quite friendly with the family, haven't you, Frankie? In fact, we all went to Napa together yesterday – it was such fun!'

'Napa? No, Frankie didn't tell me that.' Ian raises one eyebrow at me. 'Well, how very interesting . . .'

'You mean you didn't tell Ian about the phone mix-up?' Rosie goes on.

'What phone?' Ian is all innocence now.

'Oh, wait till you hear!' Rosie exclaims. 'I'll tell you about it on the way there.'

They walk out of the kitchen together, leaving me and the

rustling cereal box alone. It takes me less than a second to decide to follow them. Ian may say that Shergar is harmless but I'm still not taking any chances. Besides, I have a far greater crisis on my hands now.

Chapter Twenty-six

We're sitting at a table in Carlo's courtyard and I'm wondering if the other customers can hear my heart pounding. All around me groups of people are sharing baskets of bread and plates of olives. There are fewer smooching couples here today, more families, chattering loudly, arguing happily over the lunch menu and bursting into gales of laughter. Everyone seems to be having a wonderful time – but I am living in fear that my two worlds are going to collide any second. This is a disaster: there's no way round it and no way out of it either by the look of things.

Opposite me, Ian is alight with glee – as if he can't quite believe that he wangled his way in here. He's looking round the courtyard with curiosity, drinking in every detail as if committing it to memory. Rosie, meanwhile, is on cloud nine and is so desperate to taste Anita's cooking that she can barely contain herself. She babbled about it all the way here and, after a quick glance at the menu, already knows what she wants to eat. Now she's off exploring the place, looking at every photo on the wall, examining the small mementoes dotted around. She's even got her camera out and is taking snaps, checking them on the digital screen, smiling with pleasure at those she likes, frowning at those she doesn't and retaking them.

I have about a minute to warn Ian before she's back. I have to talk to him, tell him not to give the game away. I can't really believe we've ended up here. If it hadn't been for Rosie we would never have come – there are hundreds of other restaurants in the city where we could have been right now. Hundreds of other places where no one knows me and I can't be exposed as the liar I know I am. If Anita or John appears I have no idea if I can rely on Ian not to grill them for information. It could all come out, the truth about the situation, something that doesn't even bear thinking about.

'So, can you introduce me to Aimee's mother?' Ian says, confirming my worst fears that he's going to pump everyone he can for information about Aimee to beef up his idea for a novel based on the aftermath of her death. Oh, God – how did I ever get into this?

'I don't think she's here today,' I say, crossing my fingers behind my back and fervently hoping that Anita doesn't come near us. Is there some way I can ensure that she stays in the kitchen? Short of locking the doors or drugging Ian so that he falls into a semi-conscious state, nothing springs to mind.

'I won't ask any awkward questions, I just want to say hello,' Ian says, as if trying to reassure me that I can trust him.

'Ian, please.' I take a deep breath, bracing myself for confrontation. 'I'm asking you just to forget about this story.'

He looks at me evenly. 'Why?'

I try to remain composed, even though my insides are fluttering wildly. 'If you had come to me with this idea last month, when I knew none of the people involved, I might have thought it was brilliant. But now that I know Anita and John, it's too complicated. It doesn't feel right. I feel like I'm . . . betraying them.' I realize as I say it that this is true. I've misled them, made them believe I'm something I'm not. I have betrayed them. Utterly.

'But you only know Anita and John because I encouraged

you to meet them,' he says, staring coldly at me. 'It was a means to an end, if you remember?'

When he puts it like that it sounds so horrible. But isn't he right? Isn't that exactly what it was – a means to an end? I agreed to meet John to keep Ian happy – get some more details of Aimee's story for him, persuade him to sign on the dotted line. And now I'm having second thoughts. I *am* a grade-A hypocrite.

'You thought John was a creep or a pervert, if I recall correctly. Now suddenly you feel so strongly about his sister and his mother that you're actually forbidding me to find out more?'

'I'm not forbidding you, Ian,' I say. 'I just think it would be best to leave this alone. Let's focus on some of your other ideas.'

'You didn't play me, did you, Francesca? String me along so I'd agree to sign with you?' His voice drips with ice.

'Of course not.' I swear I can feel the unsigned contract throbbing in the briefcase at my feet. Getting him to sign it today is now starting to look very unlikely unless I row back.

'Well, that's good. Because I will sign with you, like I said. But I'm writing this story. That's the deal.'

'But the family, Ian . . . You can't just pilfer people's lives like this,' I say, desperate now.

'Writers use real people and events as inspiration all the time,' he replies baldly.

'Yes, but this is different. This family is still mourning – it would be wrong.'

'Is there something you're not telling me, Francesca?' he asks.

'Like what?'

'I don't know. But you're extremely protective of Aimee and her family for some reason. You barely know them.'

This is true. Why do I feel so protective of this story? OK, so I want him to write a sequel, get me out of a financial hole and give Gary what he wants, but is that all there is to it? Or is there something else?

'I can't explain it,' I say. 'This just feels all wrong, especially knowing as much as I do about Anita's grief. She's hanging on by a thread, Ian. You can't manipulate her anguish like this.'

Something in his face changes, softens a little. 'You didn't tell me that.'

'What?'

'That the mother was . . . hanging on by a thread,' he says.

Anita's grief-stricken texts come back to me. 'Ian, her only daughter has died. Can't you imagine how she must feel? I'm sure it's not something you ever really get over.'

'That's why she's been sending those messages,' he says slowly.

'Yes. She's heartbroken, Ian.'

'I guess I never thought of it that way,' he says, frowning. 'About how she really felt. I was just thinking about the story.'

'Never thought about what?' Rosie asks, slipping back into her chair.

'Oh, nothing,' Ian replies quickly, glancing at me. 'Let's look at this menu.'

'I know what I want already – the pizza!' Rosie says decisively. 'It looks divine!' She gestures to a couple who are happily splitting a large pepperoni, digging in with greasy fingers and wide grins.

'Yes, that does look good,' Ian agrees. 'I can't remember the last time I had a proper pizza. It must be years.'

'You don't get out enough!' Rosie tuts. 'Are all writers like him, Frankie?'

'What do you mean?' I ask.

283

'Sorta reclusive?' she says.

'I'm *not* reclusive,' Ian says.

'Sure you are! You lock yourself away in that house of yours and barely come out. It's not healthy!'

'I do come out,' he grumbles. 'I went to Alcatraz, didn't I?'

I'm still finding it hard to believe that Rosie and Ian actually went to the Rock together, but they did. Ian can't say no to her any more than I can – she has some sort of magic touch. Now they're bickering like an old married couple – as if they've known each other all their lives.

'You're practically a recluse, honey, you know you are,' Rosie says, smiling benignly at him. 'You're locked away in that big house day after day. If you had any hair I'd call you Rapunzel.'

Ian's hand shoots defensively to his receding hairline – and an image of Gary preening himself in the antique mirror in my bedroom pops into my head. I can see myself lying on the bed watching him one morning as he'd combed his hair this way and that, trying to get it just so, losing patience because it wouldn't co-operate. 'Blasted thing!' he'd roared finally, flinging the comb from him and making me jump.

'What is it?' I'd asked, taken aback by his outburst.

'I'll be bald soon.'

'Don't be silly.'

'It's true. I'm getting old.'

'No, you're not.' I knew better than to make a smartarse joke – Gary doesn't have a sense of humour about his hair. Or his waistline. Or anything that even vaguely reminds him that he might be ageing. At the end of the day, image and what others think are everything to him. Power and status are what matter most, not people. Take Ian: to Gary, Ian is just another notch on the bedpost of his career. A means to an end. Because, like me, what matters to him most is his job.

Not friends or family, not emotional connections or real people. Just self-preservation at any cost. *And you're just as bad, Frankie. Just as manipulative. Just as driven to succeed, no matter whom you hurt along the way.*

The truth hits me like a steam train. How did I turn into this person?

'I do engage with the world,' I hear Ian say, and I snap back to the present.

'Sure you do.' Rosie rolls her eyes. 'How? By watching TV?'

'I don't watch TV.' He sniffs.

'Why? Is it beneath you?' She laughs.

'Most of it is, yes,' he replies. 'All those dreadful reality shows, people eating ants for fun – it's barbaric.'

'There are more than just reality shows on TV, Ian,' Rosie says. 'You should try to have an open mind. Besides, isn't it important to keep plugged into the world? With current affairs and culture?'

'I do keep abreast of current affairs,' he says. 'I read the newspaper.'

'And what about culture? What was the last play you saw? Or movie, even?' Rosie demands.

'I don't know what you mean,' he blusters.

'Just answer the question,' Rosie replies, deadpan, her eyes not moving from his face. 'The last movie you saw – what was it?'

Ian frowns. 'It was a James Bond, I think,' he says at last.

'Which one?'

'What?'

'Who was playing Bond when you saw that movie? What actor?'

'Um . . .' Ian's face twists as he tries to recall. 'Roger Moore?'

'Oh, my gosh, this is worse than I thought.'

'Is it?' He looks a little worried now and I have to suppress a smile – he's like a big kid in some ways.

'Yes, but don't worry – all is not lost.'

'What do you mean?'

'I mean you need yourself some serious educating and I'm the gal to do it! So we're going to the movies.'

'The movies?' he squeaks.

'Yep. You can't hope to write about the world unless you're in the world. This is like your computer phobia – and you need to build a bridge and get over it. Am I right?'

Ian blinks at her, speechless.

'You lock yourself up in that house – which, if you don't mind me saying so, needs a darn good cleaning – and then you wonder why you can't write?'

'I *can* write!' Ian says. 'I *do* write!'

'Yes, but you're not happy with what you write, are you?'

'I – I –' Ian is now completely lost for words.

'So, the way I see it, you need to spread your wings, honey, come explore the world. Isn't that so, Frankie?'

I look at Ian, whose face is white at the idea that he needs to step outside his comfort zone, and don't know what to say. She has a point – Ian does need to socialize more. But only Rosie would have the guts to say that to his face. She has an uncanny knack of making people see the truth – warts and all – and I have seriously underestimated her.

'What is *wrong* with you two today?' Rosie asks. 'Cat got your tongues?'

Ian and I look at each other, neither of us sure how to respond.

'How are you guys doing over here?' a voice asks.

Anita is approaching our table. The last time I saw her was in Napa when that conversation with Roberto seemed to shake her to the core. She looks brighter today, although the shadows around her eyes are dark, as if she hasn't been sleeping.

'Anita!' Rosie calls, jumping up to hug her warmly. Rosie didn't tell me the specifics of what she and Anita spoke about in Napa – only that she's in a dark place, which I already know only too well.

'Hey, honey.' Anita hugs her back. 'It's good to see you again so soon. You too, Frankie.' She leans across to kiss me and suddenly I feel like Judas. I know how close she is to the edge.

'Anita, this is Ian Cartwright – he's an author,' Rosie says, doing the introductions.

'Well, hello!' Anita says. 'We're honoured to have an author in our midst.'

'It's nice to meet you.' Ian stretches out his hand. 'I've heard a lot about you.'

'You have?' Anita replies in surprise.

'He means you're such a legend in North Beach, Anita,' I jump in. I want to strangle Ian for being so stupid.

'I don't know if I like that term, "legend".' She laughs. 'It gives away my age!'

'You're young at heart, Anita,' Rosie says. 'I bet you go to the movies all the time, right?' She winks at Ian.

'The movies?' Anita asks, puzzled.

'This dinosaur –' Rosie punches Ian on the arm and I see him jump at her strength '– hasn't been in years. That's why we're going tonight. Do you wanna come?'

'Oh, no, I don't think so,' she replies, as if she's turning it down automatically, not even giving herself the chance to think about it.

'Are you sure? It'll be a blast!'

'No, no, thanks.' Anita looks away, ill at ease.

'Another time,' Rosie says lightly, clearly deciding not to push her. 'Well, you're coming, Frankie, aren't you?'

'Actually, I'm not sure I can. I have so much to do,' I reply. *Packing up, going home, facing Gary . . .*

'Oh, come on – please?' Rosie begs. 'One last outing before you leave? You won't regret it, I promise!'

'What won't she regret?' John appears, a platter in his hands.

'Movie night in Dolores Park?' Rosie lifts her face to smile at him as he places some complimentary *antipasti* on the table in front of us.

'Oh, yeah, that's great! I haven't been for ages,' he replies.

'Well, you'll enjoy it, then – you can come too.'

'Er, I don't think I can,' he begins.

'Course you can!' Rosie won't take no for an answer. 'Ian and I are going and so is Frankie – we can double date!'

I feel the hot blush of mortification creep up my neck. I'll kill Rosie when I get her alone – *kill her!*

'Just kidding!' She laughs when she sees my expression. 'But *La Dolce Vita* is showing. Who can resist that?'

'Not me!' Ian pipes up, ladling some grilled aubergine drizzled with olive oil on to his plate, whistling in appreciation.

'So you're going?' I ask.

'I'm not a dinosaur, and I'm certainly not Rapunzel.' He glances haughtily at Rosie. 'And I resent the implication that I am.'

'Good for you, spunky!' Rosie laughs, winking at Anita. 'Now come on, John. I just love that movie, don't you?'

'It is a good movie.' John looks to me. 'What do you say, Frankie? Are you sick of us yet?'

'No, of course not,' I reply, too mortified about the double-date comment to look at him. But it's not just mortification

288

– it's excitement too. Excitement at the thought of spending more time with him. I never felt this way about Gary – never.

'Well, then, it's settled,' Rosie rejoices. 'We're all set! John, if you could bring some of these divine titbits for the picnic it would be just peachy!'

I hear the buzz of conversation around me as the others launch into a lively discussion about suitable food, but I feel as if I'm a million miles away, lost in thought. A veil has been lifted from my eyes and I can see clearly for the first time in months. What Gary and I have is convenient, even exciting sometimes, but it's certainly not love. It's not even close. And it's no longer enough.

Suddenly I feel the hairs on the back of my neck rise. It's the strangest sensation – as if someone is watching me. Then I lift my head and find myself looking straight into John's eyes. Everything else fades, and it's as if there's only us two, locked in each other's gaze, unable to look away.

Chapter Twenty-seven

OK, Frankie, you need to pull yourself together. You do not have feelings for John Bonner and he doesn't have feelings for you. So you've shared some pretty intense looks, so what? That's because the situation is intense, not because there's chemistry between the two of you. That's all in your imagination. It has to be because you barely know each other. He doesn't like you in that way. He couldn't. In fact, if he knew the real truth about you he'd hate your guts, you know that. So, you need to forget what you thought you saw in his eyes. Full stop.

It's dusk in Dolores Park and all around us people are spreading out their bits and pieces, getting ready to kick back and enjoy the movie, as Rosie would say. John has brought a massive basket crammed with goodies from the restaurant and Rosie has another, brimful with delicacies from Sausalito, so those, coupled with the wine that Ian and I have brought, means we have enough for a small army. Mind you, I'm ravenous so I might just be able to get through the lot. Something about eating outdoors always revs up my eat-till-I-pop gene. And tonight I'm nervous as well so the combination means I'm ready to eat my bodyweight in olives and cheese.

'This is amazing,' I say, sitting down on the wool blanket that's spread on the grass.

'Isn't it great?' Rosie says happily, setting out some containers filled with food and wiping the plastic glasses, holding them to the dimming light to check for marks. 'There's no better place to watch a movie than outdoors.'

'I wouldn't know – I've never watched a movie outdoors before,' I say. I've always wanted to – ever since I saw *Grease* for the first time and sighed with envy as Sandy and Danny canoodled at the drive-in. I really wanted to be Sandy – especially when she had her makeover and transformed into a skin-tight satin-trouser-wearing smoker at the end. That looked like so much fun.

'You're kidding?' Rosie sounds astounded by my admission.

'No. The weather in Ireland doesn't quite work for this type of thing,' I say. 'I wish it did. This is great!'

There's a wonderful atmosphere as the low hum of conversation buzzes round us, so utterly different from the indoor experience I'm used to – back home it can get so tense, sitting in the dark, hoping for total silence, knowing your evening will be ruined if someone crunches their popcorn or Minstrels behind you the entire time. Here, everything seems much more relaxed. People are drinking and chatting, eating and laughing, and it all seems so Bohemian, so laid back and casual. I can't imagine wanting to box someone's ears because they're making too much noise.

'Do you think there are mosquitoes?' Ian asks anxiously, swatting the air around him.

'There might be,' Rosie replies casually.

'Oh, Jesus, Mary, Joseph and the ass! I hate mosquitoes,' he cries, panic instantly on his face.

'"Jesus, Mary, Joseph and the ass"?' Rosie rocks back on her heels and howls with laughter. 'That's too funny, Ian!'

But Ian is too busy slapping the air to hear her – obviously he reverts to his Irish brogue when he's anxious.

'So, let me get this straight,' I say to him. 'You don't mind pet mice in your kitchen but you can't stand mosquitoes. How does that logic work?'

'You have a pet mouse in your kitchen?' John asks, his

mouth twitching with amusement as he begins to unpack his basket beside me.

'It's called Shergar,' I inform him.

'Shergar? Um, what kind of a name is that?' he says.

'Shergar was a famous Irish racehorse,' Ian explains, still swatting, looking over his shoulder, as if he expects a swarm of mosquitoes to attack at any second. 'Winner of the 1981 Epsom Derby, in fact.'

'You called your pet mouse after a racehorse?' John asks.

'It's not exactly a pet,' he says.

'They have a sort of understanding,' I explain.

'You have an understanding with a not-quite-pet mouse called Shergar? I think I've heard it all.' John chuckles.

'You might not have heard it all just yet,' I say. 'Ian thinks it's perfectly acceptable to let this mouse have the run of everything in his kitchen. Like his cereal box, for example.'

'Ian, that is kind of gross.' John pulls a face.

'He's only a tiny thing,' Ian says. 'What harm can he do?'

'Maybe I should tell Mom to try that line with the health department guys when they come to inspect the restaurant kitchen.' John laughs.

'Well, at least mice don't bite,' Ian grumbles, now scratching his legs. 'But mosquitoes do and they seem to like my blood more than others.'

'They do say that mozzies go for some people in particular,' John says.

'Don't worry, y'all, I brought my special candles – they'll keep the mozzies away.' Rosie rustles in her enormous basket and pulls them out.

'Special candles?' Ian looks dubious.

'They have citronella oil in 'em – it acts as an insect repellent, so nothing will be eating you tonight, sweetpea.'

'Thank you, Rosie,' Ian says, visibly relaxing as Rosie

strikes a match and the candles glow in the fading light. All around us, people are doing the same and the sounds of fizzing matches and corks being popped float towards me on the air.

'Have you seen this movie before, Frankie?' John asks, uncorking some wine. I watch surreptitiously as he pours me a glass. God, he looks amazing.

'Yeah, years ago,' I reply, accepting the drink gratefully and taking a large swig to hide the embarrassment I feel creeping up my neck. If he only knew what I was thinking.

'Me too.'

'Mm . . . that's delicious,' I say, to fill the following silence. 'Why does wine always taste so good outdoors?'

'It's the laws of physics. Something to do with alcohol and oxygen combining.'

'Whatever it is, it works,' I say, taking another slug, letting the warmth travel down my throat and infuse my body. Relax, Frankie. He can't read your mind. Just don't let your mouth run away with you and all will be well.

Reclining here in this wonderful park, as the light fades, I can almost forget that I ever have to go home and face reality. It seems like a million miles away. Gary would hate this, I realize. His idea of going to the cinema is being invited to a VIP screening before the great unwashed public are let in. I can't imagine him here, sipping wine on a rug, enjoying the outdoor ambience, snacking on picnic titbits. But maybe he and Caroline used to do exactly this sort of thing together when they were first married. They could have gone for midnight feasts outside, maybe even to festivals, for all I know. They must have had happy times together before it all went wrong. But why did it go wrong? Did the spark between them die, just like that? Was it the stress of two successful careers, coupled with the demands of two kids, that ended it? Gary doesn't talk about it – only to say she's a total cow who's determined to prove he cheated on her and bring him to the cleaner's. But that doesn't tell me much or give me any real insight into him or their relationship.

There's so much about Gary that I don't know – that I never will know. And that used to bother me a little, but it doesn't any more. Being apart from him has created a distance between us – a distance that's far more than geographical. It was there before I came to San Francisco, I know that. But it's been even more pronounced since. I've realized more and more that I don't miss him. Not even a little.

'It's years since I saw *La Dolce Vita*,' Ian comments now, and Rosie grunts with laughter.

'It's years since you saw anything at all. That's why we're here, honey, remember?'

'You don't do movies much, huh, Ian?' John asks.

'He doesn't do anything much except torture himself with his work,' Rosie replies, on his behalf.

'Writers need solitude,' Ian responds primly. 'Everyone knows that.'

'Not *that* much solitude!' Rosie remonstrates. 'Besides, you need to get out and about, get yourself some inspiration.'

'Not necessarily,' Ian replies. He's uneasy and I know why. But before I can step in and change the subject John speaks.

'So, where do you get your inspiration from? Or is that one of those stupid questions that writers hate?'

Crap, double crap, triple crap.

'It's a tricky one, certainly,' Ian replies carefully. 'I suppose the answer is everywhere, really – other books, TV, magazines . . .'

'Not real life?' Rosie asks, plucking a juicy strawberry from a carton and popping it into her mouth.

'Sometimes,' Ian replies, darting a look at me.

'Yes, but you'd never write about real people, though, would you?' Rosie asks. 'I mean, we're not going to see ourselves in your next book, are we?'

'No . . .' Ian says, lowering his eyes, picking at the blanket beneath him.

Oh, God.

'Now, I don't have an objection, of course, but if you *are* going to base a character on me, can you make me taller? And thinner? And I'd quite like black hair, straight, please,' she says, throwing back her head and laughing raucously, her auburn locks tumbling from her neat chignon into a rippling waterfall down her back. God, she's got good hair. Shampoo-ad hair.

'Your hair is gorgeous as it is,' Ian says immediately.

It's heartfelt, I can tell – he really likes her: her fortune cookie prediction is coming true for sure, it seems.

'Oh, honey, this old mop? I can't stand it! No, I want to be willowy, with jet-black hair and a hand-span waist, like a Sidney Sheldon heroine.'

'I don't like hand-span waists,' Ian replies.

'Of course you do, you silly man.' Rosie cackles. 'Now, John, what would you like to look like, if you're in Ian's next book?'

'Let me see.' John is chewing a blade of grass. 'I'd like a six-pack, please.'

'Oh, good idea!' Rosie laughs.

'And blue eyes – I've always wanted blue eyes. And fewer wrinkles!'

I look at John's chocolate irises and can't imagine him with any other colour. And he'd look far too skinny with a six-pack. He's nice just the way he is: almost-invisible paunch and all. And the way his eyes crinkle at the edges when he smiles, it's so cute . . . If he didn't have any wrinkles, that couldn't happen . . .

'How about you, Frankie?' Rosie's question interrupts my thoughts.

'Ian would never use me in one of his books,' I say quickly. 'He knows better than that.' My voice sounds calm but inside I'm all fluttery because John has moved closer. Luckily, the movie credits begin to roll and everyone turns to watch. But as the music starts my head is swimming – what's come over me, mooning over John like this? Suddenly I'm incredibly conscious that he's beside me, a finger's width away. I can smell his salty skin, hear him breathe. I shake myself mentally. I need to give myself a stern talking-to. I am *not* romantically interested in John: we are just friends. In fact, he's not even a friend, not really. He's an acquaintance – that's a better term for it. Yes, just a casual acquaintance I've been thrown together with. Anything I'm feeling has far more to do with the wine and the warm night air than reality – and I have to keep reminding myself of that.

A few hours later Rosie and Ian have gone, sharing a cab home. John and I are slowly winding our way back through the city streets. It's close to midnight and I'm acutely aware that I should just return to my hotel, but something is holding me back. I don't want this night to end.

'That was fun,' John says.

'It really was,' I reply, feeling stupidly shy.

'It's a pity they don't show movies outdoors in Ireland,' he says.

'Maybe I should start a campaign,' I joke. 'Try to persuade people it would work.'

'I don't know about that,' he says, an impish grin spreading across his face. 'Would there be much demand for outdoor movies on the Aran Islands?'

'Oh, God! That was all your fault.' I giggle. 'Telling your mother I knew Connor! If she asks me to say anything else in Irish I'll die. I can hardly remember a word!'

'Sorry about that. I totally forgot that Connor was from there. You do seem to be holding your own, though. Besides, Mom loves you – anything you say she believes.'

'That's not true,' I say bashfully.

I really like Anita. I genuinely think she's an amazing person so to hear that she likes me, too, is a real compliment.

'Sure it's true. She's always telling me how great you are. Francesca this, Francesca that. I'm sick of hearing about you.' He laughs.

'You are not!' I punch his arm and immediately regret it. Great. Now he'll think I'm a proper eejit.

'I am too. She thinks you're a *cailín deas*.'

'How do you know that phrase?' I laugh at his pronunciation of the Irish for 'lovely girl'.

'Connor taught me how to say it. I'm supposed to use it as a chat-up line.' He grins at me.

'A chat-up line, huh? Does that mean you're chatting *me* up?' I snort. Suddenly he's looking at me strangely and there's silence between us. *What made you say that, Frankie, you stupid knob-head? The poor man is mortified.*

'And what if I am?' he says softly, his eyes searching my face.

It's undeniable – now I definitely want to kiss him. What is wrong with me? I have to pull myself together. I have to shake away the mad feeling that if I just moved a fraction closer, his lips would meet mine . . . But I'm imagining the tension, that's all. This connection between us is in my head, and if I do something stupid, I'll be humiliated tomorrow. How embarrassing would it be if I swooped in and he laughed at me?

'Frankie?' he says, reaching for my hand and holding it in his, the touch of his fingers on my skin sending a jolt of electricity coursing through my body.

'Yes?' I croak, afraid to breathe. Afraid to *move*.

'I really like you.'

Oh, my God. He really likes me. Suddenly I feel stupid and awkward as if I'm fifteen again and about to be kissed for the very first time. This is nothing like I feel when I'm with Gary – this is nothing like I've ever felt with anyone. We're almost nose to nose now and it's taking all my willpower not to pull him to me. In fact, I'm gulping back an insane urge to grab him and snog the face off him. Should I wait till he makes the first move? Can I last that long? And then he reaches for me and his hands are in my hair, my arms are round his neck and we're kissing as if we never want to stop.

'Wow,' he says, when we eventually pull apart.

'Wow back,' I reply.

'I've been wanting to do that for a long time.'

'You have?' *He has?*

'Ever since we first met.'

'No way.'

'It's true. You were so mad with me – it was really cute.'

'You *liked* that I was mad with you?'

'Oh, yeah. That fiery Irish temper is pretty awesome.'

'It is?'

'Yep. But it's not just that, Frankie. I've never met anyone like you before. I can't imagine anyone else playing along with this phone mix-up like you have, helping out a total stranger like that . . . You're amazing.'

A massive tidal wave of guilt washes over me. He still believes that I'm a nice, thoughtful person who wanted to do the right thing. He has no idea of the truth. That I was in it for what I could get. I'm not nice, I'm despicable. 'I'm *not* amazing,' I say, feeling sick.

'Yes, you are,' he whispers, his breath on my face. 'You blow me away.'

Suddenly I'm overwhelmed with the urge to come clean and confess everything. If I tell him the truth now, surely he'll understand. He'll know that I didn't mean any harm. I just have to find the right words to make him see I was backed into a corner. I'm not a bad person, not really. I just made an error of judgement – there's a big difference.

But what if he doesn't understand? What if he thinks I've been using him to get information? It started off like that, yes, but that's not the way I feel now. I like him. I really, *really* like him. Not only that, but I like his mother too – it's as if I've somehow known them both all my life, as if we were supposed to meet.

But will he believe me if I tell him all that? Or will he think I'm a lying, two-faced coward? I just don't know what to think, how to tell him . . .

And then somehow we're kissing again and all the arguments swirling in my head disappear and none of it seems important any more.

Chapter Twenty-eight

OK. I'm going to tell him. That's the right thing to do. It's the only thing to do. I just have to be brave, grab the bull by the horns . . . and fight the urge not to run away. Pushing back my shoulders and taking a deep breath, I knock on Carlo's door, ignoring the *We Are Closed* sign that hangs crookedly in the window. The restaurant is shut to prepare for evening service – but I know he's in there. He was the one who invited me to come.

After a minute or so, the door eventually swings open just a crack.

'We don't open till six,' his cousin Martha, the waitress, says, smiling almost automatically, not really seeing me. But then she clocks it's me and her expression freezes.

'Hi there,' I say. I don't know why this girl dislikes me so much – if I looked like her I'd feel so sorry for everyone else that I'd be nice to them all. I'd 'pity-like' everyone.

'Hi,' she replies coldly. But she doesn't let me pass. In fact, by the way she angles her bony limbs, it's almost as if she's . . . blocking the entrance.

'Um, I'm here to see –'

'Anita isn't here. She's gone to the farmer's market in Trocadero. She'll be back later.' And then she goes to close the door on me for real.

'It's not Anita I'm here to see,' I say. What is her problem? 'It's John.'

Her cat eyes narrow to tiny slits as she surveys me, still

not budging. 'Why do you want to see him?' she asks, acid dripping from every word.

Honestly, this girl would be brilliant on *America's Next Top Model*. She has the swagger, the bitchy attitude . . . They'd love her. Trying not to feel intimidated, I look her square in the eye. OK, she's gorgeous. But she's also about twelve. I'm not going to let her mess with me. 'He invited me for coffee,' I reply. 'Although I don't think that's any of your business, is it?'

For a split second she looks startled – caught off guard, almost. And then her lip curls. It happens so quickly it's like she's been practising it at home – in fact, it could be her signature top-model move when she stops at the end of a catwalk. Narrowed eyes and a sneer – it's perfect modelling fare.

'Why don't you fuck off back to where you came from?' she growls.

'*Excuse* me?' Did she just say what I thought she said?

'Are you deaf as well as ugly?' she snarls.

OK, now the girl has gone too far. She cannot insult me just because she's freakishly gorgeous. Besides, I may not be classically beautiful – but I'm not *ugly*. I'm working my way up to a biting retort that will put her back in her box – something about eyebrows obviously – when I hear a voice call my name. 'Frankie!' It's John. 'Come on in!'

Martha stares at me venomously and then, after a significant pause where we eyeball each other and I fantasize about slapping her face, she reluctantly stands back and lets me pass. I almost brush her jutting ribcage with my belly as I go by – not to talk of her hip bones. I would kill to have hip bones like that. But her attitude needs a serious readjustment – if she worked for me I'd have fired her by now.

'Hey, you,' John says, smiling widely at me as I approach, my legs feeling wobbly. Shit. Now that I can see him I'm not as in control as I'd thought. In fact, my insides have turned to jelly. If I blush like a stupid teenager I will die. Right here on the spot.

'Hi there,' I reply, grinning like a lunatic robot to try to hide my nerves.

'Let's go through to the courtyard.' He leads the way. 'It's nice and quiet back here. You can lock up again, Martha!' he calls over his shoulder, and I glance back to see her scowling at me. If looks could kill, I'd be on the menu.

'So, about last night,' he says, turning to me and looking a bit sheepish.

Oh, my God. He regrets kissing me. It's written all over his face. Is that why he asked to meet me? To let me down gently?

'You don't have to explain, John,' I say. I'm going to get out of here with my dignity intact, pretend it meant nothing to me either, that's the important thing. Even though I've thought about nothing else since.

'Explain?' He looks confused.

'Yeah. I mean, we'd both had quite a bit to drink.'

'Frankie. You're misunderstanding me.'

'I am?' *I am?*

'Yes. I really like you. A lot. And I don't have to drink to want to kiss you. I want to kiss you all the time.'

If your heart could actually melt then mine does at that precise second. 'You do?'

'Yes, I'm afraid I do. It's a serious problem.'

I want to launch myself at him, but I don't. I have to tell him the truth first, now more than ever. But how do I start? Should I just come out and say it? *Listen, John, I only ever agreed to keep quiet about the phone mix-up so I could get information about your family for a client?* God, it sounds bad when I put it like that. No, I need to work my way up to it.

'So, em, what are you doing with all that stuff?' I ask, gesturing to a large brown box perched on the table. My mind is working overtime, trying to come up with some other way to break the truth to him, and I need to make small-talk fast.

'This? Well, you know that Aimee's one-year anniversary is coming up?'

'Yes.'

'Before she passed away she left strict instructions that we were to have a party to mark the day.'

'A party?' I say, intrigued.

'Yeah. I think she thought we'd all be in a happier place than we are. She wanted us to celebrate – "remember her with joy" were her exact words.'

'It's a beautiful idea,' I say. And it is – imagine knowing you're going to die and having the courage to want your family to celebrate and remember you. That takes guts. Guts I'm not sure I'd have if I was in the same position.

'Yeah, it is. She even put some things aside to help me organize it – she said she wanted it done properly and if she didn't leave instructions she'd never rest in peace.'

We both burst out laughing: that's exactly what I would have expected from this feisty girl.

'I think she was probably right to plan ahead,' I say, in mock-seriousness.

'And what's that supposed to mean?' he asks.

'That men are notoriously bad at planning parties.' My two brothers have been totally useless wastes of space about Mum and Dad's do. If they represent what the male of the species can manage we're in trouble.

'Well, seeing as you're so sure about that, maybe you can help me sort it out?'

'Hmm . . . What do you have to work with?' Jokingly, I put my hands on my hips.

'Well, I have all this stuff,' he says, gesturing to the big brown box on the table. 'Aimee made me promise not to open it till now – it's full of the things she wants at the party.'

'And you were able to resist opening it?' I gape. If I was given a box and told not to look inside, I'd rip it open straight away.

'She made me promise – well, I guess it was more of a threat, really,' he says, smiling ruefully.

'A threat?'

'She said if I cheated and opened it any earlier, she'd know and come back to haunt me. Scare the shit out of me when I was on the bike – make me career off a cliff, that sort of thing.'

I can't help but giggle – the girl had so much attitude. 'Go ahead and open it so,' I say.

He begins to tear open the box and I watch, almost holding my breath, as he draws out a white envelope. He opens it slowly and begins to read aloud the letter inside, his voice shaking a little.

Dude, have you put on weight? You need to stop pigging out on Mom's pasta!

So, I know you're probably pining for your little sister, but I need you to step up and be a man! This party better rock – I have a reputation to uphold, you know! I want everyone to have a blast and remember all the fun times we had together, OK? So, no whining. Whining is for losers! I've put a few things in this box to inspire you to have an awesome night – I know how dumb you can be so you probably need a helping hand!

Lots of love,
your baby sister
Aimee xxxx

'I hate to admit it, but she's right about the pasta.' He pats the invisible paunch he's always joking about. I find I have to look away to stop myself staring at it lustfully – his stomach looks fine to me. In fact it looks great.

'It's an amazing letter,' I say. 'I can't believe she wrote that when she was so ill, when she knew that . . .'

'She was dying.'

'Sorry, yes.' I lower my eyes.

'It's OK, Frankie,' he says softly. 'Yes, she *was* amazing. She had such guts – right till the very end. And, as you can probably tell by her teasing, she was a real kidder.'

'Sounds like it.' I love her sense of fun – it shines out of her letter to her brother.

'OK, let's see what humiliations my little sis has in store for us.' He takes a deep breath and begins unpacking the box. The first thing out is a party hat – it's got bright, multi-coloured stripes all over it and a halo of tiny yellow feathers dancing on top. 'Oh, God, if she wasn't dead I'd kill her! She knows I hate these damn things!'

'Well, it looks like she wants everyone to wear one,' I say. 'I think they're cute!' I reach across, pluck the hat from his hand and plonk it askew on my head. 'See? Aren't you more cheerful already?'

'If that means am I laughing at you on the inside, yes, I am!'

'Oi!' I hit him playfully. 'How dare you? I happen to know I look good in a hat – it's my thing.'

'Your thing?' he asks.

'Yes. Some women have a thing for shoes, others have a thing for handbags. I have a thing for hats. People tell me they suit me.'

'Really?' He cocks an eyebrow. 'It's sort of hard to tell. I'm not sure the feathers are your colour . . .'

'What would you know?' I pout, pretending to be stung. 'Now, come on, what else is there?'

He rummages in the box again and plucks out glasses, then tiny umbrellas, all shiny and pink. 'I know what these are for. She wants cocktails.'

'Cocktails are always a good idea,' I say. 'You can't go wrong with them.'

'And she loved hers,' he replies. 'She used to watch that show all the time – you know the one with the Cosmos?'

'*Sex and the City*?'

'That's the one! She loved it. Hated the movie, though – boy, did everyone get an earful about that one.'

'Lots of women loved the series and hated the movie,' I say.

'She said it was –'

'– watered down?'

'Exactly! Like it had lost its spark when it made it to the big screen.'

'That's exactly how I felt about it too!' I say. Aimee and I had such a lot in common. In some way, I feel as if I knew her in another life.

Next out is a 1980s greatest-hits CD. 'She loved eighties stuff.' He turns it over in his hands. 'She used to say it was the decade that taste forgot. It cracked her up.'

'This party will rock.' I laugh. 'She has all the ingredients!'

'At least she doesn't have karaoke,' he says. 'I'm surprised, though – she loved it.'

'What's that stuck to the back of the CD?' I ask.

It's a note.

I want karaoke as well, bro, don't think you can get out of it!

'That's typical of her!' he exclaims. 'Even from the grave she's getting what she wants.'

'I wish I could have met her,' I say. 'She really sounds incredible.'

'She was,' he says, hunkered down on his heels now. 'She made me laugh every day of my life – even at the end she was wisecracking. That's just the way she was.'

'How amazing to retain your sense of humour in such tough circumstances.'

'Yeah. She didn't want everyone crying round her. That's why this party has to be great – it's what she would have wanted.'

'Well, it will be great!' I say. 'We'll make it great!' Why am I saying that? I need to get out of helping, not promise to make it a huge success. Jesus – what's *wrong* with me?

He looks at me then. 'I wish you could have met her Frankie,' he says. 'She would have liked you.'

'How can you be sure?' I ask, my stomach doing that churning thing all over again. 'She might have hated me.'

'Nah.' He stands up. 'She would have loved you.'

He smiles at me, that soft, ache-in-my-heart smile, and I know I have to tell him. I have to come clean.

'John, there's something you need to know,' I say.

'You're leaving? I know, but we can make it work, Frankie.'

'No, it's not that.'

'What? You're married?' He laughs.

'No, I'm not married.'

Something in the way I reply tells him I'm being serious and his expression changes to one of concern. 'You're in a relationship?'

A fleeting picture of Gary pops into my head. 'That's not it. I mean, there is someone . . . it's complicated . . . but that's not what I have to tell you.'

His face falls. 'I'm not liking where this is going,' he says.

'Look, I'm not sure how to tell you this. So I'm just going to start from the beginning, OK?'

'OK.' His eyes are wary now.

'When I first got here, I lost my phone.'

'And you had to hire one.'

'Yes, I hired one and then I started getting messages meant for Aimee.' I take a deep breath to steady my nerves. God, this is hard.

'But I know all that, Frankie.' John looks confused. 'I agreed to meet you . . .'

'. . . so I could explain the situation to you,' he says. 'You took a chance on a complete stranger – like I said last night, you're amazing. I'm not going to let you get away now, Frankie – we can do the long-distance thing, can't we?'

Oh, God.

'No, John, I'm not amazing.'

'What are you talking about?'

'I didn't meet you for the reasons you thought. I only met you because Ian thought Aimee's story and the phone mix-up would make a great novel. He thought the way her old phone number was reassigned when she died and I happened to get it by chance was fascinating. All the messages from your mother to her – the way you wanted to keep in touch with her in some way, even though she'd passed away . . . So he asked me to find out more . . .'

'What? What are you talking about?' His face is working overtime as he processes what I just said.

'Ian Cartwright. I've been trying to get him to sign with me, with the agency. I happened to tell him about the messages I was getting and he asked me to . . . to find out more. That's why I met you, why I kept on meeting you – to keep Ian sweet. I'm so sorry, John.'

There's a horrible, doom-laden silence as he looks at me, his face first puzzled, then disbelieving and finally angry. 'You were *spying* on us?'

'I know it sounds terrible, but I didn't mean any harm, I swear!'

John's face twists. 'Are you telling me . . . are you telling me that you hung out with me to get information for this guy, for his novel? Is that what you're saying?'

I nod mutely.

'So, you pretended to like me to get a deal done, is that it?'

'No!' I say. 'I mean at first, yes, I was pretending. But then really quickly I liked you for real . . .'

'Hang on. You promised me to keep quiet about Mom's messages to Aimee just so you could find out more, didn't you? This was all business to you.'

'At first it was just business. But I really like your mother, John – I think she's wonderful –'

'I don't want to hear any more.' His hands are shaking. 'Please leave.'

'John, please give me a chance to explain. I know what I did wasn't right, but if you just –'

'I can't believe I'm hearing this.' His face is like thunder.

'John, please, listen to me. Yes, I met you initially to get information for Ian, but that was just at the start. Then I really began to like you, I swear.'

'Wow!' he spits, furious. 'I guess I should consider myself lucky.'

'Please try to understand,' I beg. 'I really needed Ian on board. My agency is in serious trouble – if I didn't get him to sign, it was going to go to the wall.'

'So you were willing to do whatever it took, is that it?' he says.

'Yes! No! I mean, at the beginning, yes, but when I met you and then Anita, everything changed –'

'Don't!' He holds up his hand to me, his eyes blazing. 'Don't talk to me about Mom. She thinks you're an amazing

309

person. I guess she's a bad judge of character. Just like me.'

'John, please try to understand.'

'I *do* understand. I understand perfectly. Close the door behind you when you leave.'

I feel the tears slide down my cheeks as he walks away from me. I know there's no going back now. It's too late for apologies or second chances. And it's too late for us. I slide the phone from my pocket and place it beside the brown box. It's his now to do with as he likes. He was right all along – I should never have had it in the first place.

Chapter Twenty-nine

As I walk through the arrivals hall in Dublin airport, dragging my case despondently behind me, all I can think about is John. The way his fingers caressed the back of my neck as he held me, the way his lips felt on mine, the urgency of his kiss.

I can't believe I'll never see him again . . . never talk to him again . . . never be kissed by him again . . .

Stop it, Frankie.

I'm going round in circles and it's pointless: there's no use in dwelling on what might have been with John. It will never happen. It's a fantasy, and now that I'm back home I have to face what's real. And the reality is I've lost everything: my entire future has gone up in smoke.

Before I left San Francisco I called Ian and told him I wasn't the right person to represent him and that he should stay with Withers and Cole. He was taken aback, of course, as I'd expected him to be. After all, he'd got used to me pandering to his every whim in a desperate effort to get him onside. I still want him as a client – of course I do: if he signed with me, everything might change. The agency, my professional future, could be transformed. But I can't help him write Aimee's story – it was wrong of me even to pretend I could try – and if that's what it's going to take to get him on board, I have to walk away.

I called Rosie too. She was dumbfounded when I explained it all to her. I know she's severely disappointed in me, I could hear it in her voice, and that almost broke my heart because, no matter how kooky she is, her opinion really matters to me. She offered me her help and took me under her wing in a strange city and I lied and deceived her too. She's a special person, one in a million, and now I've lost her respect – and most likely her friendship too.

And then there's John.

My stomach flips when I think about how he reacted when I told him the truth. He believed I was a nice person who had agreed to co-operate about the phone mix-up out of the goodness of my heart. But now he knows what I'm really like – and he wants nothing more to do with me. Not that I can blame him: I can barely look myself in the eye in the mirror any more.

Head down, I battle my way through the throngs of people greeting each other in the arrivals hall, embracing one another with joy, thrilled to be reunited. I really don't need to see all this ecstatic emotion right now.

And then I hear someone call my name. 'Frankie!'

There it is again. 'Frankie!'

I raise my head and see my brothers waving at me frantically in the near distance. 'Eric? Martin?'

What the hell is going on? Why are they here to meet me?

In a few seconds they're beside me. 'Where the fuck have you been?' Eric roars, his face angry and red.

'I've been in San Francisco for work,' I reply, staring at him. *What is going on? What are they doing here?*

'We know that part,' Martin replies, panting with the effort of sprinting a short distance. 'Helen told us.'

'*Helen* told you?'

They were talking to Helen? When? *Why?*

'When we couldn't get you on your phone we called the office and she explained everything. But you were on the flight by then so we came straight here.'

'Why were you trying to get me?' Something's wrong, very wrong. My brothers never call me. Not unless they want something.

'It's Mum,' Martin says, sounding weary now, the anger gone.

'Mum?' My first thought is that this must be something to do with the party. But then I see the anxiety on my brothers' faces and a chill passes through me.

'Yes, it's Mum,' Eric repeats. 'She's in hospital, Frankie.'

'*Hospital?* What happened?'

'They think she's had a stroke.'

He can't be serious. Mum *couldn't* have had a stroke. Strokes happen to old people. Not to Mum. She's fit. She's healthy. She even has a pedometer. She saved up tokens for it from the newspaper for weeks – they all did it, her friends from the estate. They call themselves the Go Glow Grannies because they wear fluorescent yellow headbands and safety vests when they go power-walking together. I used to laugh at the name – it's not like oncoming traffic could miss eleven old women striding up the road, gassing as they go. They'd stop a juggernaut in its tracks. They even did the mini marathon together last year. Mum bought new trainers for it and spent weeks breaking them in before the big day. I was supposed to go and cheer her on, give her some moral support as she crossed the finishing line, except I never did: a work thing cropped up at the last minute. For the life of me, I can't remember what was so important that I had to miss her big moment. And now she's had a stroke. And I wasn't there for that either.

Everything is spinning in slow motion and I have to grip Martin's arm to keep steady.

'Dad found her last night – unconscious. It doesn't look good, Frankie.'

Oh, Jesus.

'Is she going to . . . die?' I manage to say, trying not to dissolve into hysteria.

'They don't know,' Eric says. 'She keeps drifting in and out of consciousness. She hasn't been able to speak at all. The doctors can't tell us for certain what happened until they run more tests. She might make a full recovery or she might – she might . . .'

His voice breaks and I can tell he's trying his hardest not to cry. If he's this upset it's really serious. We're not an emotional family. We slag each other relentlessly. We call each other names. We don't cry – ever. The only time I've ever seen Eric close to tears was when Frankie Goes to Hollywood broke up. He flounced around in his oversized Crombie coat with the sleeves rolled up, all red in the face, for ages after.

'She's *not* going to die,' Martin says fiercely, swinging my bag over his shoulder and herding us towards the exit. But even as he says it I know she might. Aimee died, a girl of only twenty-two, taken tragically before her time. It happens every day and it might be about to happen to us – to Mum. I might never see my mother alive again and I can't help feeling this might be my fault – because if karma is playing a part, then maybe I've brought this on us all.

Less than an hour later, I'm by Dad's side. 'It's going to be OK, Dad,' I whisper, gripping his hand tightly and trying very hard not to bawl. Mum looks so pale and tiny in the hospital bed. Her body seems almost shrunken under the white sheets, her right cheek drooping and slack, obvious even in sleep.

Dad shakes his head sadly, his eyes never leaving Mum's face. 'She just had her hair done,' he says, his voice hollow and broken in a way I've never heard it before. 'She'll be glad about that. You know how she is about her hair.'

314

'Yes,' I say, trying not to give in to the tears that are threatening to fall.

He's right – Mum is fastidious about her hair. Obsessive, even. By the look of it, she'd had it set just before it happened: it's in the settling-in stage when it looks less like a Brillo pad and more like a shaggy poodle's coat. She never likes her hair immediately after an appointment, when it's still really crazy tight and wiry, which is why she more or less stays indoors immediately afterwards, wearing a headscarf and waiting for it to loosen up. I don't know why she still gets such an old-fashioned set, actually – no one else does. She could ask for a blow dry, instead of going through the full works.

But then she wouldn't look like herself – and I can't imagine her any other way. It's like Dad and his golf sweaters. He doesn't play golf – always maintains it's a poof's game – but a friend of his works for one of the big insurance firms and is always slipping him free golf gear. Windcheaters, sweaters, hats, facecloths: all the corporate-gift stuff. Even today he's wearing a blue and white wool diamond jumper over a yellow golf T-shirt with a collar. It's quite nice, actually – not as gaudy as some of the other stuff he's worn over the years. If the insurance company logo wasn't stitched in bright green letters down the sleeve it wouldn't be half bad.

'She was always very particular about her hair,' Dad says, his voice wobbling.

Why is he saying *was*? Like she's past tense already. That is freaking me out. 'She'll be up and out of here in no time, Dad, just wait and see,' I say, trying to sound confident of this.

He looks at me, exhausted – it's as if he's aged a decade overnight. 'How do we know that?' he says.

'Because . . .' I flounder for the right thing to say. 'Because she's Mum. She'll be right as rain again soon, I know it.'

His face is gaunt, his eyes sunken in their sockets. 'I still can't believe it,' he says. 'She's perfectly healthy. Perfectly healthy people don't have strokes.'

'I know,' I whisper. Why did this have to happen?

'She doesn't drink, she doesn't smoke, she's been denying herself full-fat milk for years. I can't remember the last time she had a sausage, Frankie.'

'I know, Dad.'

Mum is careful about her weight anyway, and she's been watching it like a hawk ahead of the party. Fatty foods are a no-no. Even her beloved sausages, which we were practically reared on, along with tinned peas and instant mash, were banished once she started her latest health kick. She only uses the deep-fat fryer when we're around – and only because Eric and Martin practically demand chips. But she takes her own health and her walking very seriously, and I know that because she invested in it. Mum doesn't spend money on herself – she never has. Besides her monthly hair appointments, I can't think of one other thing she indulges in. But she invested in the walking: she'd bought the trainers and even a sports bra. Not that she ever admitted that to Dad, who never likes to hear about what he calls women's stuff, but she swore it made all the difference to her stride – it stopped her boobs swinging back over her shoulders was how she'd laughingly described it to me. Mum's stride was extremely important – she was forever talking about how you had to stretch out and keep the arms swinging to get the heart-rate up. And she was constantly checking her pedometer to see how many more steps she had to take to reach her daily target.

And now it looks as if it was all a waste of time because somehow her body has still gone ahead and betrayed her.

'We've been eating those bloody turkey sausages, you know. They were awful. Nothing like the pork ones.' Dad shakes his head sorrowfully. 'All that sacrifice for nothing.'

'What happened, Dad? Can you tell me?' I ask gently. My brothers don't seem to know the exact sequence of events and apparently it's been impossible to get any information out of Dad. He just keeps saying it should never have happened.

He looks at me blankly now. 'She was working on the party plan in the kitchen,' he says at last. 'We'd had another disagreement about the . . . band.'

'Go on,' I say softly.

'So I was watching the footie in the front room.'

'And then what?'

'She never came in with my tea. She always makes me a cup of tea at nine o'clock, even if she's, you know, cross with me. But she never came in. I went looking for her and there she was – slumped on the floor.' His voice is strangled.

'It's OK, Dad,' I whisper.

'No, it's not, Frankie.' He sobs. 'It's all my fault. I was stupidly jealous about the singer she wanted. If I'd just kept quiet I could have been there when she needed me – I could have helped. I was taping the football anyway!' He buries his face in his hands and howls.

I wrap my arms around him. 'It's OK.' I pat his back, and try not to dissolve too. That won't help him or Mum.

Dad is still crying. 'I should have helped her more. She was pushing herself too hard with that damn party.'

'Dad, everything will be OK, you hear? I know it,' I say, trying desperately to comfort him even though what I'm saying may be a lie. Bad things happen to good people – just look at Aimee and her family. Mum might never recover. Happy endings are only for fairy tales.

I can't help thinking about John now – this is how he must have felt about Aimee. He knew the horrible fear that now gnaws at my insides. He and his mother dealt with it for years, hoping that Aimee would get better, that she'd get her miracle. But she never did. What if Mum turns out to be the same? Or what if she comes round and then declines, starts to get sicker and sicker? What if it's only a matter of time? I can't bear thinking about it.

I feel a tear slide down my cheek and brush it away quickly, not wanting Dad to see.

I wish John was here now. Stupid, I know. He probably hates me – but I still wish he was beside me, holding my hand and telling me everything is going to be OK.

'Frankie?' Eric is at the door of Mum's room now, beckoning me to come and talk, so I shake away thoughts of John. I'm never going to see him again – I need to stop thinking about him, about what I've thrown away by acting so stupidly, and deal with the here and now.

The awful truth is that I've spent so much time obsessing about work that I've completely neglected my parents. I kept putting them off, thinking I had all the time in the world. I just went on cancelling lunch and dinner plans, presuming they'd always be there, that I could catch up any time, that it didn't matter that I was sidelining them over and over again. And now it might be too late to make amends.

'I'll get you a cup of tea,' I say, hugging Dad as I get up. That seems to be the only useful thing I can do. If in doubt make tea, was Mum's mantra – it *is* Mum's mantra. There's no way I'm going to start using the past tense about her – no way.

'I'm sorry I sort of shouted at you at the airport,' Eric says, shuffling from foot to foot as I close the door behind me and step into the corridor. 'I was just hassled, you know. I didn't mean it.'

His skin is grey – he, too, has aged overnight. We're all getting older, I realize with a jolt. He's not a teenager in an oversized Crombie coat listening to Frankie Goes to Hollywood any more: he's a grown man, with a bald patch. I never noticed that before – but under the hospital's harsh fluorescent lights it's quite easy to see. 'It's OK,' I reply. 'You were worried and you couldn't get me. I should have kept in touch more when I was away.'

His face relaxes a little, but the worry is still there in the lines around his mouth and eyes. 'Hey, I'm not exactly brilliant at keeping in touch myself,' he admits.

'Really?' I reply sarcastically, and he digs me in the arm.

'What were you doing in San Francisco anyway?'

'Working.' I sigh.

'You don't sound too happy about it.'

'It's complicated.' I sigh again. I'll be able to take a diploma in sighing soon, maybe teach the degree course. 'Anyway, I don't want to think about it now,' I go on. 'Mum is the most important thing. What has the doctor said?'

'She's still drifting in and out of consciousness,' he replies. 'They say that's pretty standard – the body's way of coping with the shock apparently. He says we have to wait and see what the MRI scan says. It might be minimal, it might be catastrophic. They can't tell yet.'

'Jesus. It just doesn't bear thinking about.'

'Do you think all the stress about the party made Mum ill, Frankie?' His eyes are glued to my face. 'I never lifted a finger to help her. I feel terrible. So does Martin.'

'I really don't think that had anything to do with it,' I reassure him.

'How can you be sure?' He's nibbling at his nails, just like he used to do when we were little. Mum used to paint stuff on them to discourage him but he bit them anyway. He said once you sucked the stuff off, worked your way past the gag reflex, it was grand.

'You can't blame yourself, Eric,' I say. 'Strokes happen for all sorts of reasons.' Besides, this is my fault. This is karma, I know it. I'm a bad person and someone somewhere is getting even.

'I've been such a knob-head, Frankie, you wouldn't believe it.'

'Er, I think I would know exactly how much of a knob-head you are – I've had to put up with you for long enough,' I joke.

'Shut up.' A smile spreads across his face.

'And speaking of knob-heads, where's Martin?'

He jerks a thumb behind him. Martin is deep in conversation with a doctor in a white coat further up the corridor, near the nurses' station. By the intent expression on his face, I can tell he's wrangling as much information out of him as possible.

'Wow. Martin's on the ball,' I say.

'Yeah, he's actually been pretty good for once. Usually he's no fucking use.'

'He *is* pretty useless,' I agree.

'A right useless prick,' Eric says, his mouth twitching.

'A total spanner,' I reply.

'A tool,' he says.

Just then Martin turns to us with a quizzical look, as if he's wondering what we're talking about. Eric and I explode with laughter. And then we're laughing and crying, hanging on to each other like we might never let go. And despite everything, the shock and the worry, it's the nicest feeling in the world.

Chapter Thirty

I'm back in the office, not really knowing how I ended up here, tabbing aimlessly through the names of everyone who tried to contact me when my phone was in limbo. It seems that since I mislaid it on the flight Mr Morris, the bank manager, is the one person who's been trying to contact me most. Although the dentist's receptionist came a close second – she'd called me three times to reschedule a hygienist's appointment. There are a few missed calls from clients, too, of course – and messages from Eric and Martin to tell me about Mum. But that seems to be it.

It's quite impressive in a way: even without my phone – my precious lifeline – I still managed to keep all the balls in the air. Nothing fell to pieces. I thought I couldn't function without it but, really, losing it turned out to be no big deal. It's as if some people didn't really notice I was gone . . . In fact, shouldn't there be more messages? Maybe from . . . friends?

I tab through all my missed calls again, just in case, but there's nothing. Not one missed personal call from anyone.

Suddenly it comes to me, hitting me with force between the eyes. How come I never noticed before that none of my friends call me any more? When did they stop getting in touch? Something my friend Karen said drunkenly, when we were all out to celebrate her birthday about six months ago, pops into my head.

'There's no point in calling you, Frankie,' she slurred, as she did another shot. 'You never call back! I had to leave you five messages to get you to come to my birthday party.'

At the time I'd thought she was joking – that the tequila was talking. But now that I have a real-time record of the calls and messages I received when I was away, to tab through in one swift movement, I see she meant it. She hasn't called me since then. In fact, it dawns on me now, none of my friends call me any more – not one. And I don't take the time to call them, I realize with shame. My social circle has apparently narrowed to my clients, my dentist and my bank manager. Even my family doesn't call me unless there's some sort of emergency: they know I won't have the time or inclination to talk to them. I've used this phone to keep at bay the people who should be closest to me. With call screening – my favourite phone function – I've screened practically everyone out of my life. How did I allow that to happen?

'Are you OK, Francesca?' Helen asks softly, as she places a steaming latte in front of me. She must have crept down to Starbucks and bought it without me noticing. She really is very thoughtful. And, of course, I've taken her for granted too, along with everyone else. I thought she was dim, stupid, even. But she can hold it together when she needs to. She even got Ivan Watters on TV – a minor miracle.

'Yes, thanks,' I say, coming to.

'How's your mum?' she asks tentatively.

'Same,' I reply, my temples throbbing. 'They have to run some tests and then we'll know more.'

Mum is sick, really sick. She might not get better, ever. She might never come round properly, and if she does, she might be nothing like her former self. What if she can't talk? How will we communicate? How is Dad going to cope? My head is buzzing with possibilities and none of them are good. Against the doctor's advice I've even Googled 'stroke' – and I don't like what I've read.

'You should try to get some rest,' Helen suggests gently.

'Why don't you go home and take a nap? You must be exhausted.'

'I'm fine,' I say, brushing away her concern. She's only trying to help, but I've been home already, had a quick shower, and I don't want to go back any time soon. There's no point being there, sitting alone with my thoughts. Better to be here, working and distracted. Even if the knowledge that time has run out is looming over me. I can't pay the rent. My bank account is being terminated. I'm flat broke. Bar a miracle, the agency is going under.

'Can I do anything for you?' she asks kindly.

'No thanks, Helen. You've been really great.' I smile weakly at her. Poor thing doesn't know it yet but she's going to be out of a job soon. Maybe Gary will take her on, if Marian the Rottweiler is still off. He did say she had something special – charisma. Too late, I've realized he was right.

Gary. I have to talk to him about Ian, the agency . . . everything. There's no point in putting it off – I should do it now. He's only a few floors above me – I'll just knock on his door and tell him the whole story, get it over and done with.

'Actually, can you hold the fort for a while, Helen?' I ask, pulling myself up with gargantuan effort, my limbs aching. 'I have to run an errand, but I won't be long.'

'Of course I will, boss,' she says.

Without thinking, I reach across and hug her quickly. I never appreciated her when I had her – I couldn't see past the coloured hair and her annoying love of chit-chat. I didn't recognize her potential – her brilliant way with people, how she puts everyone at ease, solves even the trickiest problems. And now it's too late.

I walk to Gary's office, my feet like lead, fatigue like a thick fog wrapped round my shoulders. When I tap on his door, he's deep in conversation with a colleague – Brendan, I think his name is. Proud Publishing has so many employees it's hard to keep track. It does seem strange not to have to battle with Marian to get to him, though. I wonder how she's recuperating after her hysterectomy. Gary hasn't mentioned her recently – it's as if, after all her years of hard work and complete devotion to him, he's forgotten about her in a heartbeat. I make a mental note to send her a card. I can't afford fancy flowers, but I can mail her a nice message, wishing her well. She was a lethal bitch, but I had a grudging respect for her too. The woman was a *warrior*.

'I can come back,' I say, as Gary's head lifts, surprise registering on his face. It seems so long since I last saw him that his features are almost strange to me.

'Francesca! No, we're finished – come in!' He looks at Brendan, who gathers up his papers and edges past me with a curt nod.

'When did you get back?' Gary asks, as the door closes behind Brendan.

'Yesterday,' I reply. 'Didn't you get my message?'

For a second his face is blank. Then he remembers. 'Oh, yes, something about your mother? Is she in hospital?'

Is she in hospital? *Is she in hospital?* How can he not know this? And then it comes to me: he never actually called me back, did he? He never phoned to see if I was OK, if I needed anything, a shoulder to cry on, a lift to the hospital. Nothing. 'Yes. She had a stroke,' I say dully. Saying it makes every nerve in my body jangle. If I say it, it must be true.

'Oh dear. How awful.' His face is working its way into an expression of sympathy. I've seen him do that look a million times: it's his fail-safe, sorry-for-your-trouble look. He never means it and I know, with full certainty, that he doesn't mean it now. He moves to where I'm standing, frozen like stone, and puts his arms around me. 'I'm so sorry, sweetheart. Is there anything I can do?'

'No,' I say, flinching as he touches me.

'Poor baby.' His fingers are moving across my arm, small circular movements caressing the skin. They're closer to my breast now – feather-light, but unmistakable in their intent. 'Let me take care of you,' he whispers, his voice husky. 'I've missed you so much.'

No, you haven't, I long to scream, instinctively knowing that's a lie. I push myself away from him and try to focus. I'm here to tell him about Ian. I have to break it to him now, before I lose my nerve. 'Listen, Gary,' I say, backing away from him, creating space between us. 'The thing with Ian . . . it didn't work out. It's not going to happen.'

He looks at me, his expression almost unreadable. 'And why is that?' he asks at last.

'He doesn't want to do the sequel – he wants to write something else.'

'Well, you don't have to worry about that for now surely.' He smiles – a smile that doesn't quite reach his eyes. 'Just get him on board and look after all the details later. I'm sure you can convince him, Blue Eyes.'

The way he says it – Blue Eyes – makes my skin crawl. It sounds totally insincere – like some awful cliché. And then I realize that's exactly what it is. A cliché. 'I can't.'

He's back behind his Regency desk now, the traffic buzzing on the street outside, as it always does. Nothing and yet everything has changed.

'Of course you can. You can make it work. What's his idea anyway? Maybe we can do something with it afterwards.'

'It's about a girl who died when she was just twenty-two.' I sigh. 'Her devastated family are still sending messages to her old cell phone a year later. But Ian can't do it – it's based on a true story and I've met the family. They're still struggling to get over her death –'

'Hey! I like it! Maybe old Ian's on to something – let's think about this some more . . .'

I shake my head to clear it. I must be hearing things. It has to be the jet lag that's doing this to me – it's always worse on the way back. That and the shock about Mum – it's jumbling my brain. 'Sorry?' I ask.

'I said there could be something in it! It needs work, yes, but the core idea is good . . . If we can get Ian to write it the way we want . . .'

His eyes are shining now and it's as if I can see euro signs lighting them up. And then, almost out of nowhere, a red mist of rage descends on me. 'Gary, you are a cold-hearted bastard,' I hear myself say.

'Excuse me?'

I see, as if from a height, the shock register on his face. 'You heard me. There is no way on earth that I'm going to encourage Ian to write this story. It's not going to happen. I told you – I've met the family. Doing this without their knowledge would be a complete betrayal.'

'Well, we could involve them somehow. I know! Maybe some royalties could go towards a charity. What did she die of – the girl?'

My head is spinning. 'She had a congenital heart defect.'

'OK, great. Well, a percentage of sales can go to a heart charity then. The public love a good sob story. Once Ian delivers the sequel, he can get to work on this. We could schedule it for a Christmas release – that could work.'

'*It's not going to happen!*' I'm shouting. I'm actually shouting at him. He stops dead and looks at me. For a split second I can see he's thinking I'm just a fly in his soup.

'But, Blue Eyes, think of the sales.'

'Don't call me that.'

'What?'

'Blue Eyes. Don't ever call me that again. It makes me sick to my stomach.'

'Babe, why are you overreacting like this?'

'I'm not overreacting. You're not listening to me. You're just thinking about the bottom line – your profits.'

He laughs, throwing his head back to reveal his perfect white teeth. 'Well, of course I am! Isn't that what it's about?'

'Not always.'

'You're just tired, darling. Why don't you go home and have a nice hot bath and a nap? We can discuss this later.' His eyes flick to his PC, checking to see what new emails he needs to read. He's done with me now and he wants me out: if I won't co-operate, I'm just an irritation.

'No, we *can't* discuss it later,' I say. 'He's not doing it. I've told you.'

'Frankie. Listen to me. You'll make it work, I know you will. You're like me – you'll do what it takes. We're cut from the same cloth.'

'We're not the same.' I shake my head.

'What is all this about?' he asks. 'Don't tell me you've gone soft, Frankie? You haven't lost your edge while you've been over there, have you?' His voice is cooler now, mocking me.

'I have morals,' I say. Suddenly I feel weary in my bones.

'Really? Well, I didn't exactly have to twist your arm to persuade you to fly to San Francisco, did I, Francesca? You were just as eager as I was to snare Ian Cartwright.'

'You're right. I was. But the difference between us is that I know when not to cross the line.'

'Even when it means that your little agency will go under?'

he says. 'Because from what I've heard that will be any day now.'

I can tell by the way he's looking at me, the disdain in his eyes, that he knows exactly how much trouble I'm in. And he really doesn't care. All he cares about is himself. 'Well, at least if I go under, it will be with my head held high,' I reply.

'Fat lot of good that will do you when you're on the bread line.'

'I'll manage.'

'How? Antonia West won't keep you afloat for ever, darling. You need me.'

'You're wrong. I don't need you.'

His eyes narrow as he surveys me. 'I see what this is about. You met someone, didn't you? You met someone in San Francisco and suddenly you're back here preaching about morals. That's it, isn't it?'

I feel my cheeks redden.

'Oh, for fuck's sake, that's pathetic!' He laughs. 'What is this guy – some sort of saint to turn you into Miss Goody Two Shoes all of a sudden?'

'It's none of your business,' I retort.

'Oh, don't worry, sunshine. I don't care! You can screw whoever you please as far as I'm concerned – I always have.'

I feel my chest shudder as I exhale. I *knew* it. He's lied to me all along – he had been unfaithful to Caroline: that's obviously why they split. She wasn't lying, trying to get more money from him. She was telling the truth all along: he'd cheated on her and, from the nasty sneer on his face, I'm guessing he's cheated on me too. No wonder he didn't want people to know about us. How many more Frankies are out there, thinking they're being discreet when really they're just being played?

'Sorry, Frankie darling, are you shocked?' he taunts.

'No, I'm not,' I say, pushing my shoulders back. 'Actually, I'm glad. Because it makes it even easier to walk away from you. I feel sorry for you, Gary – you're a smug, self-obsessed snob. Have a nice life.' I turn on my heel and stalk out of the door. I don't look back.

The rest of the morning passes in a haze.

I can't believe I've walked away from Gary. I'm shaky but relieved too – as if a weight has been lifted from my shoulders. It's the end of a chapter, I know that for sure. I just wish I knew what was on the next page. I'm getting ready to call it a day and head to the hospital when there's a knock on the door and Antonia West sweeps into the room.

Her perfume immediately fills the space. It's something expensive, knowing Antonia – she works hard for her money and likes to treat herself accordingly. It's probably some scent she had developed to order.

'Hello, darlings,' she says, as Helen and I look at each other in shock. I try to think quickly. What's this about? Sales of *The Edge of Love* have been really good, thankfully: she shot straight to number one as usual so she can't have a bee in her bonnet about that.

I look wildly to Helen over Antonia's shoulder as she leans in to kiss me, but she looks as confused as I feel. Apparently this is an unscheduled visit: Antonia has decided to drop in unannounced.

'Let's have some tea, shall we?' I say to Helen, and she leaps up immediately, looking only too happy to escape.

'My God, Frankie, you look terrible,' Antonia says, examining me openly once Helen is gone. Her sleek mane of beautifully highlighted honey hair is flowing loosely round her shoulders and she's wearing a skin-tight electric blue bandage dress and stacked heels under a camel cashmere wrap. She looks absolutely amazing and I look like a train wreck.

'Well, I'm just back from the States,' I start, 'and then my mum . . .'

But she's not listening. 'I know the perfect man for you,' she whispers. 'He's discreet and he doesn't cost the earth. Everyone I know uses him.'

'Well, actually, Botox isn't my thing,' I say.

'Botox? Who said anything about Botox?' she tinkles, her voice high as she swivels round to double check that her niece is definitely not within earshot.

'Isn't that what you meant?' I ask.

'Of course not, Frankie!' she says, doing the tinkling thing again. 'I'm completely natural, ha-ha-ha!' Then she jerks her head over her shoulder once more, to make sure no one else has appeared. 'But you know what this industry is like. It's youth-obsessed – I have to keep up. I mean, do you know that Penguin signed a sixteen-year-old last week? *A sixteen-year-old?* She's barely started her periods, for God's sake – *and* she's on the book-festival panel!'

She stares at me then, as if that's my fault, but I say nothing. The City Book Festival is still a sore subject with Antonia – and I just can't go there today.

'I hope she can stand the pace, that's all I'm saying,' Antonia goes on, her face crumpling for a second. 'She'll need the hide of an elephant to last in this industry.'

Oh, God, I hope she doesn't start crying. Because if she does, I will too.

'Anyway,' she says, visibly composing herself as she perches on the chair opposite me, 'I popped in because I was talking to Corinne yesterday.'

Corinne Banks is a good friend of Antonia's and a number-one bestselling author in Ireland and the UK. She's a real sweetheart, one of the nicest people in the business. She works hard and has absolutely no airs and graces, despite her success. But now that Antonia has mentioned her I know what this unscheduled visit is about. Advances. Or royalties. Or foreign rights. God, I hate it when authors get together and start comparing notes. It should be outlawed.

'She's just *devastated* about April's death,' Antonia goes on.

'Of course,' I say. 'I forgot she was one of April's.' OK, so she's building up to the foreign-rights thing. Or maybe it's about movie deals – I did hear that one of Corinne's novels, which April sold to Hollywood, has gone into pre-production. That'll be like salt in a wound to Antonia.

'Yes, the poor darling's been with April for donkey's years,' Antonia says, nodding her thanks at Helen, who's back and placing a cup of green tea in front of her. Antonia swears by green tea – says it soothes and inspires her. That's why she gave up caffeine years ago. Now she rises at dawn to salute the sun and starts working before seven. She claims it's the most productive time of the day.

'April *was* a wonderful agent,' I murmur.

Antonia takes a sip of her green tea and relaxes back into the chair. 'Anyway. Darling Corinne was half thinking of moving from Withers and Cole, you know. She just can't bear to be without poor April – she was so attached. So I recommended you, Frankie.'

Suddenly my heart leaps. *Oh, my God.* Corinne Banks!

'But then that bloody Bruce Makin swooped in like a vulture,' Antonia goes on, shaking her head mournfully. 'Poor April was barely cold when he called Corinne. He really is the most ghastly man!'

Of course. My hopes plummet. Bruce won't let Corinne get away so easily. He's ring-fencing April's clients, as I'd known he would. Ian will be back in the Withers and Cole fold by now as well.

'I guess it's just business, Antonia,' I say, sighing. So that's that. I may as well forget it.

'So you're giving up – is that it?' she says, looking at me strangely.

'I'm small-fry, Antonia. I can't compete with the big boys.'

She takes a sip of her tea, surveying me as she does so. 'I'm disappointed in you, Frankie. I thought you had more guts.'

I look away, not answering her.

'You're April's natural successor, Frankie. Surely you know that. If you wanted to, you could have half her list, at least.'

'I don't think so,' I say, shaking my head.

'Of course you could!' she lectures. 'I know things haven't been easy recently but I signed with you because you had a spark – fire in your belly. I believe in you, Frankie. But to succeed you need to believe in yourself. Now, this is for you.' She slides a gift-wrapped box across the desk to me. 'Go on, open it,' she says, smiling.

I tear the wrapping away and inside the box, underneath the tissue paper, lies a slim silver bangle with a delicate angel charm. It's absolutely gorgeous.

'Antonia! It's beautiful!' I say, slipping it on my arm and admiring how it sits, the charm dangling prettily.

'Look at the inscription,' she orders, her eyes strangely bright.

I take out the tiny card. '"To Frankie, my lucky charm,"' I read out loud.

'Oh, that's lovely!' Helen throws her arms around her aunt and Antonia pats her fondly on the head, the affection between them clear.

'I have something for you too, darling. I'll give it to you later,' she says to her.

'Antonia, I really don't know what to say. It's beautiful,' I whisper, overcome. She's never given me such a special gift before.

'It's my pleasure, Frankie. Thank you for everything you've done for me. I know I don't always ... make it easy.' She clears her throat. 'Now I have to go but I want you to think about what I said. And take a look at this while you do – it makes for very interesting reading.'

She passes a folded-up piece of paper across the desk to me and is up and sweeping out of the room before I can ask her what it is, her expensive perfume trailing behind her.

Wow – she's certainly full of surprises today: first a beautiful bracelet and now this. I unfold the note and scan it, but it takes a second or two for the content to sink in, for me to realize what it is. When I do I gasp out loud – I can't believe what I have in my hands. It's a master list of the names and direct telephone numbers of April's clients. This is gold dust and Antonia knows it.

But why has she given it to me? She can't expect me to call these people and make a pitch, surely. That's crazy – it would never work. Without thinking about it, I automatically open my desk drawer, slide the note in and close it firmly, putting all thoughts of what I might do with the information out of my mind.

It's sweet that Antonia wants to help me, really sweet, but it's too late. I have no more fight left in me: the war is lost and it's time to limp off the battlefield.

Chapter Thirty-one

'Frankie! Frankie!'

I hear a voice calling me and open my eyes, taking a second to get my bearings. I'm in Mum's hospital room. The lights are dim and there's noise in the background: people moving around in the corridor, trolleys being wheeled, the low hum of voices. I must have dozed off.

'Hey, Frankie, are you OK?'

There's a hand on my shoulder. It's Eric – and Martin's there too.

'I must have fallen asleep,' I mutter, rubbing my bleary eyes. I have no idea what time it is, or how long I've been unconscious. The jet lag is playing havoc with my body clock again. I could have been like this for hours, or just a few minutes, I'm not sure.

'It sounded like you were having a really bad dream. You were talking in your sleep,' Eric says, offering me some tea, the steam rising enticingly from the polystyrene cup.

'Was I?' I shake my head to get rid of the nightmare I was having about confronting Gary as I sit up, peeling myself off the side of Mum's bed, glancing at her to make sure she's not awake, that I didn't miss anything. But her eyes are closed.

'What were you dreaming about?' Martin asks, shrugging off his coat and pulling up a seat beside me.

'Oh, just work.' I don't want to get into all that now – there's a time and a place, and Mum's hospital room right now is neither.

'You work too hard,' Martin says. 'There's more to life than the office, you know.'

'You're a fine one to talk,' I say.

'Yeah, you dope,' Eric says, digging an elbow into his side. 'What about "Con Air, here to cool you?"'

'That's different,' Martin protests.

'How is it different?' I ask, wiping my damp mouth before I take a sip of the hot tea. God, I must have been drooling. How long was I asleep anyway?

'It just is,' he says sulkily, sticking out his bottom lip and looking like a truculent toddler. Martin could sulk for Ireland. He once stopped talking for a week straight because we drew straws to choose what to watch on TV and he missed the Formula One highlights. 'Anyway, I'd have a job to keep up with you. At least I'm not addicted to my Crack-Berry.'

'Ha-ha, very funny,' I say. 'Anyway, I'm not addicted to it. Not any more.'

'What?' they ask in unison.

'It's true. After I lost it in San Francisco, I realized that life still went on.'

'Wow!' Eric whistles. 'Wonders will never cease!'

'Yeah, it's a miracle!' Martin grins. 'So, what were you doing over there anyway? You never really said.'

'Trying to sign an author. It didn't work out in the end.' I can't help wondering what Ian is doing right now. Is Rosie with him? And John . . . Has he been thinking about me like I have about him? Or has he just erased me from his mind? I force myself to will the thoughts away. I can't allow myself to go there or I'll fall to pieces.

There's a short silence and I see Eric dig Martin in the ribs again as if to tell him not to say anything else. Hmm . . . Are they actually going easy on me?

'So. How is work?' Martin asks tentatively. 'The agency, I mean.'

I think about this for a second before I trot off my rote answer that everything's great – the same one I give anyone who asks. 'It's shite, actually,' I reply truthfully for once. 'Total and utter shite. I made a huge mistake leaving Withers and Cole. I'll likely be out of business in a few weeks.'

Martin and Eric smile nervously, as if they think I'm probably joking but they're not entirely sure.

'Good one, sis,' Martin says.

'I'm not kidding. I only have one decent client and even she'll probably leave me soon.'

Why wouldn't she? Antonia's been extremely loyal so far, I have to hand it to her, but I can't expect her to be loyal for ever, especially now that the Rowley Agency is going down the tubes fast. She said she came with me because I had fire in my belly – but that fire has been well and truly extinguished. She'd be better off leaving me, even I know that.

Why did I think I could make a success of my own business in the first place? Was I blind or just stupid? My tiny set-up, which I was trying to convince myself was bespoke and boutique, was a waste of time and effort. Now it's on its last legs and I'll never save it. It's over – I may as well throw in the towel and move on.

'Ah, come on, Frankie, don't say that,' Eric protests.

'Why not? It's true.' I take another sip of tea, feeling weirdly detached. Maybe it's all the tea I've been drinking – I must have it in my veins by now, I've drunk so much of it in this place.

'Stop that kind of talk.' Eric is gruffer now. 'You're a genius at what you do – everyone knows that.'

'He's right,' Martin says. 'Mum's always saying how amazing

you are – she thinks you're the best thing since sliced bread.'

'No, she doesn't. She thinks I'm left on the shelf. Barren.'

'Jesus!' Eric chuckles. 'Shut up, will you? She's always going on about you – Frankie did this, Frankie did that. She nearly exploded with pride when you set up on your own, didn't she, Martin?'

'Yeah, it was a right pain in the arse,' Martin agrees dolefully. 'She never stopped yapping about it – Dad too. You were the best in the industry, a superstar – if I heard it once, I heard it a million fecking times. They were never as excited when I set up Con Air.'

Eric is nodding vehemently in agreement at this.

I can't believe it. Is all this true? And if it is, why didn't they ever tell me?

I look at Mum, tiny and birdlike under the covers, and wish with all my heart that she'd open her eyes, just for a second.

'Come on, sis,' Eric says. 'There must be a way out – all you have to do is put your mind to it. Don't give up.'

'Yeah, Frankie,' Martin says. 'Don't give in now – you've worked too hard to let it slip away. Even if you're in trouble, there's always a way.'

I feel the tears threaten – they're being far too nice to me and I can't handle it. It's easier when we slag each other.

I'm trying to pull it together when Dad walks in, grey in the face. His golf jumper almost looks too big for him – like he's lost weight in a few short days.

'Hi, Dad.' I spring up and hug him tight.

'I've decided something,' he says, sitting down and reaching for Mum's limp hand.

'What is it?' Martin looks worried.

'I'm going to organize this anniversary party for your mother – it's the least I can do.'

'Dad,' I say softly, 'you don't need to worry about that now.'

'Yes, I do.' He turns to me, his eyes desolate. 'Do you know what I was trying to persuade her to do? Do you?'

The three of us look at each other – we haven't a clue what he's talking about.

'I was trying to get her to go on a Caribbean cruise instead of throwing a party – how selfish was that of me?'

'Er . . . I'd quite like to go on a Caribbean cruise,' Eric pipes up.

Dad shakes his head sadly, his eyes glued to Mum's face. 'So would I, but that's not the point, is it, son? This party was important to your mother. She wanted it to be perfect, and what did I do?'

The three of us look at each other again.

'I bought her a barbecue! How was that helping matters? How?'

'Ah, now, Dad. The barbecue was a steal – you couldn't pass it up,' Martin says, a little shamefaced at having played a part in that débâcle.

'I could have turned it down and I should have turned it down,' Dad says. 'But things are going to change around here. This party is going ahead, and when your mother wakes up, I don't want her to be worrying about what still needs doing. I want everything to be perfect. If I'd just helped a little more, this wouldn't have happened in the first place.'

'Dad, that's not true,' Eric says gruffly. I can see the tears shining in his eyes.

'Yes, it is. Now, I've made a list of things that still need doing.' He reaches into his pocket and pulls out a sheet of paper.

'I'll help you, Dad – whatever you need,' Martin says.

'Me too,' Eric agrees.

'And me,' I say.

Dad smiles at us, his grey face a little brighter. 'You're good children – all of you,' he says, a catch in his voice. 'Your mother would be proud of you.'

That's enough for me. I rummage in my bag for a packet of tissues so I can blow my nose and hide my tears. As I do, my hand closes on something and I pull it out.

'Eh, what's that?' Eric says.

'Do you usually carry those around in your bag, sis?' Martin asks.

'Why do you have that, Frankie love?' Dad is looking at me strangely.

It's a party hat. A multi-coloured party hat with yellow feathers on top. The hat that Aimee wanted everyone to wear to her party – it must have found its way into my handbag after that evening in the restaurant when John opened the party box. It's as if the world stops turning as I hold it in my hand. This is like a message. A message from Aimee. She was gutsy, fiery, a girl who never gave up, even when she knew her time was limited. What would she do in this situation? Would she just roll over and take it – or would she fight to the bitter end? If she could cope with all that life threw at her and be joyful even when she was facing death, shouldn't I be able to fight on too? And then there's Mum – she's fighting to get back to us, I know she is. Dad is doing his best too – even Eric and Martin are soldiering on. Shouldn't I at least try?

'It's a reminder,' I say, feeling the stirrings of hope inside. 'A reminder from someone I know.' I may be down but I'm not out. And, just like Aimee, I'm not going to quit now.

Thanks to Antonia's master list, four hours and a dozen calls, I've spoken to almost all of April O'Reilly's old clients and offered my services. No pressure. No hard sell. Just straight talking, with an offer to meet and talk some more. I'm not sure if I've managed to convince any of them to consider taking a chance on me. But at least I haven't just lain down, rolled over and given up. Thinking about Aimee's struggle – what she would have done in this situation – made me realize I had to at least try.

I've also called Mr Morris, the bank manager, and begged him for some extra time before he shuts my account. We're meeting tomorrow for a face-to-face emergency discussion. I'm not sure anything can be salvaged, but I'm not going to give up without a fight.

As for the back rent, I've accepted that nothing can be done about that. I have to face up to the fact that I can't afford to be in this building. But that's probably for the best anyway: I certainly don't want to be bumping into Gary in the lobby every day. I want to start my new chapter – wherever or whatever that will be. And if I'm going to fail, I want to know that I've done everything possible to prevent it first. If I have to fail, I want to fail well.

Helen trips into the office just as I'm figuring out what to tackle next. For the first time since I've known her, she's not smiling. Her face is drawn and worried – she knows how much trouble the agency is in because I've talked to her too. If we're to keep working together, I have to treat her as my equal – someone to be trusted, someone to confide in and lean on. OK, so she was ditzy, late, and useless at coffee-making. But she was loyal too. And good with people. And amusing and brave and fun. And she's already come up with a brilliant idea: her boyfriend Dave knows someone who has a small unit to rent in an industrial park in the suburbs. It's not very glamorous, but the price is right and he's going to help us pack up and move, if things work out and I get another chance. As Helen said proudly, when I thanked her, he's good like that.

'There's some people to see you,' she says now, and my heart lurches at the anxious expression on her face. Has Gary turned up to have another go at me? I wouldn't put it past him. I stand up, push my shoulders back and inhale. Facing him again is the last thing I want, but I will if I have to. I'll speak my mind, tell him what I think of him and then it'll be done for good and ever. Over. I want nothing more to do with Gary Elverson. In any capacity.

As I lift my head and take another deep, steadying breath, a man walks through the door. But it's not Gary – it's Ian. And right behind him, wearing a glittery green shamrock baseball cap, is Rosie.

Chapter Thirty-two

'You didn't think we'd abandon you, did you?' she says, grinning at me as Ian smiles sheepishly beside her.

'Rosie!' I bolt to her and fling myself into her arms. 'I can't believe you're here!'

'Nothing was going to keep me away when I got your message, girl,' she says, hugging me tightly.

I'd left Rosie an emotional, garbled voicemail, telling her again how sorry I was about lying to her. Then somehow I'd ended up telling her everything – how Mum was really ill and that the agency was probably going under. When I'd heard her cheery voice on her answering service it had all just tumbled out.

'But how did you manage to . . . I mean, how did you . . .' I trail away, not wanting to embarrass her in front of Ian. Rosie has no job. If she's used the very last of her life savings on this trip just because I left a hysterical message of woe, I'll die.

'I might have a story of my own to tell about that, honey.' She smiles enigmatically. 'But first things first. Now, Ian here has confessed everything. Haven't you, Ian?'

Ian flicks her a nervous look, and she glares back sternly. But it's a glare with a lot of love behind it, I can tell. These two are clearly a proper item now.

'Er, that's right,' he mutters.

'Yes. He explained it all. He persuaded you to spy on that nice family for him – I know it wasn't your fault.'

I see Ian hang his head with shame and I feel terrible. 'Hang on Rosie, I can't let Ian take all the blame,' I say.

'You can't?' He lifts his eyes to me.

'Of course not, Ian. I could have said no, Rosie.' I turn to her. 'I should have said no. It was my fault too, probably even more so. I was so desperate for him to sign with me, to write a sequel – I would have done almost anything. It was unforgivable – I'm so sorry.'

Ian smiles at me then, and so does Rosie.

'Well, honey, it's all in the past now,' she says. 'Water under the bridge.'

'Really?'

'Of course. Now, Ian doesn't want to write the sequel – you know that. But he has another idea that I know will blow everyone away. And he wants you to represent him!'

'It's not about Aimee, is it?' I ask. 'Because I couldn't do that.' Aimee's story is off limits as far as I'm concerned. It's not ours to tell – not like that.

'No, of course not,' Rosie says. 'We know that wouldn't be right, don't we, sugar?'

'Yes, we do,' he replies, smiling at her happily.

'So, go on, honey, explain your great idea to Frankie.'

'Well, it all began because of a little boy who lives close to me,' he starts hesitantly. 'I've often seen him in the cul-de-sac, cycling round on his red bike.'

'I know that kid!' I say, immediately remembering the little fellow with the blond hair, big attitude and Ben 10 helmet.

'He was knocked down the other day, right outside my house,' Ian says.

'Oh, no!' I gasp.

'Ian held his hand while his mom called the ambulance, didn't you, honey?' Rosie says.

'Yes, I did,' Ian answers quietly. 'He was so brave. And he somehow knew that I was a writer – I don't know how.'

'I told him, that first day I came to visit you,' I say.

343

'Aha, that explains it!' Ian says. 'Anyway, he asked me to tell him a story.'

'He was so sweet, wasn't he, Ian?' Rosie puts in. 'He must have been terrified inside. He'd broken his leg, poor little guy.'

'I didn't know if I could do it at first, just pull something out of thin air to distract him,' Ian goes on. 'But then, out of nowhere, I started telling him a tale about a little boy who had a pet mouse. I don't know where it came from, really.'

'A little boy whose parents had moved to the Haight in San Francisco to follow the hippie movement!' Rosie says triumphantly.

Now I get it: it's the story Ian had tried to write years ago about the hippies – he's bringing it back to life.

'Yes, his parents are hippies and he's feeling a bit lost and frightened because he's left all his friends and family behind to live in the Haight, so he befriends a tiny mouse who lives in his cereal box . . .' Ian pauses and looks at Rosie.

'Like Shergar!' she exclaims delightedly.

'Yes, like Shergar,' Ian agrees, almost shyly. 'And that's it, really. The little boy – his name's Riley – seemed to like it. He said it was awesome. He said I should write about it for real.'

'It *is* awesome, honey,' Rosie says. 'It's magical! And fun! And it has to be written!'

They look at me, clearly wanting to judge how I feel about it.

'So, Francesca . . .' Ian clears his throat . . . 'I know it's not the sort of thing my readers will expect. I've never written a children's story before, obviously, and the publishers might hate it . . . but what do you think?'

I'm gob-smacked. Totally and utterly gob-smacked. How did Ian come up with this? 'What do I think?' I say, a grin spreading from ear to ear. 'I think I love it is what I think!'

It's true. I really do. It's a bit mad, yes, but all the best stories are and I feel so excited about its potential that I know I'll be able to champion it passionately to publishers. This could be big, it could be huge, but even if it's not, even if it sells just one copy, I'll still love the idea. And I'll be willing to put myself on the line for it, no matter what anyone says.

'Really?' Ian looks shell-shocked and Rosie cheers.

'Yes, really. It's a great premise and you obviously feel passionately about it.'

'I do feel passionately about it,' Ian says. 'I really do.'

'I can tell,' I say. 'But there's one problem Ian – the Rowley Agency isn't exactly doing well. I can't promise you anything. You might be safer staying with Withers and Cole.'

'Francesca,' he's looking me right in the eye, 'I want you and I'd be honoured if you'd represent me.'

'Really?' I say, my throat feeling hot all of a sudden.

'Really. But I wouldn't blame you if you turned me down. You can't think very much of me after everything. I mean I locked on to Aimee's story like a desperate fool.'

'You were confused, honey,' Rosie consoles him. 'You were lost at sea.'

He takes her hand in his. 'You're a remarkable woman, Rosie Kelly,' he says, and she beams back at him.

'Oh, hush up,' she giggles, 'and tell Frankie the next part of our plan.'

They turn back to me.

'OK. We think you should go back to San Francisco, Francesca,' Ian says.

'Back to San Francisco? Why?'

'Honey,' Rosie says, 'the dogs on the street know that you and John are sweet on each other. It's Fate – I told you so!'

A blush is creeping up my neck. 'We're not sweet on each other,' I protest. I'm sweet on him, true. But how does he feel about me? That's hard to know – he despises me probably.

'OK, sure you're not.' Rosie rolls her eyes. 'Maybe this will change your mind then.'

With a flourish she produces a minuscule piece of paper from her bag.

My heart constricts as the tiny scrap tumbles into my palm. It can't be . . . can it? Slowly, hands trembling, I unfurl the crumpled edges and read the message. *Listen to your heart.*

'You saved the message from my fortune cookie?' I ask.

'Of course. It's Fate – I told you that. Don't you never listen to me?'

My heart is racing. 'But, Rosie, even if I wanted to, I can't. I can't up and leave again. I've only just got back.'

Yes, I admit it. The idea of seeing John again makes me shaky with excitement – I haven't stopped thinking about him since I left. But I know this is all fantasy: it can't happen.

'I'm not saying go right now, honey. Not when your momma's so poorly. But when the time is right you'll know.'

'And I can take care of everything,' Helen says, from the doorway, her dimples dimpling at me once more, her face transformed by a very large grin. 'If you trust me not to run the place into the ground, that is?'

'Of course I trust you, Helen,' I reply. 'But I can't afford to travel, even if I wanted to. The agency is broke. Stony broke. That's the truth.'

'Um, that might be where I come in,' Rosie says. 'I'm going to sponsor your trip.'

What's she talking about? She's even more broke than I am.

'Remember I told you I was a Kelly from Waterford?' she goes on.

'How can I forget?' I laugh. 'I heard about it enough.'

'Well . . .' she glances at Ian, who nods at her to continue '. . . that was only half the story. You're not the only one who hasn't been completely truthful.'

'What do you mean?' I say.

'Well, my daddy's family was Irish but my momma was a Perry from Texas,' she says. Then she pauses, as if that should mean something to me.

'I don't get it,' I say. 'A Perry from Texas – so what?'

'Momma's family was into oil,' Rosie explains. 'In a big way.'

Helen gasps. 'Oh, my God,' she says, her hand flying to her mouth. 'I've read about this – the Perrys from Texas! They're like the Ewings from *Dallas*!'

Rosie laughs, but she doesn't deny it either.

'You're not . . . you're not the heir to the fortune, are you? The multi-billionaire who left it all behind to live a simple life in secret?' Helen turns to me, gesturing madly. 'Her story was on E!.'

'Um, yes, I guess that's me,' Rosie says bashfully.

'You're a multi-billionaire?' I whisper.

'Well, now, let's not get carried away – I'm not a *multi*-billionaire. A couple of times over, maybe,' she says.

I feel faint. 'But, Rosie, you live on a tiny houseboat!' I blurt out.

'Uh-huh.' She shrugs. 'I like to keep it simple. What can I say?'

'And you travel Economy!' I go on, totally baffled. 'You sat right beside me on that flight from Dublin to San Francisco when you could have had your own private jet!' With foot massages, aromatherapy wraps, caviar on tap. Why would someone do that?

'I guess I could have.' She shrugs again, smiling now. 'But it's not much fun. If I did that I wouldn't get to meet nice folk like you – why would I sit alone on a private jet when I could be with friends?'

'So, what are you saying? That even though you've got pots of money, you choose to live – like one of us?' I stutter.

For a split second she looks hurt. 'Hey, I *am* one of you, ain't I?'

Ian puts an arm round her shoulders and pulls her to him protectively. 'Of course you are, Rosie,' he says stoutly.

Suddenly I'm laughing at the absurdity of it all. 'You know what, Rosie Kelly of the Waterford Kellys? You're a crazy woman!' I giggle. 'A complete and utter crazy woman!'

'And you hang out with me – so what does that say about you, girlfriend?' she shoots back, and we dissolve into laughter. This is nuts. Absolutely nuts. All this time Rosie hasn't been on the breadline, she's just been trying to live a simple life. Suddenly, the way she reacted when I ranted about John trying to pay me off with six hundred dollars makes sense. I thought she was uncomfortable talking about money and she was – but for a completely different reason.

'So, will you go to San Francisco, if I help you?' she says at last, wiping her streaming eyes with a tissue, hiccuping back the laughter.

'It's really kind of you, Rosie, but I don't think I can,' I say. 'I mean, what will I say to him? How can I make it right?' This is such a mess. He'll never forgive me. And neither will Anita. They won't believe that I really and truly felt for their situation, that I wasn't just hanging out with them for my own ends.'

'The boy is crazy about you, Frankie,' she goes on. 'Everyone can see it.'

'Really?' I whisper.

'Yes, really. And I think you should try to make it right, honey. I think Aimee would have wanted you to, don't you?'

Aimee. What would she have thought about it all? Would she have been able to forgive and forget? I like to think she would have known that, although I started off befriending her family for all the wrong reasons, I grew to love and respect them too. Would she want me to try to make it right? Do I owe it to her to try?

And then I look at the crumpled piece of paper in my hand. How could I have been so blind? It's from her – of course it is. It's been her all along. I just couldn't see it. Closing my fist around the note, I hold it tight, feeling it warm against my skin, as if her hand is somehow in mine. Suddenly I know Rosie's right. This is what I need to do. I know John probably won't understand or be able to forgive me – that might be too much to ask. But I have to try to make things right. For Aimee's sake as well as for mine. I know what I have to do now, what she wants me to do, and there's no going back.

Chapter Thirty-three

As the taxi pulls up to the kerb, a text message buzzes on my phone: *Go for it, Frankie!* It's from Mum. She came round a week after Rosie and Ian left. I was at her bedside, stroking the soft skin on her hands – a legacy of her lifelong love affair with rubber washing-up gloves – and telling her the complicated tale of the phone mix-up. I told her everything – Aimee, John, even Gary – reckoning it was as good a time as ever to spill the beans, when she was unconscious and couldn't lecture me.

'I'm going back when you're all better, Mum, to try to set things right,' I said finally, wrapping up the story. 'Don't worry, I'm not bankrupting myself – a friend of mine is loaning me the money until I can pay her back. I'm going to speak to John. That's all I can do.'

'Good luck, pet,' she suddenly croaked back.

I dropped her hand with fright. Had she just talked to me? 'Mum?' I said, holding my breath, not daring to hope that she was coming round at last.

'Why all the tears, love?' she asked, patting my hair.

I was sobbing with relief, my head buried in her shoulder as I rang the call button for the nurses to come. 'I thought I'd lost you,' I wailed. 'I thought I'd never have the chance to make it up to you!'

'Now, now, there's nothing to make up for,' she said. 'You're a wonderful, independent woman and I'm dead proud of you. I always have been.'

'You have?' I snuffled.

'Of course, pet. I couldn't be prouder. I want you to go and tell that John what he means to you and don't come back until you have, OK?'

'OK,' I gulped.

'And if you don't mind me saying so that Gary sounded like a right prick – you're well rid of him so you are.'

I exploded with laughter then – the enormous relief that she was conscious and making jokes welling up inside me and bursting out. 'Now, can you get your dad for me?' she went on. 'I've been thinking maybe he's right, maybe a Caribbean cruise would be better than a party.'

Then everyone rushed in at once – Dad, Eric, Martin, the medics – and all hell broke loose.

I text her back quickly now as I step out of the taxi: *Thanks Mum!*

She's been coming on in leaps and bounds, astounding the doctors, who reckon she's a bit of a medical miracle. With some physiotherapy and time she should make a full recovery. She and Dad have come to a very happy compromise about their anniversary celebrations too: they're having the party *and* they're going on the cruise in one big blow-out. If anyone deserves it they do.

As for Eric and Martin, I have to hand it to them: they've pulled out all the stops and stepped up to the plate, taking it in turns to run errands for Dad and keep Mum company. It's not all on my shoulders any more. We've become much closer in the last few weeks – even if the teasing has continued apace too. But I wouldn't want it any other way.

I think about them now as I push through the door of Carlo's restaurant, squeezing past the people waiting patiently in line. I'm quaking with nerves but determined to go through with it. I've come a very long way to do this.

The first person I see is Martha, taking people's details in her notebook. She's as gorgeous and skinny as ever, which doesn't help because I look like death warmed up after another transatlantic flight. She lifts her head as people start to mutter that I'm jumping the queue, and when she sees me her eyes narrow. 'You're not welcome here,' she spits.

Why does she hate me so much? What have I ever done to her?

'It's OK, thank you, Martha,' I hear someone behind me say. And then I twirl around and come face to face with Anita, her beautiful almond eyes wary and full of pain. *Help me, Aimee.* The thought pops into my head and I hang on to it. If Aimee is watching maybe she can make her mother see that, although I did wrong, I'm not an awful person. And I want to make things right.

'You'll have to excuse Martha,' Anita says, leading me away. 'She's slow to trust people – but maybe she's right to be.'

Her words sting, but I say nothing. After all, isn't she right?

'So, is it true, Frankie?' she asks. 'You were spying on us, like John says?'

'Anita, I'm so sorry,' I say, wringing my hands. 'I know it sounds awful and, yes, it started off that way. But I honestly truly like you both so much . . . and I didn't mean to cause you any more hurt, I swear.'

She looks at me for a long time, her eyes travelling over my face, before she eventually speaks. 'I believe you,' she says eventually, smiling faintly. 'Come, sit with me for a minute. I need a break.' She leads the way to the courtyard, where the lights are still twinkling magically, just like always.

'I remember the first time I came here,' I say, sinking into a seat and looking around sadly.

'I remember it too,' she replies. 'When we first met, there was something about you that I couldn't put my finger on –

you reminded me of Aimee in so many ways that it was almost painful.'

'I'm sorry, Anita,' I mumble.

'Don't be. My darling girl was the light of my life. Losing her has been the hardest thing that ever happened to me.'

'I know,' I whisper.

'It's been very difficult to cope. Even more so during the last few weeks – I had some very, very dark days, Frankie. I came close to the edge. Although you probably know that already, right, if you read my messages?'

I hang my head, ashamed that I read such intensely private messages from a grieving mother to a lost daughter.

'Don't worry,' she says. 'I'm feeling better now. Sending those messages to Aimee helped me when I was at my lowest – it helped me to keep her alive in some way. But I don't have to do that any more because I've finally realized something.'

'What?' I raise my eyes to hers and see the warmth in them. Can she actually have forgiven me?

'I've realized that, even if she's gone, she'll always be in my heart. As long as I'm alive she'll be here. And after I'm gone she'll live on in the memory of others – she'll live for ever. That's what I want, for her to be remembered always.'

'That's beautiful, Anita,' I say, wiping a tear away.

'I knew you'd understand. Now dry your eyes. We have work to do.'

'What sort of work?'

'Aimee's party. John never got round to organizing it – he's been positively depressed since you left.'

My heart lifts with hope. That's good, right? Maybe I *do* mean something to him. Maybe I didn't imagine what was between us. 'He has?'

'Yes, he has. But he's a stubborn boy, my John, just like his father was, so we're going to have to time things perfectly to make it right between you – and Aimee is going to help us.' She reaches across to take my hand. 'She led you to us some- how, Frankie, I know it. And now she's going to help get you two back together again. Besides, if we didn't throw this party I know she'd never forgive me!'

She throws back her head and laughs and, for the first time since we met, I see real joy in her face. But it's not just that: I see a flash of what her daughter must have been like and I know Anita's right. Aimee will help me – she's been helping me all along.

Epilogue

I'm standing at the back of the room, my heart beating fast, as Anita steps in front of the assembled crowd, microphone in hand. She looks absolutely beautiful: her hair is gathered into a loose chignon, a bright orange fringed shawl is flung over her shoulders and her skin is luminous in the fairy lights draped around the courtyard.

'I'd like to thank you for coming tonight, everyone,' she says, smiling at the crowd. 'I won't keep you long – Aimee hated long-winded speeches even more than her father did.'

People clap and cheer, and she smiles again, but I can see she's battling not to cry.

'So . . .' she takes a deep breath '. . . it's been hard, very hard, since my beautiful girl died. There were times when I wanted to die too. I couldn't imagine a world without my daughter in it. But Aimee has taught me things even since she passed away, if you can believe that. She was brave and free, she lived life right to the end, she drank every last drop of time she had – all very valuable lessons to learn.'

More cheers, as people raise their glasses in the air. I can almost feel Aimee's presence here – as if she doesn't want to miss even a second of the fun and celebrations.

'Now, it's hard to be happy when someone you love isn't here any more,' Anita goes on, 'but my beautiful girl would have wanted us to try. In fact, she would have insisted on it, wouldn't she, John?'

John steps forward to join his mother and, as they embrace,

I inhale sharply. It's the first time I've seen him since I've been back.

'The support of friends from far and wide has kept me going since Aimee died. But there are two people I have to thank especially. My son John – I couldn't have made it through without his help. Thank you, John, I treasure you.' Her voice is wobbling now as she comes close to tears and John squeezes her hand to give her strength.

'I also want to mention one other special friend.' She takes another deep breath and I see her searching the crowd for me. We lock eyes and I smile and give her a thumbs-up. 'My dear friend Roberto has stood by me through thick and thin. I love him very much and I want him to know that. The wine you're drinking tonight has been created by him in Aimee's memory – it's a beautiful tribute to her.'

I take a sip of the new cuvée that we tasted that day in Napa, unaware then that Roberto had developed it for Aimee. Around me, everyone applauds, and I see Roberto blow Anita a kiss, his face wreathed in smiles.

'Now, speaking of tributes. I have one more announcement to make. In Aimee's memory I've established a foundation in her name. The Aimee Bonner Foundation will fundraise for those affected by congenital heart defects. Our first project, kindly supported by my good friend the literary agent Frankie Rowley, will be the publication of a cookbook of all my favourite recipes from the restaurant, including the secret recipe for Aimee's favourite pasta sauce. It will be called *Every Last Drop*. I hope you all like it – I know she would have. Here's to Aimee!'

She holds her glass aloft and there's another huge cheer as she makes her way through the crowd towards Roberto, who's standing with his arms outstretched, tears glistening in his eyes. They're together at last, as they were always supposed to be. Now Anita's wonderful recipes will be her daughter's legacy. The cookbook will be a bestseller, I know it. I watch from a distance as Rosie and Ian embrace them both – another couple whom I know in my heart Aimee has brought together.

'Frankie.'

Out of nowhere, John is in front of me. My insides somersault when I see him – this is it. The part where he asks me to leave, get out of this restaurant and never come back. At least I tried. I don't have any regrets. Even Aimee would have been happy with that.

'Hi, John,' I manage.

'I knew Mom couldn't have done all this alone,' he says.

'I only helped a little. She did most of it herself.'

There's a silence, and I almost hold my breath. He's going to order me to leave, I can feel it. 'I'm so sorry, John,' I say. All I really want is for him to know that.

'I'm sorry too,' he says.

He's going to *apologize* to me and then throw me out? Not exactly what I expected. And why is he smiling at me? That's weird.

'You? What for?' I ask, trembling now from head to toe.

'For judging you. I should have known better. I was right about you all along – you are amazing.' He takes my hand in his and, even though the courtyard is thronged, it could be just us two. Suddenly I know it's going to be all right.

'I like your outfit,' he says at last, his eyes moving over the purple embroidered silk jacket that I bought in Chinatown with Rosie. It seemed to be the perfect thing to wear tonight – a fitting nod to Aimee who, I know, is watching somehow.

'Thanks,' I say. 'I wanted to dress in something bright and cheerful.'

'Well, you're really a *cailín deas* in that,' he says softly. 'Now, I want to show you something.' He reaches into his pocket and pulls out a photo. It's me, at Alcatraz, my hair blowing in the breeze, a stupid, goofy smile on my face.

'Oh,' is all I can say.

'I've been carrying it around since that day,' he says, smiling. 'Does that make me a stalker?'

'I don't think so.' I shake my head, smiling back at him. 'A little creepy, maybe.'

'I was wondering,' he says, his eyes searching mine now, 'would you like to do a duet with a creep?'

'Excuse me?' I say.

Duet? Duet on what?

He produces a microphone from behind his back. 'On karaoke? Rosie told me her favourite song is "Islands in the Stream". I promised her we'd sing it together.'

I look to where Rosie is standing, arm in arm with Ian, waving at me, a big fat grin on her face. 'Listen to your heart,' she mouths at me.

'All right,' I agree. 'But you have to sing Dolly's part. I want to be Kenny.'

'It's a deal.'

And then he leans to kiss me and I know it might be crazy but, as the music starts to play, I swear I can almost hear Aimee sing along.

Acknowledgements

Warmest thanks, as always, to those who worked behind the scenes to get this book on the shelves: the Penguin teams in Ireland and the UK; Simon Trewin and Ariella Feiner at United Agents; Alison Walsh and Hazel Orme.

My family are simply the best: Mam and Dad, Martina and Jean Christophe, Eoghan and Jessie and, of course, baby Finnean. Thank you for everything, you all mean the world to me.

I have some wonderful friends: thank you for the support and the laughter, ladies – my life would be a lot duller without you!

An enormous thank you to Caoimhe, Rory and Oliver. I am the luckiest woman in the world to have you in my corner.

Finally, heartfelt thanks to you, dear reader. I lived in San Francisco some years ago and have treasured memories of that magical time. In this novel I have tried to give a sense of what this amazing city meant to me – if there are any errors or omissions, they are mine alone! I do hope you enjoy the read and that it succeeds in transporting you for even a short time to that great city by the bay.

www.niamhgreene.com
www.facebook.com/niamhgreenebooks
www.twitter.com/niamh_greene